What readers are saying about Catching the Wind

"In *Catching the Wind,* Physioc allows us to continue the journey with Sam Cloud-Carson, understand his complexity and watch him mature. The attention to detail, development and intrigue are captivating. Catching isn't a read…it's an experience."

Scott K. Fehnel, P.E.
Lieutenant Colonel (Retired), U.S. Army

"While reading through the pages, it is easy to visualize Sam Cloud-Carson carving through opposing lineups with ease with his abundant arsenal of high-quality pitches – and he seems to know precisely which one to throw depending on the situation."

Jeff Montgomery
Kansas City Royals Hall of Fame Pitcher

"I am very grateful Steve chose me to read his book. He was very respectful of our Ute culture and truly understands that our spiritual beliefs and songs are what kept us going. When you find your inner spirit, you will find your peace."

Hanley Frost
Former Sun Dance Chief and Southern Ute
Cultural Education Coordinator

A NOVEL

STEVE PHYSIOC

"Listen to the wind,
It talks.
Listen to the silence,
It speaks.
Listen to your heart,
It knows."

Native American Proverb

CHAPTER ONE

Playa La Boquita, Nicaragua

September 2011

"Well, look who's comin' out of the twilight zone!" Whiplash McCracken yelled from his sun-bleached-green 1998 Jeep Grand Cherokee. The silhouette of the lone man walking his way on the black sand beach with a backpack on one shoulder and a large travel bag on the other was easy to recognize. The square jaw, broad shoulders, and athletic stride gave him away.

"Could it be"—McCracken shouted again as he leaned across the front seat and opened the passenger door—"the Phantom of the Hindu Kush!"

Sam Cloud-Carson grinned broadly as he threw his bags in the back and sat down next to his old friend. "Snow leopards don't carry a yoga mat, dirty laundry, and toilet paper with them. They just leave their scat and get back to the hunt."

McCracken started the Jeep and headed back through town, weaving his way through intoxicated tourists and college students weary from partying all weekend at the beach. The streets were littered with plastic cups, spilled beer, and tequila, and the salty ocean air was tainted with tobacco and marijuana.

Sam had spent the last month alone in the forests and on the black rocky beaches just north of the music, chatter, and hustle of Playa La Boquita in Nicaragua. He'd needed this time to be alone, to decompress from all that he had experienced as a reconnaissance tracker for DiamondBar Security in Afghanistan. It wasn't easy going from tension to tranquility, from two years of extreme awareness, ever alert, searching for danger, witnessing the pain and suffering of a country torn apart by three decades of war to suddenly being alone on a quiet beach.

This last month had been one of letting go and reconnecting with nature: hiking, hunting, fishing, studying the land and animals, figuring out which plants were edible and which ones were not. But Sam also gave time to his future, to getting his body back in baseball shape and disciplining his mind with quiet meditation.

While he had believed his deceased sister's advice about the importance of meditation to be true, he'd usually found something more important to give his attention. Whether it was school or baseball or Mesa State coed Lindsey Ellison, there was always something else.

That all changed his last year in Afghanistan. After rescuing an Afghan girl from certain rape by a Taliban leader, he'd had a nervous breakdown and had wound up in Bagram Air Base's military hospital. From there, Army Special Forces Colonel Bart Tomlinson had introduced him to the Friends of Everyone Hotel, a service mission in between Bagram and the capital city of Kabul.

The FEH had no religious affiliation, for its creator, his good buddy Whiplash McCracken, believed that proselytizing in Afghanistan was too dangerous. Sam's introduction to Friends was the beginning of his surrender, and in that letting go, he began to meditate and discover a power within.

Today I welcome the beauty of life, the sights, sounds, and smells of nature;
of the mountains, the ocean, the sky, and the light to heal my soul.
Thank you, God, for the magnificence of everything. Thank you for opening
my soul so that I may realize the wonder of You.

The words were from Jenny's Journal of Inspiration. Sam had meditated on them over the last hour. His sister had written an entire notebook of spiritual thoughts for him before she died at age sixteen from complications of kidney disease. The elders of their Ute tribe believed Jenny to be a medicine woman, one whose dreams were to be respected. Many of her visions had been about lessons her brother would have to learn in his life, and how, despite the difficulties, he needed to learn those lessons before he could move on.

Now, after thirty days in the wild, it was time to return to civilization. He had packed his backpack and travel bag with all his worldly possessions and headed south, to meet up with Whip.

"Ain't it grand to be back in culture and sophistication?" McCracken winked as he slowed around a couple dancing in the middle of the street and then sped up the road that would take them to the Estevez Orphanage.

Sam smiled but didn't respond.

"Man oh man, Hunoon was happy as a clam at high tide when I told her about you joinin' us in Nicaragua."

"Did you guys get married?"

"We cain't without you!" McCracken slapped him on the knee. "I needed a best man by my side, and Hunoon needed a maid of honor. You fill both vacancies."

Sam gave him a sidelong glance. "I take it you don't know anybody in Nicaragua."

"I know Cheslor Estevez."

"Oh yeah, the guy who owns the casino and baseball team."

"And finances our orphanage." McCracken winked again. "His daddy made millions in real estate, and his son wanted to thank the neighbors by creating jobs and helping kids."

"You're good at helping kids."

"And Cheslor's interested in a stud pitcher like you helping his team."

Sam rubbed his right shoulder. "I haven't pitched competitively in more than two years, Whip. I don't know if this old wing can fly anymore."

"Don't sell yerself short, EssCee. I caught yer side pieces at the Friends of Everyone. You got it, brother—you got *it*."

Sam chuckled. *EssCee* was the name the Afghan children at McCracken's mission called him when they played the greatest game in the world. "EssCee" for his initials, and he did love baseball.

"So when do I meet the distinguished Duke of Diriamba?"

"Tryouts are tomorrow. Señor Estevez built a ballpark onto the backside of his casino. Seats two thousand. You can walk straight from the blackjack table to Diamond Club seating."

"They have a Diamond Club?"

"Bleachers in the shade and all the free popcorn and tostones you can eat."

"Tostones, huh?"

"Deep-fried plantains … mm, mm, good."

Sam smiled as he thought of playing competitive baseball again: the laughter, the teasing, the chatter of the game … *focus and fire … good hustle, kid … turn two … bring him home* … ah, the joy of being part of a team again. College baseball had been the best time of his life.

He was Mesa State's MVP as a sophomore, and much was expected his draft-eligible junior year. The Mavericks were predicted to win it all. Sam Cloud-Carson was the preseason pick as Division II Player of the Year; and he was dating the prettiest girl on campus, Lindsey Ellison.

That all came crashing down the day he came home for Christmas break in 2008. He remembered it being a perfect day. He had aced his finals, had thrown well in a session before three pro scouts, and Lindsey had told him she loved him. The sun was shining and seemed to shine brighter on everything Sam touched. Until …

A shiver ran up his spine as he stared down at the hands that intuitively guided a baseball with incredible precision. They were also the hands that had pulled back the arrows on the bow that had taken the lives of two men that same day.

It didn't matter that Billy Cutthredge and Rob Marcus deserved to die. They were evil. They were responsible for his mom dying in a car accident and for kidnapping his friend, Teresa Songbird. But Sam's decision to go after Billy and Rob instead of telling the police had changed his destiny from chasing his baseball dream to working for a man he despised. Drake Dixon … the owner of DiamondBar Security, who had happened onto the crime scene and blackmailed Sam into working for his private military company in Afghanistan.

Even thinking Dixon's name rattled Sam, and he inhaled a deep breath before asking, "Did Dixon make the charitable donations I asked for?"

McCracken gave a thumbs-up. "Two hundred fifty grand for Islamic Relief, two fifty for Mother Teresa's Missionaries of Charity, and a hundred grand for the Southern Ute Cultural Center. None of the checks bounced, and the American press gave him tons of love for being such a benevolent dude."

Sam stared out the windshield into the now black night.

"When's the last time you talked to Colonel T, Sammy?"

"Last week. He said there's been no further construction on the road to Hazrat's mountain."

"Colonel's a good man," said McCracken, and Sam nodded respectfully.

Colonel Bart Tomlinson was more than good. The Special Forces commander at Bagram Air Base had been his guardian angel during his time in Afghanistan. The colonel had mentored him in reading aerial photographs and satellite images, protected him from jealous DiamondBar coworkers, counseled him during his emotional breakdown and had introduced him to the man who was now driving him to his new home.

Whiplash McCracken, Colonel Tomlinson, and an Afghan village chief named Abdul Hazrat were the men he had entrusted with sealed letters, each revealing the story of what happened that tragic day on Pargin Mountain. Sam had given the men strict instructions not to open the files unless he was killed or disabled by one of Dixon's goons.

"Colonel has a good gut when it comes to reading people," McCracken continued. "He told me before I even met you that Drake Dixon was a snake—"

"Snakes aren't vindictive!" Sam snapped. He immediately regretted his outburst, for McCracken had been a godsend, a friend who had helped him conquer his depression in Afghanistan, and now, who was helping him find work in Nicaragua.

"Sorry to bark at you, Whip."

"No worries."

Sam sighed, recovering himself. "The colonel's not only been updating me about Hazrat's mountain. He's been keeping an eye on Dixon too."

"Smart man. There's a helluva lotta money in the private military contracting business … and not all of it done for the right reasons."

It was time to change the subject. Sam needed to talk about anything else because of the deal he had made with Dixon—he would never talk about his time working for DiamondBar as long as Dixon made the charitable donations Sam demanded and stayed away from Hazrat's mountain. He mumbled some unintelligible but affirmative grunt, settled back in his seat, and closed his eyes.

Healing doesn't mean the damage never existed.
It means the damage no longer controls your life.

For the second time that day, words from his sister's journal came to him. The damage had been done. He had lost his parents and sister since first meeting Dixon seven years earlier.

The man had conned both father and son into working for DiamondBar; the first time, promising Daniel Carson a kidney transplant for his ailing daughter, and the second time, blackmailing Sam into tracking for his security team in the mountains of Afghanistan. But he would no longer let Dixon control his life or his mind. He would simply honor their agreement and keep his mouth shut.

CHAPTER TWO

Stilwell, Kansas

September 2011

Sydney Harrison sat on her parents' couch, in Stilwell, Kansas, looking through old family photo albums. She turned a page, then another, and another. Nothing.

"Hey, Mom! How come there are no baby pictures of me?"

Vivian Morgan came out from the kitchen and gave her daughter a puzzled look. "Sure there are, honey. They're in that album you're going through."

Sydney slipped a twenty-four-year-old photo from its yellowed plastic protection and held it up for her mother to see. "All of these are *after* my cleft surgery. I was looking for a picture *with* my cleft to show my students."

Vivian hesitated, then her hand fell on a second album that was open on the back of the couch. Inside were pictures of her daughter several months after her first surgery, who, despite a haphazard clutter of crooked teeth, twisted nose, and a scar from nose to lip, had a bright, unaffected smile lighting her face. The physical imperfection had all been repaired over the years by the best orthodontists and plastic surgeons in Kansas City, save for the one still tiny visible line that curved from Sydney's upper right lip to her nose.

"Why do you need a picture from before the surgery?"

"Because it's my history class, Mom. I asked my students to write about their personal histories, complete with pictures from their newborn, elementary school, and now high school years. I think it's important that I share my story with them too. Plus, there's a girl in my class who has a cleft and is very aware of it, and consequently, very shy. I thought if I shared my past, well … y'know."

Her mother nodded.

"Were you embarrassed about having a child with a cleft?"

"No," Vivian said defensively. "Of course not. I just didn't think about taking any pictures before the surgery."

Sydney's hand reflexively went to her mouth, her index finger tracing the scar from lip to nose and then back again. "It's part of who I was, Mom … and part of who I am today."

Her mother's face tightened, and she stared down at the albums with an expression somewhere between guilt and shame. "I'm sorry, honey. I was sure we had pictures of when you were born … at least we have some from after the doctors fixed your lip."

"But none *of* my first birthday. No cake or opening presents or blowing out a candle because it showed my gross scar."

"Don't say that. It was so long ago, I can't even remember."

Sydney turned another page in the album. They were all joyful memories from a childhood of love, laughter, sports, family, and faith. Sydney and her younger brother, Tom, now in his first year of law school at Loyola of Chicago. The album of their youth: Sydney's first day of kindergarten, Tom's first day of kindergarten; Sydney as an altar server at St. Benedict's Catholic Church, Tom as an altar boy; Sydney receiving the Girl Scout Gold Award, Tom as an Eagle Scout; Sydney, captain of the Blue Valley High girls soccer team, Tom, co-captain of the football team. There were plenty of baby pictures of Tom and his perfect smile, but none of Sydney before her first surgery She knew her mom loved her, but was there a part of her mom that felt guilty about her past? Maybe she thought her daughter's cleft was God's punishment for getting pregnant before marriage. Her mom had to feel some guilt for raising a child who was sired by a man other than the father who raised her.

"Do you have any pictures of my birth father?" Sydney asked.

Her mother slapped one of the albums so sharply that several pictures fell on the floor. "Of course not! Why are you being so hurtful today?"

"I'm not, Mom. I just want to share my story with my class."

"Well, that's part of my past that I'm not proud of. I'd appreciate it if you'd leave that out. Now, tell me, how's Blake doing?"

The question caught Sydney by surprise. "What?"

"Blake? You know, your husband. Did he see the doctor?"

Sydney pushed a strand of her long black hair away from her face and gave a dismal nod. "Dr. Duncan wrote him another prescription for pain."

"He should have quit football after high school. He's never gotten over that knee injury."

It was true. Blake had torn his anterior cruciate ligament on the first play of the second half of Blue Valley's 5A State Championship game in 2006. He was the senior All-League tight end. It was a simple dive play. But the opponent's defensive end had gone low and pinned Blake's leg backward, ripping the ACL completely away from the bone. Season over. Division I scholarship gone. He accepted a partial to Pittsburg State University, tore the knee again, then the other one, and his football career was finished. But the agony remained, which led to pain pills, then to marijuana and late nights at the bar.

Blake had always been a charmer, a high-energy, life-of-the-party guy, and the new pharmaceuticals took his buzz to the next level. Just the type of guy her friends had warned her about … yet she had not listened.

She had fallen for Blake as soon as he showed the least bit of interest. Why would a boy as popular as Blake Harrison ever be interested in a girl as unremarkable as Sydney Morgan? History Club Sydney Morgan. Sierra Club Sydney Morgan. Soccer midfielder Sydney Morgan. Cleft lip Sydney Morgan.

When Blake fell on hard times in college, she believed she could fix him. Even gave up her soccer scholarship to Kansas State University and transferred to Pittsburg to help him through his depression. Sydney Morgan, loyal girlfriend to the end. Only now, five years later, and two into a marriage that had experienced more than its share of ups and downs, she wasn't quite sure about anything anymore.

CHAPTER THREE

Diriamba, Nicaragua

September 2011

The baseball spikes were at least two sizes too big, but with an extra pair of socks and pulling the laces tight, not a bad fit. Sam nodded to McCracken, sitting in the stands, grabbed his baseball bag, and jogged out to join the rest of the men trying out for the Diriamba Dukes. The Dukes were relatively new to the Nicaraguan Baseball League and still scrambling to find talent. Consequently, they'd finished dead last in each of their first four seasons.

Today's hopefuls came in all shapes, sizes, and ages. From a sixteen-year-old string bean who worked on a nearby plantain farm to a forty-one-year-old car mechanic who looked like the Looney Tunes cartoon character Yosemite Sam, complete with the long handlebar mustache. At six-foot-four, Sam was by far the tallest among the tryouts and the player the Dukes' owner seemed most interested in.

"So you are the one Weeplash talking bout?" Cheslor Estevez said as he stepped out of his lime-green-and-navy-blue golf cart, the same colors as his beloved Dukes. "The All-Amereecano from Colorado."

Sam couldn't help but grin as he shook the man's hand. "Nice to meet you, Señor Estevez. *Yo hablo español.*"

"No, no, no." Estevez shook an index finger at Sam. "I need to work *en mi ingles.* Two *beisbol* teams de Managua have *americano* players. I want *americano* too—but he must be bueno."

"I still have to try out, señor."

"And you shall!" Estevez gave him a hearty slap on the back and pushed him toward the playing field. "Ahora, uh, now, I see you peetch!"

Sam stopped midstride and looked back at the owner. "Do you mind if I stretch first?"

Estevez looked confused. "Stretch?"

Sam windmilled his right arm in a circle and said, *"Estirar."*

"Stretch! But of course!" He clapped his hands at the rest of the athletes who were there for the tryout. *"Todos ustedes! Estirar con EssCee Carson!"*

*   *   *

Sam felt every eye in the ballpark watching him as he reached into his glove for the baseball. It felt great to be on the mound again, that beautiful white pearl so comfortable in his hand, fingers finding the red seams like two old friends reconnecting after … how long had it been since yesterday's throwing session on the beach? Sixteen hours?

But this was different. This was competition. An audition. Trying out for a team.

He nodded to his catcher, inhaled a deep, calming breath, and exhaled an easy, uncomplicated windup and delivery that culminated with a resounding *thwump* as the ball hit the very center of his catcher's old leather mitt. Ah, the sound of pure heaven.

It wasn't until Sam's eighth pitch that someone finally spoke.

"Creo que haras los Duques." I think you will make the Dukes. It was his catcher, Yosemite Sam, the car mechanic, grinning broadly as he tossed the ball back to him. *"Muy bien, mi amigo."*

Sam smiled back and then rolled his glove forward, letting Yosemite know his curve was next. The delivery was the same as his fastball, but at the last instant, Sam hooked his wrist, pulling down on the ball, letting the spin, gravity, air pressure, and humidity do the rest. Yosemite missed catching the ball by a good six inches as it ricocheted off his shin guard and rolled toward third base.

"Lo siento!" an embarrassed Yosemite called out. *"Tiralo de nuevo, lo etrapo esta vez." Sorry, throw it again, I'll catch it this time."*

He did, and Yosemite caught it, tracking the ball carefully into his glove.

Sam threw two more curves, a slider, and a changeup before Cheslor Estevez waved both arms over his head and hurried out to the field, the look of a prospector who had just discovered a gold nugget in a mountain stream lighting his face.

"Muy bien, EssCee Carson!" He clapped enthusiastically. "Your tryout is *terminado.* Be here *mañana, ocho*–uh–morning."

"Shouldn't I meet the coach first?" Sam asked.

"And you shall! Rafael Vargas will be here *mañana.*"

Sam scanned the stands where thirty to forty people were watching. "Coach Vargas doesn't pick the team?"

Estevez gave another look of confusion.

Sam repeated his questions in Spanish. *"El entrenador Vargas no elige el equipo?"*

This time Estevez's two bushy eyebrows drew together in anger. *"Por supuesto no! Soy dueño del equipo. Elijo a los jugadores!" Of course not! I own the team. I pick the players.*

Sam stared at him, speechless, then he walked off the mound, gathered his gear, and followed Whiplash to his Jeep.

*   *   *

"I only threw about fifteen pitches," Sam said as they drove up the hill to the Estevez Orphanage. The old abandoned church was only a mile from the casino, but one would never know it from the seldom-used dirt road and overgrown trees, weeds, and bushes that spilled out over the path.

"He saw enough of you that he don't want word to git out that his Dukes have a secret weapon." McCracken stopped the Jeep to remove a branch that had fallen across the road. "When yer not throwin' no-hitters for Señor Estevez, I'd like you to fix this road so the dairy truck don't have to drop off our milk at the casino."

"I'll start tomorrow."

"Not until after the Dukes practice." McCracken grabbed one end of the branch, and Sam the other. Together, they threw it off the road. "If yer as good as I think you are, it'll be a win-win situation for the orphanage. Estevez said he'd buy us an air conditioner for the children's sleeping quarters if you help the Dukes win."

"Thanks for the pressure," Sam said as he hopped back in the Jeep.

"No problemo, buddy. By the way, how the heck did you throw fifteen perfectly located pitches after hibernatin' on our beaches and jungles the last month?"

"I bought ten baseballs, a small rug, and a Sharpie when I arrived in Managua. Built a sand and dirt mound about sixty feet from a tree with a low-hanging branch, hung the rug on the branch, and drew a strike zone on the rug. I threw ten balls at the target, picked 'em up, and did it again. Twenty times is two hundred pitches."

"Pretty ingenious," said McCracken as they continued up the bumpy trail. "Hopefully more of that resourcefulness will come in handy when you fix this road."

*　　*　　*

The church property was nothing special. It had been abandoned in the late seventies after Nicaragua's earthquake and then a civil war brought down the Somoza family dictatorship. The change in government drew outlaws and con men to the region, and those living near the church fled to the refuge of the bigger cities.

The local clan, which owned over five hundred acres, was pushed out, and Cheslor Estevez's father, Hernaldo, a banker from Managua, came across the property deed and purchased the land for one-tenth of its value. Hernaldo built a casino that brought money from nearby Diriamba and

Jinotepe, and the Estevez fortune flourished. But the forty-acre church property northwest of the casino was left for dead.

The old stone chapel seemed to have grown out of the jungle, with vines climbing up the outside walls and roots from eucalyptus trees pushing against the steps of the church, making the entrance look swollen. A small creek was south of the property, some fifty meters downhill, lined by beautiful citrus trees with overripe fruit. There was a long house, where the orphans slept and meals were served, connected to the side of the sanctuary.

"It's got potential," Sam said when they pulled up next to a gravel path. "Maybe it will look as beautiful as the Friends of Everyone Hotel someday."

McCracken smiled. He had started the Friends mission in Afghanistan, after war broke out in 2003, and turned it into a much needed destination for refugees escaping the horrors of both terrorism and counterterrorism. Whiplash's way of preaching was simply through service; he believed that ministers of God came from all religions and no religion, that they could teach by actions or thoughts, words or silence, prayers or meditation, and that each and every form of service could benefit both giver and receiver.

"I'm making you my Dean of Physical Collaboration." McCracken winked. "You'll be in charge of landscapin' church grounds, fixin' the road, and teachin' the children the importance of sports and movin' yer body."

"That's a lot to do along with playing ball, Whip."

"But you'll have twenty-five of the most energetic kids to help git the job done—" McCracken paused when the front door of the church opened and out stepped a woman wearing a brightly colored, full-length sundress with a blazing aquamarine shayla scarf covering her head and shoulders. "Led by my Professor of Interior Design, the lovely Hunoon Sanjari."

Hunoon hurried down the steps of the church and threw her arms around Sam.

"It is so good to see you again, Samuel!"

After two and a half years in Afghanistan, Sam was more than surprised by Hunoon's expression of gregarious affection. Most Afghan women were not even allowed to shake hands with a man outside their family, but Hunoon was well past that religious restriction as she pulled his hand up to her cheek. "As Whiplash would say, you are a vision for sour eyes."

"You mean … a sight for sore eyes?" Sam corrected her.

"Sore? Sour? Whatever."

Sam bowed in respect. *"Wa-Alaikumussalam wa-Rahmatullah." May the peace, mercy, and blessings of Allah be upon you.*

"Yes, yes, yes, of course." She turned him to face the children, who were now all gathered on the steps. "I have told the children of your excellence in baseball, and they are very excited to have you coach their Little League teams."

Sam's mouth fell open. "You—what? When am I gonna have time to coach?"

Hunoon reached into the pocket of her dress and pulled out a note card. "I have your schedule right here, Samuel. Wake up at five a.m., coffee at five oh five." She smiled cheerfully up at him. "Don't worry, I'll have the coffee ready for you. Five fifteen prayer time, five forty-five yoga, six thirty set table, seven a.m. breakfast, seven thirty fast walk to Estevez Park. Eight a.m. Dukes practice, noon lunch. One p.m., children will join you at stadium as Señor Estevez has given us permission to use the big field for practice."

McCracken slapped him on the back. "Cheslor's just as fired up about havin' a Little League champ as he is about havin' a Big League weener. Said he's gonna donate all the old equipment from last year's Big Dukes and buy his Little Dukes new uniforms complete with their lime-green-and-navy-blue colors. It's gonna be awesome!"

Sam eased himself down on the bumper of the Jeep. "There aren't enough hours in the day for me to do what you're asking."

"Ah, but your day is not over yet, Samuel." Hunoon beamed. "Little League practice is from one to three, then come home for a short nap before working on road and helping children pull vines off side of the chapel, then weeding and building a new garden from four to six." She clapped her hands. "Must work quickly, dinner is promptly at six thirty, reading at seven thirty, and lights out eight thirty."

McCracken put a hand on his shoulder. "That's just the first month, Sammy. We'll back off when Dukes' games begin in November."

Sam didn't speak for a long time as his gaze panned from the church to the road, to the citrus trees, and then finally back to McCracken. "I'm already exhausted."

CHAPTER FOUR

Stilwell, Kansas

September 2011

Sydney looked over her shoulder at the cars parked in the Overland Park Soccer Complex. No 2008 navy blue Chevy Camaro. No husband who had dropped her off at the field, then promised he would return from an errand in time to watch her Tigers battle the Jaguars before they went to dinner. It was only club soccer fall ball, but this was Blue Valley vs. Blue Valley West, rival high schools in south Johnson County, who had played to a 1-1 tie at the half.

Sydney's goal was to make club soccer less regimented than the regular season. She wanted the parents to know how much she cared about their support and that the serious competition would be in the spring when the Eastern Kansas League season began. Fall soccer should be about fun and teambuilding: laughter, friendship, and developing trust.

Sydney took off her sunglasses, wiped the sweat from her brow, and glanced down at her watch. Her skin was almost the same color as the bronze leather band. That glow was part of her Lakota heritage; a past she knew little about. Her mother had only told her a few details about a relationship she'd had in the summer and fall of 1986.

She had been on a church mission at the Rosebud Indian Reservation in South Dakota. An affair with a young man of the Sicangu Lakota tribe resulted in Vivian's pregnancy, and when church officials found out, they immediately sent her home to have baby Sydney. Six months later, her mother met her future husband at a Catholic Bible study, and they were married within a year.

Jeffrey Morgan was a good man. A good Christian, husband, and father. He doted on little Sydney and later his own blood child, Tom. Coached them in soccer, softball, basketball, and football, and never once did Sydney feel as if she was unloved. They were family. Her mom had said there was no need to dig into the past, for there were no dark secrets, no mysteries about her biological father. The unmarried couple had sinned, been forgiven by God, and had moved on with their lives. But now, as an adult, Sydney had unanswered questions. Did her biological father ever think about her? Did he even care?

"Hey, Coach! Who do you want starting the second half?"

The question from her captain and midfielder jolted Sydney back to the now, and she glanced one more time at the parking lot, still absent one blue Camaro. She looked down at her notebook.

"Alexis, Kristin, Taylor, forwards," she said softly, suddenly feeling very tired. "Elliot, Grayson, Ryan, Julia, midfield. Katie, Peyton, Meg, fullbacks, and Carly in goal."

"Are you okay, Coach?" Her captain, Ryan, asked innocently.

Sydney nodded, inhaled a deep breath to get her mind back to where it needed to be, and waved for her team to gather round. She went to one knee and pulled out her dry-erase board. "Let's continue to attack the Jags' left side." She drew lines from one *X* to another. "I think if we can stay wide right, Tay can draw their inexperienced left fullback, which should open up the middle." Her eyes scanned her team, then locked on her captain. "Bring 'em in, Ry."

Fifteen fists joined as one, with Ryan shouting, "Tigers!"

Sydney's eyes followed Ryan as she led her teammates onto the field to start the second half. It reminded her of her own Blue Valley days, when her coach had selected her to lead the team. He said he had chosen her as captain for three reasons. She was the Tigers' most competitive player, and her teammates respected her. But she was also the most introverted. He needed her to speak up, encourage her teammates, and fire up the Tigers if they were going to make it to postseason. She did. And the Tigers did.

*　　*　　*

"Out wide! Out wide!" Sydney shouted as her Tigers pushed the ball forward. "Now!"

Right wing Taylor Layne, hearing her coach, sprinted to the sideline, accepted the pass from Grayson Garcia, eluded a Jag defender, dribbled down the sideline, and then lofted a perfect pass to midfielder Elliot Loren, who headed the ball into the right corner of the goal.

"Yeah!" Sydney shook her fist to the sky. "Great teamwork, ladies!"

The small band of parents and friends in the aluminum bleachers behind her shrieked with delight. She turned to give them a thankful smile and froze. Blake was in the parking lot, leaning against his Camaro, chatting with the older sisters of two of her players. He took a sip of whatever it was he was drinking, and then, as if knowing his wife was watching, he raised his cup to her and winked.

She managed a nod, then turned back around to watch her team celebrate their goal on the field. The Tigers led 2-1 with only minutes to play, but she couldn't even smile, couldn't even think in a straight line, as the image of her husband flirting rattled through her mind.

*　　*　　*

"Are you finally ready to go?" Blake asked as he opened the trunk of his car. Sydney's Tigers had won, and she had stopped to visit with parents about where to dine for the postgame meal.

She tossed her ball bag in and closed the trunk. "We're meeting at Jalapeños."

Blake leaned back against his car and groaned. "I don't want to have dinner with a bunch of teenagers and their parents. C'mon, I've got us a table at Crazy 8's."

Sydney gave him a sideways glance. "I told you this morning we were having a team dinner."

"I don't remember that conversation."

"I forwarded you Mrs. Goldman's email invite two days ago."

"I didn't see it. It must have gone to spam."

"Don't do this, Blake. It's our first team dinner in months. I'm the coach. I have to go."

He ignored her as he slid into the driver's seat and brought a red plastic cup to his mouth.

"Let me drive," she said. "It's not only against the law to drink and drive but also to bring alcohol to the soccer complex."

"Oh God. Here we go again. It's only one beer. Don't make it a big deal."

"But you could get my team suspended."

"They won't suspend you. You're a Final Four coach. Why do you stress about everything? Shit, all our friends think you're way too sensitive."

Sydney went silent as she tried to think of a response. Was Blake right? Was that true? Did other people think she was too serious and no fun anymore?

Blake started the car and patted the passenger's seat as he looked up, his eyes dancing with that sweet, mischievous, Cheshire twinkle. "Sit down, baby. Y'know I'm only doing what you asked."

She raised a quizzical brow.

"Don't you remember? You told me to make friends with my new coworkers. So I asked Phil and the guys who work the line to join me for drinks."

She nodded innocently, still confused, and sat down next to him. She sort of remembered telling him to get to know his new coworkers. After Blake had lost his last two sales jobs at Sprint and the Chevy dealership, her father had convinced his boss to hire Blake as a salesman for the Best in Field produce company. It was a midsized family business, only forty employees, down by the Missouri River bottoms. At first, it seemed like a perfect fit with Blake's natural gift of gab making everyone laugh and enjoy his company.

But over time, his corrosive nature surfaced, and her father was concerned that Blake was spreading untruths about salespeople above him. Sydney thought her dad the kindest man in the world, almost too kind, and it pained her to watch people take advantage of him. Jeffrey Morgan was a strong Christian who believed that if an individual accepted Jesus Christ as his Lord and Savior, it was his responsibility to stay with that person through any difficulty they might have. Unfortunately, there were people who used her father's religious conviction as a way to benefit themselves. She worried that her own husband might be one of those exploiting her father's kindness.

"Here's what we'll do." Blake said as he grabbed her hand. "I'll drop you off at Jalapeños for one hour. That should be enough time for your players parents to fawn over you, and then Uber over to Crazy 8's." He squeezed her hand to emphasize his point. "But no more than one hour."

She felt her shoulders give a little. She didn't want to do this right now. She just wanted to be with her team.

"Okay," she finally said, then slipped her hand free.

CHAPTER FIVE

Diriamba, Nicaragua

November 2011

Juan Carlos Pineda had no chance. As Sam sliced a low-and-away slider, the right-handed hitter threw his bat at the ball in a futile effort to make contact. The bat ricocheted off the sunbaked dirt of Estevez Field and almost hit his teammate in the on-deck circle.

"Watch it, man!" Fernando Soto ducked out of the way. "You trying to kill me?"

It was only an intrasquad game, but the Dukes' owner, standing behind the safety of the home-plate screen, shook his fist to the sky. "That's seven straight strikeouts by my American secret weapon!" Estevez roared. Then he leaned into the dugout and whispered to his manager, Rafael Vargas, "Just wait until that arrogant damn Indios' owner sees my EssCee this Sunday in the season opener. They won't touch him."

Vargas' jaws tightened, but he didn't answer. Everyone in Diriamba knew that Estevez hated the owner of Nicaragua's best team. Indios del Bóer had won both the Nicaraguan Professional Baseball League Championship and the National Championship of Superior Baseball of Nicaragua each of the last three years and had embarrassed the Dukes in every single game. Eighteen losses. No wins.

Sam fired a fastball past another baffled Dukes hitter for his eighth-straight strikeout.

"Fantástico!" Estevez clapped. "My Dukes are ready to take the crown!"

Vargas stepped down into the dugout and hid behind the concrete wall. His right hand shot to his forehead and squeezed his temples.

"Yo, Vargie," Sam called out as he jogged off the field. "How do you like being the front runner?"

His manager released a frustrated exhale. "You'd better kick ass on Sunday, gringo."

"Gringo?" Sam laughed. "I'm not welcome on any team unless I pitch well. The pressure's on *me*."

Vargas gave him a wry smile. It was true. All the pressure was on the *americano.* There was talk at the sports bars in Diriamba that the Dukes had brought in a hotshot pitcher from the States. Some former college star from the Colorado mountains. Where he had come from and why he wasn't pitching for some Major League organization were questions everyone had been asking.

And, while Estevez refused to allow Sam to talk with the press, the Dukes' owner was stirring the proverbial promotional pot with dramatic stories of his newfound discovery, telling local writers that, before EssCee tried out for his Dukes, he was seen by local farmers throwing rocks at coconuts, knocking them off palm trees from distances beyond two hundred feet. Estevez said the spin of EssCee's curveball hissed like the wicked fer-de-lance pit viper of Central American jungles and that his cutter had broken so many bats that Estevez had to take out a loan from Banco Lafise Nicaragua to buy new ones.

No way, the sportswriters wrote. The gringo couldn't be that good. It was all typical Estevez hype, exaggeration, and grandiose publicity to get people to come watch baseball at his stadium and spend money at his casino.

Sam hadn't read the papers, but his new teammates teased him about the owner's hyperbole and the kids at the orphanage demanded to hear his curveball *hissss.*

*   *   *

"Let's go, Coach EssCee! Let's go!" the children cried out when the Big League intrasquad game ended. It was time for the Little League Dukes to practice.

Sam nodded wearily, put on his best smile, and trotted back out onto the field. After a two-hour practice game, where he had pitched five of seven innings, his body *and* mind longed for the thirty-minute nap that Hunoon promised him every day. But Whiplash had brought the kids early so they could watch the final inning of Sam pitching, and the *ooos and ahhs* when he struck out batter after batter fired him up. He couldn't dare ask for a break with twenty-five children's faces pressed against the chain-link fence, pleading to take the field. This was their once-a-day break from school and working the church grounds to play the game they loved.

Baseball. The great equalizer. A game where it didn't matter how big or fast or rich or poor you were; it only demanded toughness. Could you square up a round ball with a round bat? Could you handle disappointment? How would you walk back to the dugout after striking out, or could you throw a strike after walking the bases loaded, knowing every eye on the field was watching you? The kids of the Estevez Orphanage had all experienced their share of hardship in life, but for a couple of hours a day, they could forget all their troubles and just play.

Baseball had become their refuge, and the anticipation of their first winter-ball game on Saturday only juiced their excitement more. There was no way Sam was going to tell them he was too tired to coach.

"Hey, Whip," Sam called out to his co-coach. "Why don't you work with the older kids on infield drills while I take the younger ones to the outfield?"

"Will do." McCracken rubbed his right shoulder as if in pain. "But could you throw BP, cuz my wing's about to fall off from all the throwin' I done this week?"

Sam snorted, but not without sympathy. He pinwheeled his own arm over his head and said, "I think I have another inning in me. Why don't you have Carlita throw two innings of up-downs to get her ready for Saturday."

Carlita Rapino's eyes went wide. "I'm starting on Saturday, EssCee?"

"If you keep pounding that strike zone like you have all week, you the man." Sam slapped his face in mock chagrin and then bowed to Carlita. "I beg your pardon, señorita … you the *lady*."

She giggled with both excitement and bashfulness as Sam winked at her and then took the younger kids to the outfield.

The Estevez Casino Little League Dukes would have two teams playing on Saturday. The eight- and nine-year-olds in the first game and the ten- through twelve-year-olds in game two. McCracken had to petition the Diriamba Little League to include six- and seven-year-olds to play or they wouldn't have enough players to be able to compete.

It was coach-pitch for the little guys and nobody kept score, so no big deal, but the older kids had to provide their own pitcher, and while Carlita Rapino didn't throw as hard as some of the boys, she threw strikes.

*　　*　　*

"All right, everybody, line up!" Sam called out in English. He thought coaching was a great way to teach kids a new language. As the ten six- to nine-year-olds spread out in front of Sam in two perfect lines of five, he continued his instructions in both English and Spanish.

"*Saltando Jacks!*" he said in a low, gravelly, pretend-mean voice.

They all laughed and yelled back, "Jumping Jacks!"

"*Uno dos, abrocha mi zapato!*" he yelled out as they threw their arms over their heads.

"One, two, buckle my shoe!" they answered.

"*Tres, cuatro, cierra la puerta!*"

"Three, four, shut the door!"

"*Cinco, seis, recoger palos!*"

"Five, six, pick up sticks!"

"Siete, ocho, una gallina grande y gorda!"

"Seven, eight, a big fat hen!"

The training and laughter went on for the next thirty minutes before Sam turned it over to one of the older boys. Teddy Zapata, at fifteen, was too old to play, but he was also a victim of polio that had left him with a terrible limp. Sam made him his assistant coach.

"I have to throw BP to the big kids," he said to Teddy. "Run a scrimmage and put them in the positions you'll have them start on Saturday."

Both of Teddy's brows rose. "Where should I play them?"

"Wherever you want." Then Sam leaned close so only Teddy could hear. "Just put somebody who can catch the ball at first base. I don't want any broken noses in the first game."

*   *   *

Sam felt revitalized, the weariness of his morning work at the orphanage and three hours on the ball field suddenly gone. As McCracken loaded the kids on an old school bus the casino owner was rumored to have acquired through a somewhat shady transaction, Sam waved for Whip to go on without him.

"I thought you were beat?" McCracken yelled out of the driver's side window. "Hunoon offered one of her famous shoulder massages when you git home."

"I caught my second wind. And it's time for my afternoon meditation. Thought I'd focus on Jenny's message for the day."

"I'll keep yer supper warm." McCracken winked, then put the bus in gear. He drove about ten feet before slamming on the brakes. The door opened and out jumped Carlita Rapino.

"Can I walk with you, Coach?"

"As long as you don't mind me not talking."

*   *   *

Sam explained to Carlita why meditating was important to him. How it was his way of not only reconnecting with his source, but also with his deceased sister. He told her how Jenny had been tormented throughout her life by a kidney disease and how, despite her suffering, she had started a support group to help other children. His sister had never complained, only inspired, and she had startling visions so accurate that the elders of their Southern Ute tribe believed her to be a medicine woman.

He told Carlita about Jenny's Journal of Inspiration and how she had left him with a book of quotes, thoughts, and suggestions of how best he should live his life. Most of them were downright simple, ancient wisdoms and sayings that had always been true, but too often invisible to a busy or closed mind.

"What did you read today?" Carlita asked.

Sam looked up at the sky. The sun was setting but still fifteen minutes from dipping below the tops of the western trees. "We all have good medicine in us. But the key is figuring out how we'll use our good medicine to help others."

She gave a puzzled look. "What's good medicine?"

"In most cultures, Carlita, medicine is some potion or pill you take to treat an illness. But in my culture, medicine means spiritual power. To me, even though my sister is gone, her words have spiritual power … good medicine."

They walked on, quietly now, up the dirt road and into the tunnel of trees, past bright green laurel, bushy cedar, and thick native shrubs until Sam froze and put an index finger to his lips. He turned very slowly to the spot where his eyes, ears, and nose were telling him to go. He motioned for Carlita to follow him as he turned off the road and headed into the woods. At first, she reached for him, as if fearful of the darkness, but the intent focus on her coach's face made her curious.

The wind changed, and Sam turned his head with it, studying, listening, waiting. Then he moved on, carving his way through some unseen path. A minute later, he paused and knelt down, brushing grass away to reveal a cat's paw print.

"I saw one of these near the beach," he whispered and Carlita drew closer. "I think it's jaguarundi. We don't have them in Colorado."

She didn't say anything, but the look on her face told Sam this eleven-year-old girl had no interest in meeting a wildcat in the jungle.

"Don't worry, jaguarundi won't bother us." He separated his hands by about two feet. "They're not very big–only eat small animals."

She gulped. "I'm small."

"No, you're not. You're strong and tough. That's why I picked you to start on Saturday."

His words didn't seem to make her feel any better, so he turned his back to her and bent low. "Climb on, kid. I'll get us out of here."

She did climb on. As fast as she could.

When they returned to the road, he let her down and brushed the leaves off her back. "Sorry to worry you, Carlita. I just got a little excited about seeing my first jaguarundi track."

The rest of their walk was a quiet one, but it seemed as if the little girl was more aware of the sights, smells, and sounds on their journey home. When they arrived at the gravel drive, near the edge of the church property, Carlita touched his arm.

"Coach EssCee, does anything scare you?"

He paused in thought, his dark eyes distant. Her question drew him back to his past, back to Colorado, back to Afghanistan, back to the man who had almost ruined him.

"Does anything scare me?" he said, as if asking himself the same question. "Fear does visit me from time to time, particularly when I see people hurting other people. That's my reminder to get quiet and seek what my sister asked me to find–good medicine. The good medicine that frees me from the past and from being afraid."

CHAPTER SIX

Washington, DC

November 2011

Drake Dixon adjusted the Fabergé jade-bladed letter opener on his desk to be precisely in line with his Montblanc soft leather desk pad. The owner of DiamondBar Security liked his office to look perfect. From his personalized rosewood-and-silver pen holder to his 24-karat gold-plated banker's desk lamp, to his Lalique Victoire glass sculpture, Dixon wanted his tenth-floor suite overlooking the Pentagon to exude pure power.

There were pictures covering the walls of Dixon with every important person in America's capital. There was Dixon with the president, Dixon with the vice chairman of the Senate Appropriations Committee, Dixon with the governor of Virginia, and Dixon with the manager of his favorite baseball team, the Washington Nationals. There was also a dark-walnut bar in the corner with his favorite scotch demanding to be opened.

"If Congress doesn't approve this contract, we could go bankrupt," Dixon said to his lawyer as he snatched the bottle of Highland Park eighteen-year-old single-malt scotch off the top of the bar and broke the seal.

Barry King handed his boss two glasses filled with crushed ice and watched him pour the scotch to the brim. "You'll get it, Drake. After all your family's done for Senator Richardson through the years, he still owes you. He got a twenty-eight-million-dollar severance package when he retired as CEO of Dixon Industries to run for Senate, and he still gets plenty in deferred compensation from your company. That's why he made sure DiamondBar received no-bid contracts to work Afghanistan."

"This is different. We're only a year away from a presidential election, and the doves want us out."

"If we pull out of Afghanistan now, it'll start a civil war." King paused to make sure his boss heard his next words. "Ed knows our government is fundamentally inefficient to get anything done in that hellhole. He knows that America needs contractors like DiamondBar to do the job. And like I said, he owes your old man."

Drake nodded absentmindedly as he looked out his bay window to the Washington Monument. His father may have been dead twenty years, but Dean Dixon had left his only child a sizable inheritance. With help from politicians in his home state of Oklahoma and the oil and gas industry, his father's company had made millions producing the equipment and chemicals used in hydraulic fracturing.

"Ed did a fine job running my dad's company after he died," said Drake.

"And you kicked ass in the private military industry."

Dixon raised his glass. "Thanks to 9/11."

King nodded. "When the Twin Towers and the Pentagon were attacked by terrorists, Washington reached out to companies like yours. America needs DiamondBar."

Dixon finished his drink and poured himself another. "We wouldn't be having this conversation if we had secured that mineral rights deal in the Nuristan Province."

"We were so close," King muttered, "and then the kid found out what we were up to."

Dixon's right hand shot up to quiet his lawyer. He didn't want to talk about how one of his own employees had blackmailed him into ending construction of his Nuristan project. How one twenty-four-year-old rogue idealist had ended his chance to carve billions of dollars' worth of rubies, emeralds, lithium, and other precious natural resources out of a mountain in Northeast Afghanistan. The loss of both money and power still infuriated him.

It had all started out so well after Dixon's low-budget/high-return plan to use human trackers out in front of his security teams in Afghanistan. They would not only use their skills to discover where improvised explosive devices had been planted, but they'd also track potential trouble in rural regions and report their findings back to DiamondBar and Army Special Forces for an immediate response to protect American interests.

DiamondBar was well-respected within the private military community. Their training facility was only a four-hour drive from his office in DC and was top of the line in everything, complete with both indoor and outdoor firing ranges and urban reproductions of what one might find in the troubled areas of the Middle East and Afghanistan. The only thing Dixon thought the elite security company lacked was instinct. Having someone who didn't need to rely on the sophisticated technology of the twenty-first century to track down terrorists who were making life miserable for US forces, diplomats, and the Provincial Reconstruction Teams. Insurgents had success sending small bands in for quick strikes and then retreating back into the mountains; their times were so random that it made it impossible for satellites to track them. That's when Dixon happened on to SJ Outfitters in Ignacio, Colorado.

It was a simple hunting trip, something Dixon did at least four times a year. But on this excursion, he stumbled on to the most gifted wildlife trackers he had ever encountered. Daniel Carson and his son, Sam. Instinctive. Intuitive. Mystical.

The Carsons tracked on a completely different level than other guides. They would pause at the most random times, and instead of looking down, their heads would be erect, much like birds of prey, taking in sights, sounds, and smells. Then they'd move on in an almost clairvoyant manner.

Dixon had been impressed and immediately began to recruit the father. Unfortunately, Carson rejected his offer, and leverage was needed to change his mind. The bargaining chip dropped onto Dixon's lap when he found out the Carsons had a daughter with health issues. It took his

IT team only twenty minutes to hack into the Durango Medical Center's computer to find out the severity of Jenny Carson's kidney disease. They also found that the family's insurance plan didn't cover preexisting conditions. Dixon offered his company's premium plan, promised to get little Jenny a transplant, and the father reluctantly agreed.

"We're fortunate Senator Richardson didn't blow a gasket when we lost the mountain," King said.

Dixon's face tightened. His lawyer had obviously been thinking right along with him. "Ed understands war. When the Taliban bombed our bridge, he knew it was time to cut our losses and go straight to damage control."

"Our PR guys did a helluva job spinning failure into some glorious triumph."

Dixon smiled at the memory of how the story was presented on the national networks that week. "We had every member of the media singing our praises with the dramatic capture of that high-ranking Taliban official."

"And no mention of Carson being the hero," King added.

"Fuck Carson!" Dixon snapped. "He's the reason I'm in this financial mess! If he had simply brought Abdul Hazrat's children back to Bagram, we would've had the bargaining chips needed to take that mountain."

The mere mention of Carson's name always sent his mind spinning off to some dark place. Why had Carson chosen that day to disobey orders? Dixon was sure that he could control the gifted Ute tracker the same way he had controlled all of his past insubordinate employees. Break them with money or blackmail.

He had pressured Sam with both, but the kid had proven to be too brash, too headstrong, too rogue. He should have known what Carson would do once he discovered Hazrat's kidnapped children at the Taliban hideout. He would defy orders and return them to their father. That decision had potentially cost Dixon billions.

"We never should have brought Carson on board," King muttered.

Dixon glared at his lawyer. "I don't remember you objecting when he was keeping trouble away from the Provincial Reconstruction Team that was building our road."

"But I told you this might happen if he found out that Billy and Rob worked for you."

Dixon cursed under his breath. His lawyer was right. When Carson discovered that the men he had killed on Pargin Mountain were former DiamondBar employees, it wasn't hard for him to figure out that Dixon himself had covered up their deaths to blackmail Sam into working for him.

"That son of a bitch better not try and double-cross me," Dixon grumbled.

King inclined his head slightly, as if he was a trial lawyer needing to explain some already obvious detail to a judge. "Carson only went after Cutthredge and Marcus because they kidnapped his friend and Robbie was about to rape her."

"He'll have to prove it."

King nodded. "Unfortunately for Carson, he has no defense. Both Billy and Rob were unarmed when he killed them in cold blood. We have the video. We have the arrows with his fingerprints. The son of a bitch is a murderer."

"But *we* covered it up, Barry. Both of us could go to prison if this information gets out."

"You should have made him sign a contract to keep his mouth shut."

"He refused. Said his word was good enough. He promised to never talk about his time in Afghanistan."

King had expected this and was prepared for his rebuttal. "We do have the national security nondisclosure agreement he signed when he started with us. That should be enough to keep him quiet."

"I'll ruin his life if he says one word about what happened."

"We need to stay on top of this, Drake. Where's Carson now?"

"I don't know. I thought he'd go home to Colorado, but he never showed up. And no one from his tribe seems to know where he is." Dixon turned back to his lawyer. "Or maybe they do, and they refuse to tell me."

CHAPTER SEVEN

Managua, Nicaragua

November 2011

"Ball four!" shouted the umpire.

Sam bit down hard on the side of his mouth to calm his growing irritation. He had thrown sixteen perfect pitches. All, he thought, were strikes, yet all were called balls, and now his Dukes trailed Indios del Bóer of Managua 1-0 in the bottom of the first.

"This is bullshit!" The Dukes owner screamed from behind the backstop. Cheslor Estevez's face was scarlet with fury as he shook the mesh netting and continued his tirade at the home-plate umpire. "Every single one of those pitches has been a strike! I'm going to file a protest with the league office about you screwing my team!"

The owner's rage ignited a fire both on the field and inside the dugout as Dukes players and coaches now directed their indignation at the umpire.

Only Sam and his catcher, Erasmo Ortega, seemed to understand what was happening. Sam, because he expected it, and Ortega, because he knew if he complained about balls and strikes, he'd be kicked out of the game. They were testing Sam. He was a gringo. An American pitching on Nicaraguan soil whose skills had been overblown by his owner. There was no way that some damn foreigner was going to come into their capital city and show up the country's best.

He inhaled a deep breath and motioned for his catcher to give him the sign. Ortega did. Fastball right down the middle. Sam nodded and came set. He would throw a batting practice fastball, no more than seventy-five miles an hour as a way to tempt the Indios player to swing. He delivered a pitch that basically screamed, *hit me*, and the Indios player chopped the ball by the Dukes' distracted shortstop, who continued to yell at the ump as the ball rolled into left field. Two runs scored, 3-0, Indios del Bóer.

Sam asked for another ball, and the ump gave him a devilish grin as he flipped him a new one. This was a hazing. He was sure of it. It was his job to prove to both the ump and the league that he could take it. He smiled back at the ump and then motioned for Ortega to give him the sign. Another fastball down the middle. Come set, glove at chest, and ...

"Balk!" the ump yelled out, and the Indios runner at third base trotted home. 4-0, los Indios. The home fans roared; the small contingent from Diriamba hissed.

"He didn't move!" Estevez shrieked and shook the backstop screen again. "You bastard! How much are they paying you to throw this game?"

The ump spun around and pointed at the Dukes owner. "You"—his right hand shot forward as if slinging a javelin out of the stadium—"are gone!"

The meltdown of the Dukes owner would be shown on every television station in Nicaragua that night. It took four security guards to pull Estevez out of his box seats and drag him up the stairway to the stadium holding cell.

Sam gritted his teeth as he watched the entire episode, suppressing his own urge to charge the home-plate umpire and wipe that damn smirk off his face. Instead, he waited for the energy in the park to settle down and then called his team to join him on the mound.

"Listen," he said when they all gathered around. "They only want to see how the gringo handles a little pressure."

"A little pressure?" snapped shortstop Mauricio Cardenal. "We're all getting screwed by that little shit!"

"He's a cheat" ... "Motherfucker" ... "Bastardo!" several other Dukes grumbled.

Sam raised his hand to calm them. "I'm sorry you guys have to take it because of me. Let's just stay cool and get through this first game."

The ump came halfway to the mound and clapped his hands. "All right, break it up! Time to play!"

"Fuck you!" snapped Cardenal.

"Kiss my ass!" growled outfielder Juan Carlos Pineda.

The ump snorted, pointed at both players, and jerked his thumb skyward. "You're gone!"

And then all hell broke loose. Cardenal charged the umpire. Sam tackled his shortstop just before he reached the man, but he couldn't stop Pineda. The ump bolted down the right-field line, the Dukes' outfielder in fast pursuit. Both benches cleared, one to attack the ump, the other to protect him. It was as if a swollen dam had finally broken as stadium security poured onto the field, clutching at players, coaches, and fans. The crowd howled. The public-address announcer screamed for everyone to calm down and return to their seats. Two security men finally caught the Dukes' left fielder just before he claimed his prize, knocking Pineda down and handcuffing his hands behind his back.

Sam watched it all while lying on top of his shortstop, holding him down so he couldn't join the fracas. Finally, he shook his head and sighed. "I'm just glad our Little Dukes weren't here to see this."

The tension in Cardenal's body suddenly softened.

"*Sí,*" he said quietly. "This wasn't a good example of how to play as a team."

*   *   *

It was only a ninety-minute bus ride back to the Estevez Casino and Ballpark that night, and there was little conversation. Guys were still in their uniforms, dirty, sweaty, and stinking, some blood-stained from both the game and fight. Sam had an ice bag on his right shoulder from pitching six innings, and Pineda had one on his left eye from taking a security guard's fist to his face. Sam glanced about the bus and slumped down in his seat. He felt miserable. His teammates had expected so much more after all the hype Estevez had spread about his All-American from the States. He had let them down. Yeah, he got screwed by the umps, but he had done nothing to calm his teammates' fury and the melee that followed. He was sure his teammates were thinking, *If EssCee Carson gets blown out, what hope is there for the rest of us?*

Right now, hope seemed quite lost.

*   *   *

They arrived to the sounds of the Estevez Casino: rock music blaring, roulette and blackjack players cussing after a loss, and the *cha-ching-ching-ching-a-ling* of a slot-machine victory. There was also one friendly, familiar voice calling out from the parking lot.

"Shoot-fire!" Whiplash grinned when Sam and his teammates stepped off the bus. "You Dookees sure git after it! What a game!"

At the sight of the team, a stream of fans came out of the casino, clapping, whistling, and patting the players on their backs.

After a small, confused hesitation, Sam looked over at McCracken. "Ya know, Whip, we did lose the game?"

"Win? Lose?" McCracken shrugged happily. "These folks don't care. They're just happy their Dukes are a scrappy bunch. Dang, they've had their butts kicked by los Indios for years, so to see you fight for them was way cool."

"It was?"

"Heck yeah! How many of yer hombres got tossed today?"

"Seven Dukes kicked out—and, uh, one Indio."

"Holy smokes, you played shorthanded and almost beat 'em."

"We lost by seven, Whip. 9-2 isn't almost beating them."

McCracken put his arm around Sam and turned him toward the crowd. "Look at this, dude. Fans who don't have TVs drove from miles around to watch the highlights at the casino."

"Highlights of the fight, I'm sure."

"It was great!" McCracken laughed. "Highlights of the Dukes' owner being dragged out of the ball-yard, highlights of their left fielder chasing after the ump, highlights of you tackling your shortstop—the kids thought it was hilarious."

"You let our Little Dukes see the fight?"

"I couldn't stop 'em. We was listening to the game on the radio when the fight broke out, and they all ran the full mile to the casino to watch the highlights."

A disappointed Sam pushed a hand through his black hair and exhaled. "Geez, Whip, that's a real fine teaching moment."

"It will be if we use it as a *what not to do* moment." McCracken gave him a playful shove. "But the kids also saw their coach battle. They saw you not back down to Nicaragua's best team even though most of your fellow Dukes got kicked out. They saw a man who didn't complain when he got screwed by the umps, who only bowed his neck and fired six innings of hard-fought, grind-it-out, give-up-six-runs, take-one-for-the-team in a seven-run defeat. Shoot-fire, it was a beautiful thang."

As though finally catching McCracken's words, Sam stopped to watch the crowd. Some were parents, wives, and girlfriends, arriving to pick up their Dukes; others were complete strangers, beaming proudly, shaking hands, asking for autographs. It made Sam smile.

McCracken nudged him with his elbow. "Admit it, dude—it felt good to be back on the bump again, didn't it?"

He gave his friend a grateful nod.

"That's the attitude I was lookin' for!" McCracken laughed again. "Win or lose, just play the game right! I told our Little Dukes they got one up on you. Our eight- and nine-year-old team only lost 5-2, and our ten-through-twelves lost 6-2, while you got whupped 9-2. Even sweet Carlita was chirpin' like a blue jay when I told her she gave up three less runs than her hee-ro."

Sam shook his head. "Dang, Whip, you could make three-day-old roadkill sound like French cuisine."

McCracken smacked him on the back, and together they walked over to join their new fans.

CHAPTER EIGHT

Overland Park, Kansas

December 2011

"Thanks for coming with me." Sydney's voice was strained with worry as she opened the door to the doctor's office at the Overland Park Medical Plaza. She let her friend, Mary Beth Markman, go in first, then paused as if debating whether to follow, her eyes flickering from her friend to the office manager and back again.

Mary Beth reached for her hand. "I'm sure everything's all right."

Mary Beth was Sydney's oldest and dearest friend. They had met in third grade, were in the same Girl Scout troop, played on the same youth sports teams, were teammates on Blue Valley's state semifinal soccer team, had been bridesmaids at each other's weddings, and Sydney was at the hospital when Mary Beth gave birth to her first child. That was two children ago. Now Sydney wanted her friend by her side.

Sydney had had a miscarriage the year before and was nervous about this second pregnancy. She had been excited when she missed her first period and didn't even mind being nauseous or that her breasts were sore, or that she had to pee all the time. The mere thought of a new life growing inside warmed her soul. It would be a new beginning. A fresh start for Sydney and Blake. She hadn't told her husband yet, but she was sure that a baby was exactly what they needed to reignite the love they had discovered as seniors at Blue Valley High.

"Hi Sydney!" Dr. Goldman's office manager greeted her enthusiastically. "Just sign in, have a seat, and I'll pull your records."

"Is it okay if Mary Beth comes in with me?"

"You know the rules, just immediate family. You should have brought that hunk of a husband with you."

"He … has to work late this week."

Mary Beth squeezed her friend's arm. "Don't you worry, Syd, I'll be right here looking for all the hidden pictures in the *Highlights* magazines."

Sydney forced a smile and sat down.

*   *   *

It was the same old routine. Take your weight, pee in a cup, and wait for Dr. Goldman. The waiting was the hard part. One minute seemed like five, five seemed like thirty, sending her mind scattering into doubts: about Blake, about the baby, about why she'd had blood in her urine the last two mornings. It wasn't that much, barely enough to turn the color, but enough to worry. Finally, there was a knock on the door and in came Dr. Goldman, a bright smile lighting his tanned face.

"How's the best coach in Johnson County!" he exclaimed.

She stood up to give her midfielder's dad a hug. It was like this about everywhere she went in Stilwell and south Overland Park. Friends she had played with or parents whose children she had coached would call out her name at restaurants, grocery stores, and in this case, the medical center.

"I think we can win it all this year," Dr. Goldman said proudly. "Ry Ry can't wait for spring. My little girl gets up early every morning, doesn't matter how cold or snowy it is. She's out the door, running at least five miles to get ready for the season."

Sydney nodded and inhaled a deep calming breath. She loved talking about her soccer team, but her mind was occupied by only one thing. *How is my baby? Please tell me you can hear the heartbeat. Please, please, please.*

Instead, she politely listened as Dr. Goldman quizzed her about the

Tigers' returning starters, the upcoming talent on the JV team, and of course, their archrival and Kansas State Champions, Blue Valley West. He chattered away, only stopping to listen for brief moments through his fetal doppler, for the baby's heartbeat. The pauses became longer, the icy silence winding the knot gripping her heart tighter.

She knew. She knew when Dr. Goldman's face went from the joy of talking about their Tigers to the strain of a medical expert searching for the sound of a fetus.

"The baby might be hiding," he finally said, and then put on a stiff smile. "Why don't we get an ultrasound to get a clearer reading?"

*　　*　　*

Sydney leaned her face against the passenger window as Mary Beth drove her home. It was cold and sleeting on this gray December night. Only the wind and the wipers scraping ice and rain from the windshield broke the silence. Mary Beth reached for her hand. Sydney let her have it but continued to stare out at the blur of lifeless trees, branches heavy with ice, some broken, others clinging futilely to the trunk. A huge sycamore had toppled over near the side of the road, as if it had simply given up.

"*. . . can't hear a heartbeat … I'm so sorry … we can do the D&C today … need to remove the tissue from the uterus … uterine anomaly … I'm so sorry . . .*" Dr. Goldman's words echoed inside her head as she wiped a tear from her cheek and placed her hand on her belly, imagining what her baby might have looked like had it survived. Would it have had her dark brown eyes, black hair, chiseled jaw, bronzed Native American features?

She'd never know.

*　　*　　*

"Let me make you dinner," Mary Beth said as she pulled up in front of Sydney's townhouse.

"No, thank you." Sydney bit the side of her mouth to keep from crying again and then hugged her friend. "I need to be alone right now."

The walk to the front door was treacherous. Sydney slipped on frozen pavement and grasped the icy railing. She had forgotten her gloves, her hands now cold and stiff. After fumbling with her purse and searching for her keys, she looked down at the doorknob. *Oh no, frozen shut.* The sleet was coming down harder now, ice and tears stinging her face, until finally the enormity of the day was too much.

"Dammit, God!" she banged her fist against the door. "Why are you doing this to me!"

The door suddenly opened.

"Where the hell have you been?" Blake said. "I called your phone like ten times. Why didn't you pick up?"

"I was at the doctor's office." She shivered, then stepped by him to get out of the cold.

"You went to the doc? Shit, what's wrong with you now?"

Her face tightened, but she wasn't going to let him see her cry. Not after all she'd been through. She looked around the living room. It was a mess. Blake's winter coat on one chair, the newspaper and sports magazines strewn across the couch, an open bag of Fritos on the coffee table, next to a bottle of scotch and a glass of ice. She shook her head sadly, hung her soaked wool coat on the hook by the door, and headed to the bathroom to dry her still ice-drenched hair.

"I asked you a question." He followed after her. "Why'd you go to the doc?"

"I don't want to talk about it." She grabbed a towel off the rack and began to dry her hair.

"C'mon, baby." He touched her back, tracing a line with his pinky finger, down her spine. "Tell me. Is it female shit again?"

She couldn't see him, but she felt him leaning closer as she continued to towel her hair. He was probably glaring at her, that fierce look he would give before demanding an answer. Finally, she swept the towel off and looked him square in the eyes. "I miscarried, and Dr. Goldman doesn't think we'll be able to have any children."

Blake leaned back against the bathroom sink to steady himself. "What the fuck are you talking about? Doc didn't say you had any damn problems when we went in for checkups last year?"

"It's called a uterine anomaly. There's scar tissue on the walls of my uterus, making it difficult for the baby to grow."

He gave an irritated shake of his head.

"I'm sorry," she whispered.

She reached for him, but he recoiled as if she was some kind of threat and stormed out of the room. She chased after him, through their bedroom, into the living room, where he grabbed the open bottle of scotch and poured himself a drink.

"Talk to me, Blake," she said, her voice shaking. "This is devastating for me too."

He took a long drink and glared at her, his face etched with resentment and disgust. There was silence for a long time, and then her eyes looked down in shame, at loss, a dream now gone.

"I can't be with you right now." He downed the last of his drink, grabbed his car keys, and headed for the garage. She started after him, then stopped when she heard him mumble, "You're fucking worthless. What the hell was I thinking when I married you?"

CHAPTER NINE

Diriamba, Nicaragua

December 2011

Today you will listen to the Great Spirit's guidance.
Jenny's Journal of Inspiration, page 57

Sam concentrated on his sister's message as he sat in front of his locker in the Diriamba Dukes clubhouse. He had asked his manager for five minutes of quiet time before he warmed up in the bullpen, before the Dukes game against the Tigres del Chinandega.

His life had completely changed since he had left Afghanistan. He'd gone from being alone in the Hindu Kush mountains, tracking for DiamondBar Security, no human contact for days, even weeks, to the nonstop, chaotic, bustling humanity of Estevez's casino, ballpark, and orphanage. The noise was constant: babies crying; children chattering; ballplayers strategizing; Little League; Big League; teaching; coaching; working on the road, the garden, and the church.

But, at the end of the day, tired as he might be, it was a good exhaustion, a contented weariness of accomplishment and service that always left him feeling grateful. Despite his fatigue, he always found time at the beginning and end of his day to reflect on one of his sister's daily inspirations about love, spirit, balance, unity, vision quests, and the importance of strike one.

At this moment though, with the rest of the Dukes on the field and the clubhouse empty, he only wanted five minutes of quiet to meditate about his second start of the year.

He closed his eyes and inhaled deeply, imagining his breath scraping away any negative thoughts that would keep him from doing his job of throwing the baseball exactly where it needed to go. Fastball spin, slider break, curveball drop, changeup fade, all part of today's project of location and movement. He exhaled any doubt and focused on the space between his brows … inhale … exhale … inhale … exhale …

He was soon lost in the flow of his own breath, going deep within, transcending into the beauty of pure nothingness and—

"Where is my starting pitcher!" A shout from beyond the clubhouse door broke Sam's meditation. The door blasted open, and Cheslor Estevez hurried in, followed by a camera crew from Managua's biggest TV station, Canal 2. "There he is! *Mi americano superestrella!* The reason we are sold out today."

Sam rose from his stool and shook his owner's hand, but kept his mouth shut. Why was Estevez bringing a TV crew into the clubhouse fifteen minutes before first pitch? He glanced at the clock on the wall and then back at Estevez.

"I'm sorry, señor," he finally said, "but I'm about to warm up."

"*No hay problema, EssCee.* This won't take long."

Sam gritted his teeth and shook hands with the reporter from Canal 2. "It's very nice to meet you, sir, and I'd be more than happy to visit with you *after* the game. But right now I have a job to do. Thanks for understanding." He then grabbed his hat and glove and headed for the door, his team owner chasing after him, down the hall and past the trainer's room.

"EssCee! EssCee! I demand you to stop!"

He did, just before opening the door to the dugout.

"You embarrassed me, EssCee. Do you know who that man is?"

Sam shook his head.

"That's Chase Maxwell-Cortez. He's the most influential sports reporter in our country. This is the first time he's ever been to my ballpark. He only came because of what happened last week at Dennis Martinez Stadium. That fight is still the buzz of Winter Baseball, and now Canal 2 has sent their top man to do a story on my team. Cortez can make this a great day for our community, for my Dukes, and for the Estevez family name."

Sam put a hand on his owner's shoulder. "Then let me do my job. Let's not turn this game into a circus, or about just one player. If we win today, Señor Cortez will come back. And, if we keep winning—don't worry—he'll keep coming back."

*   *   *

A loud cheer came from atop the bleachers when Sam started his walk to the bullpen with his catcher, Erasmo Ortega, by his side. They looked up to see the kids from the orphanage waving excitedly down to their coach. Sam took off his cap and shook it at them.

"*¡Atención!*" Ortega grinned and gave his pitcher a playful shove.

"Time to win," said Sam.

"We win with no ... uh ... chicanery."

Sam cocked his head. "Chicanery?"

"*Si. Deshonesta. Sofistico.*"

"Then why not just say *sofistico*? *Sabes que hablo espanol.*"

Erasmo shrugged his shoulders and then pulled his catcher's mask over his face. "Señor Estevez wants me to talk inglés with you. He thinks it will help our ..."

"Communication?"

"*Si, comunicación.*"

Sam looked over his shoulder as he walked to the bullpen mound. "*¿Por qué no nos quedamos con el español?*" Why don't we just stick with Spanish?"

"*Lo que tu digas, mi hombre.*" Ortega squatted down behind home plate and pounded his fist into his glove. "*Hablaré el idioma que quieras mientras los árbitros llamen huelga.*" Whatever you say, my man. Speak any language you want while the umpires call strikes.

Sam transitioned to Spanish and let loose his first warm-up pitch. "With today's crowd, Erasmo, I believe the ump will be more inclined to call a strike, a strike."

* * *

Sam was right. Estevez Park was packed. Twenty-two hundred fans jammed into the two-thousand-seat stadium with another three to four hundred enjoying the sunshine in the outfield berms, beyond left and right fields. Cheerleaders danced on top of both dugouts. Pep bands were drumming and bugling as fans called out for beer, popcorn, and tostones.

The late-autumn sun carved shadows of the ballpark roof from the visitors' dugout to the Dukes' first-base dugout, splitting home plate and the pitcher's mound. Sam glanced back at center field and smiled. There was a bright glare on the dark green wood of the hitter's background.

So that was why the owner had moved the game time from one o'clock to three. Estevez wanted the shadows to benefit his *americano* pitcher in the first couple of innings as the ball moved from bright sunlight to the shadows in front of home plate. And the glare off the center-field background would make it even more difficult for a hitter to pick up the spin on his pitches and decode whether they were fastballs, sliders, or changeups. Talk about major chicanery.

Yeah, it would help the Chinandega pitcher as well, but the fans and Canal 2's Chase Maxwell-Cortez had come to see EssCee Carson and the fighting Diriamba Dukes. It was time to use both the glare and the Dukes' fanatical devotion to his full advantage. But first, he had to make sure the home-plate umpire was going to give him the calls.

* * *

Sam and Erasmo had agreed to start the game with a four-seam fastball, easy for both the Tigres' right-handed leadoff hitter and the umpire to track. Low, outside corner. He figured the hitter would take it, and the darn ump better raise his right arm. Inhale, exhale, easy windup and delivery.

"Stee-rike!" the ump shouted. His catcher smiled, but Sam only motioned for Ortega to return the baseball to him quickly. He liked to work fast: get the sign, windup, and pitch. No reason to let the Tigres' hitters think on his time. He repeated the process.

"Stee-rike two!"

The top of the first took all of three minutes. All fastballs. Ten pitches, nine strikes, two strikeouts, and a weak groundout to third. The fans went crazy as he walked off the mound to the dugout.

"How's the glare?" he asked his catcher.

"It's like staring at the ocean when the sun is setting." Ortega snorted. "I can barely see your sinker when it dips out of the shine."

Sam sat down next to him. "Then we'll keep throwing it until they prove they can hit it."

*　　*　　*

Both pitchers dominated early. Nothing–nothing going to the sixth, one bloop hit by each side, nine strikeouts by the Chinandega pitcher, ten by Sam. With the shadows now covering most of the outfield and the glare diminishing, Sam threw his first breaking ball. It was a simple, slow, get-me-over curve that froze the Tigres' number-five hitter for strike one. Sam followed with a two-seamer that was chopped foul for strike two and then threw his first slider for a swing-and-miss strike three.

Tiny shrieks of joy erupted from the last two rows of the left-field stands, where the Little League Dukes were stationed.

"I did not know our Samuel was this good?" Hunoon said to Whiplash as she mimicked Carson's windup and delivery. "He just—*whoosh*—throws the ball by them."

Hunoon was right, thought McCracken. *Yeah, his friend had taken advantage of the batters' eye glare to control the Chinandega offense, but the shadows had now passed. The Tigres were still having trouble making contact with his pitches. That last slider he threw almost screwed the hitter into the ground. Dang, his buddy was this good.*

"Hey, Carlita!" he called down to the Little Dukes' eleven-year-old pitcher, who was charting Sam's every pitch. "How many pitches ya got for EssCee?"

The little girl looked down at her scorecard for a long moment and then back up. "Fifty-five pitches, forty-six strikes." She paused as Sam threw a two-seamer that creased the outside corner at the knees for strike one. "Make that fifty-six and forty-seven, Coach."

"Wow," McCracken said under his breath. "Dude's throwin' eighty-five percent strikes."

Hunoon raised both brows. "Is that good?"

"Heck yeah, it's good. Seventy percent strikes is good. Eighty-five is stupid dealin'. And now he's mixin' in his breaker. Shoot-fire, he's turnin' los Tigres into pussycats."

"I'm very happy for Samuel," she said in her thick Afghan accent. "It could not have happened to a finer human."

"Yeah, it could've." McCracken winked. "It could have happened to me."

*   *   *

"Strike three!" the ump jerked his right arm up.

The Chinandega batter cursed under his breath and slammed his bat down.

Sam needed only eight pitches to get out of the eighth inning. Two groundouts, one strikeout, but still no runs for either team.

"Are you tired?" his manager asked when he returned to the dugout.

"No, I'm good."

"Why do you keep asking him if he's tired?" Ortega handed the charting sheet to Vargas. "Look at this? EssCee's only thrown eighty-five pitches, seventy for strikes. Shit, man, he just threw his first breakers, and they didn't touch them."

"I don't want to take him out," Vargas said defensively. "Señor Estevez wants to know."

Sam glanced over at the dugout phone and then back at his manager. "The owner calls you during the game?"

"He calls every inning. He wants to know how you are feeling and to tell me who I should warm up if you get tired."

Sam's jaws flexed in anger, and he stepped up to the top of the dugout. He waved up at the only luxury box in Estevez Park, a posh three-hundred-square-foot extravaganza decorated in the lime green and blue of his Dukes. Estevez waved back. Sam put his right hand to his ear and motioned for Estevez to call the dugout.

"*EssCee is muy bueno,*" he said succinctly. "Totally fine. But, if you call down to the dugout again, I'll cancel my interview with Canal 2." He then hung up and sat down in between his manager and catcher. "All right, we got their two, three, four guys coming up. None of them have seen my curve, so I'd like to start the first dude off with a slow hook, then go two-seam in on his hands. He'll more than likely hit a grounder to third, but if he misses, it's oh and two, and we'll finish him off with a slider."

Vargas sat still, mouth half-open, stunned by all that he had just heard. Then his eyes flickered from Sam to the dugout phone and back. "Um, okay, but the only way to keep that phone from ringing is to keep putting zeros up on the scoreboard."

Sam didn't answer, his complete concentration already focused on the pitching chart. In his mind, he'd already recorded the first out of the yet-to-be-played ninth inning. Now it was on to plan how they would get the final two outs.

*   *   *

The Dukes' third baseman, Ronny Molina, walked to open the bottom of the eighth. Juan Carlos Pineda struck out, but Mauricio Cardenal executed a perfect hit-and-run single to right, to put runners on first and third. Hansel Belmonte dropped a perfect safety squeeze to score Molina, and Estevez Park erupted. Fans roared, bugles blared, drums pounded, cheerleaders danced, and tiny little voices from the last two rows in the left-field seats squealed with delight. One–nothing, Dukes.

*   *   *

"Plan your work, work your plan," Sam whispered to himself as he headed out to the mound for the ninth. Execute he did, spinning a slow curve over for strike one, then jamming his sinker in on the Tigres' hitter, who hit a weak grounder to third. One out.

"Just like you predicted!" his catcher yelled as he ran halfway to the mound. But Sam didn't hear him, his concentration already centered on his next battle, Chinendega's number-three hitter. *Right-handed, open stance, dives into every pitch. Can't touch my sinker.*

He didn't, striking out on the third pitch.

Cleanup hitter. *Left-handed. Likes it down and in. No way I'm going there, big boy. Check out this sinker.* Down and away, swing and a miss, strike one.

Let's go back there, maybe an inch farther off the plate. Fouled straight back for strike two.

Sam took his cap off and wiped the sweat from his brow. "Dude was looking for that pitch," he mumbled to himself. "He thinks I'm gonna go back there again." He put his cap back on and snuck a glance at the crowd. They were all standing, stomping their feet so hard that they were drowning out the band noise, the cheerleaders' glee, and a fiery Cheslor Estevez, who was on his feet, leaning out of his luxury box, waving his arms wildly, imploring his fans to get even louder. Canal 2's Chase Maxwell-Cortez, was, of course, by his side.

Can't let him go back to the capital without a good ending, Sam thought as he stared over the top of his glove to get the sign from his catcher. Ortega dropped one finger inside his left thigh. Sam shook no. Two fingers for a change. No. Three for a slider. No. Then a bright smile lit Ortega's face as he motioned up with his right hand. Sam nodded and reached into his glove, his fingers naturally finding their way across the red seams.

Four-seam fastball. Let 'er rip. The Chinandega cleanup hitter swung too low and too late. Game over.

The crowd went crazy as Sam walked off the mound, his back to a flashing scoreboard that blinked out the resounding message of: "Dukes win! Dukes win!"

CHAPTER TEN

Diriamba, Nicaragua

December 2011

"Time!" Sam called out to the ump and jogged to the mound to talk with his struggling Little League pitcher. "What's up, Carlita?"

"I–I–I can't throw strikes," she stuttered, her lower lip trembling as she glanced around at the loaded bases.

There were about one hundred people at the southwest Little League Field in Diriamba. Some were moms and dads there to watch their kids play for Pepe's Auto Sales, but most had come to meet the new star of the Big League Diriamba Dukes, EssCee Carson, coach of the Estevez Casino Little Dukes. After Sam's two-hit, fifteen-strikeout, complete-game, 1–0 shutout of Chinandega on Sunday, the Dukes' owner was calling every reporter and local TV station to sing the praises of his new discovery and to tell them EssCee would be coaching his Little Dukes on Wednesday. Estevez would do anything to drum up interest so fans would mosey on over to his casino and ballpark next Sunday when the Dukes hosted the Orientales de Granada.

Now, only two innings into the game, the Little Dukes were already trailing 7–0.

"I've walked six and hit three batters." Carlita sniffed, staring into her glove.

Sam suppressed a smile as he remembered a strategy his college catcher and best friend, Jose Lopez, had used on him after one of his own near meltdowns on the mound. He took the ball out of Carlita's hand and waited for the little girl to raise her vision.

"Who lives in a pineapple under the sea?" he asked.

Carlita gave him a look of absolute confusion.

"Who lives in a pineapple under the sea?"

She wiped a tear from her cheek. "SpongeBob."

He nodded. "Do you smell it? That smelly smell that smells smelly?"

She blinked a few times, and then the side of her mouth began to curl into a slight smile. "You're weird."

Sam winked and dropped the ball into her glove. "Go get 'em, kid." He then walked off the mound, singing the final line of the cartoon the kids watched on Saturday mornings. "SpongeBob SquarePaaaaaaants! A-ha-ha-ha-ha!"

*　　　*　　　*

The Little Dukes lost the game, 10–3, but Carlita gave up only one of the last three runs and finished the final two innings in right field. It was near four o'clock when the game ended. Sam signed a few more autographs before he stepped onto the team bus and sat down in the front seat, next to McCracken. It was quiet for the first ten minutes of the drive home, but there were grumblings from the back, soft, teasing murmurs that Sam tried to make out. All seemed to be directed at the Dukes' female starting pitcher. He casually turned around to tell them to knock it off, only to see Carlita leap across the aisle and punch her third baseman in the face.

"Fuck you!" she screamed and hit him again.

Sam ran to the back, pushing kids aside who were now staring at the fight. He'd never heard a child Carlita's age use such language.

"I'll fucking kill you!" She slammed her fist once more into the little boy's face before Sam was able to wrench her off Anthony Villanueva and drag her to the last seat on the bus.

Carlita was sobbing now, wildly flailing her arms and legs, lost to a fury and shame that scared even Sam.

"Settle down, Carlita," he whispered in her ear, as if trying to calm a frightened colt. "Please, settle down." Finally, she gave up in a drained, quaking, exhaustion of tears, curling up against Sam into a ball of both sorrow and embarrassment.

*   *   *

"How much do you know about Carlita?" McCracken asked when they returned to the orphanage that night.

"I know she loves baseball," Sam said as he carried two bat bags to the wooden toolshed behind the church. "But practice and games are about the only times I see her. She seems pretty happy and together. That's why what she did today shocked the heck outta me."

"Naw, actually that's pretty common with cutters," McCracken said frankly. He took a ball bag from Sam and hung it up on a side wall.

Sam's face tightened as he tried to make sense of what his friend was telling him. "Cutters?"

"Kids who cut themselves because of depression or a relationship problem," McCracken explained. "And if yer an orphan, yer likely dealin' with some kind of crappy relationship issue. ... Hunoon and I had a few cutters in Afghanistan. It sucks when kids get rejected or lose a loved one. Some feel they deserve the pain."

Sam hadn't been expecting that, and he looked back at the kids who were heading to the cafeteria for dinner, Carlita trailing behind, head down, all alone.

"That's why Carlita's always wearing long-sleeve shirts, Sam. She don't want anyone to see the cuts on her arms. Hunoon and I talked with her about it. She claims the church cat scratched her, or she got pushed into the rose bushes, but we know." McCracken paused for a long moment. "We also know she's had it rough. Dad left when she was a baby. Mom was a cocaine freak, who gave her away when Carlita turned seven."

"She's been here four years?" Sam said.

"And me and Hunoon only been here four months. Carlita still don't trust us completely. She's still moody and distant when we give her chores to do, but"—he hesitated as if to make sure Sam heard his next words—"she sure lights up whenever yer around."

"I'm her coach."

"You ain't wondered why she changed her delivery?"

"What?"

"It's a carbon copy of yours, Sammy. Deep inhale, slow exhale, takin' both hands over the head, glove touchin' the back of the neck, high leg kick, follow through. She even jogs off the field like you, side-steppin' the foul lines before comin' into the dugout."

Sam thought back to the first time he had seen Carlita Rapino throw. It was from the stretch, a natural, uncomplicated, smooth delivery. But she *had* changed … and he hadn't even seen it.

What was the first thing his dad used to tell him when they went hunting? *Be aware of your surroundings. Intuition is just as important as sights, sounds, and smells. If we depend only on our senses, we'll believe that the physical world is our only reality. Yet Mother Nature is trying to teach us that there is so much more.* Why hadn't he seen Carlita copying him?

"Baseball's her peace," McCracken said, breaking Sam's moment of reflection. "It's the only time I see Carlita smile. And now she wants to be just like her *HE–RO.*" He dramatically separated each syllable to emphasize his point. "Then you show her up by throwin' a complete-game shutout while she gives up eight runs, feels like crap, and takes it out on a teammate."

"Oh God, I should have seen it coming. I could have prevented it."

"Don't beat yerself up, Sammy." McCracken closed the toolshed door and turned back to his friend. "We all have lessons to learn. For some, the lessons are harder than others. Life's like baseball. It ain't fair."

Sam let out a long breath and stared out at the horizon. The distant call from a macaw seemed to be intended for him.

He turned back to his friend. "Hey, Whip, would it be okay if I took Carlita for a walk after dinner?"

McCracken nodded.

*   *   *

The cafeteria reverberated with the chatter of children, laughing, joking, and teasing, save one little girl all alone in the corner, quietly finishing her meal.

Sam snatched an apple out of a bowl and walked over. "Hey Carlita, have you ever seen the Pacific Ocean?"

She shook her head.

"I usually go this time of the day to a cool overlook that has a beautiful view of the water. Do you want to go with me?"

Carlita looked outside. The sun was gone, and the trees were jagged silhouettes against the night sky. "You mean like . . . right now?"

"Yeah. It's a short walk through the woods."

Her dark eyes darted from Sam to the woods and back again. "Can we go tomorrow when it's light out?"

"Sure," said Sam indifferently. "I'll ask Anthony if he wants to go."

"No!" Carlita jumped up. "I'll go. Let me . . . put my dishes away."

*   *   *

They entered a trail into a forest of cedar and pine, Sam pushing aside low branches and cobwebs to give Carlita an easier path. He could feel her behind him, her breathing higher up in her chest, the result of fear.

"It's--It's dark in here"-- she said.

"Yep."

"Are there any snakes?"

"Probably."

"What about ... you know?"

"Jaguarundi?"

"Yeah, those big cats."

"They're not that big."

"I saw a picture of one in the uh—"

"Encyclopedia?"

"Yeah--they're pretty big."

Sam stopped and turned around. "If you're scared, we can go back."

"I'm not scared," she said defiantly.

She glanced back down the path where they had come. It was dark. No sign of any light from the church or a nearby farm. An insect buzzed by her ear and she almost fell down trying to swat it away. "I just want to get out of the woods."

He nodded and continued through the trees. She ran after him and grabbed the back of his shirt. "Not so fast, Coach. I don't want to get lost."

"I'd never let that happen, Carlita."

Finally, they reached the end of the forest, and Sam pushed aside the last pine bough. "There you go, kid . . . the biggest ocean in the world. The mighty Pacific."

Carlita stood frozen, her eyes locked on the dark expanse of water some twenty miles away. "Wow . . . that's amazing."

They walked to the edge of the bluff and sat down.

"I love how everything in nature serves us," Sam said. "The oceans share their food and water. The water serves the earth by raining down on our plants and trees. The trees share their oxygen, and the sun shares its warmth and light. We, too, are designed to serve."

She didn't respond.

"I never saw an ocean until I played baseball in college," he said with a faraway look. "My tribe is from the mountains of Colorado."

Still, Carlita said nothing.

"We believe that it's our duty to respect nature. That everything happens in a circle. The Earth revolves around the sun in a circle. Birds make their nests in a circle. The wind whirls in a circle, and what you give in life will be returned. If you give kindness, it will return to you. If you give anger, it, too, will come back to you."

In the silence, Sam tried to collect his thoughts. "What happened on the bus today, Carlita? Why did you hit Anthony?"

She looked down. "I don't know."

"Whatever you give, you will receive. That's the promise of the Great Spirit."

The little girl tensed up at his last words. "I hate God."

"Why?"

"Because He made my mother and father hate me. So I hate Him."

Sam let out a long breath and moved close to her. He knew her hatred well. Had been there before. His mind traveled back to Pargin Mountain and his own personal losses. As he looked at Carlita, with her head bowed in shame, he knew he had to say something to let her know she wasn't alone.

"I hated God, too, when my mother, father, and sister died. I blamed Him for their deaths and demanded He take me as well."

The bowed head rose up.

"I even tried to kill myself," he continued. "But thankfully, I failed. I was lucky to have someone watching over me." Carlita swallowed hard but remained quiet, as if wanting to hear more.

"It was my sister, Jenny. She knew that I would suffer after she died. I told you about the journal of inspirations she wrote for me. Jenny hoped they would comfort me whenever I was sad or angry."

She reached out to him, and he took her hand.

"Jenny reminded me that I wasn't alone. And over time, I discovered that there were lessons I still needed to learn." He turned to face her. "These were not lessons handed down by God. They were simply events that happened. I came to realize that every experience in my life, both good and bad, was a lesson to remember the Great Spirit's presence in my life."

"It's still not fair."

"All of us suffer in some way, Carlita. No one gets through life without challenges. That's why we need each other. To learn and to grow." He pointed again at the horizon that seemed to have no end. "Everything happens in a circle. The earth is round. The moon is round. The planets are round." He smiled down at her. "And a baseball is round. The stitches on a baseball remind me that we're all tied together. If one stitch is broken, it can send the entire ball off in the wrong direction. We need each other. Our teammates need our unique gifts and we need theirs."

"What are my gifts?"

"I think one of them is the way you help Whip and Hunoon when new orphans arrive—and the other gift is your ability to throw a baseball."

She made a face like she had just bitten into a lemon. "I suck."

"You do when you change your delivery to throw like me. I think, if you go back to your old style and practice the right way, it will help the entire team."

"You don't think I practice right?"

"I never just play catch, Carlita. I always have a target. A knee, a hip, a shoulder. I'm always training my body to throw the baseball precisely where I want. So, at tomorrow's practice, I want you to go back to your old delivery and throw to a target on every single pitch." He paused to make sure she heard his next words. "I also want you to practice being the best teammate you can be."

"What if they're mean?"

"Let it go. It's like being on the mound. Bad stuff's going to happen. Teammates are going to make errors. You're going to throw a good pitch, and the ump's gonna call it a ball. Or the hitter's gonna bloop a base hit. But it's up to you on how you react to trouble."

They sat quietly for a spell, gazing out at the enormity of the Pacific. From twenty miles away, it seemed so tranquil, yet Sam knew the power that loomed underneath, the currents and tides and reefs roiling with danger. Was it that much different than a man when tested with adversity? Would he fight the currents, or would he let them carry him where he needed to go? He didn't know if Carlita followed his message, but there was a part of him that believed she did.

A cool December breeze suddenly swept in off the ocean, sending a chill through him. He turned to look down at Carlita. The little girl was shivering, hugging her knees to her chest for warmth. But she didn't speak, her eyes remote, still locked on the Pacific, as if searching for something in its depths.

"You ready to go back?" he asked.

His words seemed to snap her out of a trance. She nodded and slowly stood up and looked around: at the ocean, at the moon, at the shadows, and then back at the forest's darkness.

"Coach?" she said, a bit of fear creeping back into her awareness. "Will you give me a piggyback ride home?"

He smiled, turned his back to her, and crouched down. "Hop on, kid. Let me show you what being a good teammate is all about."

CHAPTER ELEVEN

Stilwell, Kansas

Christmas Eve, 2011

The snow was coming down in big flakes as Mary Beth turned onto the Tomlinson property. The long driveway had been recently plowed, and the lights from the truck pushing the snow still shined brightly, as if directing them which way to go. Bette Tomlinson's land was typical of most southern Johnson County farms: about a hundred acres of rolling plains, of flint and silt loam, not the best for wheat or corn, but fine for a good-sized garden and a small herd of cattle.

Bette's property stretched all the way to the Little Blue River, complete with chickens, ducks, dogs, and a stable of eight quarter horses that were as lovable as Labrador retrievers.

"Won't they cancel because of the weather?" Sydney asked as her friend squinted through the flakes to make sure she didn't veer off the path the snowplow had carved for visitors. Even though it was Christmas Eve, a day for family and office parties, they hadn't seen one car on their drive to the Tomlinson farm. Sydney had stopped by Price Chopper that morning to buy stickers and cookies. It was the least she could bring as gifts for these inner-city kids, many of whom had never been to a farm.

"You don't know Bette Tomlinson," Mary Beth said. "Tough old battle-ax in her early seventies. Her husband passed away ten years ago, so she lives alone and runs the place like an Army base. Every few months, some developer comes by and makes her an offer, and she shoos 'em off like a cow tail swatting flies."

They finally made it to the main house, a simple two-story structure, probably four bedrooms, two or three baths, with a full basement. The snowplow driver waved for them to follow, and they did, snaking their way through an archway of sycamore, oak, maple, pine, and cottonwood, all the way to the horse stable and corral. There was a yellow school bus parked out front, and several kids were running around inside the corral, trying to catch snowflakes in their mouths.

"What did I tell you." Mary Beth laughed. "Ole Mrs. T pulled on somebody's holiday heartstrings to bring the kids in this snowstorm. She wanted to make sure these boys and girls have a new Christmas memory."

"Just park it there!" yelled the snowplow driver. "Ain't nobody else comin' today."

"Is that her?" Sydney asked in surprise.

"Yep," Mary Beth said as she put her car in park, turned off the engine, and stepped out to greet Mrs. T.

The woman was all of five foot two and wore a sheepskin coat that was much too big for her, a purple Kansas State University scarf, and denim overalls tucked into red rubber boots that climbed all the way up to her knees. Atop the haphazard throw-pillow style apparel was a Dakota Dan Trooper ear-flap cap with fur lining that snapped underneath the rosiest cheeks, roundest chin, and most inquisitive blue eyes Sydney had ever seen.

"Howdy, Coach," Bette said and reached out a hand. "You've done a fine job with our Tigers. Three straight postseasons."

"Oh, thank you." Sydney felt herself flushing as she shook the woman's hand. "I didn't know you were a fan."

"Both my boys went to Blue Valley, and my grandson graduated last May. I follow all Tiger sports."

"Jamie Tomlinson is your grandson? He was in my history class—really nice boy—one of my better students."

"Of course he was." Bette snorted, as if her grandson being a good student was a foregone conclusion. She put an arm around Sydney's shoulders and led her to the stable. "Jamie's at K-State now, got a 4.0 his first semester. His daddy's a Special Forces colonel who had three tours in Afghanistan. He's back in the States now at Fort Lewis, Washington."

*   *   *

The Tomlinson stables were clean but needed plenty of work. Many of the cottonwood stalls were old and fractured, with dirty flakes of white paint peeling off the wood, but they looked strong enough to keep a well-behaved quarter horse safe. Despite the cold, stepping into the tack room warmed Sydney's spirits. It was a space of dusty antique chairs, smooth, timeworn leather, horse sweat, lanolin, beeswax, saddle soap, and a hint of honey.

The familiar aroma drew a pleasant smile from Sydney, and her thoughts drifted to years gone by, of riding horses with her father and brother for hours, then returning to the stables to rub down their horses and meet up in the tack room to clean saddles, bridles, and leathers, and to have silly family chats.

No fair! she remembered her brother Tom complaining. *You go too fast! I always get the slow pony!* Dad would come to her defense, saying Sydney was just a natural in the saddle, as if she had been born to ride.

"You know how to prep?" Bette's voice snapped Sydney back to the now, and she nodded innocently.

"Brushes are on the top shelf." Bette pointed to the far wall and then headed to the first stall with a brush in one hand and a blanket in the other. "Only one child and horse in the corral at a time. My homeowner's insurance don't cover kids getting kicked in the head."

*   *   *

The air outside was frigid yet invigorating as Sydney led a quarter horse named Leo into the corral. The fourteen-year-old chestnut gelding stomped for a moment, then lowered his head and sniffed. *Yeah,* Sydney thought, *Leo was used to this kind of weather.* He was comfortable with snow and wind and, more importantly, kids.

As she tied Leo to the rail, she thought about why Mary Beth had insisted she come with her today. Obviously, MB was concerned about her after she miscarried in November. It had been one month of depression, four weeks of numbness, thirty days of wondering why God was punishing her. Nothing seemed to lift her from her own personal hell. Her baby was dead … and she may never be able to have another.

She drew a deep breath of frigid air and brought the brush up to Leo's withers. It felt good to be with something, or someone, who didn't care how she felt. She was tired of her mom's incessant, *How are you feeling?* and *You've got to let it go and move on.* Or her dad's text messages of scripture and a minister's phone number. But most of all, she wanted to be away from the look of resentment she saw in her husband's eyes. Her failure to give him a child was just one more reason why Blake was coming home later from work.

"Can I ride now?" said a little girl who was eagerly watching from behind the gate.

Sydney turned and smiled. "Hi. What's your name?"

"Maria."

"Well, Maria, you can ride Leo after I finish brushing him."

"Why do you have to brush him?"

"It's important to get the loose hair off because horses sweat under the saddle."

"So?"

Sydney swept the brush across Leo's shoulder and then paused. Her dark brown eyes softened as childhood memories of summers at the stables came rushing into her mind. Summers of fishing and hay rides and horses.

"If a horse's back gets wet, he may shake to get the hair off and shake the rider off too." She gave the little girl a wink. "That happened to me when I was about your age. So it's important to brush the hair off before we put the blanket and saddle on."

Despite being peppered by question after question from Maria, it took Sydney no more than five minutes to prepare Leo and walk the little girl over to the mounting block.

"Climb up those steps, and I'll help you on."

The excitement in Maria's eyes made Sydney smile. This seven-year-old was practically vibrating with the thrill of taking her very first pony ride. She helped Maria onto the saddle, placed her boots in the stirrups, and began to lead them around the corral.

The snow was falling heavier now and sucked in every sound, except for the occasional snort from Leo and horseshoes crunching on frozen ground. Sydney was suddenly aware of everything around her: of gray clouds heavy with snow, flakes swirling, biting her face, tree branches pulled low from winter's white. She paused near a lone small pine, heavy with powder, seeming to struggle to reach up through a drift toward an illusory sun. It was as if something familiar, some ancient memory, was putting an arm around her shoulder to let her know that she would be all right.

*　　*　　*

Three hours later, the Christmas Eve ride ended. Twelve elementary school students, all squealing with delight, calling out their horses' names, and waving goodbye to the women who had led them, climbed back onto their school bus. Sydney waved back but didn't speak for a long time, her eyes fixed on the bus as it pulled away, its red taillights glimmering softly in the twilight before dissolving into nothingness, the memory of the children's laughter and the low rumble of the bus's engine a last reminder of their day at the Tomlinson Ranch.

"Did you ladies forget something?" Bette asked as she headed back to the stables.

"Christmas presents!" Sydney cried out, and she and Mary Beth bolted for their car.

Bette raised a hand to stop them. "Don't go chasing after them now. You're more likely to wind up sliding into some ditch than you are of catching that bus. Plus, you already gave those kids a gift."

"We did?" Sydney asked.

"You gave them your time. That's more precious than any darn toy."

Neither of the two women said another word as Bette continued on to the stables, muttering under her breath, "You can give 'em the stickers and other crap when you come back next week. I'll need a little help when we teach the kids how to clean stalls."

*   *   *

The drive home was treacherous. The snowstorm had ended, but a thick fog dropped down, making it difficult to spot any black ice. Twice, Mary Beth's car almost slipped off the road, and she had to back her car up to get a faster run at making it over an icy hill. The main road back to Stilwell was practically empty, save for a few daring souls risking it for some Christmas party. Yet, despite the danger, despite her still frozen nose, toes, and fingers, Sydney felt happy.

Mary Beth slowed the car at a four-way crossing and glanced over at her friend, who was beaming broadly. "So I take it you enjoyed our little adventure?"

Sydney's smile somehow went wider. "Oh, MB, it was wonderful! The kids, the horses, the snow, the trees, just being out in nature again and seeing those children smile—I can't wait to go back."

Mary Beth laughed and continued up the road. "Mrs. Tomlinson loved you, said you were a magnet with the kids."

"So were you."

"No, Syd, you're different. I'm good with *my* kids, but you're good with *all* kids. I think that's why you're such a good coach."

Sydney didn't reply, taken aback by her friend's words.

"You always seem to say the right thing to lift another person's spirit." Mary Beth glanced at her friend. "Perhaps it's time to lift your own."

Mary Beth said no more, and an awkward silence hung between them until the *ping* of Sydney's phone broke the quiet.

"Oh no!" Sydney exclaimed as she searched for her phone. "I told Blake I'd be back by five, and it's now seven."

There were five text messages and three voicemails, all from her husband.

The first text: *Where are you?*

Second text: *Did you forget it's Christmas Eve? Everybody's waiting for us at Crazy 8's!*

Third text: *The roads suck and now the fog's rolling in. WTF*

Fourth text: *Thanks for ruining my one night to party.*

She didn't even read the fifth text as she frantically scrolled down to find Blake's number.

"Sydney," Mary Beth reached over and took the phone out of her hand. "We're only a mile from your house."

"I need to let him know why I'm late."

"You know he's already had several drinks, and he's pissed. Not a good combo with Blake."

Sydney looked at her friend guiltily. "Because of the baby."

"Bullshit." Mary Beth stopped the car in the middle of the road and turned to face her. "He's a control freak. He looks for reasons to put you down. C'mon, Syd, how many times has he come home late without calling you?"

Tears welled up in Sydney's eyes and rolled down her cheeks. Her day had gone from one of total joy to crushing regret. She sniffed hard and reluctantly nodded. Mary Beth returned her phone, and Sydney quickly texted: *Almost home. I can explain.*

CHAPTER TWELVE

Diriamba, Nicaragua

January 2012

On a pleasant mid-January morning in Nicaragua, Sam sat on a stone ledge overlooking the Pacific Ocean. The sun, barely creasing above the tree line, sending streaks of soft light, stretching to the mighty water, was behind him. He loved this quiet time.

There was so much going on in his life right now. The winter garden was ready to bloom; the children's sleeping quarters needed to be painted; the road to the orphanage wasn't finished; and both the Little League and Big League Dukes had made the playoffs.

The Dukes had shocked the Nicaraguan baseball world by making it to the championship round, finishing second in December's round-robin with an extra-inning win over Chinandega. With the excitement of game one just hours away, he needed this time alone, to let go of any anxiety, to align his mind, body, and spirit, and then to go beat the crap out of the defending league champion, Indios del Bóer.

Sam set his watch and flipped open Jenny's Journal of Inspiration to page fourteen:

O Great Spirit, help me always to speak the truth quietly,
to listen with an open mind when others speak,
and to remember the peace that may be found in silence.
Cherokee prayer

He closed his eyes, inhaled deeply, placed his uplifted palms on his thighs, and focused on the prayer, letting his breath take his mind where it needed to go. He saw his father, studying a track on Pargin Mountain; saw his mother, dancing the Bear Dance outside their Colorado home; saw his sister's face on a white buffalo, the same confident, crooked, wry smile he'd always adored. Their spirits would be with him on this day.

*   *   *

The alarm on his watch *pinged* the end of his meditation. Now it was time to begin the half-mile trek back to the orphanage, grab a quick breakfast, and head to the Estevez Ballpark, where the team bus would take them to Managua for their first playoff game.

He put his sister's journal away in his backpack, stretched his arms over his head, and suppressed a smile. He knew they were watching him. He had heard their careless footsteps snapping twigs and dry leaves as they stealthily followed him to his favorite meditation spot. He could hear them now, failing to quiet their tiny giggles as they hid in the woods.

The wind changed, drawing heavy clouds and early morning fog with it, so Sam felt it important to get the kids back to the church without anyone getting lost. As he pushed aside two branches and entered the forest, there they were—seven little kids sitting on a log, mimicking him, legs crossed, palms on their thighs, hands upturned, eyes closed, lips pressed together tightly in an effort to smother their snickers.

"You're not that funny," muttered Sam in mock annoyance, and the children burst out laughing.

As he moved past them into the woods, they jumped off the log and raced after him. It only took ten minutes to get home, seven panting, wheezing, out-of-breath tadpoles following his every step, afraid if they lost him they might be devoured by some wild forest creature, perhaps a jaguarundi.

Carlita was the first to catch up with him and gave him a playful shove. "You go too fast."

"You go too slow."

He counted out six more heads to make sure every child was accounted for and then winked down at Carlita. "Just because you won your last two games doesn't mean you can slack off on your running."

She shoved him again. He laughed, pulled her in, and gave her a noogie rub on her head. "Come on, kid, let's get breakfast. Coach Whip wants everyone well-nourished before he takes you to the game."

"Why can't I go with you?" She pleaded and fluttered her eyelashes. "I promise not to talk on the bus or in the dugout."

He put his arm around her and led her to the church cafeteria. "Not today, Carlita—today's a business trip. Total concentration. Just like you had when you struck out the side to beat Diego's Casa de Hamburguesas last week."

She giggled and gave him one more shove.

*   *   *

There was an uneasy quiet the first half of the bus ride to Managua. Then Manager Vargas wobbled down the aisle and handed Sam his pitcher-catcher scouting report. It was never very good, the usual fastballs up and in, breaking balls low and away, nothing as detailed as Coach Elba's scouting report at Mesa State, but Vargas had put in the effort so it was important that Sam show respect and give it a look.

He glanced up and saw that a few of his teammates had moved closer for a better view of the simple one-page directive. Third baseman Ronny Molina was in the seat in front of him and turned around for a peek; second baseman Delwin Rodriguez hovered over Ronny's shoulder; even right fielder Hansel Belmonte, a timid introvert, seemed interested in what was on the page.

It was the first time Sam had seen any nervousness on his teammates' faces. These were simple men who were professional ballplayers by name only. All of them worked second jobs. Molina was a car mechanic, Rodriguez worked on the city street crew, and Belmonte raised pigs.

Even the most experienced player, shortstop Mauricio Cardenal, sold auto insurance. They were all guys who were still playing because they loved the game.

Winning had been secondary. No one had ever expected much of the lowly Diriamba Dukes, the laughingstock of both the Nicaraguan League and the spring circuit, who had finished last every year of both leagues' existence.

But now the Dukes were good. They had a winning record for the first time in their short history and had made the finals. There was something to play for, a greater purpose and pride, and with it came a more pronounced anxiety to win, both for their community and for their families.

Sam held up the one-page memo. "Anyone want to go over the scouting report with me and Erasmo?"

"*Sí!*" came the replies and he waved them over.

"Vargie puts a report together every game on how he thinks we should attack our opponent." He passed the sheet around. "He takes into consideration not only my strengths as a pitcher, but also the opponent's weaknesses. Accordingly, it will help our defense on how to play each hitter. As an example, the Indios del Bóer leadoff hitter will likely be Humberto Abreu. He's a lefty, not very big, but fast and has quick hands. He likes to slash the ball to the left side. Vargie suggests I pound him in early with four-seamers and then go away with two-seamers and changeups, so Ronny and Mauricio have to be on their toes when Abreu's up."

"That's why you're always moving us, EssCee?" his third baseman said. "Because you guess where they hit the ball?"

Sam raised one dark brow. "We never guess, Ronny, but if we execute our pitches correctly, there's a higher percentage that a respective hitter will hit it the way we're defending. I believe if we all do our jobs today, los Indios won't have a chance."

There was a sarcastic snort from the back row. It was outfielder Juan Carlos Pineda.

"We've played them four times already, gringo, and lost all four. What makes you think today will be any different?"

Sam straightened up in his seat and looked directly at Pineda. "Because we're a better team now. We're no longer playing for ourselves." He opened his hand wide. "Each of these fingers has a bit of strength. But when I draw them into a fist, I have greater power." He clenched his hand and then opened it wide again. "We're going to win today because we're going to do all the little things very well." He looked at his first baseman. "We're going to win because Jairo is going to dig a low throw out of the dirt." He turned to his second baseman. "We're going to win because Delwin is going to turn a nice double play." He glanced at his shortstop. "We're going to win because Mauricio is going to set up perfectly for cutoffs from the outfield." Sam nodded for his shortstop to continue.

Mauricio smiled broadly and tapped their third baseman on the shoulder. "We will win because Ronny will take a hot shot off his chest and throw that damn runner out!"

They all laughed, and then Ronny looked at their right fielder. "We will win because Hansel will hit the cutoff man!" More laughter.

Hansel nodded to their center fielder. "We will win because Darvin will drop a perfect bunt."

Darvin turned to their left fielder. "We shall win because Juan Carlos will shorten his swing and hit a sacrifice fly."

They all turned to Juan Carlos, who let go a loud sigh, as if surrendering his earlier doubts. He nodded to the Dukes' catcher. "We will win because Erasmo will call a good game."

Ortega smiled broadly and then winked at Sam. "We shall win because EssCee will follow Vargie's game plan and throw many amazing strikes."

Sam laughed at that and threw his hands in the air, his fingers stretched wide. He looked directly at each one of his teammates as he drew his fingers into a fist. "We shall win because we are all one." He opened his hands again. "Alone, we are nothing." He drew his fingers back into a powerful fist. "But together—we are the mighty Dukes of Diriamba!"

"Duuuuuukes!" they all roared, and the anxiety of ten minutes before was now gone.

*   *   *

It was a nothing–nothing game through five innings. The ball was coming out of Sam's hand in an effortless manner, each throw biting, cutting down and away from the meat of the Indios del Bóer bats. He had retired the first fifteen batters on a ridiculously low thirty-nine pitches. Eleven groundouts, one popup, three strikeouts. Much like they had talked about on the bus, his Dukes were playing flawless defense. Third baseman Ronny Molina had taken a hot shot off his chest, first baseman Jairo Espino had dug Molina's low throw out of the dirt, and Erasmo Ortega was calling a great game.

"You got it going, EssCee," Ortega said when Sam finished the fifth and plopped down next to him on the dugout bench. "All we need is one run to win this game."

"Then let's get that one run right now." Sam took his cap off, wiped the sweat from his brow, and glanced over at his shortstop, who was picking a bat out of the bat rack. "If their third baseman plays back like he has all day, we could start a rally."

Mauricio Cardenal hesitated a moment, as if hearing his pitcher's words, and then headed to the on-deck circle to get loose.

"You think Mauricio was listening?" Ortega asked.

"We'll see."

Whether the Dukes' leadoff man took the suggestion, or it was the team's continued focus on playing for each other, Sam's words seemed to have their desired effect. Just before the first pitch, Cardenal peeked over his left shoulder. The Indios third baseman was playing back. Cardenal dropped a perfect bunt, and the Dukes' lead man was on. Rodriguez followed with a hit-and-run single to right. Pineda shortened his swing and hit a sacrifice fly, Belmonte roped a double to left, and the Dukes led the mighty Indios 2–0.

"Check out Señor Estevez." Ortega motioned to the front row behind home plate, where the Dukes' owner was wildly dancing and high-fiving fans next to him. "He can almost taste his first win ever over the great Indios del Bóer."

"Then let's finish the job," said Sam as he opened his scouting notebook and began preparing for the bottom of the sixth. "Los Indios get overaggressive when they're behind. Let's see if we can expand their strike zone."

One hour later, the game was over. Sam flipped a slider that was a good foot outside the zone. The Indios cleanup hitter swung futilely at the illusory strike, and the Dukes claimed their first ever Nicaraguan Baseball League playoff victory. It was only one win, and they needed four to take the series, but this would indeed be a night to celebrate. The Estevez Casino ran out of booze by eleven o'clock.

CHAPTER THIRTEEN

Washington, DC

February 2012

"We found him, sir!"

Drake Dixon looked up from behind his desk at the pimple-faced intern who was knocking on his open door. He knew exactly who this young man was talking about, but he wanted it to look as if the information was inconsequential.

"Excuse me?"

"We found Carson, sir!" the young man gushed again, and then bit his lip to calm his nervousness.

Dixon completely understood his intern's jitters. All of the rookies his staff had recently hired reacted the same way when finally getting a chance to meet the important private military contractor the *Washington Weekly* had recently called *one of the most dynamic leaders in America's fight against international terrorism.*

It didn't hurt that Dixon's PR people had saturated the press with positive stories about DiamondBar's dramatic capture of a Taliban leader, photos of his contractors handing out food to Afghan refugees, and his generous donations to two Afghan charities. What wasn't reported was how close DiamondBar was to bankruptcy after Dixon was forced to end his bid to steal the mineral rights of a mountain in the Nuristan Province.

Very slowly, Dixon rose out of his black leather chair, walked around his desk, and offered his hand to the young man. "And you are?"

"William Jacobs, sir." The intern shook Dixon's hand enthusiastically. "I'm a senior at Georgetown. It's—it's an honor to work for you, sir."

He gave the young man a respectful nod and then closed the door to his office.

"It's nice to meet you, William Jacobs." Dixon continued to downplay his interest in the whereabouts of Sam Cloud-Carson. But he had to know where his enemy was in case Sam broke his promise and began to leak unsavory information to the press. The last thing he needed was for a disgruntled former employee to expose what had happened in Afghanistan to some ambitious investigative journalist.

Dixon flashed a bright veneer smile, leaned back on the edge of his desk, and began his lie. "I like to take care of my people. The Christmas bonus I sent to Carson's old address was returned. I wanted to make sure he got my gift for his service to our country."

"Of course, sir," Jacobs beamed, his confidence returning. "That's why I kept digging on the internet. They had all of Carson's stats in college. All-American, Rocky Mountain Conference Tournament MVP, Final Four All-Star team, but nothing more after he signed on with DiamondBar."

"What did you find?"

"I googled Sam Cloud-Carson and baseball, and at first all I got was the same Mesa State baseball stuff, but then I googled international baseball and winter ball. All of a sudden, this EssCee Carson started showing up." Jacobs looked up at Dixon, searching for approval. "Anyway, I thought, EssCee—you know, for the initials *S* and *C*—and as soon as I clicked, the same guy who was picked to be the D-2 National Player of the Year showed up. Sam Cloud-Carson is pitching for the Diriamba Dukes in Nicaragua, sir."

Dixon played it cool. "He was indeed a good ballplayer. How's he doing?"

"Very well, sir. There are only five teams in the Nicaraguan League, and the Dukes finished second at fourteen and eleven, which is by far their best finish ever. Before this year, the most wins they ever had was three."

"This was their first time making the playoffs?"

"Yes, sir. But unfortunately, they lost four victories to two, to the perennial champion Indios del Bóer." Jacobs looked up at his boss. "Los Indios are like the Yankees of Nicaragua."

Dixon gave a patronizing nod. "I take it Carson was instrumental in the Dukes' improvement?"

"He was their best pitcher, sir. Five and two with a two and a half ERA. Sixty-two strikeouts and only eleven walks in sixty-four innings. Most of the walks came in the first game." Jacobs handed Dixon a newspaper story he had printed. "Carson won both of their games in the final series. He only gave up one run in eighteen innings."

Dixon raised both brows. "You know your baseball, Mr. Jacobs."

"I was the Hoyas stats and student manager, sir," Jacobs said proudly and then returned to his notes. "Mr. Carson threw a complete-game four-hitter in the Dukes' win at Estevez Park. The pictures in the Diriamba newspaper were hilarious, sir. It looked like the whole town was at the game, and they stormed the field to celebrate the Dukes' win. They carried Carson off on their shoulders to the local casino and–"

Dixon's right hand shot up to quiet his intern. "But they lost the series, Mr. Jacobs. Everything in between means nothing. The only thing that anyone will remember is who won the championship."

Jacobs gave an embarrassed nod.

"Did you get any personal info on Carson?" Dixon folded his arms over his chest. "Like a phone number? How much he's being paid? Who he's shacking up with?"

Jacobs winced, not sure he'd heard right. "Excuse me, sir?"

"Do you have an address for him?"

"No, sir, all I have is that the spring season starts soon and EssCee Carson will be starting against some team from … uh … Man–Man–"

"Managua," Dixon muttered. "It's the capitol of Nicaragua." He paused to show his disappointment. "If you want a full-time position with DiamondBar, Mr. Jacobs, you'll have to do a better job with your research—addresses, phone numbers, contacts."

Jacobs looked up at his boss, embarrassed but also confused. "I'm sorry, sir. I thought you only wanted to send Mr. Carson his Christmas bonus?"

Dixon glared at his young intern. "Just get me his address."

CHAPTER FOURTEEN

Diriamba, Nicaragua

May 2012

Sam fell into a methodical routine at the Estevez Orphanage. Up every morning at five: coffee, meditation, breakfast with the kids, feed the thirty chickens and four goats, expand the garden, work on the road, and finish his personal project, building a baseball field in the pasture behind the church. His Little Dukes wouldn't have to hike the mile to practice at Estevez Park anymore. The kids could play ball whenever they wanted.

He spent most evenings playing for Cheslor Estevez's Pomares League team. Neither the pay, nor the talent of the spring-summer circuit was as strong as the Nicaraguan Pro League, but it was still baseball, and for that he was thankful.

"Pretty nice of Señor Estevez to scrape the dust off his wallet and buy us a backstop," Whiplash said as he tightened the chicken wire to a rusted metal pole. The mesh would hopefully save the windows of the chapel from most stray foul balls. Not all, but most.

"Buy?" Sam gave a look of skepticism and then adjusted home plate to make sure it was in line with the pitching mound. "I think that's the same chicken wire I saw in the casino store room. Y'know, the wire that was next to the air conditioner he gave us last month for the kids sleeping quarters."

"He's gotta cut somewhere after spending so much on new players in his quest to beat his arch enemy, Indios del Bóer," Whiplash said. "Stole the best reliever from Chinandega, overpaid for the Leones big first baseman, and signed that eighteen-year-old slick fielding shortstop from Managua who everybody thought would ink with los Indios."

"Still have to come together, Whip. We're just a bunch of talented guys until we prove we're a team."

"You won last night over a pretty good Jinotega outfit."

"You weren't there. Twice, our outfielders overthrew the cutoff man, and our new first baseman, Mairena, ignored a bunt sign and swung away."

"Don't tell me that was the RBI double he ripped in the sixth?"

Sam frowned. "Señor Estevez wants to be the George Steinbrenner of Nicaragua. He thinks he can buy a championship."

Whip cocked his head to the side. "Kinda like you buyin' a Little League crown."

Sam didn't respond, not quite sure he'd heard right.

"Shoot-fire, Sammy. You done bought our lil Dookies the snazziest uniforms, the shiniest cleats, the most expensive bats and gloves—we are an orphanage, y'know?"

Sam tore off a piece of duct tape with his teeth and handed it to his friend. "What's that old saying, Whip? Dress for success?"

"Yeah, well yer spendin' your entire paycheck on the kids and then buyin' gloves and caps for every team they play." Whiplash fastened the duct tape to the pole and chicken wire backstop and pressed down firmly. "Just like baseball, dude, you cain't do it alone. You cain't outfit all of Nicaragua on the peanuts you make."

Sam stretched his arms from one side of the church property to the other. "What else am I gonna spend it on when you give me free room and board at this palatial estate?"

"Hmph," Whiplash snorted. "I know the Pomares League don't pay as much, Sammy. How much did Estevez cut you?"

"I got fifteen hundred a month during the Nicaraguan Pro season, and now a thousand a month with the Pomares League."

"That's five hundred less than that big slow first baseman he just signed. Geez, Sammy, yer the best pitcher in both leagues."

"He's got leverage." Sam winked. "He knows I'm a lousy negotiator who's tied to you."

"Yeah, well, yer the number-one reason Estevez Ballpark attendance quadrupled this year. You deserve more."

*   *   *

The spicy aroma of gallo pinto filled the air of the church kitchen as Hunoon prepared the traditional Nicaraguan beans-and-rice dish. Carlita moved in front of her and sprinkled cilantro, sautéed onions, and sweet red peppers into the pot.

"It smells good," the little girl asked. "Should I put salt in now?"

"Why don't we let everyone salt to their own taste," Hunoon answered. "Some people like their food salty, and some like it not so salty."

Carlita gave a happy nod, which made the matriarch of the orphanage smile. Hunoon had watched the eleven-year-old orphan from crime-infested Barrio San Judas transform from a withdrawn, distrusting, defensive child with severe abandonment issues to one who had become a leader both on and off the baseball and soccer fields. It certainly helped that Carlita was having a terrific Little League season. The Little Dukes pitcher had won all of her starts and was batting over .400, leading her team to a second place standing in the Diriamba Little League. She had even befriended her third baseman, Anthony Villanueva, the boy she had attacked on the bus after being teased about a bad pitching performance some six months before.

"May I set the table now?" Carlita opened the silverware drawer.

"Forks on the left–" Hunoon said.

Carlita cut her off. "Spoons and knives on the right. I know, Ms. Sanjari, I'm not five."

They laughed until the phone rang, then they both raced for it. Hunoon slowed at the last second to see how Carlita would answer.

"Friends of Estevez Orphanage!" she gushed breathlessly. "How may I help you?"

Hunoon beamed as she watched the little girl listen carefully.

"Yes, sir." Carlita's face tightened as she seemed to have difficulty understanding the person on the other end of the line. "Yes, sir, I will get Coach EssCee for you, sir."

Carlita held her hand over the mouthpiece and whispered, "His Spanish is not very good—says his name is Jose Lopez."

Hunoon smiled. "That's Samuel's best friend from America!"

As Carlita ran off to find her coach, Hunoon laughed into the phone. "Hola, Señor Lopez! Is the new papa diaper trained yet?"

*   *   *

Carlita was back at the stove, stirring the gallo pinto, but also trying to stifle her giggles as she overheard the silly conversation between her coach and his old friend.

"Don't call your baby mud butt." Sam laughed. "He'll get a complex … nooo … Winnie the Poop is a bad name too … C'mon, Jose, be patient, you'll probably have two more years of diaper duty, so only about four thousand more Code Browns." He paused mid-conversation and winked at Carlita. "This poo shall pass."

Carlita couldn't contain herself any longer and cracked up laughing. Her English wasn't the best, but she knew enough to understand words like butt and poop.

"When can you guys come to Nicaragua?" Sam asked Jose. "Yeah … January? That's seven months away … I know, but … okay … Take two weeks off. I'll pay for the trip. That'll be my Christmas present to you and Teresa … No, I insist. That way you'll have to come … You're right, hopefully our Dukes will be in the playoffs when you get here." Sam paused for a long moment as the conversation suddenly took a more serious tone. "What? Someone's been asking about me?"

Carlita stopped stirring and stared at her coach. He didn't look happy anymore.

Sam's hand went to his temples and squeezed. "You think it's Dixon? What's he want now? … We have a deal . . ."

Carlita didn't hear anymore as she slid the gallo pinto off the stove and ran to her coach's dorm room in search of help.

*　　*　　*

Sam sat alone in the kitchen, his head in his hands, and closed his eyes. He had finished his conversation with Jose and was trying to think calmly, trying to settle the anger that was boiling inside. *Drake Dixon.* The name was like an arrow piercing his heart. He hadn't thought about the man in months, and now Dixon was trying to find him. Likely seeking leverage, control, power, pressing at some crack in the wall that Sam had carefully built to keep thoughts of Dixon out of his mind.

He and Abdul Hazrat had agreed to communicate every three months by email or phone whenever the mountain leader went to Parun to pick up supplies for his village. There had been no more construction on his land. That was a relief. *Why is Dixon trying to find me? What does he want? I'm getting my life back … playing baseball again … and playing well … will I ever be able to escape Dixon?*

He opened his eyes and found that Jenny's journal had been placed before him.

"Coach?" a tiny voice said cautiously, and Sam turned to see a look of worry on Carlita's face. She pointed to the book. "You told me you read this when you're sad."

He forced a smile. "I read it every day whether I'm happy or sad."

"You said her words help you."

This time he didn't have to force a smile as his mouth curled up happily. "Open it, Carlita. Open it to any page."

She peeled back the old, weathered journal and pointed at the words.

Forgive everyone who has hurt you … not for them, but for yourself.
Let go of the memories and sorrows that scar your heart and seek counsel
with Spirit. Your past, your mistakes, do not limit who you are
or what is possible for you now. Get quiet and seek peace.

"Is it a good one?" Carlita asked.
He put his arm around the little girl's shoulder. "It's perfect."

CHAPTER FIFTEEN

Overland Park, Kansas

May 2012

Sydney looked down at her wristwatch to see how much time was left in the game. Two minutes. Two minutes to the 6A Kansas Girls Soccer Semifinals. Her Tigers were leading archrival Blue Valley West 2-1 in the Regional Finals. She couldn't remember a team that she had played on or coached that she'd been more proud of. After losing their first two games of the season and struggling with their confidence, this group of Tigers had fought back to win thirteen straight.

It had all started on a road trip to Wichita in late March. Two games in two days, in brutal weather. Temperatures in the low thirties, and sleet that came down sideways off the howling Kansas prairie, biting her players' faces and legs as they skidded through ice and mud in search of a waterlogged black-and-white ball. It was a frigid scrum, a battle of wills, until the Tigers' right wing, Taylor Layne, broke free of the pack and left-footed a shot past a diving Wichita South goalie for the only score of the game. Blue Valley survived, 1–0.

But instead of climbing back into their two vans and hustling back to the Holiday Inn to defrost and go to dinner with their parents, Sydney told her team to meet her at the hotel conference room after they cleaned up. They arrived to find a sign posted on the front door: *Coach Sydney's Spaghetti and Garlic Toast Grill.* Their coach had ordered take-out from a local Italian restaurant for her players and their parents.

Something happened that night. Sydney started it by flipping a slice of garlic bread at her captain, Ryan, who then tossed it at a shy junior who rarely played. That ignited the laughter, and a food fight began. Sophomores tossed bread at seniors, who pelted juniors, who fired toast at their parents and coaches. The giggling and squealing continued until Sydney waved her hands to stop.

"Let the games begin." She feigned a melodramatic seriousness. "I've been practicing, so I doubt there's anyone in this room who can beat me." She picked a noodle out of her bowl of spaghetti and held it up. "Competitors must dangle a noodle out of your mouth and write, in cursive, the word win on a piece of garlic bread. Whoever finishes first gets to pick the music on the drive home after we beat Wichita East tomorrow."

"Yeah!" her Tigers shouted, and the competition began. The scene of heads bobbing back and forth as the girls tried to suppress their laughter with a single noodle dancing uncontrollably from their lips was too much. There was no winner, but a bond was formed that night in the Holiday Inn conference room. Call it trust, chemistry, unity, there was a commitment to each other.

The next day, despite the cold and more rain, Sydney's Tigers played with a togetherness that was unbeatable. Their breaks were sharper, their passes more accurate, and their ball movement like clockwork as they overpowered the number six team in the state, 4–0. Junior Grayson Garcia was selected by her team to pick the music on the drive home.

Now, two months later, with the season on the line, Blue Valley was leading the defending state champs by one goal with ninety seconds to go. Sydney was surprised she wasn't nervous as she watched her team. Her Tigers were playing with a confidence that came when minds and bodies worked together.

Sydney didn't even have to coach as that was being done by her senior captain, Ryan, who was directing her teammates as they moved in unison to defend their goal, rotate the ball away from trouble, and play keep-away from the Panthers. Ryan to Katie, to Taylor, to Elliot, to Grayson, and back to Ryan. It was perfection.

Sydney glanced at her watch again, and a smile began to crease her face, waiting for the moment. The whistle blew, the referee raised his arms, and the game was over. The Blue Valley Tigers were moving on to the Kansas 6A Final Four.

*　　*　　*

The last congratulations had been given, the last handshake, the last hug, the last high five, the happy walk to the parking lot with her proud parents before they said goodbye. And then Sydney stood alone, searching for the one car that wasn't there. She wondered why her mom or dad hadn't asked, "Where's Blake?" They probably already knew. No reason to pour salt on her wound. It was a sensitive subject, and yet her folks, such strong Christians, believed that faith alone would get their daughter and son-in-law through this tough time.

She unlocked her car and reached for her phone in the side console. There were about twenty-five texts. All but one congratulating her for leading Blue Valley High to the state semifinals. The other text was from her husband.

I left at halftime. You guys were playing so well that I didn't think you needed me. I headed to Crazy 8's to jump-start your party.

What? She didn't want to go to a bar. Her captain's parents had invited everyone over to their house after the game. She was sure she'd told Blake.

She texted back: *We won 2–1. Party at Dr. Goldman's. I'll meet you there.*

Thirty seconds later came Blake's reply: *Borrrring. I've got a table for twenty set up, so tell everyone to come here.*

Her fist reflexively went to her mouth, biting down on the first knuckle. She inhaled a deep breath and typed: *No. I told you if we won the party was at the Goldmans'.*

His reply: *You told me the party was WITH the Goldmans not AT the Goldmans'.*

That's not true, she thought. She was sure she had told him it was *at* the Goldmans'. Blake seemed to use this strategy all the time, getting her to doubt what she had said. For a moment, she hesitated, her fingers hovering over the keys. Then she wrote: *I said AT the Goldmans'. These are 17- and 18-year-old girls who shouldn't be at a bar.*

Don't make this a big deal. They're not going to be drinking, just having a little fun. The bar manager is even saving a bottle of champagne for us. The whole place wants to celebrate your big win. Can't wait to see you.

She was furious. She didn't want to go to Crazy 8's. She wanted a simple party with just her team and their parents. Her hands were shaking as she typed: *I'm going to the Goldmans'. You are welcome to join me.*

Then she slammed her phone down onto the passenger's seat, started the car, and with more than a bit of anger, sped off to join her victorious Tigers.

*   *   *

Ten days later, Blue Valley was back on the bus, driving from Olathe after losing the championship game to number-one-ranked Olathe East. For most, it was a very successful season. Sixteen wins. Three losses. Runner up in the top division in all of Kansas.

But for Sydney, there was a sense of failure. What more could they have done? What else could she have said? What strategy could she have changed that would have catapulted her Tigers over Olathe East?

The final score, 3–2, had said it all. Her girls had given everything. Twice as many shots on goal than East, more interceptions, greater time of possession. And yet it wasn't enough—they had lost.

It was a quiet drive back to Blue Valley High, with Sydney sitting in the bus's first row, her head turned toward the window, her gaze on nothing in particular, her thoughts flying from what might have been to what she would do now.

Teaching and coaching had been her eye in the middle of the storm that awaited her at home. The end of school and the soccer season meant more time with Blake, which meant more criticism or the silent treatment and more time with his friends. And she, of course, would be asked to prep the parties, cook the food, and hand them another beer. No, thank you.

She closed her eyes, settled back into her seat, and let her mind take her someplace else. Someplace happy, someplace innocent, someplace peaceful.

Suddenly, she felt something touch her cheek, then her forehead, then her hair. Her hand reflexively went to swat the bug away, but the intruder did not leave. Giggles followed and another something on her face. She swatted again and opened her eyes to find her entire team surrounding her, laughing hysterically. Their captain, Ryan, had opened a bag of spaghetti noodles and had been very carefully placing each one on their coach's face.

"Noodle power!" Ryan cried out, and Sydney couldn't help but laugh as well, as the giddiness turned to bliss, and all was right with her world again.

CHAPTER SIXTEEN

DiamondBar Headquarters, Southern Virginia

August 2012

Dixon clicked off his phone and tapped on the glass that separated his DiamondBar office from the rest of his staff. A contented smile began to spread across his face as he motioned for legal counsel to join him. Barry King hurried over and closed the door.

"Guess who I just got off the phone with?" Dixon asked.

"I have no idea," King replied, "but from the look on your face, it was good news."

"It was the second Major League general manager to call me today." Dixon leaned forward and flipped back a page of the yellow legal pad he'd been writing on. "They both wanted to get a character reference for a player their scouts saw in Nicaragua."

Both of King's brows rose in interest. "Carson?"

Dixon nodded. "He threw a complete-game five-hit shutout to lead the Diriamba Dukes to a fourth-place finish in the twelve-team CNBS League. Apparently, there were four Major League scouts in Managua, and one of them remembered Carson as the prospect who pulled himself off the market to work for me in 2009." Dixon paused to look down at his notes. "Had a helluva year too … eight and two record. Ninety-one strikeouts, only eleven walks in eighty-three innings."

"What did you tell the GMs?"

Dixon gave a smug laugh. "I told them he was a bad guy—that we had to let him go because he wasn't a team player. Fought with his coworkers, disobeyed orders, and there were rumors he might have been involved with drugs and prostitutes."

"But none of that's true."

"Truth isn't important, Barry. Only getting people to believe what I say is important."

"You don't think he'll find out what you're doing?"

"No. GMs will talk with other GMs, who will tell their scouts, who will tell other scouts that Carson is cancer. You know how people like to share bad news over good, even when they have no facts. GMs won't care who started the rumor. They'll just be glad they didn't spend money on some asshole who will divide their clubhouse."

"Even if they discover the rumors aren't true?"

"If Carson was an eighteen-year-old phenom from the Dominican Republic, they might investigate further. But they're not going to dig into the backstory of a twenty-four-year-old turd they saw on some sandlot in a third-world country."

"Are you sure *all* the scouts will back off?"

"Both GMs I talked to today thanked me for my honesty and said they'd pull their scouts from his games." He winked at his lawyer. "The last thing we need is for Carson to come back to the States and start talking to our press." Dixon leaned back in his chair and clasped his hands behind his head. "Nothing would give me greater joy than to see him rot in the baseball hell of Nicaragua."

CHAPTER SEVENTEEN

Diriamba, Nicaragua

January 2013

Sam asked the umpire for time and slowly walked out to the mound. Carlita Rapino didn't have her best stuff today, but she had been battling. Until this moment. The twelve-year-old was one of the best pitchers in the Diriamba Little League, but she had been kicking at the pitching rubber and talking to herself this inning. Carlita had led her Little Dukes to a second-place finish in the summer-league season and now had her team on the cusp of winning the winter-ball crown.

All she had to do was get by Porfi Dario, the biggest kid in the league, already six feet tall and over two hundred pounds. Nickname, el Bufalo. He was two for two against Carlita today, with both hits massive home runs over the center-field fence. And now, it was the sixth inning, with bases loaded and two outs. Carlita was struggling to protect a two-run Dukes' lead.

"*¿Como te va, piña?*" *How's it going, pineapple?* Pineapple was Sam's pet name for Carlita after their *Who lives in a pineapple under the sea?* mound conversation from a year ago.

The little girl clenched her jaws so her coach wouldn't see her chin tremble. "El Bufalo has my number, EssCee." She then glanced at Dario in the on-deck circle. "He makes me so mad when he pounds his chest after hitting a home run."

Sam peeked over his shoulder at the opposing batter, who did seem to have a cocky grin on his face as he windmilled a weighted bat over his head. Heck, the bat itself probably weighed more than Carlita.

"Why don't you pitch him differently?" Sam suggested.

"I threw him a pitch six inches off the plate last time, and he hit it all the way to the parking lot."

He put a hand on Carlita's shoulder. "It's impossible to pitch to two strike zones, *piña.*"

She narrowed her eyes as if not sure what her coach meant.

"You've been pitching to el Bufalo's strike zone. Watch him when he gets in the batter's box. His hands are in the true strike zone, allowing his long arms to reach any pitch off the plate."

She nodded as if she were beginning to understand.

"Pitch to *the* strike zone." He went down to one knee and faced both pitcher and catcher. "Eduardo, I want you to set your target on the inside corner of the plate. Carlita, I want you to throw your four-seam fastball hard through Eduardo's glove. Not *to* Eduardo's glove, but *through* it." Sam had all of his pitcher's attention by now, his eyes locked on hers, exuding confidence in the little girl. "Throw your four-seamer with conviction. Don't worry about hitting him."

"Let's go, guys!" the umpire interrupted.

Sam popped the ball firmly in Carlita's glove. "Let her rip, *piña.*"

*   *   *

Carlita dug her right foot against the pitching rubber, bent low at the waist, her jaws clenched defiantly as she stared in to get the sign from her catcher. Eduardo dropped one finger and then set up on the inside corner. Carlita wound up and let her fastball rip. It tailed at the last second, toward the batter's head. El Bufalo dove out of the way, landing on his ample butt. The crowd *oooed*, and Carlita jerked around in search of her coach.

Sam clapped his hands and gave her a thumbs-up.

The high heater did the trick, wiping the smile off el Bufalo's face as he cautiously rose up from the dirt and dusted off his pants.

Carlita was already back atop the hill, jaw set, eyes narrow slits as she nodded to her catcher's pitch selection and location. Another fastball in.

El Bufalo reluctantly placed his right foot on the back line of the box, a not-so-confident look this time as he readied himself for the crazy girl's next missile.

Carlita let fly another heater inside. El Bufalo tried to get out of the way, but the ball hit the handle of the bat and fluttered innocently toward the mound. Carlita caught it easily, glared at the batter, and then pounded her fist against her chest. "Get back in your corral, el Bufalo!"

Sam spun away from the field and covered his mouth to muzzle his laugh as he fell back on the dugout bench, next to his assistant coach.

Teddy Zapata buried his face in Sam's shoulder and said, *"Esa chica tiene unas bolas." That girl's got some balls.*

*   *   *

Light and joy and peace abide in me.

Those were the words that came to Sam as he sat on a beach in La Boquita, listening to the sounds of waves crashing, seagulls squawking, and children laughing. The light was the brilliant late afternoon sun's rays flickering gently off the water, the joy was kids playing tag in the surf, and the peace was what filled Coach EssCee's heart.

This trip to the tropical Pacific seashore was his promised reward for the Little Dukes winning the Diriamba winter-ball title. For many of the orphans, it was their first trip to the ocean: first time swimming, first time tasting saltwater, first time making sandcastles. Polio-stricken Teddy was floating on his back, no longer tormented by the pain that came from walking. Everth, Jonathan, and Elena were building a sandcastle, and Carlita was donning a bathing suit, finally abandoning the long-sleeve shirts she always wore to cover the self-harm scars.

Sam had never talked with her about it, figuring that was Whiplash and Hunoon's territory; he had only encouraged her through baseball and by asking her to help coach the seven- and eight-year-olds' T-ball team. He found that the more responsibility he gave Carlita, the more she thrived.

"Heckuvayear," said Whiplash, always seeming to slide his words together in his south-midland Arkansas drawl. "Lil' Dukes champs 'n' Big Dukes goin' to the Nicaraguan Series on Sunday."

Sam smiled, more interested in watching the kids play in the surf than discussing postseason.

"Yer a natural with kids, y'know. Bees to honey in Afghanistan, and the Lil' Dukes think yer about as fine as frog hair split four ways."

"What does that even mean?" Sam asked Hunoon.

"It means you are a good coach," she laughed, and then despite her thick Afghan accent, she attempted to mimic her husband. "And as a ballplayer, yer as sweet as cherry pi–yie."

Whiplash straightened up on the sand and became serious. "Speakin' o'which, Sammy, why ain't more scouts talkin' to ya?"

Sam shrugged as if it didn't bother him.

"C'mon, bro, you got more wins, the lowest ERA, and the best strikeout-to-walk ratio, yet all the scouts want to talk about are Gonzalez of los Indios and Valdez of los Tigres."

"They're probably younger than me."

"So what? The scouts could have at least stayed to watch you pitch. I asked 'em why they was leavin' before your game, and they said they"– Whiplash raised his fingers and gave the proverbial air quotes–"gotta look at some dudes in Venezuela. That was the day you threw the three-hitter against los Gigantes with eleven strikeouts."

"They'll be back for the playoffs." Sam hesitated, then said, "And what are you and the kids going to do if I sign with a Big League club?"

"You don't think I already planned for that?" Whip scoffed. "Sisters Lidia and Catherine from San Caralampio come twice a week and told their monsignor they'd like to be transferred full-time to work our orphanage, and you've been training Coach Teddy to take over the Little Dukes for more than a year–"

Sam's phone rang, and he was relieved for the distraction. Did he want scouts to see him? Damn straight he did. He knew he was good. Knew he could help some team. Yet none of the few Major League scouts who saw his games had even talked to him. He let go a soft sigh and looked down at his phone.

It was Jose!

He clicked on and said, "Waddup, meat! Are you calling from Houston?"

He paused to listen, a renewed happiness lighting his face. His Christmas present to his best friends, Jose and Teresa Lopez, was a vacation in Nicaragua. Even booked them rooms at a La Boquita beach resort. Teresa's mom was watching their fifteen-month-old son, Joey, while they were away, so it was going to be perfect.

"Is your flight on time?" he asked. "Okay, yeah, I'll be there … Eleven thirty p.m. arrival? No problem … It's only a couple of hours from the airport to the resort … Don't worry, I'll be ready to go on Sunday … Yeah, I'm starting … All right, dude, I'll meet you at baggage claim."

Then he clicked off and beamed a smile so bright his face practically glowed.

Light and joy and peace abide in me … indeed.

"Will you look at Sammy," Whiplash crooned. "Grinnin' like a possum eatin' sweet taters."

CHAPTER EIGHTEEN

Santo Domingo, Dominican Republic

January 2013

Roberto Francisco stood behind the chain-link backstop at the Kansas City Royals Dominican Academy, watching sixteen- and seventeen-year-old boys run the bases. He had already watched these prospects hit and field. Now he wanted to check their speed; time them from home to first, first to third, first to home. Francisco was beginning his fourteenth year with the Royals organization, but this was his first in his new role as Coordinator of Latin American scouting.

He had started as a part-time scout and coach for the club's rookie-league affiliate in Surprise, Arizona, then worked as an area scout, covering Arizona, Utah, Colorado, and New Mexico. The promotion meant more money, but it also meant more time away from his wife and two sons. If he could finish this last day of scouting in Santo Domingo by four, he might be able to make the six o'clock flight through Houston and get home in time to have breakfast with his family.

His general manager, David Wilson, was a family guy too, a man who bent over backward to help his staff spend time with loved ones. Particularly scouts like Roberto, who were constantly on the road, hustling to Puerto Rico, Venezuela, Cuba, Mexico, and, of course, the hotbed of baseball, the Dominican Republic. Wilson had built one of the strongest minor league systems in the game, opened a new academy in the Dominican, and now wanted to expand to other Latin American countries.

This was an important year for the Royals. After nearly three decades of losing, they were on the cusp of contending. A group of talented prospects had all come up together, winning a championship in A-ball, another at AA, and two years ago winning the Pacific Coast League's AAA crown. Most of those kids were now with the Big League Royals and playing well. They were great defenders, athletic, fast, and just beginning to scratch the surface of a dynamic offense. The only thing Kansas City lacked was starting pitching. That was Roberto's job. Find arms. Anywhere he could.

He tapped his stopwatch as the second-to-last prospect swung the bat and broke for first base. He tapped again when the boy hit first. 4.2 seconds from the right side. Not bad. He glanced at his wristwatch. 3:50 p.m. It was gonna be close. Then the phone rang. It was the boss.

"Hey, David, just finishing up tryouts at our academy."

"Any you like?"

"Just clocked Victor Hernandez four point two, home to first, from the right side. Kid's got power potential too. I don't see him staying in center though, probably a corner outfielder once he fills out."

"How about arms?"

"Saw a kid yesterday. Older prospect, turned nineteen in November, throws mid-nineties but has no idea where it's going yet."

There was a long pause from his GM on the other end of the line. *Uh oh.*

Finally, Wilson said, "You're gonna hate me, Robbie, but I need you to go to Nicaragua—as in tonight. Their championship series starts tomorrow, and our headhunter in Managua had a death in the family."

Roberto grimaced in disappointment. "Totally understand, sir. Is there any particular player you want me to focus on?"

"Eddie said los Indios has the best team and that we should check out their pitcher, Gonzalez, and some of their eighteen- and nineteen-year-old prospects ... I don't know anything about Diriamba. They're a surprise to even be in the series. I'll let you be the judge on who you like ... sorry about this, Robbie, I know you've been away from family for a long time, but I'll make it up to you. I promise. Emily's got you on a six thirty flight through Miami, getting to Managua at midnight."

*   *   *

The foot traffic to Dennis Martinez Stadium was chaos as Francisco dodged fans and then a bicyclist who almost crashed into a street vendor selling deep-fried plantains. It seemed like all of Managua had turned out to watch their home team, los Indios, overpower the underdog Diriamba Dukes. He bought a program and a savory bean-and-rice dish and headed to his seat, stopwatch around his neck, notebook in his back pocket, and three colored pens dangling from the string that held his pass. Typical scout. All he needed was a Tommy Bahama shirt, binoculars, and a radar gun. Unfortunately, all three had been in the luggage the airline had lost somewhere between Santo Domingo and Managua.

Roberto settled back in his seat and opened his program to the stat page. Indios del Bóer easily won the regular season with a 23–7 record, and the Dukes snuck in through the round-robin after a 16–14 finish. *How'd they do it?*

His index finger went down the page to see if any stats jumped out: batting average, homers, runs batted in for the hitters; wins, ERA, strikeouts to walks for the pitchers. *Wow, who's this EssCee Carson dude?* 6–1 record in 7 starts, 50 innings, 28 hits, 51 strikeouts, only 6 walks, 1.5 ERA. *Damn, that's impressive … and he's starting today.*

"Looks like KC's charting new territory," said a voice off to the left.

Roberto turned to see two other Major League scouts come down his aisle and plop beside him. "Hi, Geno. Hey, Pedro." He shook each man's hand and then said, "Our area birddog had a death in the family, so David asked me to check out the series."

"There's a few guys to keep an eye on," said the Dodgers' scout, Pedro Juarez. "Some big arms on los Indios and a couple of young dudes on Chinandega."

Roberto nodded thoughtfully, then glanced down at the stats page and back to Juarez. "What about this EssCee Carson? Unbelievable numbers."

"Apparently, there's a lot of baggage with that one. Bad attitude, drugs, hookers, cancer in the clubhouse." Juarez shook his head. "It's a shame too because he's by far the best prospect I've seen. But when the boss says stay away, you close your scouting book when he's on the mound."

The Dukes went three up, three down in the top of the first. As the Dukes' pitcher threw his warm-up pitches, Roberto straightened up in his seat. He'd seen this delivery before. *Loose, confident, smooth.* He turned to the Tigers' scout. "Hey, Geno, can I borrow your binoculars for a second?"

Geno obliged, and Roberto brought the glasses to his eyes. He twisted the focus to get a better image. All the color drained from his face.

Holy shit. It's him. EssCee is SC. Sam Cloud-Carson. The kid I first saw at Ignacio High. Then Mesa State All-American. We would have drafted him if he hadn't quit the game after his mom died some three years ago. This boy had seen more than his share of tragedy. Roberto lowered the glasses and glanced over at the scouts next to him. *They said he was a cancer in the clubhouse, into drugs and prostitutes? No way. I knew his family. Great people. There has to be more to the story.*

*   *   *

As the game went on, Roberto fixated his attention on only one player. How did Carson react after a call didn't go his way? How did he interact with his catcher, his teammates, his coaches? They all seemed to like him, no discontent from his infielders when their pitcher moved them before certain los Indios batters. One moment in particular intrigued him. Third inning, one out, man on first, right-handed batter at the plate. Sam motioned for his third baseman to move two steps closer to the line. He then delivered a perfect sinker, down and in, that was hit directly to third for an easy 5-4-3 double play. It was beautiful. Individually, the Dukes weren't nearly as talented as los Indios, but collectively they were better.

In the top of the fifth, Juan Carlos Pineda homered to give Diriamba at 2–0 lead. Roberto's gaze went to the visitors' dugout. Carson was high-fiving teammates as Pineda circled the bases, and then he was the first Duke to congratulate him after he touched home plate.

Bad teammate? Really?

Meantime, Sam was dealing on the mound. Shutting out mighty los Indios on two hits through five. No walks, seven strikeouts.

After a swing-and-miss strikeout on a four-seam fastball to end the inning, Roberto peeked over at Geno's radar gun. *93 mph. Not bad. More velo than he showed in college, and he still had that incredible late-life control, and the best changeup in college baseball. Not one batter had truly squared up one of his pitches.*

A tap on the shoulder brought Roberto back to the present.

"Mr. Francisco?" asked the stranger, who looked familiar. Roberto nodded.

"I thought it was you." The man reached out to shake his hand. "Jose Lopez, sir. I was Sam's catcher in high school and college."

Startled, Roberto jerked up from his seat and shook Jose's hand. "Of course, I remember you." Roberto angled his body to block the inquiring eyes and ears of the two scouts who now seemed more than interested in what EssCee Carson's friend had to say. "I remember a home run you hit"—he glanced back at the Dodgers' scout who was leaning his way, straining to hear the conversation—"to help Sam win a game in Denver."

"Good memory, sir." Jose nodded toward the visitors' dugout. "Do you like what you see from Sammy?"

Roberto didn't want to answer. Not now. He needed to know more. A fan got him off the hook.

"Abajo en frente!¡No podemos ver el juego!" Down in front! We can't see the game!

"Lo Siento. Culpa mía." Roberto apologized, and then put his hand on Jose's shoulder. "Where are you sitting? I'd like to catch up."

Jose waved for him to follow and then pointed one section over. "I'm with my wife and the entire Dukes Little League team." He winked. "They're the ones making the loudest racket whenever Coach EssCee strikes somebody out."

Bad guy Carson coaches kids? Roberto thought. *Something doesn't add up.*

* * *

"You remember Teresa?" Jose took him around to meet the fans sitting in the Diriamba section. "She was always sitting with Sam's mom at our games."

"I do remember." Roberto shook their hands and then paused in reflection. "Susan Cloud-Carson. She was a great lady."

Teresa seemed to shrink back on the bench, as if the mere mention of Susan's name pained something deep inside. Roberto noticed and changed the subject.

"Who are these beautiful children?" he motioned up to the lime-green-and-navy-clad kids behind them.

"They're Sammy's winter-ball champion Little Dukes," said Jose, and then he pointed to a middle-aged couple one row away. "And these two are the team's vice presidents of love and kindness, Whiplash and Hunoon McCracken."

Whip put his arm around his wife. "Marry a woman with brains enough for two and you'll come out even."

They all laughed, except for Hunoon, who narrowed her eyes at Roberto. "Are you a scout?"

He nodded. "Kansas City Royals, ma'am."

"Why haven't you signed Samuel? He's the best pitcher in this country and not one of you scouts have even talked to him."

Roberto took a step back, a bit surprised by Mrs. McCracken's candor. He winked at Jose. "Is she any relation to Agent Jenny?"

Jose laughed. "You remember Sammy's sister?"

"How could I forget her? She grilled me about Sam every time I saw him pitch."

Jose put his hand on Hunoon's shoulder. "Well, this lady's just like her. She fights for the people she loves."

Roberto pointed to the seat next to Hunoon. "May I?"

She slid over on the wooden bleacher.

"This is only my first day in Nicaragua, ma'am," Roberto said as he sat down. "Tell me everything you can about your client."

*   *   *

They talked the rest of the afternoon, Roberto less interested in the outcome of the game than the Diriamba faithful. Dukes' fans surrounding him stomped and cheered every time their hero got two strikes on a batter, and then he rewarded them with a strikeout or weak groundout. In the end, the Dukes prevailed, 4–1. Coach EssCee struck out eleven in a complete-game five-hitter.

As they headed down the aisle, the man called Whiplash tapped him on the shoulder. "Where ya holed up tonight?"

"Don't know yet. Stayed at the Airport Best Western last night. But they're sold out tonight. I'm on a waiting list."

Whiplash steered him toward their exit. "Yer comin' with us, brotha. Hunoon's cookin' her famous nacatamal."

"Naca—what?"

"Pork, smashed taters, veggies—y'know—good stuff."

"Will Sam be there?"

Whiplash gave him a sideways grin. "Is a pig's ass pork?"

Roberto didn't know what the heck that meant but assumed it was the affirmative. He accepted the invitation.

*　　*　　*

The drive to the Estevez Orphanage in a rusted, dented, wire-and duct-taped-together old yellow school bus was filled with the sounds and smells of twenty-five laughing, singing, sunbaked, sweaty children. Roberto grabbed the first row next to Jose and Teresa.

"I've barely had a chance to visit with you two after talking with the McCrackens the last three innings."

"Completely understand," said Jose. "They're super people. I think you'll enjoy seeing what they've built in the jungle."

Teresa leaned across her husband and said, "Sam's been a big part of the rebuild."

Roberto gave an understanding nod. He had yet to ask anyone about Sam's alleged dark side. This was a time to simply observe, gather information, and put together a solid and honest report for his GM. He'd seen plenty of scouts fail by asking probing questions too soon, putting a prospect or his family on the defensive and getting no true understanding of a player's character.

"You've played with Sam from Little League through college," he said to Jose. "How do you think he's grown into the player we saw today?"

"You can't see it on the outside, Mr. Francisco, because he looks so cool and calm, but there's a fire that burns inside that dude that's as hot as ten thousand suns. He had trouble controlling it when he was younger, couldn't understand why we couldn't play the game with the ease that he did. He seemed to have this internal compass whose needle would focus on a singular target. While the rest of us would be horsing around the basketball court, jacking up threes or trying to dunk, he'd be working on cuts or coming off screens. Same with baseball. We'd be done with practice, exhausted, gear packed, waiting in the parking lot for Sam to finish"–he paused to give air quotes–"his routine. Nothing he ever did was random. Whether it was tracking or pitching. He had this ability–I don't even know how to explain it, but he could see, or feel, beyond the physical to make things work for him. In the wild, it was his ability to read nature: the terrain, animals, wind, weather. He could bring every element together to serve him."

"I remember Jenny telling me that the mound and the mountains were his churches."

"Those are the places he feels most at peace." Jose's face brightened. "When he was in high school, he didn't know how to channel his competitiveness and would yell at umpires about bad calls or get a technical in basketball when he thought he'd been wronged."

"But he learned to let it go?"

"He was forced to let it go." Jose's eyes darkened, remote with memory. "You saw what he went through, Mr. Francisco–losing both parents and his sister in a two-year period. That's the only time I've seen Sam struggle in sports, be a poor teammate, and fall to the depths of attempting–" He didn't finish the sentence as Teresa squeezed his hand.

Roberto noticed and wondered if there was more they were holding back.

Fall to the depths of attempting what?

"We were going to win it all in 2010," Jose went on. "Sam was our rock, a guy who had created something special at Mesa State. And whether he did it consciously or not, we believed we were great. When he finally learned to live with his grief the second half of his sophomore year, we took off. Sam was not only our best player, he was our leader. He would say just the right thing to pick up a struggling teammate, calm a temper, hold guys accountable." He drew his hand into a fist. "He connected us—and we followed him."

"And then his mom died in that car accident."

Jose drew in a deep, shuddering breath. "We weren't the same team without Sam."

"And yet I still can't understand why he quit baseball and school to join DiamondBar. After all that he had been through, why would he choose that path?"

"I think"—Jose glanced at his wife, then back at Roberto—"I think I should let Sam answer that question."

*   *   *

As they drove down the tree-lined dirt road and pulled into the orphanage lot, the children rushed to the front of the bus to congratulate the Dukes' winning pitcher. Sam was on the church steps, still in his dirty uniform, bags of ice tied around his right shoulder and elbow. He hugged the kids to him and then shaded his eyes to fight off the sun's glare, reflecting off the bus windows, so he could see who the stranger was inside. Then suddenly, his entire face brightened.

"Mr. Francisco!" He ran over and gave him a warm hug. "What are you doing here?"

"The Royals are looking for pitching"—Roberto opened his arms to display the people behind him—"and your advertising agency did one heckuva job selling you."

CHAPTER NINETEEN

Nicaragua

January 2013

"I'm telling you, David, the rumors are not true!" Roberto yelled into his phone from the top row of Estevez Ballpark. It was likely the final game of the Nicaraguan Series with the Dukes leading three victories to one. Sam was back on the mound against los Indios, one victory away from a shocking upset. Roberto stuck his index finger into his left ear and pressed the phone to his right, straining to hear his general manager over the crowd, pep bands, and cheerleaders who were dancing atop both dugouts.

"I talked to Mr. Dixon this morning, Roberto. He said Carson was trouble. Disruptive with coworkers and disobeyed orders."

"That's not the Sam I know, sir. I've spent the last week living at the orphanage and going to every game. I've watched him coach the kids, work with the people who run the place, with his teammates, with fans—"

"Did you ask him about the accusations? About drugs and prostitutes?"

Roberto winced. He remembered Sam's face during that conversation. It wasn't angry or even distressed. It was blank, distant, unreadable, and Roberto had wondered if there was more that Sam wasn't telling him.

"Of course we talked about it. He told me he's never used drugs or disrespected women in his life, and the two missionaries who run the Estevez Orphanage were with him in Afghanistan. They said he spent all his free time at their mission and that he was a positive influence with the children. I've got their numbers if you want to talk with them."

There was a long pause. He knew David was thinking about it, knew that his GM trusted his evaluations. Heck, they'd worked together for almost two decades, and David was the reason he had been promoted to coordinator of Latin American scouting.

"Ownership doesn't want us taking chances on questionable guys," his GM finally said in a weary, almost regretful tone. "We've built something special in KC. Chemistry, teamwork, and leadership is all coming together. I won't bring anyone into our clubhouse that will disrupt that harmony."

"I'll bet my career on Sam, David. He's one of us … he's a connector."

Another long pause. And then, despite the crowd going crazy around him, he heard a long, loud exhale from the other end of the line.

"Okay, here's what I'll do," Wilson said. "We're three weeks from pitchers and catchers reporting. I'm trying to sign two veteran free-agent starters coming off injuries who hopefully will help us until our prospects are ready. Tell Carson to be patient. If these guys don't work out and he keeps pitching well and stays clean, we'll try him out at the end of camp."

"The Astros and Marlins are here today, David. I'm not sure he'll still be available."

"Sorry, Rob. That's the best I can do right now."

*   *   *

Roberto was pissed. He needed to take a walk and let go of the fury he was feeling. He didn't know why he believed in Sam so much. Was he guilty of the biggest mistake made by any scout? Was he letting his personal feelings get in the way of the Royals' best interests? Probably.

He was the scout who had discovered Sam in high school, bonded with the family, been charmed by his little sister's nonstop commentary on everything from baseball to God, and he was the only scout who had been to all three Carson funerals. Yeah, he had let his personal feelings affect his evaluation … and he still wanted to sign Sam. More than anything.

He stormed past vendors and fans drunk on both Toña pale lager and the Dukes' stunning success, weaving his way through the concourse, glancing up occasionally at the television monitors overhead. Sam was dealing. He could hear the tiny shrieks of delight from the Little Dukes above him every time Sam struck a batter out. *Why can't he suck just for today so Houston and Florida will lose interest?*

By the time he did two laps around the stadium, the Dukes were up 4-0. A Pineda home run made it 6-0 in the fifth, and the party was on. The final score was 8-2 with Cloud-Carson pulled after seven shutout frames.

Roberto stood in the aisle, watching the celebration. Security had already given up trying to keep fans off the field as they poured over dugouts and outfield berms to dance with players, cheerleaders, and local politicians. Owner Cheslor Estevez had confiscated the band leader's hat and baton and was leading the ensemble in the Dukes' fight song. The only people heading to the exits were the Astros' and Marlins' scouts. They'd appraised the talent, questioned Sam about his previous employer's allegations, and were off to file a report on the best pitcher in Nicaragua.

Holy shit, I could lose the next Greg Maddux.

* * *

Diriamba looked like a ghost town as Sam drove Roberto to the airport early the next morning. The community had never experienced a sports championship before, so Sam didn't know what kind of delays they might have after last night's wild celebration. Several Diriamba streets were closed for cleanup, and others were littered with liquor bottles, plastic cups, and beer cans. A *Vamanos, Dukes!* banner still stretched across Avenida Central, flapping proudly in the January breeze.

Roberto tapped his right hand anxiously against his leg as he thought about how he could draw Cloud-Carson into conversation about his meeting with other Major League scouts. He glanced over at his driver, who still had an impassive, calm expression on his face—the same look he'd shown to los Indios batters less than twenty hours before.

Finally, Roberto cleared his throat and said, "I'm putting this week at the very top of all of my scouting adventures, Sam. Watching you pitch, working with the kids, you taking all of us on hikes to your Pacific overlook, it's something I won't forget."

"I'm grateful to work with good people," Sam said.

"So, uh . . ." Roberto paused, searching for the right words, and then blurted out, "What will you do now?"

Sam glanced over, a slight grin on his face. "That's not up to me, is it?"

"You're right. It's not fair to ask you to be patient for another month when others are after you." He paused again to see if Sam gave any tell about other offers. He did not. "But I do believe with every fiber of my being that you have the talent to help the Royals win right now."

Sam didn't reply, just drove on, his eyes focused on the road.

"I know that Houston and Florida talked with you."

Sam nodded.

Darn it, Roberto thought, *How do I get this guy to talk?* He took a deep breath, steeling himself to what he'd say next. "Teresa told me not to trust anything Drake Dixon says."

Sam's jaws tightened at the statement. "Did she say anything else?"

"No." Roberto turned to face him. "What happened in Afghanistan, Sam? My GM needs something."

"And I gave my word that I would never talk about my time there."

"Even if telling the truth will get you to the Major Leagues?"

Sam sighed. "My grandfather once told me that the greatest compliment I could ever receive was, *There walks an honest man. He can be trusted.*"

"So you're just going to let Dixon spread lies about you? Ruin your reputation? Keep you from realizing your dream? That doesn't sound like an honest man to me."

Sam jerked the car over to the side of the road and reached in the back seat for his backpack.

"I was going to show this to you when we got to the airport, but I think now's a better time." He hauled out an old, beaten-up monstrosity of a notebook and dropped it on the scout's lap. "Jenny wrote this journal for me when she was dying. She didn't think I would handle her death very well."

His jaws flexed again, but his dark eyes softened with memory. "My sister never did anything for herself. She pushed me in baseball, sent my resumes and videos to Major League teams, started a kidney disease help-line to help others who were suffering. Even on her death bed, she worried more about me than herself. Worried about a guy whose entire life was spent pursuing his own goals: baseball, basketball, grades, even trying to save Jenny. It was all for me . . ." He stopped there, his voice trailing off as if the rest of his words were swept away by the cool morning breeze. No conclusion. No ending. No revelation.

Roberto knew there was more, and he didn't know what to say, how to respond. Here was the best prospect he'd ever scouted, a young man who had lost his entire family, his education, and his dream of baseball to work for someone he absolutely despised. He looked uncertainly from Sam to the notebook, and then back to Sam. "Are you protecting someone? Has Dixon threatened someone close to you?"

Sam didn't answer. He simply opened up the journal to a page that revealed one sentence.

Despite the challenges that confront him, a good tracker will follow the right path.

He waited for the scout's eyes to come back to his.

"Do you trust me, Mr. Francisco?"

Roberto slowly nodded

CHAPTER TWENTY

Stilwell, Kansas

March 2013

A horse whinnied. Another stomped the ground as Sydney walked down the center aisle of the Tomlinson stables. She was tired and cold, having spent the previous three hours standing on the chilly sideline of Blue Valley High, coaching her Tigers to a flat, lifeless 3–3 tie against an inexperienced DeSoto High School squad. It was a new year and a new team, one that had lost their captain and two other All-Conference players to graduation, but Sydney still felt they had more talent than today's opponent. Unfortunately, her Tigers had yet to come together as a team, had yet to establish a clear leader, and that concerned her.

It would have been nice to head straight home from the game, take a hot shower, heat up some hot chocolate, and plant her feet next to their wood-burning fireplace. But home wasn't safe anymore. It was tense, sullen, and ominous, as she tiptoed around an unhappy husband, making sure she didn't do or say something that would set Blake off. She tapped the toes of her boots against one of the stall's lining boards to get the feeling back in her feet and kicked a decaying old plank into the stall.

"Great." She sighed and then looked over her shoulder at one of the new workers Mrs. Tomlinson had hired two months before. In an effort to save money, Bette had cut a deal with the Barton House, a sober living center for men afflicted with drug and alcohol problems. The men would come once a week to pull weeds, cut the grass, and work on the barn, kind of a transitional program to help the addicts get back on their feet.

"A little help?" she called out to the man who was two stalls away, repairing a feed box.

The man got up slowly and shuffled over. He was probably early fifties but looked much older with his hollow eyes, gray skin, and decaying teeth. She remembered her orthodontist called it "meth mouth." This poor fellow was probably a victim of it.

Sydney unhooked the hammer from the wall and grabbed a handful of nails. "If you'll lift the plank and hold it against the post, I'll nail it back on."

The man gave her a look like she was crazy. "Nail it to what? More rotten wood?"

"It's going to have to do for now."

He lifted the plank into place and squinted at her. "My daughter had a cleft."

She dropped the hammer, and her right hand shot up to cover her scar. It was a response she'd done a million times before, starting in elementary school when the first of many curious students would ask, *"What happened to your lip?"* The question was so common from children that it didn't bother her anymore, yet it was still the tiny imperfection that always drew her attention whenever she looked in the mirror.

"Whoever your doc was did a great job," he said straightforwardly. "My daughter had a bilateral cleft, so she needed a bunch of surgeries."

"Mine was a unilateral." She picked up the hammer and tapped a nail through the rotting wood to set the panel. "My folks searched high and low for the best doctors and plastic surgeons to make me look … typical."

"Wish my daughter had your parents," he said, but there was regret behind his words. "Unfortunately, her dad was me."

She was unsure how to respond. She rose up from her crouch and extended her right hand. "I'm Sydney."

He shook it. "Nice to meet ya, Sydney. I'm Roger … been sober ninety-three days."

She smiled, and together they walked to the corral to prep the horses for the waiting children.

"My daughter's name is Maggie," he muttered, as if talking more to himself than to Sydney. "She lives in Emporia. Married, one child. We haven't spoken in two years. I write letters … apologizing for being a poor father."

"That's all you can do," she said softly.

"Number nine of the twelve steps of AA. Make amends with people we've hurt."

Roger kept talking, quieter now as they helped the children onto their saddles. It would be a simple half-hour ride through the woods, next to the Little Blue River, on this cool afternoon in mid-March. Sydney leading one line of horses, and Mary Beth leading the other.

Her friend was already saddled and waiting. She smiled at Sydney for taking the time to listen to the man. He must have noticed, because as Sydney swept her right leg over the horse's flank and onto the saddle, he winked up at her. "Thank you for letting me complete number five."

She gave him a curious look.

"Admit to God, myself, and another human being the exact nature of my wrongs."

*   *   *

The trail was an easy one, and the seasoned quarter horses made it even easier. They'd been on this path hundreds of times before: straight for fifty yards, left at the bur oak, parallel the river, climb a small bluff, cut through a stand of sycamore and cottonwood, and circle around to the backside of the corral. For Sydney, it was simple but wonderful. She imagined being here two centuries before, part of a Native American tribe, perhaps the Osage, Black Bob, or Shawnee, living peacefully by the Little Blue.

For a moment she caught a reflection in the river, as if someone were watching her, and it made her think about her biological father. The young man from the Lakota tribe her mother had met two and a half decades before. She'd never met him, rarely thought about him. Why? She already had an adoptive father whose love she never doubted. But on this day, on this trail, by this river, questions surfaced. *Where was he now? What had he done in his life? Did he ever think about her?*

*   *   *

The sun was low when they returned, harsh streaks of light shooting through still-barren oak, elm and cottonwood limbs, forcing Sydney to shade her eyes to see the trail. A lone figure stood on the second rail of the fence, waving for them to hurry in.

Sydney inhaled a startled gasp when she saw who it was. Blake. Why wasn't she happy to see him?

"Let's go!" he called out, more than a bit irritated. "Did you forget Dean's birthday?"

"What?" She had no idea what her husband was talking about. Dean was a guy Blake worked with, hung out with after hours, but someone Sydney had never met.

"You do this all the time," he grumbled. "Forgetting dates, times, stuff I told you."

She jumped down from her horse and tied the lead rope to a corral post. "I have no idea what you're talking about, Blake. What party?"

"I told you about it this morning. Right before you left for your game."

She searched her mind. She didn't remember Blake saying anything about any party.

He grabbed her by the upper arm. "C'mon, let's go. We're already late."

She wrenched free. "I have to help the kids off the horses and then unsaddle and brush—"

"Roger and I can do that." Mary Beth stepped down from her horse and glared at Sydney's husband. "I mean, God forbid you're late to one of Blake's drunkfests."

"Shut up, MB." He scowled. "You're such a bitch."

"And you're a jerk."

"Stop it!" Sydney's hand flew up for quiet. She turned to her husband and mouthed the words, *"Don't say bad words in front of the kids."*

He exhaled loudly. "I'm sure they've heard it before. Don't be so sensitive."

"I'm not."

"Yeah, you are. Overreacting again. Drama queen." He grinned up at the children, twirled his index finger around the side of his head, and then pointed to Sydney. "Cuckoo, cuckoo."

The kids giggled, which only infuriated Sydney more. She bit down hard on the side of her mouth.

"I'm just joking, Syd, but that's what everybody says about you. Always making a mountain out of a molehill." He walked out of the corral. "I'll meet you in the car. I'll text Freddy that we're on our way."

She paused to compose herself and then helped a child down from her horse. A hand touched her shoulder. It was the recovering addict, Roger.

"Let me do that," he said softly. "You go on with your husband."

She gave a defeated nod and handed him the reins. As she started to leave, she heard Roger whisper, "I hope he knows what he has. You're a real fine person."

CHAPTER TWENTY-ONE

Diriamba, Nicaragua

March 2013

Sam placed one knee on the jungle floor and pointed to an animal track. "Jaguarundi," he whispered, and the three children crept closer to their instructor. It was the third day of Sam's tracking class for kids interested in uncovering the secrets of nature.

"Carlita and I found a similar track over a year ago when we were coming back from baseball practice."

The little girl nodded proudly because she had been a part of something that the other two had not.

"You've probably heard them," Sam continued. "They have an odd chirp, a hissing growl, or a scream that sounds like this: *Yeeowww!*"

The children moved closer, Carlita hugging his left shoulder, Anthony on his right, and Joey practically crawling on his back. Sam steadied himself to keep from falling over and brushed aside dead leaves that were hiding another track. "Here's the main foot pad, and these are the four lobes. They keep their claws withdrawn until they're ready to attack."

Anthony gulped. "What do jaguarundis eat?"

"Small mammals, rodents, lizards."

"But not people?"

"None this week." Sam suppressed a grin as he pointed to Anthony's dirty hands and fingernails. "But I've heard that jaguarundis are drawn to kids who don't use soap."

They giggled at that, even Anthony, whose laugh seemed a bit forced.

Sam moved on about ten yards and found another print. "This is the cat's left front paw. Notice how it's easier to read than the last one?"

They all nodded.

"That's because he likely paused to listen. Something may have startled him—was it a predator or his lunch? Either way, he has to be quiet, let the jungle tell him what's up."

"How do you know it's a boy?" Carlita asked.

"Good question, Carlita. I don't know exactly, but this is the largest track I've seen, and most male jaguarundis are bigger than females."

They continued on, Sam having to remind them more than once to be silent the rest of their journey. It was time to listen to the woods, the scolding of the birds, the screech of a howler monkey, the rustle of brush and tree branches. Only their quiet and keen attention would lead them to their goal.

Sam paused and went to one knee. "We're close," he whispered. "He picked up the scent of his prey here—look how his gait changed as he began checking under each bush and then went up that bank." Sam drew his monocular from his side pocket and slithered on his stomach up the hill. The children quietly followed, mimicking their teacher's every move, patiently waiting for some sign or signal of what to do next.

Very, very slowly, Sam's gaze went right to left, pausing occasionally to study and then move on again. He stopped and smiled. Lowering the monocular from his right eye, he handed the eyeglass to Carlita. "Dark area, left side of the tree, with the broken limb that looks like the letter *J*."

She swallowed once and nodded.

"About halfway across that limb is your jaguarundi."

The little girl brought the glass up to her eye and searched. Sam imagined her seeing the jaguarundi for the first time: soft gray fur, long slender body, short rounded ears, and penetrating blue-black eyes that looked like the wildcat was staring into your very soul.

"Wow," Carlita said in a hushed tone. "She's beautiful."

Sam smiled. "I guess it's a girl."

*   *   *

They arrived back at the orphanage a little past noon, tired and hungry, but excited to tell their friends what they had seen in the jungle. As the kids ran off to the lunchroom, Whiplash waved for Sam to join him.

"Ya might wanna check yer phone, Sammy. It was chirping like a jealous blue jay the whole time you was gone."

Sam gave him a quizzical look, and together they headed over to their living quarters.

"Maybe the Astros or Marlins upped their offer," Whip said.

Sam shrugged. Both teams had invited Sam to spring training but had only offered a two-thousand-dollar signing bonus and plane ticket. He had turned both down. It didn't feel right. There was no connection.

He wanted the Royals. KC scout Roberto Francisco was a man who had been following him since high school, had cared about his blood family and his new one in Nicaragua. He trusted Roberto and trusted his gut. Intuition didn't always tell him what he wanted to hear, but it often told him what he needed to hear. *Be patient,* Francisco had said. Sam had been.

"Señor Pop-u-lar," Whiplash said as he peeked over his friend's shoulder when Sam checked his phone.

Three texts from Francisco and a text and voicemail from the Royals GM, David Wilson.

He read Francisco's first: *Hey, Sam, got some good news. Call me.*

He scrolled down to Wilson's. It was buttoned up and formal. *Hi, Sam, David Wilson of the Royals here. Call me ASAP.*

Impatience got the best of him, and he didn't even listen to the messages. He immediately called the Royals GM. Wilson answered on the third ring.

"Hi, Sam, congratulations on your Dukes winning the series."

"Thank you, Mr. Wilson. The team came together at the right time."

"As you probably know, my coordinator of Latin American scouting is a big fan of yours. Roberto brings your name up in every meeting we've had at spring training."

"I'm a big fan of his too, sir."

"He also doesn't believe any of the rumors."

Sam didn't respond.

"Roberto's sticking his neck out for you, son. Don't let him down."

"I won't, sir."

"All right, here's the deal. We have only two more weeks left of spring ball, and we've had a few injuries to some vets in camp. We need pitching depth. We'll fly you in for a look. I can't promise anything more than that right now."

"I understand, sir."

"Good. Here's what we're willing to do. Minor league deal, with a May fifth out. If we don't call you up by May fifth, you can opt out to sign with another team or choose to stay in our system. I'm also offering a five-thousand-dollar bonus to sign."

"Sounds great, but could you give my bonus money to the Estevez Orphanage?"

"Sure, who's the contact?"

"Their director is ... just a moment." He placed his hand over the mouthpiece and whispered to his friend, "What's your real name?"

Whiplash gave a look like he had just bitten into a lemon. "Harold."

Sam snorted back a laugh and slid his hand off the mouthpiece. "Harold McCracken, sir."

"That's very kind of you, Sam. I've never had a ballplayer sign over his bonus to an orphanage. But, quite frankly, after all Roberto's told me about you, it's not surprising."

"Thank you, sir."

"Okay, we need you here, ASAP. I'll have my executive assistant, Emily Sanders, email you flight information. Is tomorrow too soon?"

"Tomorrow is perfect, sir."

"Great. I look forward to meeting you, eight a.m., Saturday, March sixteenth. See ya then."

Sam nodded dumbly at the phone and then broke into a stupid grin.

"You"–Whiplash laughed out loud–"are the worst negotiator ever. I mean to tell ya, you ain't got the sense God gave a goose."

*   *   *

"May I have everyone's attention!" Whiplash called out when they walked into the lunchroom. The place quieted as Hunoon's staff and all twenty-five children turned to face them.

He put his hand on Sam's shoulder. "Yer lookin' at a bonafide Big League prospect. Coach EssCee has been invited to try out for the Kan-Sas! Cit-Teee! Roy-Als!"

The kids cheered and then rushed to hug their coach. All except one. Carlita, whose face went ashen, sprinted out of the dining hall.

*   *   *

Sam knocked on the door of the little girl's dorm room. No answer. He knocked again. Nothing. He cracked the door open and peeked inside.

"Carlita?"

She was on the lower bunkbed of a room she shared with three other girls. Her back was to him as she stared at the wall.

Sam sat down and put a hand on her back. "I have to go."

"Then go," she whimpered. "Everybody leaves me."

He closed his eyes and exhaled. "I'm not leaving you, Carlita. I'm following the dream I told you about when we first met."

Tears welled up in her eyes as she turned to face him. Sam could see that she was biting down on the inside of her cheek to keep from crying. "You'll become a star and forget about us."

"Forget about my Little Dukes who won the Diriamba Crown? Impossible."

"You'll never come back."

"Yes, I will."

"No, you won't. No one ever comes back for us older orphans."

Guilt curled up against his soul. He knew what she was feeling. He had been there himself after losing all three members of his family, each death ripping away a piece of his heart.

"Do you remember me telling you about my sister?"

She nodded.

"I believed that through sheer willpower I could keep Jenny alive. And when I didn't, I blamed myself for her death. Yet it was Jenny who had told me that she was ready to walk on, that I held onto her even though she didn't belong to me. Jenny believed that the power of the world is a circle, that our lives are a circle, from childhood to childhood."

He could tell that Carlita didn't quite understand.

"It means that, even when I'm gone, I'm still with you. And you are with me. Always. Our spirit goes with the ones we love." He slipped the Nicaraguan Series Championship ring off his finger and gave it to her. "I want you to have this. May this ring be the circle that connects us forever and ever. It's my promise that as soon as the season ends I'll come back."

The little girl's eyes went wide as she slid the oversized gold-and-diamond band onto the fourth finger of her left hand.

"And one more promise," Sam said. "When I get called up, I'll fly you, Whiplash, and Hunoon to KC for an entire week of games."

She wiped a tear from cheek and looked up at her coach. "Do you really think you'll make it to the bigs?"

A bright smile lit his face. "Yes, I do, piña. Yes, I do."

CHAPTER TWENTY-TWO

DiamondBar Headquarters, Southern Virginia

May 2013

A group of men in olive-drab camouflage uniforms finished their special-weapons-and-tactics demonstration and jogged off the field, pausing only to wave up at the man who had been watching them from his observation tower. Dixon gave them an indifferent nod and moved back into the deck's shadows. There were only fifteen new recruits worthy of sending overseas to provide security for America's never-ending war against terrorism. It was a quarter of the number of candidates DiamondBar had trained just two years earlier. But with more and more private military companies being created, so too grew the competition for soldiers, for leaders to train them, and for lucrative contracts from both foreign and domestic governments.

Dixon closed his eyes and rubbed his temples. A migraine was likely on the way. Not much was going well in his life. His empire was crumbling. His wife had recently filed for divorce, and even with a strict prenuptial agreement, he'd have to give Liz at least 20 percent of everything.

Damn it, there was a time he was a billionaire. Not anymore. His net worth had fallen to less than $200 million after the 2008 crash, the huge expense of running a PMC, and of course, his monumental disaster in Afghanistan. If only Sam Cloud-Carson would have responded the way all the others had and accepted the bribe. Taken the money. It solved everything. He just upped the price until he finally broke them.

But not Carson. He was too idealistic, too prideful, too enamored in the ways of an old, dying world. A world that no longer existed. Ancient history that some thought sacred, but that Dixon thought foolish. There had to be a way out of this nightmare, one that would not only get Dixon back in the game to win Hazrat's mountain, but one that would also claim revenge on his enemy.

"Excuse me, Mr. Dixon!"

The shout from below broke him out of his trance, and he looked down at the young man whose name he couldn't remember.

"May I help you?"

"Your secretary wanted me to give you a message, sir."

"Let's have it."

"She said to let you know that a Sam Cloud-Carson was just called up to the Major Leagues."

Dixon's hand immediately went to his temple. The migraine had arrived.

CHAPTER TWENTY-THREE

Kansas City, Missouri

May 2013

Sam couldn't stop smiling. He was close. Close to being inside his second Major League ballpark. He'd been to Coors Field in Denver with his college girlfriend the summer he played for a wood-bat league, but that was it. This was going to be different. Instead of being in the stands watching, he'd be on the mound, all eyes on the new guy just called up from the minors.

He'd made three starts for Double-A Northwest Arkansas and pitched well each time out--only three runs allowed in fifteen innings of work. The Royals' front office had hoped to bring him along slowly after his heavy winter workload in Nicaragua, but now they were desperate. A team that many expected to contend for the American League Central title had gotten off to a terrible start. Eight wins. Eighteen losses. The problem? Starting pitching. An earned run average over seven. Time to take a flyer on the kid who, six weeks ago, was pitching in Nicaragua.

The four-hour drive from Springdale, Arkansas, had flown by. He had called everyone close to him: Jose and Teresa; Grandpa Douglas; Whiplash, Hunoon, and the kids; Estevez; Roberto Francisco; Mesa State's Coach Elba; several of his high school, college, and Dukes teammates; and last, he had called Army Colonel Bart Tomlinson.

He had been communicating with the Special Forces officer he had assisted in Afghanistan every three months to not only share his conversations with Abdul Hazrat, but also to make sure no construction had resumed on the road to Hazrat's mountain. Sam figured the colonel would appreciate hearing about his promotion to the Majors.

The colonel was now back home with his family in Fort Lewis, Washington, and was thrilled to hear from Sam. He even encouraged Sam to call his mom in some small town about thirty miles from the ballpark. Stilwell, Kansas. Said she had a cottage on her eighty-acre property that he might be able to rent.

Sam had laughed. This call to the Big Leagues was temporary. Royals General Manager David Wilson had been honest. Two starters were down with injuries, their young prospects weren't ready yet, and Sam had a May fifth opt-out in his contract. Wilson needed someone to bridge the gap until the veterans returned from the injured list.

He glanced down at his GPS. Stadium Drive. One mile ahead. This was it. Everything that had happened to him in his life, both good and bad, had led him to this moment. He suddenly felt incredibly grateful. Grateful for every experience and every person who had helped him on this journey. To his mother and father and sister. He felt their spirits as he drove up the exit and turned right.

There it was. Kauffman Stadium. Major League ballpark. A silver and blue and white cathedral shimmering beautifully in the two o'clock sun.

*   *   *

Ninety minutes later, Sam was in the video room with pitching coach Andy Phillips and catcher Tony Ramirez, going over the scouting report and watching highlights of the likely Minnesota Twins hitters he would face in three and a half hours.

"Roberto says your strength is command," Phillips said. "What say you?"

"I can throw the ball where I want," Sam said matter-of-factly.

Both of Phillips' brows rose at Sam's candid response. "How would you rank your pitches?"

"Two-seam, change, slider, curve, four-seam."

"Your four-seam is fifth best?"

"I don't rank them, sir. But I like to use my four-seam as a change *up* in velocity when I feel the hitters are looking low. I can ride it up and in on both righties and lefties."

"Better not leave it over the plate against the Twins. They're a darn good fastball-hitting team."

"I won't, sir."

Phillips glanced at Ramirez, who grinned, then back at Sam. "How would you pitch the lineup you'll likely face tonight?"

"Leadoff man, Pena, free swinger, fastballs in early, soft away both change and slider. Number-two hitter, Johnson, leads team in homers and extra-base hits, grounds out at a lower clip than most hitters, curves early to disrupt his timing, save the fastball for later in the count. Number three, Wilfredo Encarnación, good plate discipline, loves a firm fastball, but vulnerable to sinkers low and away. Setting up a fastball with an off-speed pitch could be an effective way to get him out—"

Phillips hand shot up to stop Sam. He snatched the scouting report off his desk and stared at it. "That is literally word for word what I wrote in my report. Do you have some kind of photographic memory?"

Sam nodded. "It comes in handy third time through the order."

Ramirez snorted back a laugh. "Let's hope you make it that far, rookie. We could use a pick-me-up."

Phillips leaned back in his chair and clasped his hands behind his head. "Now, is there anything we can do for you before your first Big League start?"

"Is there someplace quiet I could meditate for ten minutes before warm-up?"

"You can use this room," Phillips said. "Be here at six twenty-five, and I'll knock on the door at six thirty-five."

Sam nodded one more time. "Thank you, sir."

*   *   *

"Did I miss anything?" Roberto Francisco burst through the door of David Wilson's suite.

"Nope." Wilson patted an open chair for his coordinator of Latin American Scouting.

Francisco sat down and put his hand on his chest to catch his breath. He had been in the Dominican Republic when Wilson had called him back to see Carson's debut. This was the player he had been selling to his GM since Sam's Ignacio High School days. He was a winner: tough, determined, competitive, intelligent, focused—and a young man with a tragic history.

Wilson leaned toward Francisco. "I hope he brings us good luck."

*   *   *

Sam carved the initials of each member of his family into the dirt on the back of the mound and stood up. It was go time. *Calm breathing. Narrow focus. Trust the gift God gave you.*

His first pitch was a sinker, low outside corner for strike one. Second pitch was identical, grounded to short, an easy play for slick fielding shortstop Enrique Hernandez. But, for the first time all year, Hernandez bobbled the ball, and the Twins' leadoff man was on. The next hitter grounded the first pitch to third. Routine double play. Unfortunately, Rex Blackwell rushed his throw to second. The throw clipped off Terry Ayers' glove, and Minnesota had runners on first and third with nobody out.

The crowd groaned. The GM slammed his fist against the wall. The radio announcer's voice could be heard throughout the concourse. "Tough way to begin your Major League career. Let's see if the kid can get out of this jam."

Sam inhaled a deep cleansing breath and asked the ump for time. He reflected on a line from an old Ute prayer.

Earth, teach me stillness as the grasses are stilled with light.

"Minimize the damage," he said to himself, and then pointed to his shortstop to let him know the throw would be coming his way if the ball was hit back to the mound.

Sam thought back to the scouting report. *Wilfredo Encarnación, good plate discipline, loves a firm fastball, vulnerable to sinkers low and away. Setting up a fastball with an off-speed pitch could be an effective way to get him out.*

First pitch, sinker, down and in, taken for strike one. Second pitch, changeup, low and away, for a ball. *How about that low-and-away two-seamer with a little middle-finger pressure right here?* The pitch was perfect, tailing at the last second. Cardenal swung mightily but hit only the top half of the ball, chopping it up the middle. Sam leaped, snared it, and came down on the back of the mound. He calmly threw to second to begin an easy double play. A run scored, but he minimized the damage when he got the Twins' cleanup hitter to pop up to end the inning.

*   *   *

Up in the general manager's suite, Wilson breathed a sigh of relief. "I like that he didn't panic."

"Even in high school, he pitched to the situation," Francisco said. "Only went for the strikeout if the team needed it."

*   *   *

They would need one in the fourth. After the Royals took a 2–1 lead on a Cimoli home run, the Twins' Max Carter doubled to lead off the fourth and went to third on a groundout.

Sam's catcher trotted out to the mound. "This guy's patient," Ramirez said. "Likes the ball middle away and won't try and pull. How about we start him with four-seam, up and in, then that sweet change you've been throwing down and away?"

Sam covered his mouth with his glove. "After we get to oh and two, I'd like to finish him off with a two-seamer in."

Ramirez took a step back and grinned. "I'm liking you more and more, amigo. You got guts."

"*Será mejor que tengas agallas para jugar a este juego loco.*" Sam winked. *You better have guts to play this crazy game.*

Sam did precisely what Ramirez wanted. Got a foul off the first pitch for strike one, a swing and a miss on the off-speed for strike two, then threw the nasty two-seamer that looked like it was going to hit the left-handed batter in the hip before it broke a good twelve inches to graze the inside corner of the zone. Strike three. Two outs. The next batter flied out to center, and the Royals were out of the inning, still leading 2–1.

Both manager Skip Charles and pitching coach Phillips were waiting at the top step of the dugout when Sam jogged off the field.

"Good work, kid." Charles patted him on the back. "Where the hell'd you get the movement on that two-seamer?"

Sam shrugged. "They had a half-off sinker sale at the Managua Airport gift shop."

"Ha!" His manager laughed and gave him another hearty pat on the backside.

As Sam walked to the far end of the dugout and buried himself in the scouting report to study the hitters he would face in the fifth, Ramirez pulled his pitching coach to the side. "I know it's only four innings, Andy, but I like this guy. Not intimidated at all. *He* called the pitch that struck out Suarez—and then threw it *exactly* where he wanted."

The Royals won 7–3, snapping a five-game losing streak. Sam got the win, allowing no walks in seven innings with five strikeouts. He was doused with beer in the clubhouse. Even took a sip before heading to his hotel room off Interstate 70.

CHAPTER TWENTY-FOUR

Stilwell, Kansas

May 2013

"How about a big hand for our two-time Eastern Kansas League Coach of the Year!" Cindy Goldman called out from behind the buffet table. It was the Tigers' season-ending team banquet, and it always choked Sydney up when it was time to say goodbye to the graduating seniors she'd coached the last three years.

She waited for the applause to die down and then nodded to the Tigers' team mom. "Thanks very much, Cindy. Thanks for hosting our postseason party at your beautiful home, and thanks to all the parents who supported our girls this year. We had the youngest team in our conference and still made it to the Regional Finals before barely losing to the second-ranked team in Kansas. I'm very proud of the way our Tigers growled this year—"

"Growled?" her husband interrupted from across the outdoor patio. "That's a good one, honey."

Some of her players giggled, which bothered Sydney. She forced an uncomfortable smile. "Despite a rough start, our Tigers stuck together and won seven of our last ten to make it to postseason."

"Blah, blah, blah," Blake continued to tease. "Let's get to the trophies."

"I'm getting there, Blake. Please be patient."

She saw her father lean over in his lawn chair and tap her husband on the shoulder. He put an index finger to his lips to quiet his son-in-law. Blake rolled his eyes and waved for Sydney to continue.

By the time the ceremony was over and all the postseason awards had been given, it took every fiber of Sydney's being to stay calm. Her husband had embarrassed her … again. Some of her players and even their parents probably saw it as silly kidding between husband and wife, but this was disrespectful. He had made her feel small in front of her players.

Blake seemed to know every single button to push to make her doubt herself, as a wife, as a coach, as a human being. His barbs always seemed innocent: *I'm just joking … you're overreacting … you're so jealous … even your parents think you're too sensitive.*

Was she too sensitive? She wasn't sure anymore.

An arm came around her shoulder and gave her a squeeze.

"Wonderful party," her father said, then kissed her on the cheek. "One more week of school and then summer break. What are your getaway plans?"

Without thinking, she blurted out, "I'd like to get away from Blake."

Jeffrey stepped back in surprise and led his daughter over to a quiet spot on the other side of the pool. "What's going on, honey?"

She couldn't look her father in the eyes. He wouldn't understand. He had a good marriage. Adored her mom. Lived by the Golden Rule. Treated others the way he wanted to be treated. And believed that every challenge in life could be answered with some Biblical verse. She knew one was coming.

"Marriage isn't always easy." He raised her chin and looked her in the eyes. "It takes work to make it work."

"You don't live with him, Dad. I shouldn't have to worry about everything I say when I'm with my husband."

"He's going through a tough time. I invited him to our men's Thursday Bible study."

"You asked him two months ago. Has he shown up yet?"

"Have faith, Syd."

"Oh, Dad, he criticizes everything I do. He's drinking more, coming home later—"

He raised a hand to quiet her and smiled sweetly. "You'll get through this. I know my little girl. She's a fighter." He put his arm around her shoulder again and led her back to the party. "God is our refuge and strength, a very real present help in trouble. Psalm forty-six, one."

She nodded, raised her vision, and stopped dead in her tracks.

There, in the middle of the celebration, stood Blake, secretly pouring something from a brown paper bag into the red plastic cup of one of Sydney's players.

*　　*　　*

"What the heck's wrong with you!" Sydney snapped when they drove home that night. "Sneaking a drink to one of my players! Carly just turned eighteen!"

"Oh, lighten up." Blake groaned. "She's going to college in three months. I was just breaking her in before she goes to her first bar."

"Why can't you be a role model for once, instead of some lecherous old creep!"

He jerked the car over to the side of the road. "Jesus Christ, Syd! Don't make this a big fucking deal."

"It is a big deal. These girls are my responsibility. I'm their coach. This was an awards banquet honoring Carly and her teammates."

"Aw, shit, here we go again." He leaned back in his seat and shook his head. "It was one little drink."

"I don't care if it was one little drink. This is my team, and these are my rules."

He grabbed her upper arm and squeezed. "Would you stop being a whiny little bitch."

She tried to pull free, but he tightened his grip, making her wince.

"Take me to my parents' house."

He immediately released her arm, and his entire face softened. "They don't need to know about your problems, Syd. Let's just go home and forget that we ever had this conversation."

"Not until you promise that you'll respect my team rules."

"I promise," he mumbled, but his eyes held a definite note of warning. "And I'm sorry you think that what I did was a big deal—because it wasn't."

She held his gaze for a long moment. "Perhaps, in the future, it would be best if you didn't come to any of our team parties."

Neither of them spoke again on the drive home.

CHAPTER TWENTY-FIVE

Stilwell, Kansas

May 2013

"Only five hundred dollars a month?" Sam asked Bette Tomlinson as she showed him the small cottage at the far end of her property. "That doesn't seem fair to you, ma'am."

"My son said you were a good boy." Bette opened the door to the screened-in porch and stepped inside. "All I want is a renter I can trust who knows horses. Bart told me you were both."

"I grew up with horses, ma'am. We always had at least three on our land in southwest Colorado. Backed up to the San Juan National Forest, so we had plenty of places to roam."

"We don't have mountains." She raised her arms to display the view from the wooden porch. "But these woods are pretty and grow all the way to the Little Blue River just south of here."

It was perfect. He'd gotten antsy living in a hotel room next to I-70. The constant noise of trucks thundering down the highway and streetlights bleeding through the curtains bothered him. He pined for the peace and quiet of the country, and with his good start with the Royals, he figured they might keep him around a little longer. Three straight wins to open his career wasn't too shabby, and the team had taken off as well. 8–4 record in the two weeks he'd been with the club. Maybe he'd arrived at the right time.

"I'll be gone to visit my son at Fort Lewis for a couple of weeks, so I'd like to get this done today." Bette opened the inside door. "Let me show you the place."

It wasn't much. A one-story cottage that looked like it was something out of a fairy tale. All white, gray trim, gray wooden floor on the front porch, and oak wood floors on the inside. There were only three rooms. A kitchen/dining/living area, a bedroom, and a bathroom. All furnished. *Thank God for that.* He hated to shop. Just wanted to play ball and work the farm.

"There's no basement or attic," she continued, "so if you have anything to store, you'll have to keep it in the barn."

"I travel light, ma'am. I only have a yoga mat and one bag of clothes and essentials."

"Smart. Having a lot of junk can get in the way of what's truly important. Now to the stables."

The stables were down a dirt lane, through an archway of huge oaks, maples, elms, and cottonwoods, about seventy yards from the cottage. The breeze was soft and easy, bringing the smells of the barn with it: horse sweat and hay, dust and leather, urine and manure. *Ah, home sweet home.*

"Eight quarter horses is all I have," Bette said as she led him inside. "Friendly as Labrador retrievers. Perfect for a program I have that connects inner-city kids with nature."

"That's a lot of work, Mrs. Tomlinson."

"Naw, I gotta couple of gals who volunteer to help me during the summer. One comes more often than the other." Bette arched one gray eyebrow. "I think she might be havin' trouble on the home front, if y'know what I mean."

He didn't respond.

"Would you tell 'em yer my new tenant and that you'll be taking over for the Barton House boys?"

He gave her a sideways glance. "Barton House boys?"

"Men's sober living center, who charge me six hundred a month for their less than inspiring work. Now, I know you have a full plate pitching for our Royals, but if you clean the stalls, give the horses fresh water and hay, and fix up and paint this stable, I can end my deal with Barton and you get your solitude shack for half of what I should be charging."

Sam scratched his chin as his mind went back to his time in Nicaragua, to all his responsibilities working at the Estevez Orphanage *and* playing baseball. But he was in the Major Leagues now. He had to be ready and focused every day.

"Ma'am, you do know that we go on the road every other week?"

"And I got those two girls and a neighbor's son who can help me on the weeks you're gone. For crying out loud, Sam, don't be a wuss. I only got eight horses. You're barely gonna have to work one, maybe two, hours a day."

He leaned back against a stall, thinking about what he should do, until the nose of a horse nuzzled the side of his neck. Without even turning around, he reached up and rubbed the horse's nose.

"That's Jenny," said Bette. "She's partial to men."

"Jenny?" Sam smiled as he extended his hand. "I like that name. You got yourself a deal."

CHAPTER TWENTY-SIX

Kansas City, Missouri

May 2013

It was bound to happen. He had to lose sometime. Unfortunately, it was to the first-place Detroit Tigers, 6–4. He didn't pitch that badly. Four runs in six innings. But a mistake with a poorly located fastball to Tigers slugger King Dillman resulted in a three-run home run that landed in the Kauffman Stadium fountains.

The loss infuriated him. He spent five minutes alone in the trainer's room to cool off, then took a deep breath, stepped out into the clubhouse, and answered every reporter's question respectfully. He showered, dressed, and headed for the door.

"Where the hell do you think you're goin'?" first baseman Kevin Cimoli called out from across the room.

Sam shrugged. "Home."

"I don't think so." Cimoli walked over with third baseman Rex Blackwell, designated hitter Manny Morales, and pitcher Willie Kahal.

"You shouldn't be alone after your first Big League loss." Morales put an arm around his shoulder. "You're coming with us."

Sam wanted to say no. Really should say no. It was already eleven o'clock. Tomorrow would only be his third day working for Mrs. Tomlinson, who was off visiting family. She hadn't given him any set schedule, yet he liked to work early and get everything finished before the kids from the Urban Wildlife Academy showed up … But this invitation came from four leaders on the team. No way could he turn them down.

"Okay," he said.

"Have you been to the Plaza?" Blackwell asked.

"I haven't been anywhere."

"Follow us." Cimoli winked. "We stylin you tonight."

*   *   *

Gram & Dun off Ward Parkway was packed, but somehow the maître d' found the five Royals a prime table outside with a nice view of Brush Creek. It was a typical late May evening in the Midwest: pleasant, cool, a slight breeze from the south.

Cimoli ordered a pitcher of Boulevard Farmhouse Ale and leaned back in his chair.

"So, Kid Carson, tell us about yourself. You barely say anything at the yard."

Sam shrugged. "I figured it's better to keep my ears open and mouth shut."

"Smart rookie," said Kahal.

"You ain't getting off that easy," Cimoli cut in. "You only went out with us one time in Chicago and didn't say boo." He nodded at Kahal. "Willie here thought you were a deaf-mute until he overheard you talking with Tony about where to set up off the plate for your slider."

Sam smiled but didn't answer. Despite Cimoli only being in his third Big League season, Sam had noticed that the Royals' tall first baseman from South Carolina was highly respected by his teammates. His words carried weight, and he always seemed to say the right thing to encourage a player or call him out.

"C'mon, kid. Backstory. History. Where you grew up. Hearts you've broken. What the hell took you so long to help our asses out of the cellar?"

They all laughed. The beer came, Cimoli poured for everybody, and then raised his glass to Sam. "Let's have it, rook."

"Nothing special," said Sam. "Raised in Colorado. Southern Ute reservation. Family ran an outfitting business, college, work—"

Rex's hand shot up. "Hold up. You hunt and fish?"

Sam nodded. "Some of the best fly-fishing in the world is in Colorado. South Platte, Animas, Gunnison Rivers—"

"How about hunting? You ever bagged a bear, elk, moose?"

"I've led hunts for bear and moose, but never taken one myself. I don't kill an animal unless I'm going to eat it. So mainly elk, deer, turkey, rabbit, and—y'know."

His teammates leaned forward in their chairs, mesmerized by Sam's stories about stalking a black bear in the San Juans, matching the hatch to lure a trout, and waking up to a cool breeze coming off a mountain lake. He carried on not only to connect with his guys, but also to steer them away from asking any questions about Afghanistan or why he quit school with a semester left in his draft season.

Several newspapers had already done human-interest features on him after his second win, but he deflected questions about working for DiamondBar with boring answers like, *It was typical security stuff,* and *Just did my job,* and the proverbial *I wasn't near any war zones* to get them to move on to another subject. The *Kansas City Star* had reached out to Drake Dixon, but the call had not been returned. Thank God. He didn't know what he'd say if his former boss attacked him in the press.

They stayed till closing time, Sam slowly nursing one beer in the two hours they were on the Plaza. By the time he got home, it was two in the morning. Seven a.m. was fast approaching, and Bette Tomlinson's horses would be waiting. He set his alarm and went to bed.

*   *   *

The sound of the phone buzzing on her nightstand woke Sydney. She had finally fallen asleep around three in the morning, worried about the whereabouts of her husband. They had barely spoken since their argument following the Tigers' banquet. Now, almost two weeks later, she found herself lying in bed, mentally reliving the argument. *Should she have said something to Carly? What if her parents found out, or other players, and they went to school officials to file a complaint? Did Blake understand the ramifications of his actions? Did he even care? Why hadn't he come home last night?*

Blake had texted after he got off work, a brief message that he was: *Going out with the boys. Will call later.* She didn't see the message for an hour and had immediately texted him back, but no answer. Eight phone calls later and still no response. She called his coworkers, checked the internet for any traffic accidents, called the police, but nothing.

The phone buzzed again. She looked at the screen. Didn't recognize the number. Fear gripped her as she clicked on. "Hello?"

"Morning, babe!" Blake said happily. "I'm at Eddie's. Lost my phone."

"What—where?" She didn't know what to say. She was just so relieved to hear his voice.

"I went to the Royals game with some friends. My phone must have slipped out of my pocket or something."

Sydney sat up in bed, her breath coming back and her mind finally clearing. "Why didn't you call me on someone else's phone? I've been up all night, worried."

"I did call. Texted you too."

"I didn't get anything."

There was a long pause, and then Blake said sweetly, "Uh oh, made a mistake. I just looked at Eddie's phone. I typed in eight-five instead of eight-six as the last two digits of your number. So somebody got my message to you. That's funny."

"I have a personal message on my phone, Blake. Didn't you figure that out when someone else's voice came on?"

"Shit, Syd, don't do this. I went out with the boys, had too much to drink, and crashed at Eddie's. Do you want me to drink and drive again? Get another DUI like last year, when you made me come to another one of your fucking games?"

"No," she said defensively. "I—I was just worried."

"You? worried? What a surprise. Same shit over and over with you. Whatever. All right, I gotta go. Eddie's gonna give me a ride to where I left my car."

A car horn honked outside, and Sydney jerked out of bed. It was Mary Beth, coming to pick her up, to go to Mrs. Tomlinson's and prep the horses for Bette's children's program. They had agreed to help more this month with school and soccer over and Bette gone visiting family.

"Blake, Mary Beth's outside. We have our children's program this morning."

"Of course you do. Can't be there when your husband gets home, but your bleeding heart will be there for every poor kid who wants to ride a fuckin' pony."

"That's not true—" she started to say, but her husband had already clicked off.

*   *   *

Sam's eyes fluttered open. He rolled over on his side and glanced at the window. The sun's rays cutting through the blinds were a little brighter this morning. *My alarm should be going off any second.* He reached over and checked his phone. 8:33.

"What the heck!" He jumped out of bed, tripped over the pants that he'd left on the floor, and stumbled to the closet. *I set my alarm for p.m. and not a.m. Thank God Mrs. Tomlinson's on vacation.*

He threw on a pair of workout shorts, a wrinkled Hawaiian shirt, and flip-flops and started for the door, pausing momentarily to glance at his reflection in the window. *Yikes!* It looked like a bomb had gone off in his hair, each strand exploding in a different direction. *Kids are coming this morning. I don't want to scare them.* He grabbed a floppy bucket hat off the kitchen table, slipped on a pair of sunglasses, and headed to the stables.

*   *   *

"Of course they're late!" Sydney's voice was sharp with frustration, anger simmering over the way Blake had treated her, and now rising even hotter because the men from the Barton House hadn't shown up yet. The stalls were a mess, and the place reeked of the staggering ammonia smell of urine.

"The one day they need to be on time, and they don't show up," she continued to rant. "I'm so sick of selfish jerks thinking only of themselves. This is so unfair. The kids will be here in twenty minutes."

"I'll tie the horses in the corral while you clean the stalls," Mary Beth said as she began to lead a horse named Leo outside.

Sydney snatched a rake and shovel off the wall and got to work, scraping some gross combination of urine, straw, and manure onto the shovel. As she turned to dump it into a wheelbarrow, she caught the silhouette of a man approaching the barn.

"Sorry I'm late," the man said.

"Of course you are!" she snapped. "That's the excuse all you guys have. Sorry, sorry, sorry. Always sorry for all the people you've hurt."

The man quietly unhooked another shovel from the wall and walked over.

She didn't recognize him. He must be new to the Barton House. He looked awful. Stupid floppy hat and sunglasses, likely trying to hide his bloodshot eyes. This guy was probably hungover and worthless, returning from an all-night bender. *Great. Just what I need.*

"You're an hour and a half late," she grumbled.

"Sorry—I mean, I set my alarm wrong."

"Sure you did. How often do you use that excuse? You had car trouble. You lost your phone. You dialed the wrong number. The dog ate your homework. Right."

The man's mouth hung open, and so did Mary Beth's. She'd returned from the corral to halter the next horse.

Sydney was aware of them both: her friend, staring at her, shock still etched on her face, and the stranger, who had picked up a shovel and was now quietly shoveling manure into the wheelbarrow. He seemed to know what he was doing too. There was a strength and ease to his movement that belied any hangover. She didn't even know this stranger, didn't know his backstory, or what may have led him to the depths he had fallen.

"I'm sorry," she finally said, her shoulders slumping forward in both guilt and regret. "I've had a bad morning. I shouldn't have taken it out on you." She leaned her rake and shovel against the stall and extended her hand. "I'm Sydney."

The man took off his sunglasses and smiled. His eyes weren't bloodshot. They were the most riveting chocolate-brown eyes she had ever seen, intense yet soft, focused yet remote, approachable yet impossible to read.

He accepted her hand and said, "Kids call me EssCee."

For a moment she stood frozen, mesmerized by the intensity of his gaze—until the sound of Mary Beth clearing her throat snapped her out of her trance.

"Kids call me MB," Mary Beth said, extending her own hand. "It's short for Mighty Brilliant." She snorted out a laugh, which brought the same from Sydney, whose right hand shot up to cover the tiny cleft scar on her upper lip.

"Nice to meet you, MB and Sydney," he said. "Why don't you guys ready the horses, and I'll clean the stalls." He cocked his head to the side and looked directly at Sydney. "And, if you don't mind my saying again, ma'am, I'm truly sorry for being late."

It was the last time they would talk that day, the new guy busy in the stables, and she and Mary Beth riding with the children. When they returned at noon, he was gone, but he had left a note on the stable's corkboard. *Cleaned stalls, fresh water and hay, replaced three boards in Leo's stall and will finish the rest tomorrow. I promise to be on time. Have a great day, EssCee.*

She looked around the barn. The place was spotless. The middle path had been swept, the floor of each stall was clean, and the tools and wheelbarrow had been washed and put away. Despite being an hour and a half late, the new guy had gone above and beyond what was asked of him. Unfortunately, none of it made her feel any better.

*   *   *

He was already there when she and Mary Beth arrived two days later. Same workout shorts, same goofy floppy hat and sunglasses, only a different T-shirt with the words *Diriamba Dukes* emblazoned across the front. He stood up from what he was working on, hammer in one hand, wooden plank in the other, and a three-inch nail dangling from his lips.

"Mornin'," he mumbled.

"It is a beautiful morning," Mary Beth agreed. "But it's going to be a hot one today. That's why we came early."

He let the nail fall from his mouth and deftly caught it with the same hand that was holding the hammer. "I love mornings. Peace and quiet. Starting a new day with the promise that something good's about to happen."

"You're a morning person?" Sydney blurted out. "I figured you guys were night owls." She regretted her words as soon as they left her mouth.

"What do you mean by *you guys*, ma'am?"

"I'm sorry. I don't know why I said that. I thought with you … living at the Barton Sober House and everything–"

Both his dark brows shot up in surprise. "What? I don't–"

Mary Beth cut him off by raising both hands. "I think now's a good time for my friend to shut up, Mr. EssCee. I've never heard Sydney talk like this before. She's actually a decent human, rarely having to stop so often to take her foot out of her mouth."

Sydney's face went a bright shade of crimson, astonished herself that she would make such a callous statement. *What was wrong with her? Why was she behaving this way in front of some addict or alcoholic? She might be married to one. Was she drawn to these types of men?*

She caught her breath for a beat and looked up at the man, "You have talent, EssCee. I mean, how about what you've done here. The place looks good. You know horses. I'm sure you could get a job at any ranch in south Johnson County."

"Thanks." He took off his sunglasses and smiled in a way that said he knew something that she didn't. "May I use you as a reference?"

"I didn't mean it that way. I just … What did you do before … y'know?"

"Entertainment business," he said, then pursed his lips tightly to hide an ever-growing smirk, which only frustrated her more.

"Of course you're in the entertainment business," she bristled. "That's why you're in this predicament."

"Sydney!" Mary Beth splayed a hand to her chest. "What's wrong with you?"

But she couldn't stop. This guy was laughing at her. Not literally, but his chocolate-brown eyes certainly were. And every time he opened his mouth and flashed those perfect white teeth against his bronze skin, he was mocking her. Yes, he was. She didn't have to take this. She was already dealing with it at home.

"You can change anytime you want," she said defiantly. "Why don't you start by choosing better friends."

"You don't approve of my friends?"

"I don't know your friends."

"But I need to choose better ones?"

"Obviously, or—or you wouldn't be in the mess you're in."

"Oh yeah, I forgot I was such a mess."

Darn it, there was that teasing grin again. He was baiting her. She knew it. She curled her fingernails into her palms and forced herself to say, "You need to believe in yourself, EssCee. You have talent. You can fix things. You know your way around horses. You're not bad looking. You have good teeth—"

"Are you building my resume or prepping me for auction?"

That brought a snort from Mary Beth, and when Sydney turned to scold her friend, MB's hands were covering her mouth, her shoulders shaking as she tried to stifle her amusement. She spun back around to find that EssCee had pulled the plank he was holding against his face to mask his own laughter.

This wasn't fair. They were ganging up on her. Her best friend and some recovering addict she hardly knew. *But was she at fault here? Was there some unconscious reason she was behaving this way?* She had barely spent twenty minutes with this man, yet she acted like some awkward schoolgirl blurting out thoughts and judgments she normally wouldn't think of saying. *Were they subliminal intentions she wanted to tell her husband but felt more comfortable saying to a complete stranger?*

"You don't know me," she finally said. "You don't know what I've been through."

"No, ma'am, I don't. Nor do you know me."

"At least—at least I didn't quit."

His smile faded, and his eyes no longer laughed at her. Instead, they were warm and understanding. "I think most people don't change until they face some kind of crisis."

Stop with the psychobabble, she thought.

"Most need crisis before they can see a higher perspective."

"Thanks. Did you get that from one of your AA meetings?"

"That's enough, Syd," Mary Beth cut in, but EssCee held up his hand to quiet her.

Sydney's chin quivered as she fought hard not to cry. *She did it again. Speaking without thinking. How unbelievably insensitive. What was it about this man that made her talk this way?*

"I'm sorry." Her voice cracked. She felt as if she couldn't breathe. She had to get out of here before she started bawling in front of him. She was about to speak when he bailed her out.

"The kids will be here shortly, ma'am. I brought the horses to the corral, but they still need to be saddled."

CHAPTER TWENTY-SEVEN

Detroit, Michigan

June 2013

The Royals' manager, Skip Charles, closed the door to his office at Comerica Park and sat down across from his GM, David Wilson. The four-time defending Central champion Tigers had dominated the Royals in recent years, winning twenty-four of the last thirty, including five straight this year. They blew out KC, 11–1 on Friday, then walked them off last night on a broken-bat blooper, 6–5. It was a lucky hit, but it was another reminder that the Royals weren't as good as the Tigers. And now they were sending a rookie to the hill, to try to break the curse.

"We've played darn good ball the last month," Wilson grumbled. "Took two of three from Cleveland, swept the Twins, confidence was high, and then bam—Detroit."

"I know we can beat them." Charles nodded toward the clubhouse. "But those guys gotta believe it."

"Today is a big game, Skip. Interest is up all over KC. People care. Ticket sales are rolling. TV ratings are high. Fans think we've turned the corner."

"And now we're asking a guy who was throwing in the jungles of Nicaragua two months ago to beat the champs."

Wilson shrugged. "He's been our best starter in this run."

"But this will be his second time facing Detroit. They're veterans. They'll adjust. Does Sam have what it takes to adjust back?"

"What do you think?"

"I don't know." Charles shook his head. "He's a difficult read. Barely says a word in the clubhouse, doesn't really hang with any one guy or group, but Andy loves him."

"Why?"

"Says he's low maintenance, executes the game plan, asks good questions, has great recall, and has an innate ability to read hitters."

The Royals GM sat quietly for a spell, as if trying to understand his newest player. There were still those statements from Sam's past employer that worried him. *Cancer in the clubhouse. Selfish. Drug problems.* Those rumors concerned owner Jonathan Ewing too. If those rumors were true, this experiment could all blow up in their faces. Wilson cleared his throat and asked, "Have you talked with Sam about his past?"

"I've tried to. Had him in twice. He's very good at turning the conversation away from himself." Charles leaned back in his chair. "I asked him about losing his parents and sister … All he said was that it was tough and that they were great people. Then he asked me about my family, my hobbies, what I liked to do in the offseason."

"I remember him doing the same thing on a KC radio interview. The host asked him pointed questions about growing up on a reservation, what he learned from his folks, about his time in Afghanistan. He answered in boring clichés, praising his teammates and coaches, talking about how much Andy had helped him, and then he turned the interview around and asked the reporter where he grew up, what sports he played, where he met his wife. It was funny but odd."

Wilson glanced at the clock on the wall. Twenty minutes until first pitch. He let go a deep sigh and stood up. "I pray he's not hiding something because I really like the kid. There's an edge to him that our pitching staff was missing. The guys know Sam's a big reason for our turnaround, and they're counting on him to break the Tigers' curse today."

*   *   *

"You suck!"

"You'll never beat the Tigers!"

"Grab some pine, rookie!"

"Sweep! Sweep! Sweep!"

Sam ignored the jeers from Detroit fans as he walked down the dugout steps, accepted high fives and pats on the back from his teammates, and then shook the hand of his manager.

"Way to battle out there," Charles said. "You kept us in the game."

He nodded thanks and then sat down next to his pitching coach, who thankfully gave him a moment to calm down.

Sam was pissed. He knew how important this game was for the team, and he'd pitched like crap. Yeah, he was able to make it through six innings, but it was a grind. He was being pulled with the Royals trailing 4–2. *Shit.*

Detroit was good and they knew it. Confident, talented, experienced, and just enough swagger to get into the minds of both their opponents and the umpires.

"Tigers changed their approach from last week," Phillips said as he handed Sam his stat sheet.

Nine hits, three walks, four runs, 110 pitches. Way too many throws. Dammit. Gotta be more aggressive.

"They know you like to work quickly," Phillips continued, "so they called time, stepped out, slow-played you, and the ump did nothing to speed 'em up."

Sam looked down the dugout at his teammates. Where was the boldness, the joking, the eye contact, the fun that was so prevalent after sweeping the Twins? It shouldn't abandon them this quickly. They needed a spark, a statement, a message to let the Tigers know they weren't afraid of them.

But he was a damn rookie; in the Big Leagues barely a month. *Don't talk. Just listen. Ears open. Mouth shut.* What could he do? He glanced over at his first baseman, Kevin Cimoli, and saw that he was watching him. Kevin winked as if he knew what Sam was thinking. *Let's win this game. Any way possible.*

*   *   *

Enrique Hernandez rolled a single up the middle to open the top of the Royals' seventh. Two outs later, Terry Ayers singled and Mason Falls walked, bringing Cimoli to the plate.

"This is it, fellas!" Charles clapped. "Salami Cimoli! Right here!"

First pitch, fastball. Big swing, fouled straight back. Strike one.

Next two pitches in the dirt. Hitter's count, 2–1.

Sam stepped up to the top step of the dugout and rested his arms on the railing. Something great was about to happen. He could feel it. Three other teammates joined him, including his catcher, Ramirez.

"This is your pitch, KC," Sam said softly.

"You calling long distance?" Ramirez asked.

Sam nodded.

Cimoli swung. *Crack!* Maple on cowhide. The ball took off like a rocket. The Tigers' right fielder took two steps back and then stopped as the ball soared past, gone. Grand slam. The ballpark went silent, save for the men in the visitors' dugout, who were now dancing and high-fiving like miners who had struck gold.

Ramirez hugged Sam. "You called it, baby! You called it!"

The Royals' glee lasted all of about thirty seconds as the very next pitch from the frustrated Tigers' hurler missed designated hitter Manny Morales' head by inches.

"What the hell!" screamed Cimoli, who bolted out of the dugout with his teammates in pursuit. Both benches emptied, players leaping over the railing, coaches tripping up the stairs, bullpens sprinting in from beyond the outfield to support their mates.

Sam stood alone, outside the melee, arms crossed, watching the pushing and shoving, listening to the insults fly.

"This is our house!"

"You don't throw at his fuckin' head!"

"We're the champs! Take yer pussies back to KC!"

More shoving and yelling, but no punches thrown.

As soon as order was restored, Sam meandered over to his pitching coach.

"I got one more throw in me, Andy."

Phillips' head jerked around. "We're not headhunters, Sam."

"Neither am I," he said through clenched teeth. "But they threw at Manny's head. Thirteen-year vet. Nicest guy in the league. They can't get away with that."

Phillips's mouth curled into a proud smile. "I'll tell Skip."

*   *   *

It wasn't something Sam wanted to do, but it was something he had to do. A team was family. And families needed to be protected. Much like his Ute family, the baseball family was made up of warriors; not warriors who attacked, but warriors who supported one another. Sometimes they hugged and teased or yelled and threw things and pounded on their chests in anguish or joy—and other times they sacrificed themselves for the good of others.

Sam was already on the mound when the Detroit coaches realized what was going on. Ramirez pounded his glove like a prizefighter waiting for the bell, and Cimoli was firing his between-inning warm-up throws to his infielders like he was Nolan Ryan. His infielders were rifling the ball back even harder.

Tigers' slugger Eduardo Suarez seemed reluctant to get into the batter's box as he glanced back at the home-plate ump and then down at Ramirez.

"Hey, Tony." He winked. "We cool, right?"

Ramirez hammered his fist in his glove again. "Get in the box, bitch."

Suarez did. Tentatively. He looked to the mound. The pitcher's eyes appeared glazed over, as if he were some maniacal assassin in a zombie movie.

Before Suarez could even get comfortable, Sam was already winding up. Suarez threw up his right hand, pleading for time. The ump didn't give it to him as Sam's fastball came sizzling inside, drilling the Tigers' hitter perfectly on his left butt cheek.

Sam glared at the Tigers' dugout and shouted, "That's where you hit him!"

The ump jumped in front of Suarez, who was pointing his bat at Sam. "What the hell's wrong with you, rookie!"

The ump splayed his left hand on Suarez's chest, pointed his right at Sam, and jerked his thumb skyward. "You're gone!"

Sam didn't answer as both benches and bullpens bolted for the diamond again, shoving, jabbing, and swearing, but like ten minutes earlier, no punches were thrown.

The Royals won that day, 6–4. There seemed to be a new swagger in the clubhouse after the game. The way they talked to the media, the look in their eyes as they deadpanned boring clichés … *We play hardball … We're here to win … Pitch got away from Sam … We don't want to fight, but we won't run from one either …*

As they walked to the team bus, Cimoli put his arm around his rookie pitcher's shoulder.

"If war breaks out, Sammy, I want you in my foxhole," the Royals' unofficial captain grinned. "Cause you are one bad motherfucker."

CHAPTER TWENTY-EIGHT

Stilwell, Kansas

June 2013

Sam tossed a bale of hay off the loft above the stables and climbed down the backside of the barn. The team had landed in KC at a respectable hour, and he'd come straight home, despite his teammates' pleas to join them for a few cold ones at the Power and Light District. They were still jazzed about the way they fought to win the final game in Detroit, but Sam told them he was tired and needed his beauty rest if he was going to fight for them tomorrow. They teased him unmercifully as he headed to his car. The truth was he had no interest in drinking and driving. That truly could cost the team.

As he cut the twine to the first hay bale, he heard voices coming from the main path to the stables. He recognized them immediately.

"Thank God for my dad," he heard Sydney say. "He saved Blake from getting fired and talked the boss into only suspending him one week."

"It shouldn't be that hard to get along with your coworkers," replied Mary Beth. "Why would he spread lies about his supervisor?"

"He does it to draw favor from management."

"Until they figure his act out."

He heard Sydney release a heavy exhale. "He blames everyone. Including me. Last night was the third straight evening he drank himself to sleep … I don't know what to do."

Sam knew he shouldn't eavesdrop, but he couldn't help himself. He sat down on the edge of a hay bale and leaned toward an open stall.

"Why don't you come out with us?" Mary Beth asked. "All you do every day is go for a run, come to the stables, work out your team, and take care of your husband."

"Blake needs me."

"No, you need you. You've changed. You're not the same fun girl I grew up with. Come out with us. Let's go to the Plaza, the Crossroads, to a Royals game—shoot, did you hear about yesterday's game?"

"No."

"It was hilarious. I didn't see the highlights, but I read in the *Star* that their rookie pitcher hit the Tigers' best hitter in the ass and all hell broke loose. We won and cut the Tigers' lead to only nine games."

"Nine games?" he heard Sydney groan. "Big whoop … maybe when they get out of last place, I'll go."

"They're out of last place, Syd. They've played really well the last month to pull within two games of third. C'mon. Let's go."

"I'll think about it," said Sydney. "Where's that new guy? He took off all last week, and now he's late his first day back—geez—what a loser."

Sam bit down on the side of his mouth to keep from laughing. This was too good. It was time to have some fun with the angry girl. Very cautiously, he raised up, tiptoed back to the front of the stables, then cleared his throat loudly and walked inside.

"Good morning, ladies!" He opened his arms as if welcoming the new day. "And it is a beautiful morning. The sun's shining, the birds are chirping, and the horse manure has the perfect hint of hydrogen sulfide. Mmm, good."

Sydney gave him a disappointed maternal look. "And after a week off, the help is late."

"But only by a half hour and in good spirits."

"Probably after you had too many spirits last night—" Her hand shot to her mouth in shock. "Oh gosh, I'm sorry. I shouldn't have said that. That was … very insensitive."

Mary Beth chuckled, and so did Sam, who gave Sydney a look as if she was the funniest girl in the world.

"Why don't we start over?" He extended his hand. "Señor EssCee. Here to work your hacienda, ma'am."

She barely touched his hand in a poor attempt to recover. "I–I have no idea why I'm saying these awful things to you. I–I don't say them to anyone else."

"I'll take that as a compliment."

"It's not a compliment–" she stopped midsentence, her ears burning a brighter shade of red. "No, that's not what I meant. I don't know what I meant. I'm–I'm sorry."

"Don't worry about it. I'm glad you feel comfortable speaking your mind with me."

Sam watched her. She looked like a mouse caught in a trap, glancing down at the ground, then over at the rake on the wall, then up at the rafters, looking at anything but him. He could tell she was searching for words to string together that might not be so insulting. There was something about Sydney, dressed in her overall jean shorts, her wiry legs sticking out, her black untamed hair whipping wildly about her face in the Kansas breeze that he found adorable. He decided to let her off the hook and clapped his hands sharply.

"What do you say we get to work? I'll get fresh water and hay if you guys release the horses to the pasture."

Sydney nodded dumbly and immediately took off for the stall farthest away.

"Mary Beth?" Sam whispered. "Could you help me with something?

"Sure."

They went outside the stables to a place where Sam had both a good view of Sydney and where they were far enough away that she couldn't hear their conversation.

"There's something I need to tell you," he said with a crinkle-eyed grin. "I'm not who you think I am."

Both of Mary Beth's eyebrows drew together in interest.

"I don't live at the Barton House. As a matter of fact, I've never taken drugs in my life." He pointed down the dirt road toward the Blue River. "I'm renting a cottage from Mrs. Tomlinson at the end of that trail. Part of my rent goes to working her farm so she could end her deal with the sober living center."

"Why didn't you say something earlier?"

"I tried to, but you guys never let me explain. Every time I opened my mouth, Sydney would rip me a new one for living an undisciplined life or choosing the wrong friends or working in the entertainment industry."

"What is it you do, EssCee?"

A wry smile twitched at his mouth. "Well, to start with, my name's not EssCee. Those are two of the three initials of my name—S. C. C. I wasn't late this morning. I was actually early, working on the other side of the barn, and I overheard your conversation about the Royals game in Detroit."

"Did you see it?" Her face brightened. "They almost had a big fight because our new guy threw at the Tigers' best player."

"I had to hit him," Sam said matter-of-factly. "They threw at Manny's head after Kevin's slam gave us the lead."

Her mouth fell open, and she took a step back. "You . . . play for the Royals?"

He took off his sunglasses and floppy hat. "Yes, ma'am. Sam Cloud-Carson—they pay me to hit guys in the butt."

She stared at him as if he was some Martian who'd just stepped out of a spaceship.

"The League fined me five-grand for hitting him, but no suspension, and we won, so it was worth it. Now, if we could get back to what I wanted to talk with you about?"

Mary Beth's stunned look didn't change.

"Judging by your personality, Ms. Mighty Brilliant, I thought you might want to have a little fun with your friend, who's been trashing me the last two weeks."

She blinked once, twice, and then swallowed. "Okay."

"I start Friday night against Seattle. I'll leave you tickets. When they announce the lineups on the center-field scoreboard, they'll show my mug and surprise the heck out of Sydney."

Mary Beth let loose a belly laugh that carried all the way to the pasture, causing Sydney to turn their way.

Sam put an index finger to his lips. "Mum's gotta be the word on this one, MB. And, if you guys have time after the game, I'll get you passes to meet me in the clubhouse lobby. Win or lose, it'll be funny. Maybe we'll even get a smile out of Sydney."

His words wiped the grin off Mary Beth's face. "She hasn't had much to smile about lately."

"I figured"—he nodded reflectively—"I went through a tough time a few years back. I was lucky to have good friends who helped me through it."

"I want to be that friend for Sydney. She's really a very good person."

"I'm sure she is," said Sam as he glanced over at the young lady, all alone, brushing one of the horses. "I'm sure she is."

CHAPTER TWENTY-NINE

DiamondBar Headquarters, Virginia

June 2013

Dixon checked his phone for the fifth time. He was waiting for a call from the vice chairman of the Senate Appropriations Committee. Senator Richardson had promised to update him on Chinese companies pursuing Afghanistan's vast natural resources. How dare they? China had no right to bargain for Afghanistan's mineral wealth after US and NATO forces did all the fighting to stabilize the war-torn country.

Damn it, America deserved those rights. China had given nothing to help Afghanistan—no troops, no equipment, no funds for security—while America had fought for those rights with both blood and gold. There was no way Drake could let China steal what belonged to him. Hazrat's mountain in the Nuristan Province would have been his if not for the man who was now starring in the Major Leagues.

Drake picked up the sports section of Monday's *USA Today* and glared at the headline and picture on the front page.

Royals' talented rookie, Sam Cloud-Carson, moves his record to 6–1 with a hard-fought, emotional win over the Detroit Tigers.

"You son of a bitch," Drake said under his breath. "Your luck is about to run out."

"What's that?" Barry King looked up from across the room.

"Nothing," Dixon muttered.

His lawyer likely knew what he had said. Barry was at every meeting, every DiamondBar strategy session, spying on every conversation Dixon had. King didn't like to leave his boss alone with the other staffers because he worried about how they might influence any decision he'd make. His lawyer thought it unwise to slander Carson to Major League general managers inquiring about signing him. But Dixon knew better.

Aggressiveness was needed. Pull the splinter before it festered, rip up weeds before they took over the garden, cut out the cancer before it spread. Carson was Dixon's tumor. Dangerous if left alone. And this was personal.

Carson had cost him millions and was still a threat because he had discovered DiamondBar's illegal activity in the Nuristan Province. Carson had to be controlled.

Unfortunately, one team had not heeded his warning. The Kansas City Royals. Despite telling their GM that Carson was selfish and divisive and that there were rumors of drug use, the Royals had signed him two weeks before opening day and then called him to the Majors only five weeks later. King had warned him that a character assassination was a bad idea. If Carson succeeded both on and off the field, Dixon's personal attacks could come back to haunt him.

The phone rang, and Drake snatched it off his desk and checked the identity. *Washington, DC.* He clicked on.

"How's my favorite senator doing on this lovely day?" Drake said with an overdramatic enthusiasm.

"Busy running the country," Ed Richardson replied. "Just got off the phone with the State Department. Afghan Oil and Gas cut another deal with China in the Logar Province, south of Kabul. Now they're bidding on mineral rights up north."

"Nuristan?" Dixon asked.

"You guessed it. They're cutting into our territory. And to add insult to injury, our troops are providing security for the Chinese companies by patrolling the regions they're working."

"That's bullshit. That's *our* land. That's *our* blood and sweat in those hills."

"It's geopolitical, Drake. China and Pakistan are both concerned about India's growing influence in Afghanistan, so all these corporations are coming in, trying to strike a deal for natural resources believed to be worth almost three trillion dollars."

"How can the Afghan government sell a mountain to the Chinese when Hazrat still owns the mineral rights?"

"I don't know, Drake, you tell me? You're the one who cut and ran when the going got tough in 2011. Taliban came in, blew your bridge, captured a few of your workers, and you put your tail between your legs and left millions on the table."

Dixon pinched the bridge of his nose. He couldn't tell Richardson what had really happened. Only a few DiamondBar employees and that traitor Carson knew that Dixon had put a killing bounty on an Afghan village leader who owned land that he wanted. Dixon had screwed up. Big time.

"Maybe the Chinese found a loophole in Hazrat's treaty," he said.

Richardson snorted back a laugh. "I remember you telling me a few years ago that Afghanistan was like the Wild West, Drake. That treaties were only good until those in power changed their minds."

Dixon didn't speak for several moments. He was thinking about all of the ramifications of what would happen if he went after Hazrat's mountain again. He still had allies within the Afghan government who could be bribed, and there were warlords in the mountains who owed him. There was no way he could let some Chinese company come in and steal his mountain.

He believed that if private military companies were given the power to take over the war in Afghanistan, an idea supported by many on Capitol Hill, they could also control the abundant natural resources in the country. DiamondBar deserved those mineral rights. After all, he had poured enough of his money into super PACs to support at least four senators with close ties to the mining industry, or companies that sold heavy construction equipment overseas.

Like many in the US private military contracting business, he had benefited from the Supreme Court's 2010 decision in *Citizens United vs. the Federal Election Commission*, which introduced a loophole that made US elections and politicians vulnerable to both foreign and domestic interests. Dixon was taking full advantage of it. No longer did he have to disclose his identity as he hid behind the 501(c) nonprofit and gave money to powerful politicians who would do his bidding.

It was DiamondBar who had provided the security for the Provincial Reconstruction Teams. It was his men who risked their lives guarding the construction workers who would build the roads and bridges in the Nuristan Province. Dixon was the one in power. Not China, not the US government, not Afghanistan, and certainly not some disgruntled former employee.

It was time to break his agreement with Carson and bury him. He wouldn't even have to do it directly. He would have others do the dirty work for him by attacking Carson with accusations, rumors, and lies. Hell, most people loved hearing about a young star getting knocked off his pedestal. There was no way Carson would divulge the truth of what happened in Colorado and Afghanistan to the press. Not anymore. The boy was a star now. He had too much to lose. Even if Carson was willing to blow up his baseball dreams to stop him, Dixon knew how to silence him. Threaten someone he loved. Simple as that.

"Drake, are you there?" Richardson said.

"Yeah."

"What are you thinking about?"

Dixon squeezed the phone and said, "I'm thinking about breaking a treaty."

CHAPTER THIRTY

Kansas City, Missouri

June 2013

"Oh my goodness, how did you get these seats?" Sydney's voice was happy with surprise as she, Mary Beth, and Mary Beth's husband, Phil, walked through Kauffman Stadium's plush Diamond Club and down an aisle to row four behind home plate. Her eyes were wide as she sat down and looked around. "I've never seen a game this close before. I feel like royalty."

Mary Beth and her husband pursed their lips to keep from laughing. They were both in on the practical joke set up by Sam. Sydney still thought he was a client of the Barton House and was completely unaware that he would be the starting pitcher for tonight's game.

"You are royalty, Syd," Phil said and then waved to a waiter to bring them menus. "Food is courtesy of our friend too."

"Who is this mystery person?"

"You'll see him in due time." Mary Beth grinned mischievously.

"Something's going on here." Sydney narrowed her eyes. "You guys are being really, really weird."

Phil handed her a menu. "Just eat."

She opened the menu. "Whoa, look at this: curry chicken … strawberry spinach salad … veggie burger."

"We're at a ballgame, Syd. Please, just once, eat like a normal fan."

"Then, I'll have the Beyond Burger." She winked. "It's vegan, plant-based meat on a gluten-free bun."

"Of course it is." Phil shook his head. "Anything to drink?"

"Lemonade, please."

He turned to place their order, and Sydney opened the program on her lap. Mary Beth immediately snatched it away.

"Give that back, MB! I like to keep score. My dad taught me how when I was in second grade." She gave a shy grin. "I also like to circle the pictures of the cute players."

MB gave a heavy sigh. "You're like a kid in a toy store, Syd, having to open or touch everything."

"I feel like a kid tonight!" She opened her arms wide. "I mean look at this place. We're in the Diamond Club! The grass looks greener, the sky's bluer, the scoreboard's bigger. I want to take in every moment and—"

She paused when the music started, and the public-address announcer boomed out, "Here are the starting lineups for tonight's ball game. First, for the visitors from Seattle . . ."

Sydney turned back to her friend. "Thanks for talking me into coming with you tonight. I didn't want to at first because … you know. It's Friday, Blake's favorite day of the week. He'll be out late—Westport, Crossroads, I don't know—we may even beat him home after the game."

Mary Beth elbowed her in the side and pointed up at the scoreboard. "Would you just chill? Let's check out our guys."

Curiosity lit up in Sydney's eyes. "What's going on, MB? You and Phil are both real oddballs tonight."

The scoreboard flashed a picture of the Royals' second baseman, batting ninth.

"He's cute," Mary Beth said.

"Uh, okay?" Sydney turned to face her as the announcer bellowed, "And on the mound for your Kansas City Royals … Sam … Cloud … Carsonnnn!"

Mary Beth slapped her friend sharply on the knee and jerked her thumb at the scoreboard.

Startled, Sydney straightened in her seat and stared up at the image that took up the entire display beyond center field.

It couldn't be, could it? No way.

"That looks like"—she paused, as if mulling it over—"EssCee from the sober living center."

Both MaryBeth and Phil exploded in laughter, causing fans around them to turn in their seats to see what the commotion was about.

"You're an idiot!" Mary Beth cried out. "It is him! EssCee is Sam Cloud-Carson. He plays for the Royals."

"So he ... finished his rehab?"

"No!" Mary Beth snorted back another laugh. "He never used drugs, Sydney! He rents a cottage from Mrs. Tomlinson. He wanted to pull a practical joke on you after all the grief you gave him when you accused him of having a substance-abuse problem."

Sydney tried to swallow but could not, mortified by her past behavior as she watched the man jogging to the mound. All she could think of were the terrible things she had said to him.

You're late ... You need to choose better friends ... Of course you're in the entertainment business. That's why you're in this predicament ... You're late again ... Car trouble ... Lost your phone ... Dialed the wrong number ... The dog ate your homework ... What a loser.

Oh my God, she thought. *I am an idiot—and a cruel one too.*

She wanted to drop her head into her hands, but she couldn't take her eyes off Sam, now warming up. He was an athlete, that she could tell. And a very skilled one with his smooth, unhurried, almost effortless delivery.

As the catcher fired down to second base, she watched Sam nod to each one of his infielders and then turn his attention to home plate. A tremor ran up her spine as his expression suddenly changed from serene to absolute concentration. As a coach, she had seen this look before in the elite ones, a complete absorption into the present, distancing themselves from the outside world, the crowd, the music, the opponent, as if every fiber of their being came together for one singular purpose—*to win.*

Another elbow to her side snapped her out of her trance. "We got ya good, didn't we?" Mary Beth snorted.

Sydney nodded but turned her attention back to the game as Sam delivered a first-pitch fastball on the outside corner for strike one.

"I was holding my breath all week long hoping you wouldn't catch on to our plan," Mary Beth said. "I even stole your morning newspaper when Sam's picture was on the front page of the sports section."

Sydney didn't respond. She leaned forward in her seat as the next pitch was fouled off.

"He called me on Wednesday to say he was leaving Diamond Club tickets for us."

Third pitch outside for a ball.

"Phil and I couldn't wait to see your face when you saw him on the scoreboard."

Fourth pitch, sinker, outside corner, Sydney's right arm jerked up in unison with the umpire's. *Strike three.*

Mary Beth laughed out loud. "Look at you! Into the game. Welcome back, Sydney!"

But she wasn't listening. She was busy pulling a pen out of her purse and reaching for the program that her friend had stolen earlier.

"Can we talk at the end of the inning?" she said with a serious expression. "I need to keep score."

*　　*　　*

Peace eluded Sydney.

As the game wore on, the more random thoughts zipped through her mind. *Who was Sam Cloud-Carson? Where had he come from? Where was Blake? What was he doing tonight? Should I tell Mom and Dad about tonight? Would they approve? Would they think this prank pulled by an unmarried man was funny? Why did I say he was unmarried? That's none of my business. I don't know anything about him? He probably has a girlfriend. I wonder what she looks like? Stop it, brain! Stop thinking so much. But ... but Mary Beth said he wanted to see us after the game. What would I say? What should I say? Should I just apologize for the millionth time and then go hide under a rock?*

She looked down at her scorecard and shook her head. It was a mess. An incomprehensible scribbling of 6-3's (groundout to short), F-7's (flyout to left) and K's (strikeout). But there were also plenty of WWs (wasn't watching) when her mind was a train wreck of haphazard thoughts as she watched the game.

Sam was dealing too. His innings barely lasted five minutes as he threw strike after strike, piling up a myriad of groundouts before his manager finally pulled him after eight innings, with the Royals leading 8–2. He was good. Better than good. Every pitch he made had a purpose.

And the Royals appeared to be united. They seemed to like each other, playing for one another: sacrificing, stealing bases, executing hit and runs, turning double plays. It was a fun group to watch, and the thirty-one thousand fans in attendance on this Friday night were into it as well. They all stood the entire ninth inning, and when the ball settled softly into center fielder Alonzo Hawkins' glove for the final out, the crowd roared.

She joined them in cheering for the victorious Royals until she realized her palms were sweaty. And it wasn't the summer heat.

Uh oh. It was time to meet the man who'd pranked her.

She wiped her palms against her jeans and turned to her friend.

"Ready?" Mary Beth was holding three passes that obviously would take them down to the clubhouse lobby.

"Sure," she said, her voice higher than usual.

Okay, okay, okay. Why are you so nervous? You can do this. Just breathe.

*   *   *

They stood in the lobby between both clubhouses, surrounded by the players' families and friends waiting for their loved ones to come out. The first to exit were those who didn't play that night.

Phil leaned in close to Sydney. "That's Mario Fuentes, he's one of our starting pitchers … and that's reliever, Willie Kahal … and that's—"

Phil paused when the clubhouse door opened and out came Sam with a huge ice bag on his right shoulder and another on his elbow, his eyes searching the room for the woman he had pulled the practical joke on.

"Hey, Sydney!" he cried out, and every head in the lobby turned to see who that night's winning pitcher was calling out to.

Her face went beet red, and she shrank back behind Phil.

Sam grinned as if overjoyed to see her and spread his arms wide. "Did I choose better friends?"

Even though she was beyond embarrassed, she couldn't keep herself from laughing. And not just any laugh, but a laugh from the very depths of her belly, the kind of laugh she hadn't let go in more than a year. Her face was still bright red as he walked over and extended his hand.

"Sam Cloud-Carson, clean and sober. Nice to meet ya."

She was still giggling uncontrollably as she shook his hand, but she couldn't look him in the eyes. Not yet.

It was only when he was busy giving high fives to Mary Beth and Phil for their successful shenanigans that she had the courage to finally look up at him.

"You got me good," she said, attempting to hide her huge, idiotic grin. "And I deserved it."

"Don't hold back." He winked. "It's nice to finally see your beautiful smile."

She gulped and felt her pulse notch up. It was time to change the subject.

"Mary Beth, uh, said that we're going to meet you, uh, at Brio?"

"Sounds good to me. I'll go shower and meet you guys in thirty."

*   *   *

It was a lovely summer evening on the Plaza, with a gentle breeze cutting through what would have been oppressive humidity. From the second floor balcony of Brio, they had a perfect view looking down at packed Nichols Road. Sydney checked her watch. 11:17. Sam should have been there by now. She wondered if he'd even show, and then she saw a man sprinting down Nichols their way. She could tell it was him. Tall, athletic, black hair slicked back, probably still wet from his shower. *Shut up, brain. You're taken. Just shut up.*

He arrived out of breath. "Sorry I'm late. I got pulled over on Blue Parkway."

"Speeding?" Mary Beth asked.

"No." He frowned in concern. "It was weird. The officer said they received an anonymous call that someone driving a 2004 gray Prius with my plates was speeding, driving erratically, and looked drunk."

"What?"

"Thankfully, the officer had been listening to the game and knew I didn't have time to drink and drive. I offered to take the breathalyzer test, but he thought the whole thing may have been a prank from some disgruntled fan." He eyed Sydney. "It wasn't you, was it?"

"No!" She said defensively, and then her brows drew together in interest. "You drive a Prius?"

"Bought it last week. Only ninety-five thousand miles on it. Gets forty-five miles a gallon. I'm an environmentalist."

She brightened. "Me too. I have a 2003 Civic Hybrid. Averages forty-two."

"I tested one of those, but the emergency brake's on the console so my right knee kept bumping into it."

"I'm only five-foot-six, so that's not a problem."

"How's it handle in winter?"

"Front-wheel drive, so not bad, just have to watch for black ice."

Mary Beth waved a hand in front of their faces. "Hey, guys, Sam was almost arrested. Why are you talking about whether you need chains for your enviro-vehicles?"

Phil handed Sam a menu. He looked it over.

"In case the authorities have it out for me"—he winked—"I'd better have a lemonade."

"That's what I'm having." Sydney held her glass up. "It's almost as good as the one I had at the ballpark. Fresh-squeezed."

Mary Beth rolled her eyes and mumbled, "Hybrids and lemonade. Why don't we put both of you on the cover of *Boring Illustrated*."

*   *   *

The party only lasted until midnight. All four of them had to be up early on Saturday. Mary Beth and her husband were visiting family in Wichita, leaving Sam and Sydney to prep Mrs. Tomlinson's stables for the KC Urban Wildlife Academy.

Sydney was alone in the back seat of her friend's car, absentmindedly flipping through her phone to check messages. Nothing. Then she glanced at the rearview mirror to make sure no one was watching and touched the icon for the internet. A wave of guilt rushed through her veins as she quickly typed in his name. Who was Sam Cloud-Carson? He'd barely said anything about his past tonight. She had to know more. At the top of the page was a feature done by the *Kansas City Star*. She clicked on and skimmed through.

All-American at Mesa State … worked for some company named Diamond-Bar Security in Afghanistan … Grew up on the Southern Ute Reservation in southwest Colorado.

Interesting. He's Native American, and I'm half Native American. We have something else in common.

She scrolled down to read more when her phone pinged, startling her so that she tossed it in the air as if it had suddenly caught on fire. It landed between the front seat and console.

"I'll get it for you," Mary Beth said and turned in her seat.

"No!" Sydney jerked forward, but her seatbelt wouldn't let her claim her lost prize. In near panic, she twisted through a strap and stretched her left arm as far as it would go. But her friend reached it first. The screen was dark.

She let go a thankful sigh.

"What's wrong with you?" Mary Beth handed the phone to Sydney. "Did Sam spike your lemonade?"

"No!" The truth was her head was spinning. She didn't know what she was feeling. Yesterday, she thought Sam was a loser, and now, less than twenty-four hours later, she was seeing him in a completely different light. She shook her head as if to rid herself of those thoughts and typed in her code to read the text. It was from Blake.

Where are you? I came home early to enjoy my wife and … no wifey?

She texted back. *I'm with MB and Phil. We went to the Royals game.*

Fifteen seconds later, he replied. *Thanks for inviting me.*

She didn't know how to respond. She hadn't given Mary Beth a definitive answer that she'd even go to the game until Wednesday night. And MB didn't extend the invite to Blake because … she didn't like him. Didn't like the way he treated Sydney. Finally, she typed back:

Sorry. I'll be home in twenty.

He was asleep, passed out on the couch, when she opened the front door, a half-finished cocktail on the coffee table, along with an open bag of pretzels. She cleaned up the mess, covered her husband with a blanket, and went to bed.

*　　*　　*

The loud groan of Blake entering their bedroom and laying down next to her jarred her awake. It had taken her at least two hours to fall asleep after thoughts of the previous night sped through her mind. A bleary-eyed glance at the clock showed that it was seven thirty. Less than two hours before the kids would arrive at the stables. Time to go. Very cautiously, she peeled back her blanket to slip out, and then felt her husband's arm come around her.

"Where you goin', baby?" he whispered into the nape of her neck.

"Stables," she said, without enthusiasm. "The kids will be there soon."

He pulled her close. "They can wait. I came home early to be with you."

She tried to peel his arm off, but he strengthened his grip.

"Please, Blake. I have a responsibility–"

"You have a responsibility to me." He climbed on top of her. "It says so in your Bible. Wives, submit to your husbands."

Gritting her teeth, she resisted the urge to push him away. Yes, she was his wife, but she didn't want to be with him right now, didn't want to argue, didn't want to fight, didn't want to …

She just wanted to leave, so she simply laid back in bed and closed her eyes.

*   *   *

Sam checked his watch again. 8:37. Sydney was late. She'd said she'd be there by 8:00 to prep the horses. He'd already cleaned the stalls, spread new hay, changed the water, and brought all eight horses to the corral and brushed them, but he didn't want to overstep his bounds by saddling them until the boss lady arrived.

He waited another ten minutes and then saddled all eight.

Sydney arrived at the same time as the children, looking like she'd slept in her car.

"Thank you! Thank you! Thank you!" she cried out to Sam as she ran up the dirt path, sneakers untied, one strap of her overall jean shorts dangling down, uncombed jet-black hair frizzed about her face.

She looked lost, her head on a swivel, swinging from the kids getting off the bus to Sam and back, as if a compass needle spinning wildly, searching for some kind of true north, some path to find her way home.

"Mornin'," Sam said, and then he led the first horse to the mounting block.

"I'm so sorry," Sydney gushed, wiping at her swollen eyes. She obviously had been crying. He remembered Mrs. Tomlinson saying there was trouble on the home front.

"Thanks for getting everything ready, Sam. This isn't like me. I'm always on time. I'm so sorry—what can I do?"

He handed her the reins. "Just help the kids on and we'll go for a ride."

Tears welled in her eyes as she nodded dumbly. He knew she was trying desperately to hold it together and waited a beat before pointing down at her shoes.

"You might want to tie those first."

*　　*　　*

They had the first group ready within five minutes, save for one little girl who screamed in terror as her mother pulled her inside the corral.

"C'mon, Brianna," the mom pleaded. "Riding ponies is all you've talked about this week. There's nothing to be afraid of."

But the girl wailed louder, which caused the horses to stomp and snort, ears back, tails swishing wildly. As Sydney did her best to calm the horses, Sam walked over to the mom.

"May I have a word with Brianna, ma'am?"

Releasing a frustrated exhale, the mom gave Sam her daughter's hand and took a step back.

He knelt down on one knee and looked the girl squarely in the eyes. "Do you like horses?"

Brianna's sobs softened, and she ran her arm across her runny nose.

"Much like you, horses are sensitive." He pointed to the mare next to the mounting block. "That horse has the same name as my little sister." He smiled brightly. "Jenny."

A hopeful smile twitched at the little girl's mouth.

"Jenny's a sweet girl. She likes to be brushed and go on walks and have kids ride her. Do you know how I know she's happy to see you?"

Brianna shook her head.

"Stay right here and I'll show you." He walked over to Jenny and began stroking the horse's neck. "Like all of God's creatures, Jenny responds to love. If I give her love, she'll love me back. But if I yell or hit her, she'll cower or fight back. So I give her plenty of love."

The mare nudged Sam's back with her nose. "Jenny just told me she wants a hug." Sam hugged the horse's neck, then gently slid his right hand down to her nose. "Come here, Brianna."

She took four steps closer but remained a comfortable distance from the horse.

"Look how Jenny's nostrils and lips are relaxed, and her tail's not swishing back and forth anymore. That means she's happy—happy to see you—happy to let you ride her. But you have to show her that you're a confident rider." He motioned her over. "Put your hand on her neck to let her know that you're her friend."

The little girl did, cautiously.

"Horses' senses are very keen," Sam said as the mare leaned down to sniff Brianna.

"Her nose is soft." She giggled.

"That's Jenny's way of getting to know you, through smell, sight, sound, taste, and touch. Her entire body is as sensitive as your fingertips. She can feel a fly on a single hair and can also sense whether you're calm or afraid. That's why it's important to show you're confident when you're near Jenny so she's confident to have you ride her."

"I'm ready." Brianna beamed.

As Sam lifted her onto the saddle, he glanced over at Sydney, who was staring at him with the sort of intent interest his Little Dukes showed whenever he talked about baseball or tracking jaguarundi.

"Do you want to lead, Syd, or do you want me to?"

"I—I'll do it." She shook her head as if trying to clear her mind.

"I was hoping you'd say that. Because I don't know where we're going—and it's hard to lead if you don't know where you're going."

"It's the Blue River Trail." She straightened up in her saddle. "Only a mile or so."

"Well then, lead on, Ms. Sydney." He swept up onto the saddle behind Brianna with the same ease that he'd displayed on the pitcher's mound the night before. Smooth, natural, self-assured, as if he'd done it a million times before.

*　　*　　*

They followed the trail through a tunnel of willows to the river, then turned north underneath giant sycamores, whose roots curled toward the water. It was well shaded, but there was no breeze, and the humidity was so thick Sam's cotton T-shirt soon stuck to his back. Sensing his mare's growing comfort, he handed Brianna the reins and guided Jenny with his knees along the trail.

"We had horses where I grew up, Brianna."

"What was your horse's name?"

"Red Cloud. My mom's maiden name was Cloud, so we had Red Cloud for my horse, and because my dad's last name was Carson, we called my sister's horse Johnny—for Johnny Carson."

"Who's he?"

"Famous late-night talk-show guy before your time."

A boy some two horses ahead of them yelled back, "The Royals have a pitcher named Cloud and Carson. He won last night's game."

Sydney turned in her saddle and grinned at Sam, who put his finger to his lips to stay quiet. She shook her head mischievously and said for every child to hear, "That's the same Cloud-Carson who's riding with Brianna."

The boy jerked around in his saddle and stared at Sam. "No way!"

"Yes way," Sydney deadpanned with a victorious smile. "I was at the game last night. EssCee is very good."

Upon hearing her emphasize his nickname, he chuckled. "I probably deserved that."

"Yes, you did."

Brianna looked up at him. "Do you really play for the Royals?"

"Yep," he said with a slight drawl.

"Do you have a girlfriend?"

"Nope."

She practically glowed as she asked, "Can I be your girlfriend?"

He glanced at Sydney, who was covering up a laugh, then back down at Brianna.

"Okay."

*　　*　　*

The rest of the ride was filled with teasing, laughter, and a nonstop barrage of questions from the little riders about baseball and beyond.

"How fast do you throw?"

"Fast enough."

"Have you ever hit anybody?"

"Yep."

"Does it hurt?"

"Yep."

"Do you have a cool car?"

"2004 Prius."

"They're lame."

"Gets me where I need to go."

"Do you ever have to go to the bathroom when you're pitching?"

"Yep."

"What do you do?"

"Pitch fast. Get out of the inning. Go to the bathroom."

"Have you ever peed in your pants?"

"Just once."

All the kids giggled at that. Even Sydney's shoulders shook with silent amusement as she led them through another stand of willows. He was glad to see that the young woman's mood had lightened from the distress of her morning. There was some kind of tension at home—that he was sure of—and there was nothing like a little trail ride in the woods with children to soften one's pain.

They were back at the corral by 10:45. They helped the kids down from the horses, handed them off to their moms and chaperones, and started to uncinch the saddles when they saw a familiar figure striding their way.

"Hey, Mrs. Tomlinson!" Sam called out. "How was Fort Lewis?"

"Wonderful!" she yelled back. "My son sends his regards."

"He's a good friend," Sam said. He could tell by the look in his landlady's eyes that she knew more about him than she was letting on. Colonel Bart Tomlinson was good at keeping secrets, but moms had a way of reading their children best when executing a full interrogation. They obviously had talked about him.

"Bart said the same about you." She opened the corral gate and stepped inside, glancing at Sydney and then back at Sam. "Nice to see that you two have met."

"Yes, ma'am. Ms. Sydney's a fine horsewoman."

"Heckuva soccer star too," Bette said respectfully as she uncinched a saddle. "All-State midfielder at Blue Valley High and now their coach. Took our Tigers to the playoffs all three years she's been the boss."

Sam gave Sydney a sideways look. "Soccer star, huh? What else haven't you told me?"

"I'm gullible to juvenile pranks."

He laughed. "Hit a grand slam on that one, I did."

Bette's eyes switched from Sam to Sydney and back again, as if evaluating their new friendship.

He noticed. "Long story, ma'am. Sydney didn't exactly respect my skills when we first met, but I evened the score last night, so all is forgiven."

Sydney snorted. "I never said I forgave you."

He put his hand on his heart and looked up to the sky. "Then ye shall be the one who bears the burden of unforgiveness, m'lady."

She rolled her eyes. "You're a goofball."

"Mr. Goofball to you."

They pulled off their saddles and blankets, threw them over their shoulders, and headed to the barn. He followed, pausing only to sniff under his arm and wince in disgust. *Geez, I reek of horse and sweat. Good thing I left a clean T-shirt in the tack room.*

He tossed his gear onto the saddle rack, peeled off his sweat-drenched shirt, tossed it to the side, and reached for the dry one he'd hung on the wall. He slipped the clean shirt over his head and started to pull it down across his chest and abs only to find Sydney staring at him, mouth slightly open.

"Sorry about the smell," he said.

She blinked once, twice, then leaned back against her saddle as if to steady herself. "Would you, uh, care to"—she forced a swallow and leaned back even farther—"care to join me and the kids for a picnic by the river?"

The saddle slipped off the rack, and Sydney fell with it, banging her head against the wooden bench as she fell to the ground. She sat up quickly, her ears burning with embarrassment, and felt the side of her head to assess the damage.

"All-State in soccer, huh?" Sam chuckled as he reached down, hauled her to her feet, and brushed the dirt off her back and shoulders. "You must have been great on sliding tackles."

She rubbed what appeared to be a knot on the side of her head and sat down in a chair.

"On any other day I'd join you," he said as he walked across the tack room to the mini-fridge and pulled out a bag of ice, "but the Royals' community relations department asked me to visit kids at the children's hospital."

"I almost forgot"—she winced as he placed the ice on her injury—"that you had another job."

"It pays the bills."

She looked up at him, her dark eyes shining. "Thanks … for the ice."

"Ahem," said a loud voice near the door. It was Bette, hands on hips, head cocked to the side. "There's four more horses that need to be taken care of, and I'd be happy to take Sam's spot for lunch."

"Of course." Sydney stood up too quickly and bumped her head on Sam's chin. He stumbled backward but caught himself against the saddle rack.

"Wow, you're gonna put both of us on the injured list before the day's over."

"Sorry." Sydney's hand shot to her mouth, to hide another spasm of embarrassment, and she spun around to face Bette. "You can … teach the children the history of your property?"

"History?" Bette's brows rose as if confused by the question. "It's just farmland."

Sam saw Sydney's discomfort and said, "Everything's got a history, Mrs. T. As a matter of fact, I found an old arrowhead down by the river last week. I read where the Black Bob band of the Shawnee used to hunt this land."

Sydney gave him a brief smile of thanks.

"What about your history, Syd? Where do your people come from?"

She took a step back. "I beg your pardon?"

"I figured, with your features, you have a bit of the people's blood in you?"

She paused for a long moment and then said, "Lakota. My biological father was Lakota."

Sam nodded.

"I haven't met him." Sydney looked down. "I think it would hurt my parents."

"That's too bad. You'd enjoy Lakota history, especially reading about He áka Sápa."

"Who?"

"He's more commonly known as Black Elk. Holy man of the Oglala Lakota." Sam put his hands on his heart. "At the center of the universe dwells the Great Spirit. And that center is really everywhere. It is within each of us." He smiled at her. "I think Black Elk is way cool."

For the third time that day, Sydney stared at him, mouth slightly open, as if contemplating what Sam had said. There was a moment of awkward silence until Bette cleared her throat.

"That's real fine, Sam, but we got work to do and I'm hungry." She pointed down the main hall of her barn. "When you gonna finish my stalls?"

"At least three weeks, ma'am. Stilwell Lumberteria was out of Southern Yellow Pine and the stain you like. I ordered some more, should be here on Monday."

"Then pick it up, and we'll start early on Tuesday."

"No can do, Mrs. T. We're in Baltimore and Boston this week, so—"

"I'll pick it up," Sydney interrupted. "I don't have a lot going on this week and my dad has a truck."

Bette gave her a sideways look. "That's a lot of wood for a scrawny girl like you."

"I'll get help."

"Blake?"

"Huh?"

"Your husband?"

Sydney flushed slightly and glanced at Sam, then back at Bette. "I'll find someone."

"Let me get you the work order," said Sam, who opened a drawer and pulled out a pen and paper.

"What's your phone number? I'll text you the info and call the guy at the lumberyard to let him know you'll be picking it up."

"913"–she hesitated, her gaze catching Bette's, whose grim old mouth twisted into something like a smile–"555-6846."

Sam tore off a piece of paper and handed it to Sydney. "Here's my number if you need me." He swept past her and headed for the door "Better go shower. I stink."

"I've smelled worse," Sydney said, then grimaced at her statement. "That's–that's not what I meant."

"No worries." Sam kept walking.

"Good luck this week!" she called after him, her voice higher than normal. "Go, y'know, break a leg!"

He didn't even turn around, only shook his head and chuckled. "This ain't Broadway, Sydney. Nobody's gonna drop a beam on me."

CHAPTER THIRTY-ONE

Kansas City, Missouri

June 2013

Sam stood up from the chair in front of his locker, stretched his arms over his head, and yawned. It had already been a full day: cleaning Mrs. Tomlinson's stables, prepping the horses, going on the trail ride, and visiting with children too sick to get out of bed.

He'd loved the children's hospital experience—giving gifts, encouraging, listening, signing autographs—he even met a little girl who was going through the same kidney-dialysis procedure his sister had gone through. He sat with her the longest, listening to her story and then praying with her. The nurse said that it was the first time the girl had smiled in days. Sam gave her a Royals hat, a pennant, and batting gloves, and he promised to come back.

It was off to the field now, to get his off-day-workout in and to cheer on his teammates, to hopefully take another win from Seattle. The team had played well after what the media was calling the Showdown in Motown. They had won four of five to move into third place in the American League Central, eight games back of first-place Detroit. Sam intentionally drilling the Tigers' slugger last week seemed to unify the team, draw them closer, like bees working a hive, completely focused on only one goal—the success of the entire colony.

As he left the clubhouse to go out and stretch, the Royals vice president of communications, Walt Swanigan, stopped him.

"There's a writer from the national paper, *The Sporting World*, wanting to talk with you. His name's Bob Dalley."

"Okay," said Sam. "Can it wait until after I workout?"

"Of course, but … just watch what you say. Dalley likes to dig up dirt."

"Thanks, Walt. I appreciate the warning."

Sam ran up the dugout steps, smiled at the reporters waiting to visit with his manager, Skip Charles, and joined his teammates.

One reporter stuck his hand out. "Hello, stud. Bob Dalley. Got time for a chat?"

Sam shook the man's hand. "I have to stretch and shag, but I'll finish around five."

"Can we talk while you stretch?"

"Sorry, sir. Team rules."

Dalley nodded but continued to hold Sam's gaze. "I flew in from Vegas, where I met an old coworker of yours."

Sam's jaws clenched, and he did his best to hide his curiosity. "Who's that, sir?"

"Frank Weber."

There was a long silence before he answered. "I'll see you at five."

*   *   *

He stretched, jogged from pole to pole, did sixty-yard sprints, and then shagged fly balls in the outfield, the entire time thinking about one name. *Frank Weber.* They had served together in Afghanistan. One twelve-year veteran of private overseas security … and one well-paid novice. Weber never liked Sam, didn't like the fact that he had no experience and made more money. Weber had hazed him from the very first day, picking fights, pointing a gun in his face, bullying him in the field, and ignoring his tracking intel.

It came to a head one day near a bridge the Provincial Reconstruction Team was building in the Nuristan Mountains. That day when Weber rejected Sam's judgment before a Taliban attack, and the result was four men dead. Now, nearly two years later, Sam wondered what Weber had told this national sports writer.

The clock struck five, and the coaches waved the players in. Sam waited for his teammates to clear the field and head to the clubhouse to shower and dress for the 6:05 start. No need for any Royal to hear this conversation. He motioned for Dalley to join him at the end of the dugout.

"What can I do for you, sir?"

"I'm doing a feature on the hot rookies in baseball."

"We've been playing good ball."

"*You've* been playing great ball, kid. Seven and one in your first eight starts is pretty impressive."

Sam glanced at the clock on the scoreboard. 5:05. Even though he wasn't starting, he wanted to be with his team, not out here talking about himself, particularly about his past.

"I've only got ten minutes, Mr. Dalley. Fire away with your questions."

"All right, son, not a whole lot is known about your time in Afghanistan–"

"Like I told our local media, I can't talk about my time with DiamondBar. It's an agreement I made with their owner."

A smile curved the writer's thin lips. "Drake Dixon."

Sam didn't respond.

"I find it extremely odd that you would sign on with his company only days after you gave an enthusiastic interview with a Grand Junction TV station about your excitement for Mesa State's upcoming baseball season." He paused for effect. "You remember–the day your Mavericks were picked to win the National Championship, and you were the pick to win National Player of the Year."

Again, nothing from Sam.

"Did your mom dying in a car accident that same day have anything to do with you changing your mind?"

The side of Sam's mouth twitched, but he held the writer's gaze. "That's none of your business."

"Sorry, son, just trying to write a story."

"Don't call me son. I had a mother and a father."

"Both gone though. And you refusing to talk about it makes people think?"

"Let 'em think."

Dalley exhaled loudly. "You're a tough cookie. The big mystery of the Major Leagues in 2013. A star in college, likely a high draft pick, threw it all away to work security in Afghanistan. Then all of a sudden, you show up out of nowhere in Nicaragua, leading the worst team in the league to the championship."

Sam glanced at the scoreboard clock again. "You have five more minutes, sir. Do you have any questions, or are you just going to run down the timeline of my life?"

Dalley straightened up on the dugout bench. "Tell me about Frank Weber."

"We were coworkers for DiamondBar."

"Did you get along?"

"I gave my word to Mr. Dixon that I wouldn't talk about my time overseas."

Dalley slipped off his sunglasses and smiled. "As I mentioned earlier, I met Mr. Weber in Vegas yesterday."

"Good for you."

"He said that you cut off his ear in a knife fight."

Sam shook his head. "And you believed him?"

"I don't know what to believe if you don't tell me anything."

"You want to talk high school, college, Nicaragua, playing for the Royals, fine. But I can't talk about Afghanistan."

"Then I don't have story."

"That's not my problem."

"Aren't you at least interested in what Frank's doing now?"

Sam gave a disinterested shrug

"He's a bouncer at a strip club, lives in a trailer east of Vegas."

"And out of the blue he calls you to talk about a former coworker?"

"A former coworker who could be this year's Rookie of the Year," Dalley said. "C'mon, Sam, give me something. Tell me about Weber. Did you cut off his ear?"

Sam stood up and checked the clock one last time. "I'm done here, Mr. Dalley. I've got to pack for a road trip and be with my team." He started down the dugout, then stopped abruptly and looked back at the writer. "But you might want to do a little more research before you write a story based on quotes from a guy who works at a Vegas strip club."

CHAPTER THIRTY-TWO

Stilwell, Kansas

June 2013

Sydney, glancing up at the television each time Sam threw a pitch, slowly stirred her homemade salsa. It was a tense game at Fenway Park. A pitchers' duel between Sam and the 2012 Cy Young winner, Josh Henry. 1–1 in the bottom of the seventh inning, man on first, one out. She stopped stirring when Sam came set to deliver an important 2–2 pitch, her hand frozen to the spoon in the salsa, her eyes glued to the TV.

"Hey, baby, we're hungry in here!" Blake yelled out, and Sydney's hand jerked forward, spilling half the salsa on the kitchen counter. She grabbed some paper towels and wiped up the mess.

Sam's pitch barely missed outside. Full count. Tension increase.

Her husband looked over his shoulder and held up an empty basket. "We need more chips too. Pronto. Big moment for our boys in Blue."

Next pitch, fouled off.

The drama was indeed building. For the first time in decades, the Royals had become fun to watch; they were athletic, competitive, energetic, and exciting. The potential of the best minor league system in baseball was finally being realized. Former high draft picks Kevin Cimoli, Rex Blackwell, Terry Ayers, and Bo Chapman had emerged as rising stars, and the international signings of Mario Fuentes and Tony Ramirez were paying off. The only thing the team was missing was an ace. A number-one pitcher who would bow his neck in times of trouble and stop losing streaks. Shockingly, that ace had fallen onto their royal laps in a low-budget gamble out of Nicaragua.

Cutter inside, fouled off.

"Damn, we're only a game out of second place," Blake's friend Tyler said. "We haven't been in second place in June in five years."

"And we always screw up at Fenway," Blake grumbled. "Ya gotta know how to pitch 'em in this park. Everything away."

All eyes turned back to the TV as Sam threw a perfect two-seam fastball that brushed the outside corner. Called strike three.

"Yakka!" yelled Blake, but this time Sydney didn't spill any salsa as she gently placed the bowl and the basket of chips on the coffee table.

"Outside corner! That's what I'm talking about!" He grabbed a chip, dipped it in the salsa, and shoved it in his mouth. "This son of a bitch can flat pitch."

Sydney flinched at her husband's words.

"There aren't too many Native Americans playing in the bigs," said Tyler.

"He's Ute," she said softly. "His teammates call him EssCee."

Blake gave his wife a sideways glance. "How do you know that?"

She hesitated. "I, uh, read it somewhere."

Tyler gave a tomahawk chop with his hand and roared, "C'mon, Chief EssCee! Let's scalp those Red Sox!"

"Back off, T," Blake muttered. "My wife's got Indian blood in her."

Sydney glowered at her husband as Tyler mouthed, *Sorry.*

"She's real sensitive about it." Blake swept another chip into his mouth. "Her mom had an affair with a Lakota dude years ago, and the result was Sydney."

"Shut up, Blake." She wasn't quick to anger, but damn it, her backstory was none of their business. She started to stand up, but Blake pulled her down next to him.

"Did I hurt my sweet little squaw?"

Infuriated, she twisted free and started back toward the kitchen until she heard all four men shout in alarm. She spun back around to find their faces twisted in anguish as they stared at the TV … at the image of a Royal writhing in pain on the ground.

Sam.

*   *   *

"Where did it get you?" Royals trainer Jimmy Austen asked.

"Right side of my lower thigh." Sam pointed to a spot above his knee. "It didn't get me square. I think I got part of my glove on it. … I should've caught it."

His manager was kneeling next to him and snorted back a laugh. "That ball came at you over a hundred miles an hour. You can't catch what you can't see."

"I saw it." He tried to sit up, but Austen put a hand on his chest and pushed him flat.

"Would you not move until I check for any structural damage?"

He looked up at his manager. "Where'd the ball wind up?"

"It ricocheted into left field like a pinball hitting one of those flippers. Sox have runners on second and third."

"No problem. Delvecchio's up. He couldn't hit a slider to save his life."

"You're done, Sam."

He twisted away from his trainer, struggled to stand up, and said through clenched teeth, "I'm good, Skip. I can get this guy."

"I admire your grit," said Charles, "but you're at a hundred and seven pitches. I was coming to get you anyway. Go get some ice on that leg, and we'll get that final out for you."

Sam had no sooner sat down on the training table in the clubhouse when he heard the roar of the Fenway crowd. He looked up at the tiny TV monitor to see both Red Sox runners touch home plate. Reliever Willie Kahal's first pitch had been drilled off the Green Monster, and Boston was up 3–1.

"Dang it," Sam muttered. "If I'd caught that ball, we'd still be tied."

"Oh yeah?" his trainer said. "And if that line drive was three inches lower, we'd be carting you off the field with a broken kneecap. Consider yourself lucky."

*　　　*　　　*

Blake's friends finally left at one in the morning. It took Sydney another hour to clean up the mess that they said they'd take care of. Yeah, right. She heard Blake snoring even before she washed the first glass. Thanks for the help. Sleep was difficult, and she crept from bed at seven thirty. She dressed for a run, slipped out the front door, and took off in a dead sprint, as if trying to run away from her thoughts.

Ten minutes later, she found herself standing in the middle of the street, head on a swivel, not sure which way to go. She'd been up most of the night, thinking about a man other than her husband. That wasn't right. God would punish her for even thinking such thoughts, but there they were, flying through her mind like a spider monkey swinging from branch to branch in search of the fruit of temptation. Sin always started with wicked thoughts.

But … how was Sam? Was he hurt? He'd had to be helped from the field. *Did he break anything?*

The Royals had lost the game, and Sam was hurt. It was her fault. Why had she said it? Why had she told him to *break a leg* when she last saw him at the stables? That was stupid, and now, he'd probably never forgive her. What an idiot.

She should apologize, shouldn't she? That was the right thing to do … but a married woman texting a single man? That wouldn't look good, would it? But, but, but *he* had texted her earlier in the week, sending her information on when to pick up the wood and stain from Stilwell Lumberteria. She'd responded innocently with:

Mrs. Tomlinson's neighbor is going with me to pick up supplies.

He answered with: *Thanks. You're the best!*

What did he mean by *You're the best*?

It had taken her nearly three minutes to choose the right emoji to reply.

Smiley face (innocent enough). Baseball (that's okay too). Girl holding a hammer (perfectly understandable). No one would read into that text.

Dang it, why was she acting like one of the girls on her sophomore team? She and Sam were friends. If Sam was a girl, would she be acting this way? Of course not. But he was so nice. She saw it in his eyes when he calmed Brianna before the pony ride. There was a gentleness about him that was uncommon in most elite athletes. Was it possible to be a champion without being ruthless?

Her husband told her that winners were like sharks: born to hunt, focused, tenacious killers who would stop at nothing to win. It was a character trait Blake said she lacked. He said she could have given more, even as an All-State soccer player, hustled more, cared more. He pointed out every flaw in her game that had kept Blue Valley from winning a state championship her senior year.

He, of course, had an excuse. A devastating knee injury was the only thing that kept him from basking in glory. But she had only herself to blame, for not wanting it more than the other players, and now as a coach, for not training her team to want it more than the other team. It was never enough with Blake.

She shook the dark thoughts from her mind and headed down the road, toward her high school, picking up the pace as she approached the athletic center, sprinting through the parking lot, past the football stadium, to the soccer field beyond. She collapsed at midfield, her lungs burning, gasping for breath. It felt good, like taking a sports car out on an empty rural road and letting the engine roar.

The feeling lifted her spirits and gave her strength for what she wanted to do. If she let another minute go by, she might lose her nerve. She reached inside her sweatshirt pocket and pulled out her phone. 8:30 ... 9:30 in Boston.

She scrolled down through her texts and stopped at her most recent one to Sam, her finger hovering over the keys. She inhaled a deep breath and typed: *I saw yesterday's game. I hope your leg is okay.*

His reply was immediate. *Unfortunately, a beam fell on me from the rafters. Thanks for your "break a leg" comment.*

Her face broke into a wide smile and she typed back: *I didn't mean it literally. Are you going to live?*

He wrote back: *The docs think they can save my leg but that I'll probably lose my job as a sock model for Macy's.*

She giggled. *Macy's is still in business?*

They'd better be. I'm running out of socks.

She giggled again. *You're weird.*

You're mean. Then ten seconds later, he added: *Gotta go. Just arrived at Fenway for treatment. EMT guys are here to medivac me in.*

Can't keep them waiting. Have a great day!

We have tomorrow off. Do you want to help me fix the stalls?

She caught her breath for a beat, suddenly feeling giddy and girlish. She waited for a long moment, thinking of something to text that wouldn't seem presumptuous. She typed back: *Sure. I don't have anything going on.*

*   *   *

The Royals escaped Boston with a Sunday afternoon win, finishing the trip with four wins and two losses to move into a second-place tie with Chicago at 41–37, still eight games back of Detroit. The flight home was a happy one: music blaring, card-playing, teasing both rookies and veterans alike. Sam sat in a row between the Latin players and the Americans, partly as a bridge of two cultures but also as a translator for pitcher Miguel Guerrero and right fielder Felipe Contreras, whose English was so rudimentary that the only words they knew were *beer, hottie,* and *he got good shit.*

The head trainer, Jimmy Austen, came waddling down the aisle to where Sam and Contreras were seated, carrying an ice bag in one hand and a jar of heat balm in the other.

"You need to keep icing that leg." Austen handed the bag to Sam and tossed the balm to Contreras. "Tell Felipe to put this on his hip. Have him warm it between his palms to liquefy and then massage it wherever it's sore."

Sam nodded and turned to his teammate. *"El señor Austen se disculpa por no llevarte a cenar primero, pero quiere que te bajes los pantalones para poder frotar tu trasero."*

The entire Latin section of the plane exploded in laughter, and Austen put his hands on his hips and glared at Sam. "What did you tell him?"

"I said that you apologized for not buying Felipe dinner first, but could he pull his pants down so you could rub his ass."

This time the American section laughed as a beet-red Austen smacked Sam on the shoulder. "Shut up, rookie, or I'll put that heat balm in your cup."

Sam threw up his hands in mock defense. "Truce, Señor Austen, truce!"

As the Royals' trainer shook his head in amusement and started back toward the front of the plane, Sam grabbed his arm. "Hey, Jimmy, would you help me with a practical joke?"

"Sure—one of your teammates?"

"Nope."

His trainer gave him a sly grin. "Is it a lady friend?"

"Maybe."

"Good. It's about time you went on a date, kid. What's her name?"

Sam leaned close. "Nunya."

"Nunya?" Austen's brows came together in curiosity. "That's a funny name."

"Yeah." Sam winked. "As in, nunya business."

CHAPTER THIRTY-THREE

Stilwell, Kansas

June 2013

"Have you seen my keys?" Blake asked as he walked to the bathroom the next morning, rubbing the sleep out of his bloodshot eyes. It was already seven forty-five. He was supposed to be at work at eight, and the office was a good half-hour drive away.

"I think I saw them on the kitchen counter," Sydney said as she brushed her hair back into a ponytail. She'd been up since six and had gone for a run, eaten her usual bowl of yogurt, granola, and blueberries, and showered.

"Already checked." He pushed past her and turned on the shower. "They're not there. Shit, I'm gonna be late again, and your dad's gonna be pissed."

She shook her head in frustration. There was no use in responding. He'd only blame her for losing his keys. This had become their daily dance. Searching for Blake's lost stuff: keys, phone, TV remote, toenail clippers, whatever, it was always her fault for putting his stuff away.

"Just leave 'em be and we wouldn't have this problem," he would say. *"How many times do I have to tell you?"*

Most of the time, she'd find his keys where he told her he had already looked. In the cupholder of his car, on the floor of the garage, underneath the couch, or, too many times, in a drawer of his liquor cabinet. She'd even built a key rack next to the door that led to the garage, where Blake could hang his keys when he came home from work. He'd rarely used it, and now, as he showered, she searched the typical spots where he might have been. Car. Liquor cabinet. Couch. Briefcase. As she went through his briefcase, she saw a text light up on his phone.

Where are you?

She looked at the name. Allison. Who was Allison? She scrolled back.

How about coffee?

Sounds great. Running late. Order me the usual.

Two sugars? Sweet like you.

She was still staring at the phone when Blake walked into the room.

"What the hell are you doing?" He stormed over and snatched the phone out of her hands. "That's my work shit."

She stood her ground. "I was looking for your keys. Who's Allison?"

He waved away her concern. "Coworker."

"Why are you meeting her for coffee?"

"What?"

"She texted, *Two sugars? Sweet like you.* What's that about?"

He threw his hands up in exasperation. "Oh, God, here we go again. Sydney overreacting. Twenty-one questions. Time to interrogate. Bring it, Perry Mason."

Startled, Sydney shook her head. "No, Blake, don't turn this on me. I was looking for your keys, and a text popped up on your phone. I saw a message from a woman named Allison. I have a right to know who she is and why you're having coffee with her."

His face suddenly changed from anger to easygoing sweetness. He gently put his hand on the side of her face. "Don't worry, babe, she's just a coworker helping me on a sales project. Don't be so paranoid."

Sydney pushed him away. "I have to go."

"Where?"

"The stables."

"Did you find my keys?"

"No."

"Well then, I need your car."

"I'm supposed to be there right now."

"It's just volunteer work, Syd, they'll understand." He snatched her keys off the key rack and looked back at her with obvious approval. "You look good today, babe. If you let this little mistake of yours go, maybe I'll come home early." He winked as he opened the door. "Just you and me, a bottle of wine, and some sweet afternoon delight."

*　　*　　*

Sam sat alone in the tack room and adjusted the knee-immobilizer brace he'd borrowed from the Royals trainer. He still had a wicked bruise where the ball had glanced off his right thigh on Saturday, but he was able to get his day-after workout in yesterday and shouldn't miss a start. The team had a rare day off, and he wanted to make his new friend laugh. The poor girl showed up in some kind of distress nearly every time he saw her.

Trouble on the home front, Mrs. Tomlinson had said. What a shame, because Sydney was nice and … she was cute, with her wiry athletic frame, carved and bronzed by hours on the soccer field, her jet-black hair sweeping across a face highlighted by dark brown eyes that seemed to smile every time he was near. Too bad she was married. He checked the clock on his phone and then looked out the window. She should have been here a half hour ago. *Late again. I hope she's okay.* He was about to text her when he saw the dust trail of a bicyclist come flying down the Tomlinson drive, headed his way. It was Sydney.

He couldn't help but laugh at the joke he was about to pull as he grabbed the crutches leaning against the wall and limped outside.

"Thanks for telling me to break a leg!" he called out when she finally arrived, out of breath, red-faced, ringlets of sweaty black hair curling about her temples.

"Sorry I'm late." She turned away from him and leaned her bike against the corral.

He stifled a grin and began to limp over. "Are you some kind of telepathic psycho who likes to injure ballplay–" He stopped midsentence when Sydney didn't turn around. Obviously, she had been through some sort of calamity this morning and needed time to recover. He stood quietly, some fifteen feet away, as she dabbed at her eyes with her T-shirt, then inhaled a deep breath, and spun around.

"You're a terrible actor," she said. Her smile was strained, and small tracks of tears were visible on her cheeks, but she presented herself as if all was right in her world. "I watched yesterday's game, and they showed you in the dugout, pain-free, joking with your teammates. The TV guys said you'd make your next start."

"Dang it." He tossed the crutches to the side. "They ratted me out. I was trying to take the lead in our weekly high jinks."

She laughed. A real laugh this time. "How many times do I have to apologize for the way I behaved when we first met?"

He gave her a playful shove. "Every day for the rest of our lives."

She punched him in the arm.

"Ow!" He rubbed his right triceps. "That's my pitching arm. Geez, first the leg, now the arm. What's wrong with you?"

"Poor baby." She clutched a hand to her heart in phony concern. "Should we get some ice on your little boo boo?"

This time it was Sam who laughed. Partly because it was funny, but also because it made him feel good to have lifted her spirits, perhaps providing a brief distraction from whatever troubled her this morning. He barely knew Sydney, yet there was something about her that put him at ease. It was as if they had known each other for years, and it was that comfortable feeling that made him want to know more.

"Let me show you what we have to do," he said and started to put his hand on her back to lead her through the stables. Then he thought better of it and instead stretched his arms over his head so she wouldn't get the wrong impression.

"You probably already cleaned the stalls and fed and watered the horses, didn't you?"

"Yes, ma'am. Those are my duties when we're home, or Mrs. T will up my rent."

He had set up everything behind the barn. Planks of Southern Yellow Pine boards lay perfectly atop several sawhorses with cans of wood stain at the end of each horse. She picked up a brush and said, "You're very responsible."

He grinned up at her. "I had a little extra time waiting for the help to arrive."

"Sorry."

"Why did you bike here?" He pried open the first can with a screwdriver.

"My husband lost his keys . . . he took my car."

"You should have called me. I would have picked you up."

"I wanted to ride. I was a little upset—needed to cool off."

He stood up and handed her the can of wood stain.

"Blake has a history of losing his keys. He doesn't like it when I put his stuff away."

Sam said nothing as he pried open the second lid, picked up a brush, and began painting the first plank.

"I think if he was more organized, he wouldn't be late all the time." She paused, as if waiting for Sam to say something, but all he did was nod at the plank that was in front of her.

"Oh yeah. Sorry. No reason to bring you into my troubles."

"I don't mind, Syd. How'd you guys meet?"

She told him about Blue Valley High, about meeting Blake in English class, about her soccer and his football, his knee injury, her transferring colleges to take care of him, about his proposal and her accepting, the wedding at St. Michael's Catholic Parish, and finally, his struggles with alcohol and pain medications. All the while, Sam listened intently, brushing stain on wood, but his eyes, soft with understanding, stayed on Sydney.

He offered a few, "mmm-hmms" and "uh-huhs" and even an occasional "sweet," but all he really did was listen. She paused every now and then to dry her eyes, but he remained quiet, waiting patiently for her to continue.

When they finished the final plank, she looked down at her watch, "Oh my gosh, it's eleven thirty. I've been prattling on for over two hours."

"That's okay," he said. "I like hearing people's stories."

"What about your story, Mr. Cloud-Carson? What about the guy the media is calling *Major League Baseball's Mystery Man?*"

"Naw, you're not finished yet. Why did you get into coaching?"

"Long story and I'm hungry. Can we talk about it over lunch?"

"Sure." He put his brush in a bucket of soap and water and motioned for her to follow. "I haven't been to the market in over a week, but I have apples, bread, and peanut butter and jelly—how does that sound?"

"Perfect," she smiled, and together they walked to his cottage.

*   *   *

They sat on old wicker chairs, on Sam's screened-in porch, quietly munching on sandwiches while listening to the Blue River gurgle by. They couldn't see it through the trees, but the sound of slow water meandering past was both peaceful and restorative. He offered Sydney a bowl of sliced apples. She took two.

"How'd you get into coaching?" he asked.

"My dad coached my brother and me when we were young, and I had a good coach in high school. We made the playoffs all three years I was on varsity, and we finished second in state my senior year. I like teaching young people the importance of teamwork."

"Sounds like my upbringing. I was pretty shy, so my parents signed me up for every sport as soon as I was old enough."

"You"—Sydney straightened up in her chair—"were shy?"

"Very. Growing up, I was fine being alone in the woods or on the mound. I could control my environment when it was just me. Team sports changed that, but it wasn't easy. Even my best friend, Jose, would answer for me when a coach asked a question."

He could see the wheels turning inside Sydney's mind. He paused to allow her to comment, but she said nothing.

"I wasn't necessarily the best teammate, but they put me on all the good teams because I was talented. They put up with my idiosyncrasies and left me alone. That's why I succeeded at pitching. I didn't need anyone else. I could do it all by myself. *I* could throw the big pitch. *I* could get out of jams. *I* could make sure we won."

"And did you?"

He gave her a sidelong glance. "You're a team coach. You know that answer."

"What did you do?"

"Withdrew into myself, didn't accept any help until–" He hesitated midsentence, thinking, *No need to go there.* She probably knew about his past, from some online story or newspaper article, about losing his parents and sister. Instead, he said, "I went through a few challenges that forced me to think of others."

She leaned back in her chair, as if trying to bring him into better focus.

"Thank God I had someone watching over me," he said.

"Who?"

"My sister," he whispered in a voice so soft she could barely hear him. He stood up, went inside his cottage, and returned with a large notebook. "Jenny was considered a shaman in our tribe. A visionary. She had dreams of trouble in my life."

He handed Sydney Jenny's journal and sat back down. "Jenny didn't write this because she was dying. She wrote it to help me survive this world after she was gone."

Sydney began to read, turning page after page; first, she read insights from a child, then a young girl chronicling her brother's sports feats, then deeper messages of peace, acceptance, and forgiveness.

Trust life, Sam. You hold onto me when I don't belong to you. Let me go. I know you thought certain things should not be happening to you, but they did. What looks like an obstacle may be an opportunity. My kidney disease has helped me grow spiritually. I'm not afraid of death anymore. All I ask is that you not be afraid to live after I'm gone. In your darkest hours, please remember that I'm only a thought away … I am with you always.

Tears welled up in Sydney's eyes and rolled down her cheeks. "What a courageous young lady."

He nodded. "Even though she's physically gone, her spirit and words still teach me."

She wiped her tears with a sleeve, but her eyes stayed on the words *Trust life.*

"I wish I was that strong," she said at last, and he touched her hand as if to give her comfort.

"I think you're stronger than you know, Sydney."

She glanced up at him, and the sheer intensity of his gaze sent a quiver up her spine. She didn't know what to do or say, so captured by the heartfelt kindness in his eyes. They continued to stare at each other, neither one of them able to speak.

Suddenly, Sam's phone buzzed. He looked down to check the call, and his entire face lit like a candle.

"Sorry, Syd, but I gotta take this. It's my friends in Nicaragua."

*   *   *

"Howdy, stranger!" Sam said then paused to listen to the voice on the other end. He broke into a huge grin.

"*¡Carlita, el amor de mi vida! ¿cómo has estado?*" *Carlita! the love of my life! How have you been?*

"Hi, Coach! I can't wait to come to America next month and see you pitch."

"*No tanto como estoy emocionada de verte mi linda piña.*" *Not as much as I am excited to see you, my cute pineapple.*

The conversation went on for a good five minutes, and then Carlita handed the phone to Whiplash.

"Mighty sweet of you to pay for our plane tickets and put us up in the Intercontinental," said his old friend.

"No big deal. The Royals have an arrangement with the hotel, so I got a good rate, and I wanted you guys to see our beautiful city. You can walk to the Nelson Art Gallery, Loose Park, and great restaurants on the Plaza. Carlita will think she's died and gone to heaven."

"Sweet, brother. We cain't wait to see ya, but there's somethin' else we need to discuss."

Sam could tell by the tone in his friend's voice that the subject was serious. He walked away from Sydney to the far corner of the porch. "I'm listening."

"Señor Estevez told me some writer from the States called trying to dig up dirt on you," said Whiplash. "Name's Bob Dalley. Said he's doing a feature on you. Started off real nice and everthin', congratulatin' Cheslor on his Dukes winnin' the title and sayin' what a good pitcher you was. Then he started askin' questions about you bein' involved with drugs and prostitutes. Cheslor said you was a first-class citizen, a leader, a role model, and a Nicaraguan champ-peen."

Sam sighed loudly and then glanced over at Sydney, who was still immersed in Jenny's journal. "Drake Dixon's behind this. He'd never call Estevez directly. He has other people to do his dirty work."

"He's a con artist, all right," said Whip. "Worst kind too. Accusations without facts, breakin' promises, prolly makin' shady deals with no contract so legal dudes can't tie him back to doin' somethin' crooked. Have you talked to Hazrat or Colonel T lately?"

"I talked to both of them last month. They said there's been no further construction on Hazrat's land."

Sam rubbed a hand across his face. This new drama made him tired. Was Bob Dalley on Dixon's payroll? What was Dixon's motivation to badmouth a former employee? Sam was a nobody. Just a ballplayer. Afghanistan was ancient history. In his quarterly phone conversations with the Afghan village chief, the news had been good. No construction on Hazrat's mountain. Dixon had not reneged on their agreement.

Was this simply about revenge, or was Dixon planning something new? Was he afraid of what Sam knew and that he couldn't control him? Dixon was provoking him, wanting Sam to lash out and defend himself. But that reaction would only jeopardize Hazrat's village. It was best to ignore Dixon's taunts.

"I'll call Cheslor," he finally said. "Thank him for defending me."

"He knows the true you, Sammy. He's mighty proud that one of his Dukes made it to the bigs, so he don't take too kindly when some stranger rips a Dookie."

"I'm grateful that he gave me a chance," Sam said. "We all should have friends like you and Señor Estevez."

"Speakin' of friends, how's that gal you told me about?"

"Fine."

Whiplash paused. "She's with ya, right now, ain't she?"

"Y-y-yep."

"Is she purty?"

"Yep."

"Be careful with wounded married women. They're fragile."

"It's not like that, Whip. But I'll be careful."

"I'll let you go, brother. Hunoon sends her love. We'll talk next week."

Sam clicked off the phone and walked back to Sydney. "Thanks for being patient. Are you ready to get back to work?"

She slowly raised her vision from Jenny's journal and then shook her head as if trying to straighten out her thoughts. "Your sister is amazing."

His face brightened, and his previous dark thoughts immediately disappeared. "I read that every day. I meditate on her lessons. It seems as if each one is perfect for whatever I'm going through."

"*Five-letter words . . .*" Sydney's voice trailed off.

"Yeah, that's a cool page," Sam said. "Those five-letter words are way more hurtful than the four-letter ones: pride, greed—"

Sydney finished his sentence. "Bully, cruel, shame, guilt." She stopped there and looked down at the journal, her fingers touching the page as if mesmerized by the words.

Sam watched her, her head down, her dark hair spilling forward to hide her face. He had been a victim of those five-letter words in the past, and so had Sydney. He had been able to shake those demons, but she had not.

"Have you experienced those five-letter words, Sydney?"

Her bowed head didn't move.

"Syd?"

She placed the journal on the table and walked out of his cottage.

He followed her. "Did I say something wrong?"

She kept walking. "Can we just go back to work?"

"Sure. I'm sorry if I said something to offend you."

She sighed and turned around. "You said nothing wrong, Sam. I'm just tired of talking about myself."

"Okay. What do you want to talk about?"

"How about you?" She put her hands on her hips. "Ever since we met, I've told you *everything* about me—my life, my family, soccer, high school, college, coaching, marriage, hardships—and yet you've shared nothing about yourself other than to show me your sister's journal."

"I thought you liked it?"

"Of course I liked it. It's incredible. But when are you going to tell me your story—your family, your friends, growing up Ute—college and Nicaragua. What about your girlfriend?"

He cocked his head to the side. "My girlfriend?"

"Carlita?" she said in a voice that sounded like a prosecutor uncovering damning evidence. "You didn't know I took Spanish in high school, did you?" She clasped her hands to her chest. *"Carlita, el amor de mi vida!"*

He bit the side of his mouth to keep from laughing. "You got me, Syd. What more do you want?"

"Tell me about the Dukes, and, y'know, Carlita?"

"She's a great girl. A lot like you. She likes sports and the outdoors."

She rolled her hand for him to continue.

"Also like you, she has dark hair and brown eyes."

"Whatever," she muttered, as if those features were no big thing.

"She's four-foot-eleven, about ninety pounds and throws a heckuva changeup."

Sydney gave a confused look.

"Carlita Rapino"—he paused—"is twelve years old. She's the captain of my Diriamba Dukes Little League team and a fine soccer player too."

Sydney's mouth fell open.

"Carlita's a great example of how sports can save us. Her father ran off before she was born. Her mom was a druggie who abandoned her, and she was passed from family shelter to family shelter and finally to the Estevez Orphanage. Carlita was a mess when Whip and Hunoon took over. Angry, afraid, defensive, fought with the other kids, cut and burned herself on purpose."

"Self-abuse," Sydney whispered.

"Then I arrived, and Whip asked me to coach their Little League team." Sam smiled at the memory. "Most of the kids had never touched a ball before, but Carlita had played stickball and soccer on the streets of Managua while her mom was inside some crack house getting high."

Sydney remained quiet.

"Baseball helped her heal. It seemed like every time that girl threw the ball she was releasing a part of her past: abandonment, anger, shame, grief"—he paused and made sure Sydney's eyes stayed with his—"and another five-letter word—abuse."

She looked away. "I'm fine, Sam."

"I hope you are, Sydney. Because it seems like every time you come to the stables, you arrive in some sort of distress. Thankfully, as the day unfolds you're like a flower opening to the light. The true *you* shows up … and it's beautiful."

She flushed in embarrassment and looked down at her hands, to the ring that marked her sacrament to Blake. Consecrated for the faithful accomplishment of her proper duties before God. Lawfully wedded, from this day forward, to have and to hold, for better—for worse.

"Don't let anyone take your spirit," he said softly. "Not your parents, not a friend, not your husband. People like you, who try to save others from being hurt, can be mighty vulnerable themselves. Make sure you take care of you."

CHAPTER THIRTY-FOUR

Washington, DC

June 2013

The conference room at DiamondBar Security's satellite office in Washington, DC, was packed with all of Dixon's allies. Seated next to Dixon were his lawyer, Barry King, and all the men who were with him on Pargin Mountain the day Sam Cloud-Carson killed Billy Cutthredge and Rob Marcus. At the far end of the table was the vice chairman of the Senate Appropriations Committee, Senator Ed Richardson, and his new chief of staff, Mark Sommers.

Richardson and his assistant were the only ones in the room who didn't know what had happened that December day in 2008. They didn't know that two of Dixon's employees had caused the accident that killed Sam's mother, or that Cutthredge and Marcus had kidnapped the surviving passenger, Teresa Songbird, or that Sam had tracked them up Pargin Mountain and ended their lives just before Marcus was about to rape Teresa.

Dixon glanced at the director of security for Alkron Metals Limited, Ethan Conway, the man Dixon had handpicked to assist one of the top international mining companies in the world in their attempt to strike a deal with Afghanistan. Conway had been one of Dixon's top security men and had videotaped the entire incident on Pargin Mountain: from the moment Sam let loose the first arrow that split Rob Marcus' cervical vertebrae, to the second arrow that shredded Billy Cutthredge's heart, to the third, which burrowed into Billy's brain, killing him instantly. Billy and Rob did deserve to die, yet that incident began a domino effect that Drake regretted. His enemy now had leverage over him.

"Let's get this meeting started." Dixon opened the manila folder on the boardroom table. "The situation in Afghanistan is at a breaking point. Two Chinese companies have brokered billion-dollar deals with the new Afghan president. One is south of Kabul, rich in copper; the other is in the Nuristan Province, near a claim we had with members of the old government."

Dixon nodded at Conway to continue the well-rehearsed presentation they had worked on the day before. It was time to convince the influential Texas senator and his chief of staff to continue to bankroll their security operations in the Hindu Kush.

"A big thank you to Senator Richardson," Conway said, "for convincing Congress to give almost a half billion dollars in aid to develop Afghanistan's mining and energy resources."

"Resources America deserves a percentage of," Dixon added, "because we're the lead country in helping them overthrow the Taliban."

Conway put his hand on his boss's shoulder. "Drake and DiamondBar have worked tirelessly training the Afghan police force, providing security for diplomats to move safely around the country, and most importantly, defending Provincial Reconstruction Teams who were being terrorized by insurgent groups."

"And now China comes in after we did all the work," Dixon grumbled. "Even if the Taliban surrendered today, Afghanistan's governance and infrastructure is so screwed up, China couldn't transport the minerals out of the Nuristan—not without using the roads that *we* built."

What Drake didn't say was that *the roads that we built* were completely funded by US taxpayers. Not a dime came out of Dixon's wallet, and all the security DiamondBar provided came from a fat congressional contract. Those roads led to incredible mineral wealth. Unfortunately, Dixon had lost his ally inside the Afghan Interior Department after Almeida Zubair was fired for accepting a five-million-dollar bribe from a Chinese energy company. That was four times what Dixon had gifted Zubair for the illegal rights to Hazrat's mountain some seven years before. But now that the province was being sought not only by China, but India, Pakistan and Iran, it was time for Dixon to kick that door open again.

"What do you think is *best* for Afghanistan?" asked the man at the far end of the table.

All heads turned toward Richardson's new chief of staff. Dixon had already done his research on Mark Sommers: Stanford political science degree, master's in environmental science, internship at World Oil and Gas, four years at the Environmental Protection Agency, and now he was working for Richardson, a former oil tycoon. *Keep your enemies close.*

"Speak your mind," demanded Dixon.

"I just think that these never-ending wars, where foreigners constantly come to stake their claim, has had a profoundly negative environmental impact on the country. Over sixty percent of Afghan forests are gone because of the wars or because they were torn down by the timber mafia. Bombs have ripped apart their water systems, making it nearly impossible to get water to rural villages, so people flee to the big cities and pollution has tripled."

Dixon flicked the air with his hand. "That's not our responsibility."

"It should be *everyone's* responsibility."

Dixon leaned forward in his chair and glared at Sommers. "My job is to train their police and protect their workers so they can become independent when we leave."

"But what kind of world will you leave them?" Sommers asked, his gaze unwavering. "The United Nations EPA director said that dealing with the consequences of war will take generations and require extreme sensitivity to the country's diverse tribal cultures."

Dixon scoffed. "Most Afghans want to be pulled out of the Dark Ages, and the hill people won't survive without our help. They're ignorant farmers and goat-herders from a by-gone era who have no knowledge of the wealth that's beneath their feet."

"But of course, *you* do?"

"Damn right I do!" Dixon pounded his fist on the table. "And if we don't dig it up for them, the Chinese or Iranians or somebody else will—using the roads that Americans built, that my company defended, that my finest men died trying to protect."

"Then why did you pull out two years ago?" Sommers asked, his gaze fixed directly on Dixon. "Why did you let the bombing of one rural bridge end the progress the PRT had made?"

Dixon swallowed hard. He couldn't tell them the truth. He couldn't tell them that Cloud-Carson had uncovered much of what Dixon was planning in the Nuristan Province: bribing government officials, ignoring regulations set up by the Minister of Mines, and putting a bounty on Abdul Hazrat's head.

If Dixon could soil Cloud-Carson's reputation, attack him with subtle untruths, hint at drug use, cowardice, and consorting with the enemy. If he could manage to drag his character so low that not even his mother, if she were alive, would believe one word out of her son's mouth, then he'd be okay, no matter what the boy said. Lie. Repeat. Lie. Repeat. Like drops of water falling steadily on granite … eventually even the strongest of rocks would break.

Dixon ignored Sommers and looked directly at his superior. "You've heard the expression *one bad apple spoils the whole bunch*?"

Senator Richardson nodded.

"Well, we had one very bad apple who brought down our whole operation. We believe he cozied up to the enemy while he was alone in the hills of Afghanistan. There were reports he was into sex trafficking and drugs. The final nail was when he helped the Taliban blow our bridge in the Nuristan Mountains."

"Why wasn't I told about this earlier?"

"Because we don't have proof." Dixon chose his words carefully. "But when you hear something once, twice, three times, from many people, and you get an ultimatum from the Afghan government to remove that employee, well, I felt it was time to end our contract or the Afghans would pull it."

"Who was this bad apple, Drake?"

"Sam Cloud-Carson."

Both of Richardson's bushy eyebrows rose in shock. "The baseball player?"

"We couldn't prove that he was working with the Taliban," Dixon said. "But he couldn't prove that he wasn't. So we came to an agreement that, in the best interest of DiamondBar, Afghanistan, and the United States, we end his contract." Dixon let go a patronizing sigh. "Unfortunately, this young man may have some deep unresolved issues from his parents' deaths. I tried to get him help after he had a nervous breakdown in the field, but he refused. Still, I don't believe there's any ill will between us."

"You're a much more forgiving man than I would be," Richardson snarled. "The son of a bitch cost you millions."

"It's one of the unfortunate consequences of my business." Dixon waved his hand as though shooing flies. "I don't want to hurt the young man anymore. He's suffered enough."

As he raised his vision and glanced about the room, Dixon felt the intoxication of absolute power. He had everyone believing his lies. Even those who knew the truth. Why? Because people loved to see stars fall. It's why tabloids sold and social media ripped.

Sam Cloud-Carson was a shooting star. One that would burn bright for a flash, but would then be snuffed out without anyone remembering his name. He was the past. From an ancient world, long oppressed, ready and willing to accept its fate again.

There was no way the people in this room could withhold the sensational details he had given them. And when those droplets of disinformation began to leak to their friends and their friends and eventually flow into the public arena, Cloud-Carson's credibility would be as good as dead.

CHAPTER THIRTY-FIVE

Stilwell, Kansas

June 2013

Life in Stilwell settled into a cautious routine for Sydney. She would rise every morning at six, put the coffee on, go for a four-mile run, return to wake her husband, fix his breakfast, and wait for him to leave. She found that the less she said to Blake, the more likely he wouldn't torment her. Being with him was like stepping gingerly onto a newly frozen pond, testing every step to make sure the ice wouldn't snap.

Why did she have to be so careful with her words when talking to her husband? She felt numb with Blake. Empty. Lost. Alone. It was as if every feeling she had for him had drowned in her tears. She was done . . .

But, as her father had suggested, she had prayed on it. Prayed on the Bible passage that she and Blake had said on their wedding day. *So they are no longer two, but one flesh. Therefore what God has joined together, let no one separate.*

Yet reciting Mark 10:8–9 had done nothing to lift the weight of guilt from her mind as she waited for her husband to leave. She peeked through the blinds to make sure his car turned off their street, before sighing with deep relief. Then she too was gone … off to work at Mrs. Tomlinson's stables.

*   *   *

"Howdy, Sticks!" Sam called out from the courtyard as he shouldered a load of wooden planks to the barn. *Sticks* had become the pet name he'd given her because of the way her wiry legs stuck out from the overall jean shorts she always wore. "Ready to get some calluses on those soft schoolmarm hands of yours?"

She laughed. "I was working this land long before you got here, buddy boy."

"And then Mrs. T hired me to fix your mistakes?"

She snatched a hammer that was hanging from his belt and acted like she was going to hit him on the head with it. "Why don't we go inside and compare calluses?"

He continued into the barn, leaned the planks against a stall, and turned around to face her. He opened his hands, palms up. "Check 'em out, Coach."

She pursed her lips to keep from smiling and leaned forward, like Sherlock Holmes studying a crime scene.

"Is that one?" She pointed, then glanced up at him. "Or is that a blister from the curve you hung last night when Jenkins hit one into the fountains?"

He laughed out loud. "Good one! Ya got me. That ball took off like a rocket to the moon." He held up his hand for a high five. She slapped his palm hard, and then handed him the hammer.

It was odd, she thought. She had barely known Sam one month, yet he was already easier to talk to than her husband. There was no way she could have teased Blake about an athletic misfortune and received even a chuckle in return. He would have given her one of his stony glares, stewed about it for a while, and then said something hurtful when they were with family or friends.

Yet with Sam, there was a natural ease to their give and take, as if he not only enjoyed her razzing him but encouraged it … even when she needled him about giving up a homer that cost the Royals a game.

"Yo, Sticks, a little help?" Sam's voice jolted her out of her reflection.

He had already nailed one of the planks against a corner post.

"Lift your end so I can see if we're level."

He squeezed in next to her and hammered her end of the plank to the opposite post.

God, he smelled good. She caught her breath. What was wrong with her? *Stop it, brain, you're going to get me in trouble.*

Sam tapped the final nail in place and gave her a sidelong glance. "You okay?"

"Yeah," she blurted out, flabbergasted at the quickening of her pulse. "I—I was just wondering how you felt after giving up that home run. I mean, I can't sleep when my team loses. I constantly think about what I could have done to change the outcome."

"Well, it took me awhile"—Sam's voice was very casual—"but the baseball and I have come to an understanding that neither of us has any control of where it winds up once it leaves my hand."

She playfully smacked him on the arm.

"It's true." He shrugged. "I made a mistake. Was I bummed? Sure. But if I carry that mistake to the next pitch, it hurts the team."

He grabbed another plank and motioned for her to hold her end up so he could hammer a nail in place.

"We humans hold on to so much of the past." He tapped the head of the nail to get it started. "I have trouble letting go of old hurts in my everyday life, but I've learned that the only way to succeed in baseball is to treat the past like a homer I give up." He slammed the hammer down on the nail, driving it flush to the wood. "The past is outta here!"

She handed him another nail. "But as a competitive person, that's not easy."

"Not for the ego, but I chose to play for a team. Once I made that choice, I had to train my mind to leave my ego in the clubhouse and do whatever I could to help the team win." He placed the nail against the board and, in another savage blast, pounded it in place. "The ego wants you to go for the strikeout. The ego wants revenge. The ego is always selfish."

"Did you always have this kind of discipline?"

"No, I was the kid in high school who cussed at the umps, froze out my teammates, and got technicals for kicking basketballs into the stands when I felt wronged."

"What changed you?"

"Life."

"That's rather vague?"

He opened his hand for another nail. She gave him two.

"I gave up a home run that cost my high school the Colorado State Championship."

"Really?"

He nodded. "I was devastated. Moped around our house for days. About a week later, my sick little sister, her body ravaged by kidney disease, asked me to go outside and play catch."

The side of his mouth curled into a slight smile at the memory. "She duct-taped two baseballs together, handed them to me, and walked back about twenty feet. She called out in her squeaky little voice, *'Throw me a strike, Sammy, c'mon!'* I gave her some dumbfounded look and told her that I couldn't throw a baseball that was taped to another one. Jenny pounded her fist in her glove and said, *'Of course you can't, stupid. So why don't you let go of that darn homer that you've been carrying around the last week.'*"

They both laughed, and then Sydney said, "That was it? Jenny's little teaching moment changed you?"

He exhaled and his face changed. Gone was the look of amusement. In its place was one distant with some old sorrow.

"Losing Jenny, losing my mom and dad, Afghanistan, Nicaragua—they all changed me."

Without thinking, she placed her hand on his, hoping her touch might soothe whatever thoughts troubled him. He had shared much of his life with her this past week: a loving family, supportive friends, hiking Pargin Mountain, his college girlfriend, and curveballs hung and driven far into the Colorado sky. Her hand on his must have worked because his smile returned.

"I've become pretty good at compartmentalizing. I give myself five minutes to cool off at the end of the game, visit with the media, my pitching coach, and teammates, and then I say one of Jenny's favorite quotes when I leave the clubhouse."

She removed her hand but held his gaze, waiting for him to finish.

"Let go. Let God."

*　　*　　*

They finished the stall in casual conversation, a request for another nail or a call to raise or lower a plank the only words from Sam. But Sydney wanted to know more, and as they walked outside, she asked, "What church do you belong to?"

He opened his arms to the canopy of trees that surrounded them. "This is my church. This is where I feel closest to the Great Spirit."

"Great Spirit?" She searched for the right words. "So you're not Christian?"

"Maybe I'm the oldest kind." He laughed. "As Jenny used to say, *'God? Wakan Tanka? Allah? Buddha? Great Spirit? I don't care what His name is. I just know He's good.'*"

"Yes, but"—she took a deep breath—"I was taught that Christianity is the one true religion."

He pointed to the forest. "How do you to get to the river?"

She gave a confused look.

"Which way to the river, Sticks?"

"There are several paths we can take."

"Exactly. We can take the path next to the corral, or the one behind the barn, or that deer trail, or the two from my cottage, but they all lead to the river—to the source of life. Is one path to the river better than the other?"

"That's not the same thing."

"I saw plenty of suffering and despair in Afghanistan. Much of it caused by religion. But I also met many people of true faith and service." He stopped and stared out at the horizon, his eyes remote with memory. "One of those people was a guy named Whiplash McCracken. He ran a mission called the Friends of Everyone Hotel. Even though Whip's a

Christian minister, he wouldn't let anyone proselytize their faith. Why? Because it was dangerous. He said religion was Afghanistan's land mine. Whoever spoke up, blew up."

It was the first time Sam had revealed anything about his experiences in Afghanistan, so Sydney didn't want to interrupt him. From his tone, this was something very important to him.

"Afghanistan's a country that's been invaded by everyone," Sam said. "The Brits, the Russians, the Americans, the fundamentalists, the not-so-fundamentalists. They all came to *civilize* the country as they bombed the villages and destroyed the land." He shook his head sadly. "Whip only came to help. He took in families displaced by the war, fed them, clothed them, and organized sports programs to give kids something to smile about. Then he, too, was kicked out."

"Why?"

"Because some volunteer forgot to take off her cross necklace when she was at a local market. The Taliban found out and bombed the mission."

Sydney inhaled a startled gasp.

"Thankfully, no one was killed, but the message was delivered. Don't bring your religion to our country."

"That's awful," she said. "No Christian would ever do that."

Sam turned to face her, and the darkness in his eyes made her pause.

"You're a history teacher, Sydney. No religion is perfect. They've all done something they're not proud of."

She didn't respond.

"Come with me," he motioned and then disappeared into the forest.

She followed him down a horse trail, ducking underneath branches of sycamore and willows, thankful for the horseshoes that had driven down the brome grasses, thorny bushes, and poison ivy that lay in their path. A flock of jays screeched at their intrusion, and the sound of some random animal skittering away made her pick up her pace. Sam moved as silently as a big cat, not even his sandals curling up against the soles of his feet made any sound.

He stopped suddenly and pulled back a low branch to let her pass. There it was. The Blue River. It wasn't much. A small, slow-moving brown stretch of water snaking its way north some forty miles before it emptied into the Missouri River.

Sam pointed down to a split heart-shaped track. "White-tail deer. Their tracks symbolize well-being, prosperity, and safety to all who see them."

She didn't know what to say other than, "Cool."

"Water is the source of all life," Sam said. "It serves everyone. Deer, rabbit, squirrel, fish, turtle, birds, raccoon, fox … they all come to quench their thirst in this water, and none of them fight over it."

She narrowed her eyes, still unsure of where he was going.

"Rivers flow by small towns and big cities, farmlands and wild, Christians and Jews and Muslims, believers and nonbelievers, always serving, never discriminating, patiently waiting for us to understand."

"Understand what?"

"That we're all one. Even the word *religion* means to tie together. Yet we've used it to separate, to fight, even to kill." He picked up a rock and leaf from the ground and tossed both in the water. "We can either hold onto our old ways and sink like that rock to the bottom, with the mud and silt and decaying past, or be light like the leaf, surrender to Spirit, and float along peacefully, joining with others who understand the way."

"What is the way?"

"Love."

He slipped off his sandals and stepped in, letting the water ripple over his toes and the tops of his feet. "I think this river is like God's love. Always flowing, always available … to everyone. But you can't feel Love's presence unless you let go and get in."

"It sounds like you've made up your own religion."

"Maybe I have." He smiled and reached for her.

She took his hand, kicked off her flip-flops, and stepped in. "It's cold."

"It's always a shock to the system when you make a change, Syd. I'm not antireligion. I'm just pro-love—a guy trying to find the universal wisdom that's in all faiths. Y'know, kindness, charity, teamwork, forgiveness, open-mindedness, gratitude. I found those qualities in our Ute ceremonies, in a Muslim village in the Nuristan Mountains, at the Friends of Everyone Hotel, at the Estevez Orphanage, and now in the fellowship with our Royals."

There was an awkward moment as they held hands, a dozen different emotions flying through both her mind and body, most of them conflicting. The biggest question was what was she doing alone in the woods, holding hands with a man other than her husband? And why didn't she want to let go?

She tried to think of something else, anything else but Sam. She directed her attention to the sounds of the river, cicadas buzzing, frogs calling from the marsh grass, and birds singing in the trees. Nothing worked. She glanced up at him, her eyes latching onto his gaze for a beat too long. Goose bumps zipped up her arms.

"Thanks for listening to me," he said. "There aren't many people I'd speak so freely with about how I believe. For some reason, it's easy to share it with you."

She hadn't been expecting that. Her mouth opened, but no sound came out. His declaration struck with particular impact, and she looked at him, unsure of how to respond.

"I hope what I said doesn't make you feel uncomfortable, Sydney."

"No—no—" she stuttered. "Of course not."

The truth was his statement made her feel great. Because he meant it. Every word of it. Sam's words were direct, sincere, and honest. There was no pretense, no attempt to impress her, no hidden agenda. She thought back to how they met—the way he took her barbs without defending himself, the delight he displayed after pranking her at the ballpark, and the light-hearted banter he had with the children when they went on a trail ride. He was indeed a man any woman would desire.

"Shall we head back?" he asked.

"Wh-what? Stunned, she gaped at him for a moment, then dropped his hand, and practically ran out of the water.

"Are you all right?"

"I'm fine. I—I think I stepped on a snail."

He chuckled, following her onto the bank. "Yeah, they're pretty ornery in this part of the river."

She could feel her ears burn with embarrassment. *I stepped on a snail? Really? That was a dumb thing to say.* She had to do something, say something, anything to distract him from her awkwardness.

"Tell me about, um, your friends growing up?"

He knelt down to help her put on her sandals.

"I've known Jose and Teresa my entire life." She felt her knees quiver when he cupped his hand around her heel and threaded a sandal between her toes. "They're visiting next month. I'd like you to meet them."

"Sure," was all she could think to say as he stood up and smiled at her.

"Ready to go?"

Completely flustered, she needed to keep him talking. "Didn't you play baseball with Jose in college?"

"He was my catcher in Little League, high school, and college—kind of a brother-slash-psychiatrist whenever I'd have a meltdown on the mound."

"You"—she stared at him for a moment, recovering slightly—"would get upset while pitching? That's hard to believe watching the calm, cool guy we see on TV."

"Experiential maturity." He grinned. "This world can either break you or make you. It wasn't until I finally stopped trying to control everything that my life began to improve."

His comment had her thinking about her own soccer team. Young girls, arriving at their first high school practice as shy, uncertain freshmen, would become confident, vocal leaders as seniors.

"What did Jose teach you?"

"That only when I learned to accept losing without being defeated would I become the player that I wanted to be."

"Wow, that's very good advice."

He absently slipped on his own sandals. "The Indian way came naturally to Jose. He lives by a moral code of kindness, respect, and harmony for everyone and everything."

"Sounds like you could be talking about yourself."

He turned to face her. "Thank you, Sydney. Being compared to Jose is the best compliment you could ever give me."

She blushed, liking that she had made him feel good. She wanted to know more. Who else besides his family had molded Sam into the man she knew today?

"What about your friends in Afghanistan and Nicaragua?"

"Bette's son, Colonel Tomlinson, Whiplash and his wife, Hunoon. Great people."

As they started back to the barn, Sydney was finally beginning to feel at ease again. This was nice. Innocent. Sweet. Unthreatening.

"How about now?" she asked. "Best buds on the Royals?"

"I don't think I have a *best* friend on the team," he said matter-of-factly. "I like 'em all the same. But if you were to ask me who was my *best* friend in KC"—he playfully nudged her in the side—"I'd have to say you."

The goose bumps returned.

CHAPTER THIRTY-SIX

Kansas City, Missouri

July 2013

Friday night at Kauffman Stadium. Game one of a three-game series with Minnesota. Ten o'clock and the temperature was still a stifling ninety-one degrees. The Royals led 3–2 with two on and two out in the bottom of the ninth. Postgame fireworks ready to blast. It was the Royals' tenth game in ten days. The team was exhausted, and the bullpen was shot. Both eighth-inning specialist Miguel Guerrero and closer Kevin Andrews were unavailable, having pitched each of the last three games.

As twenty-eight thousand, three hundred and forty-five fans rose up out of their seats, stomping and cheering for the final out, Sam peeked over his shoulder at the bullpen. Rookie Eduardo Alvarez was ready to go if he couldn't finish. After every inning from the sixth on, he'd told his pitching coach he felt great. No problem. Plenty left in the tank. Loved it hot and humid. Hum, baby. After 118 pitches, he needed one more out.

He took his cap off, wiped the sweat that was pouring down his face with his left sleeve, and planted his right foot against the pitching rubber.

Deep inhale through the nose. Slow exhale out the mouth. Come set. Windup, delivery.

Ball one.

Same sequence.

Ball two.

"Time!" Andy Phillips called out from the dugout and jogged to the mound.

Sam actually welcomed the break to catch his breath.

"Be honest with me." Phillips demanded.

Sam peeked again at the bullpen. "Alvarado's only been up one week. You can't bring him into this situation."

Phillips snorted back a laugh. "Said the guy with two months in the Big Leagues." He turned to their catcher. "What do you think, Tony?"

Ramirez glanced from Phillips to the bullpen and back again. "His velo's down, not much movement, falling behind in the count, runnin' out of gas"–he winked at Sam–"but he's still the badass I want on the mound."

His catcher's words seemed to give Sam a new resolve as he covered his mouth with his glove and said, "I can still locate my two-seamer. Let's go low and away."

Phillips put one hand on Sam's shoulder and looked him in the eyes. "Finish it, kid."

Instinctively, Sam's mind went back to work for him. As he stared in to get the sign from Ramirez, a thought occurred to him. The Twins' hitter probably knew what was coming.

Knew it would likely be his best pitch. Sinker, low and away. But the batter didn't know the guts behind this pitch, nor the trust Sam had in his teammates. If he did, he'd call time. Sam smiled, despite himself, wound up, and let the ball fly, low and away, with absolutely nothing on it. Eighty-seven miles an hour at best, screaming *hit me*.

The Twins' hitter laced a one-hop smash up the middle. Shortstop Hernandez dove to his left, knocked the ball down, grabbed it with his bare hand, and back-hand flipped it to second for the final out. Game over. Incredible. Kauffman Stadium exploded.

As Ramirez ran to the mound to congratulate him, Sam looked up at the sky and let loose a primal scream that sounded like a wolf howling at the moon.

Ramirez laughed, released his own bark, and then pointed at Sam. "You one lucky badass!"

"Yes, I am!" Sam laughed, then let go another howl.

*   *   *

Back in the clubhouse, reliever Willie Kahal cranked up the stereo and demanded his teammates join him in a victory line dance as he belted out, "*Time to … get with the dogs … get with the dogs … get with the dogs . . . Yeah, yeah, yeah.*"

Sam sat by his locker, peeling off his sweat-drenched uniform top, one eye watching the frivolity, hoping it would end before Kahal reached him. Being on the mound with the game on the line in the ninth was one thing, but being forced to dance while your veteran teammates hooted with laughter? No thanks.

The music snapped silent, and Sam looked over to see Kevin Cimoli by the stereo, grinning at him.

"Hey, rook!" he shouted. "What the heck was that howl at the end of the game all about?"

Sam's ears burned red as all eyes turned his way. Even his coaches and their manager, Charles, came out of their offices to hear his answer.

"It was a wolf howl," he muttered.

"Stand up, dude!" Cimoli demanded. "It's story time."

Very reluctantly, Sam stood up. "Well, wolves are all about family. They run in tight packs and protect each other. Their howl is the way they communicate from long distances to strengthen their bond and let each member of their pack know that I got your back."

Cimoli's dark brows rose slightly. "That's some awesome shit, Sammy." He then opened his arms to the entire clubhouse and roared, "Bring it in, boys! We're now the Royal Wolves of KC!" The entire clubhouse let loose howls that could be heard all the way up to the Diamond Club.

*　　*　　*

Honesty inspires peacefulness.

Jenny's Journal of Inspiration, page 97

Sam's eyes slowly opened from his morning meditation, and he smiled back at who was staring at him from outside his screened-in porch. It was Mrs. Tomlinson's three-year old mutt, Barney, waiting for his new friend to give him a treat and a scratch behind his ears. Bette had adopted the dog two weeks before, and after sniffing around his new property, he had found a kindred spirit in the cottage by the river. Sam rose up and so did Barney, wagging his tail joyfully as the screen door opened and the dog hurried in.

"Let me see what I have for you, kid." Sam opened his refrigerator. "Hey, we're in luck. Two hard-boiled eggs left. Ya want one?"

Barney sat patiently, eyes glued to his prize, mouth open, tongue hanging out in anticipation.

They ate on the porch. Sam scratched Barney's ears, and then together they headed to the stables to prep the horses for the Urban Wildlife Academy.

*　　*　　*

It was past nine thirty. Sam was understandably late. He had even texted them to say that he was going to try and sleep in after pitching the previous night. Mary Beth watched Sydney scramble to get everything finished before he arrived. It was nice to see her rally from her earlier despair. When she had picked up Sydney that morning, she was near tears, shaking with anger, and of course, she didn't want to talk about it.

But now, it was as if someone had switched on a bright light in a dark room. The old Sydney was back. The one she'd known since kindergarten. The All-Star soccer player. Competitive. Funny. Happy. Compassionate. Loyal ... to a fault.

"Okay, here he comes," whispered Sydney as she tightened the last cinch and motioned for Mary Beth to hide with her behind the mounting block. "You ready?"

Mary Beth rolled her eyes. "Whatever."

They both cupped their hands to their mouth and let go their best wolf howl. *"Ow, ow, ow, owooooo! Ow, ow, ow owooooo!"*

Barney bolted behind Sam, who suppressed a grin. "I guess you saw the end of the game?"

"Your *Call of the Wild* is everywhere." Sydney stepped out from behind her cover. "They've been replaying it on ESPN, MLB, local news. It's had over a hundred thousand hits on YouTube."

"No way."

"Yes way. They say it's the new Royals battle cry."

Sam closed the corral gate and walked over. "Well, okay, as long as we win."

Sydney raised her hand for a high five. "Nice CG."

He smacked her palm. "Thanks."

"CG?" Mary Beth asked.

"Complete game," Sam explained. "Sydney's decoded every single baseball initial. CG. ERA. OPS. ASSQ."

Sydney cocked her head. "ASSQ?"

"Another Stupid Sydney Question."

She threw one of her riding gloves at him. He caught it with one hand and gave it to Barney, who scurried away to the corner of the corral to chew on his new toy.

"Sam! That's my new glove."

"Well, maybe you shouldn't be using them as weapons, eh, Sticks?"

Mary Beth took a step back to study this silly banter between her best friend and the Royals star. While she hadn't been to the stables in more than a week, she knew that Sydney had been coming almost every day. Part of her was happy to see her friend's newfound joy, but another part was afraid for her. Sydney had been through so much over the past two years: two miscarriages, the diagnosis that she wouldn't be able to have children, and an abusive husband. She was at a vulnerable time and, like a moth lured by a flame, she could be drawn to any extension of kindness. And Sam was kind. But he was also a man.

Mary Beth cleared her throat. "Hey, Sam, why do you call Sydney Sticks?"

He gave her a lifted brow. "C'mon, MB. Look at her. Skinny legs sticking out of those antique overall shorts she wears all the time." He turned back to Sydney. "I didn't know Goodwill had your size?"

Sydney punched him in the right arm. "I'll have you know, EssCee, that these sticks will run circles around you on the soccer field."

He shook his head. "Strawberry milkshake says you can't get three out of five shots past me."

"You're on."

"Ooo, I'm scared."

She punched him again.

"That's my pitching arm, Sticks. What'll I tell the press if I go on the DL?"

"That a *girl* hurt you."

He gave her a playful shove and then walked over and removed her riding glove from Barney's mouth.

Mary Beth blinked twice, wondering if she should talk with Sydney about her behavior. Because there was no doubt about it. Sydney was flirting … and Sam was enjoying it.

*   *   *

Two honks from a yellow bus coming down the drive announced the arrival of the Urban Wildlife Academy, and Sydney spun around to Mary Beth. "You get the kids! Sam and I will get the riding helmets."

Sam was already striding toward the barn, boasting a wry smile as he looked over his shoulder. "Last one to the tack room has to clean the cobwebs out of the barn."

"No head starts!" Sydney bolted after him, catching him at the main gate, giggling as she nudged him to the side. They arrived at the tack room at the same time and lunged for the saddle rack. Sydney reached it first, and the sleeve of her T-shirt slid up her right upper arm, revealing black, blue, and yellow marks just above her bicep.

All the color drained from Sam's face as he stared at her arm, and without thinking, he put his hand on her bruise.

"It—it's nothing." She jerked away and pulled her sleeve down.

He raised his vision from her arm to her eyes. There was sadness in them that made her go cold, and she turned away to gather the children's riding helmets and to escape Sam's grim silence.

"It's none of your business, Sam."

His head snapped up. "It isn't?"

"No."

"What kind of friend am I if I don't make it my business?"

She removed the last of the helmets from the wall and sighed. "You said last week that I was your best friend in KC. If that's true, I'd appreciate you not saying anything."

"Really? That's what you want from a friend?"

"Yes."

"Those aren't friends, Sydney. They're enablers. People who stay silent when a husband abuses a wife."

She threw the helmets at him. He did nothing to defend himself, letting them ricochet off his body and fall to the floor.

She glared at him, panting with emotion, as he quietly knelt down to pick up each helmet. When he stood up, his gaze swept past her, to who was watching from the shadows of the barn.

Mary Beth and Bette Tomlinson.

*   *   *

Thirty-one hours later, Sam was on the Royals' charter, listening to the jet engines whine as the team was buckling in to leave for a four-game series in Houston. His feelings were in complete turmoil as he thought about Saturday. Another person he cared about had been hurt, and he'd done nothing. Instead, he had fought with a friend.

Was that all Sydney was to him? A friend? No question, he enjoyed her company. They had a lot in common. Sports. Nature. Inspiring conversations. He liked the way he could make her forget about her troubles and get her to smile, that cute little curve that started on the left side of her face and widened into absolute joy.

He'd gone out a few times in Nicaragua with sisters of teammates or girls who worked the Estevez Casino, but none had lasted more than a few weeks. He liked Sydney. Liked that when he teased her, she teased him back; liked when he asked her opinion on a subject, she didn't hold back. He liked her spirit, her stupid humor, and he liked her looks … but she was married. Married to a jerk who had physically abused her. And he was unable to do anything to protect her.

Mary Beth and Bette had seen their argument in the tack room, and he hoped they had talked with her about Blake's abuse. He had texted MB, but she had yet to reply.

Now, as he sat in the back row of the plane, his mind was filled with images of Sydney storming out of the tack room in anger. He had gone to his cottage to cool off and had been on his way back to apologize when his phone *pinged*, a reminder from the Royals' community relations department on where to meet at the children's hospital in one hour.

Scramble mode. Shower, shave, dress, visit kids, ballpark, workout, game, come home and pack for the road trip, sleep, six a.m. wake-up, quick clean/water/feed horses, shower, dress, get to the ballpark by nine thirty, workout, game, bus to the airport.

He had hoped to see Sydney at the stables, but it was Sunday, and Sundays were dedicated to church in the Morgan family. He wondered if Blake had gone with her.

As the plane taxied down the runway, he stared out the window, watching the buildings and trees and cars and roads all blur together into one. He glanced down at his phone again and saw that he still had a signal. He scrolled to Sydney's number and typed *I'm sorry.*

*   *   *

The Royals' charter touched down in Houston at seven thirty, and Sam's phone *pinged* that he received a text. It wasn't from Sydney.

MB here. Call me ASAP. Don't text Sydney.

He wanted to call her immediately but not like this. Not with fifty other men around as he cupped his hand over a mouthpiece and whispered into the phone. He'd wait until he was alone in his hotel room.

*   *   *

"You coming with us, EssCee?" Cimoli called out from down the hall.

Sam fumbled with his room key card again, dropping it on the floor for the second time. "Can't tonight. Gotta make an important call."

"C'mon, man, you never go out. I'm buying the first round."

He swiped his card to unlock the door and turned back to Cimoli. "Text me where you guys are, and I'll try and catch up."

"Yeah, right, that's what you always say—" were the last words he heard as he closed the door, sat down on his bed, and called Mary Beth.

She answered on the second ring. "Hey Sam."

"Hey, MB, what's going on?"

He heard her exhale. "I didn't know all that Sydney was going through until I overheard your conversation yesterday."

"Yeah, she was pretty mad at me."

"She's not mad at you, Sam. She's mad at herself for letting it go this long ... and for not telling me about Blake's abuse."

"What happened?"

"He blew up when she told him that she had talked with their priest. Blake said their marriage was nobody's business, and when she tried to explain, he shoved her up against the refrigerator. When she tried to get away, he grabbed her and dragged her to the bedroom. That's why the bruise on her arm."

Sam didn't respond, just sat frozen, numbly listening as Mary Beth went on.

"Fortunately, that's when I arrived, or it could have been worse. I knocked several times before the door finally opened. Blake put on his old charm, but I knew … I knew they'd been fighting. She finally told me what happened after you challenged her."

He closed his eyes and pinched the bridge of his nose. His mind went back to Pargin Mountain, to the day Rob Marcus climbed on top of Teresa Songbird. It went to Afghanistan, to the Taliban warlord about to rape a thirteen-year-old village girl. Haunting images of terrified eyes, pleading for the men to stop, and then those visions blurred into Sydney's frightened face. Beautiful Sydney. Innocent Sydney. Victim Sydney.

"Where is she now?"

There was a pause before Mary Beth answered. "She's at home. I stayed with her for a few hours, then had to go and take care of my own family."

"Is Blake with her?"

"He is now. But he came home late and went straight to their bedroom and closed the door."

"We have to do something, MB."

"Stay out of it, Sam. Don't you dare call or text her. Blake's turned into a control freak. He's taken over their finances, opens her mail, and checks her emails. I told her to delete any old texts from you. She said she already did."

At this, the color left his face, and he gripped his phone tighter. This was killing him. Someone he cared about needed help, and he couldn't do anything?

"Sydney needs help," he said in a low but firm voice. "She's a prisoner in her own home. There has to be a hotline or someone she can talk to."

"She's going to meet with Father John tomorrow, but you need to know something, Sam. Sydney's one of the most competitive people I know. She studied her butt off to get good grades in school. No opponent outworked her on the soccer field as a player or a coach. Losing crushes her. Sydney probably thinks she can fix her marriage by simply working harder, being a better wife, being more understanding—"

"Love isn't a competition, MB."

"I know that, Sam … and that's why I'm asking you to be careful."

CHAPTER THIRTY-SEVEN

Stilwell, Kansas

July 2013

The sun broke through the tops of the cottonwoods as Sam released the last of the quarter horses into the pasture west of the barn. All eight stayed close, quietly munching on the brome grasses that grew near the fence. He glanced up the drive, hoping to catch sight of Sydney's car. He found nothing but an empty dirt road. She would have been here by now. Yesterday's text from Mary Beth informed him that Sydney had not any more trouble with Blake and that she had come to the stables every morning to help Mrs. Tomlinson. But not today. Not with the Royals back in town for the final series before the four-day All-Star break. And he couldn't shake the foreboding sense that he was the reason she hadn't come.

The thought troubled him. The last thing he wanted to do was hurt Sydney. She was wounded already. He saw it the first day they had met. The sadness in her eyes. The struggle to keep from crying in front of a stranger. But then, as they got to know each other, Sydney's true personality opened like a morning glory greeting the sun on a bright Kansas day. He thought of her embarrassed smile after she discovered who he really was, her laughter on the trail ride when the kids teased him, and the look on her face when he told her that she was his best friend in KC.

He glanced one more time at the road and then down at his phone. Eleven o'clock. Time to go. Hospital visit in one hour. Sydney would have to wait.

Saturday was the same. Working alone in the stables. And, with Mary Beth and her family leaving that morning for their summer vacation to New Mexico, there was no way he was going to bother them to check on Sydney. Instead, he finished his chores, went back to his cottage, and showered and dressed for an autograph session at a local sporting-goods store.

As he started to leave, he stopped next to the kitchen table, where his sister's journal lay open from his morning meditation. Right now, he couldn't remember what her message was about. Something about the end of dreams, about waking up and realizing your connection to Spirit.

He touched the book, his fingertips drumming against the old worn pages, wondering what inspiration Jenny might have for him. He flipped the book open to a random page and read:

The Creator gives his hardest battles to his bravest warriors.

*   *   *

Sydney sat on the edge of the bed, picked up her phone, and began to type in Sam's number. She hadn't dared put his name or number in her contacts, and she'd deleted all their previous text conversations as soon as they ended. Blake knew all of her passwords and likely checked her messages when she stepped away from her phone for even the shortest of times. His increased alcohol and pain-medication use had led to greater paranoia and irrational behavior.

Was it her fault? Was she the reason for his continued struggle? She wanted to save her marriage and had dedicated this week to simply loving her husband. But each day was like a microcosm of their marriage. The mornings would begin quietly; she, waking up early, putting the coffee on, going for a half-hour run, and timing her return exactly when his alarm sounded at seven thirty. She would fix his breakfast, place the newspaper next to his placemat, and wait for him to join her. Invariably, she would make a mistake; it might be that the coffee was too cold or why were they out of cereal, but he would find something to pick on her about. From there, the comments would become hurtful, and if she asked him to stop, he'd say she couldn't take a joke. Either way, she was wrong, put on the defensive, and her confidence would erode. One of the questions he had recently asked gnawed at her.

Do you think that you'll ever become submissive to me?

When she answered, *No, never,* he replied, *Yes, you will. You're part Injun. They're a submissive culture … and you're a woman.*

She heard the sound of water being shut off, signaling the end of Blake's shower, and she quickly erased her message to Sam. It was Sunday. He would be pitching today. She just wanted to thank him for texting his apology earlier in the week and wish him luck on his last start before the All-Star break. Not now. As she watched Blake step away from the shower and begin to towel off, she put her phone on the nightstand and asked, "Are you going to church with me?"

Blake stopped and slowly turned to face her, his eyes darkening with contempt. "Really?" He shook his head. "Do you expect me to go to church after you whined to Father John about your problems?"

"My problems?" she said defensively. "They're *our* problems."

"Bullshit. Every marriage has trouble, but they don't announce it to the whole damn world." He walked toward her, towel on his shoulder, and she leaned back to get away from his nakedness. "Why don't you fix yourself? You're like some psycho, crazy-ass bitch who's trying to ruin my life."

"I am not. I'm trying to help us—"

"Shut the fuck up!" He threw the towel in her face. "Go to church by yourself. I'm going to Eddie's to watch the ballgame." He yanked his jeans off the back of the closet door and turned back to her. "At least Eddie won't bellyache every time I drink a beer."

*   *   *

It wasn't a good day. She spilled coffee on the yellow sundress she was wearing to church, drove over a nail while backing out of the garage, and then had to stop by the tire store to get it fixed. She was a half hour late to mass, and her parents wanted to know why Blake wasn't with her.

Gritting her teeth, she whispered, "Not now."

When the service ended, her dad insisted she join them for brunch, and then both her parents bombarded her with questions. *How was she was doing? Was there anything they could do? Did Father John's words help?* And, of course, they said would pray for her marriage.

She left at one thirty and drove to Antioch Park. She walked around the lake, then got back in her car and turned on the radio. How were the Royals doing? Or, more precisely, how was their starting pitcher doing?

"Cloud-Carson is on today," said the broadcaster. "After giving up a second-inning homer to Vilorio, he's retired twelve of thirteen to take a 5-2 lead to the seventh inning."

"C'mon, Sam," she whispered. "Keep throwing strikes. Your team needs you."

"First pitch of the seventh ... strike one, outside corner. That's been his safe place all game long. Low, outside corner."

We all need a safe place, she thought. Over the last six weeks, her safe place had been at the stables with Sam. He was kind, thoughtful, mature, responsible ... but he was also handsome and single. The latter two characteristics made him dangerous.

There had to be a myriad of women after a guy like Sam. A pang of jealousy shot up her spine. She glanced at herself in the rearview mirror, and her right hand immediately went to her upper lip, to her cleft, the imperfection that always drew her first gaze.

Oh well. She may not be perfect, but she didn't want to lose Sam's friendship. It was time to get back to fixing her marriage. She'd find Blake and apologize.

*   *   *

Eddie McGee lived in Westport. He was a childhood friend of Blake's, and much like his high school football teammate, Eddie loved to party. A full-time job was too restrictive, so working part-time in construction and bartending at Kelly's was a perfect fit. He rented a first-floor, two-bedroom, one-bath split-level rundown house. Sydney had only been there twice, and the way Eddie cleaned the place, she had no interest in returning.

The eighth inning had just ended when Sydney parked her car in front of Eddie's. Sam was no longer pitching, but the Royals' bullpen was more than good enough to protect the now 6–2 lead.

As she walked up the fractured cement and brick path, pushing aside overgrown tree limbs and weeds, she glanced through the screen door and saw the silhouette of a couple sitting on the couch, watching television. The man had his arm around the woman.

Sydney took two more steps and stopped dead in her tracks. Later, she would recall the difficulty she had breathing as she watched her husband pull the woman closer for a kiss.

Sydney stood frozen, uncertain what to do. Then the competitive spirit that had always been part of her DNA exploded as she shoved the door open.

"So this is why you wouldn't go to church with me!"

Blake jerked his arm away from the woman so quickly that his wristwatch caught in her tangled dishwater-blonde hair, prompting a painful shriek from the woman.

A red-faced Blake stood up in an effort to block Sydney from seeing what was on the coffee table.

"I already saw the cocaine," she said angrily. "Adultery and drugs. What an appealing husband you've become."

He raised both hands to calm her, and then forced a sweet smile. "Now, Sydney, this isn't what you think."

"Don't pull your Prince Charming crap on me. You're nothing but a damn liar. I want you out of the house tonight—out of my life! Just—just get out."

She could see indecision flicker momentarily on his face as he chose his next move. Finally, he simply gave her a smug look and stepped toward her. "I don't think so, babe. I'm the husband. The house is in my name, and all finances are in my name. You are shit out of luck without me."

She swallowed hard and braced herself, desperately trying to keep him from seeing her hands shaking.

Her effort failed as Blake's condescending arrogance returned. "Everything's gonna be all right, baby. This is just a little hiccup. Why don't you go on home and wait for me?"

As he reached for her, Sydney bolted out the door and ran to her car. Her last memory was of her husband standing on the porch, arms crossed over his chest, watching her drive away.

*   *   *

Get home. Pack a bag. Get away. Sydney wiped the tears from her cheeks as she sped south, trying to distance herself from Blake as quickly as she could. *Fix this. You're a coach. You can do this.*

She checked the rearview mirror. No Blake. Thank God. The last thing she wanted to do was see him tonight. She thought about calling Mary Beth, but she didn't want to interfere with their vacation, and there was no way she was going to call her parents. They'd put her in a full-court press of pity and sorrow. Her mom was oblivious to Blake's gaslighting, and her father believed any marital trouble could be resolved by simply applying certain scripture to equal challenge. *Maybe in time, Dad, but not right now.*

She needed a distraction, anything to take her away from thinking about her troubles. She snapped on the radio. The Royals had won, and the postgame host was playing sound bites from earlier interviews of stars of the game. First, Kevin Cimoli, who'd hit his fifteenth home run, then Terry Ayers, who'd driven in two runs, and then winning pitcher, Sam Cloud-Carson.

"I just followed Andy's game plan and trusted our defense. Blackwell made two awesome plays at third, Hawkins robbed Schmidt in right-center, and Enrique and Terry bailed me out with three great double plays."

"What are your plans for the four-day All-Star break?" the reporter asked. "Are you going home to Colorado?"

"No, I'll be resting up for our second-half sprint to catch the Tigers."

The reporter chuckled. "Seven games back at the break, Sam, do you really think you can catch the four-time defending Central champs?"

"Absolutely," answered Sam. "I know I'm just a rookie and should keep my mouth shut, but I believe in this team. We're good. We care about each other. We'll give the Tigers a run."

The rest of Sydney's drive home was a conversation with herself. Should she call another friend? Should she be alone? Should she call Sam? He and MB were the only ones who truly knew what she was going through, and Sam always made her look at the world differently, as though through some spiritual prism, comparing baseball to tracking or the river to God. He was different. And he had also said that she was his best friend in Kansas City.

*   *   *

It took her barely ten minutes to pack a bag and leave home. She was constantly looking over her shoulder to make sure Blake wasn't following. She breathed a sigh of relief when she turned into the Blue Valley High parking lot, still unsure of what to do, what hotel to check into, and how far away.

Head confused, heart beating too fast, Sydney stared at the phone in her lap. She dialed his number and felt a flutter of panic stir up her spine as she listened to each ring. Just before she was about to hang up, she heard Sam's jovial voice boom out, "Hey, Sticks, waddup?"

Her mouth opened, but no sound came out. She found herself fighting for the right words to explain what had happened.

"Sydney?" he asked again. "Sydney, are you okay?"

The entirety of the day welled up inside her and came spilling out like a dam finally breaking loose from a swollen river. "I found Blake with another woman. … I don't know what to do. I don't know where to go."

"I'm so sorry," he said, and then offered what she'd hoped he would. "I'm almost home if you want to come over and talk about it."

"Yes." She paused to collect herself. "I'd like that very much."

*   *   *

Both Sam and Barney were waiting outside when Sydney drove down the lane to his cottage. Sam was in his usual attire: flip-flops, old faded jeans, and a comfortable white T-shirt with a backpack slung over his right shoulder. He said nothing as he opened her door and offered a hand. As she looked up into brown eyes soft with understanding, her tears started again, and for the first time in their friendship, he hugged her, wrapping his arms around her, drawing her close, and letting her cry.

It felt good, natural, comfortable. No—more than comfortable, as though she fit perfectly in his embrace.

When they finally separated, Sam gave her one of his heartfelt smiles and said, "Let's go for a walk."

It was a typical July Kansas evening. Hot, humid, the buzz of cicadas ruling the night. As she walked beside him, she was acutely aware of his silence, his eyes focused, his footsteps soundless on the forest floor. She wondered what he was thinking, but he remained quiet until they curled around a stand of willows to the banks of the Blue River.

"I come here in the mornings to meditate," he said and then motioned for her to sit on the trunk of a fallen elm some ten feet from the water's edge.

"It's peaceful," she whispered.

Sam slipped the backpack off his shoulder and drew out a candle and a box of matches. "It's a lot more peaceful with a citronella candle keeping the mosquitos away."

She smiled a little, but said nothing, unsure of where to begin.

He lit the candle, placed it between them, then reached again into his backpack and pulled out a bag of peanut-butter-and-jelly sandwiches and two bottles of water, one labeled *Sam* and the other, *Sticks*.

She snickered in amusement. "Well, aren't you the culinary artist of Johnson County."

But instead of laughing with her, Sam raised his vision and looked directly at her. "Talk to me, Sydney. What's going on?"

She turned away and took a deep breath, wondering how to say it, and when she finally started, her voice was strained. But she did tell him. Of her morning argument with Blake, her punctured tire, being late to church, and then finding her husband with another woman.

He sat quietly, listening over the buzz of the cicadas and the gurgling of the Blue as it slowly drifted by.

Sydney finished her sandwich first and took a long drink of water.

"I don't know what to do, Sam."

"Do you love him?"

"No." The quickness of her response surprised even her. "But I took a solemn vow—for better, for worse."

"We all make mistakes, Sydney. That doesn't mean we have to live with them for the rest of our lives."

She didn't respond.

"I know I told you about losing my parents and sister," he said, "but I never told you of the depths that I fell to after my mother died. My father's and sister's deaths were devastating, but my mom's death absolutely crushed me. She was my rock. I don't think I had closure after she died. I fell into a deep depression—and twice almost ended my life."

She stared for a second, not sure she heard right. Then he nodded and went on,

"There are times I can still taste the gunpowder from the barrel of the pistol I placed in my mouth."

"What"—she took a deep breath—"stopped you?"

"Jenny ... I heard her voice cry out in my mind."

Sydney touched his hand but remained quiet.

"My sister used to tell me that there were three muscles I needed to exercise every day. The mental, the physical, and the spiritual. She thought

I was strong in the first two but weak in spirit. That's why she wrote the journal I showed you a couple of weeks ago."

"I put off reading it for years until I was in Afghanistan—and then, after an emotional breakdown in the field, I started reading. I would meditate on Jenny's message in the morning and keep it in my mind throughout the day. Each insight seemed perfect for what I was going through." He paused as if to make sure she heard his next words. "The last time I saw you, after we argued, I opened up her journal to a random page and found a quote that I thought was perfect ... for you."

She said nothing but was moved that he had thought of her.

"The Creator gives his hardest battles to his bravest warriors," he said softly. "I don't think that means that God or Wakan Tanka or whatever you want to call Him is giving you challenges, but that every experience in life is an opportunity, or lesson, to remember the peace that the Great Spirit already gave to us. That belief takes strength. Faith. Discipline. Daily practice." He pointed to a field of sunflowers on the other side of the river. "Which direction are those sunflowers facing?"

"West."

"And in the morning, they turn to the east, awaiting the sun, then they follow their source throughout the day. Maybe we should be like sunflowers, Syd. Focusing on the light even when darkness is closing in."

A gust of wind broke the stillness, and despite the warm evening, she crossed her arms. She sat that way for a while, thinking about what he had said, alternately looking at the sunflowers and then the river as it carried leaves and twigs and seeds to the Missouri River.

He brushed a mosquito off her arm. "Let's head back. This is the time of night not even citronella can fight off the second wave of dive-bombers."

She laughed and stood up, brushing off the bark that had caught on the hem of her yellow sundress.

He offered her his arm, and she took it, a bit sad that she would be leaving. This was a night she didn't want to end. There was something natural about being with Sam. Painless. Relaxed. Comfortable. No worrying about every word she said being criticized or laughed at.

Watching him made her wonder what he was like growing up. How he communicated with his family, his sister, his tribe. She truly had never met anyone like him. On the surface he was a baseball star, beloved in Kansas City, and obviously a fierce competitor to shine in the Major Leagues. Yet there was a simplicity and tenderness about him that calmed skittish horses and befriended even the mangiest of dogs. Heck, Barney practically worshipped Sam after only two weeks.

"Do you ever get lonely?" she asked.

"Nope."

"Never?"

"Not really. As you've probably surmised by my living quarters, I'm not much of a partier. I'll go out with the fellas on the road, but I mostly enjoy those who visit me here."

"You have visitors?"

"Sure. Barney, deer, fox, turkey, rabbits, raccoons, possum, squirrels, birds—they drop by every day."

She couldn't suppress a smile. "Those are pretty nice friends."

"We get along. The wildest animals I ever met lived in the city."

She laughed. "Boy, isn't that the truth."

They walked in silence the rest of the way. Twilight made seeing difficult, but Sam moved through the woods as if he had memorized every stone, twig, and leaf on their path. The sounds of an owl or a scampering animal didn't bother him.

She was happy that she had called him, and then come to visit. Her earlier anxiety had vanished like the wind that fluttered the tops the trees above them.

When they arrived at her car, he snuck his hand into hers, which surprised her. "Where are you going?"

"I don't know. I'll find a hotel, but I'm not going home. I can't see him right now."

"Stay here."

"No, Sam."

"C'mon. You take the bed. Barney and I will sleep on the floor."

"I'm not going to let you sleep on the floor after you pitched today. If you lose your next game, I'll feel terrible."

"Okay, you sleep on the floor. Barney and I will take the bed."

She giggled. "You're impossible."

"That's what I was going for."

They stood in silence for a time, both feeling a bit shy after the recent exchange, but she didn't move to open her car door.

"What"—she searched for the right words to keep this wonderful evening going—"What was Jenny's lesson for you this morning?"

"It was a line from a book she was reading the year she died. *A Course in Miracles*. Lesson 101: *God's will for me is perfect happiness*."

He let go of her hand, but his eyes stayed steady on hers.

"What makes you happy, Sydney?"

Without thinking, she replied, "Being with you." Her right hand shot to her mouth. She was astonished at the haste and unrestrained honesty of her answer. She tried hard not to show her embarrassment, but she couldn't stop her ears burning red as she covered up her flustered smile.

"Why do you do that?" he asked.

"Do what?"

"Cover your smile."

"Habit, I guess." Her index finger touched her cleft line.

"That's a habit you should break," he said, his brown eyes bright with mischief, "because you have the most gorgeous smile I've ever seen. And with your permission, if you'd lower your hand, I'd like to kiss you."

It was as if some universal force, an untamed tide, a wind from another world, swept her hand away, away from her scar, her flaw, her self-perceived imperfection.

"Some of us have a scratch or two on the outside," he whispered as he lifted her chin to meet his gaze. "And some, like me, have them on the inside."

His lips touched hers, barely at first, gently tracing a path to her cleft and staying there a while as if trying to make her world all right again.

Her eyes fluttered shut as she leaned back and let go, her mouth opening slightly, wanting more of him, like a sunflower wanting more of the light. She ran her hands underneath the back of his shirt and pressed him closer.

His lips left her mouth, traveling down to her chin, her neck, to the hollow of her throat. She took his hand and led it to her breast, inhaling a sensuous gasp when he found her nipple. He rose up, as if waiting for her to open her eyes, and when she did, she found his sultry stare.

Her heart was racing a thousand miles an hour as she gushed, "I've decided to accept your offer of staying tonight."

He kissed her hard this time, a long, deep, dizzying, back-bending embrace that lifted her off the ground. Then he swung her up into both arms, carried her into his cottage, and dropped her on his bed.

As she wriggled out of her sundress, Sam peeled off his T-shirt. He looked over at Barney, who was waiting by the door, tail wagging, hoping to be invited in.

"Sorry, bud. I'm sharing my happiness with someone else tonight."

CHAPTER THIRTY-EIGHT

Stilwell Kansas

July 2013

S am stirred the sautéed vegetables into a bowl of four beaten eggs and then poured it all into a hot greased skillet. The pan sizzled loudly, causing a stir in the bedroom. As he sprinkled in a dash of salt, pepper, and garlic, he peeked over his shoulder at Sydney.

"Hey, sleepyhead. I hope you like omelets."

She sat up in bed and pulled the sheet up over her breasts. Her hair was a mess of wild black static spikes twisting in the air, looking like a Kansas wheat field after a tornado had blown through.

"How long have you been up?"

"About an hour. Did my meditation and light stretching. Thought I'd wait for you to do yoga … if you're interested, of course."

"Sure." She rubbed her eyes, and the bed sheet slipped. She quickly pulled it up again.

"Really, Sticks?" He cocked his head to the side in amusement. "After the performance you put on last night, now you're gonna act like the shy girl-next-door?"

She turned bright red and pulled the sheet completely over her head. But he could tell she was laughing underneath.

"If I lose my next start, it's because you wore me out."

The bed sheet shook with greater hilarity.

"Barney still hasn't returned after all your screaming."

"Enough!" She threw the sheet off her, jumped out of bed, and in her complete nakedness, marched to the bathroom.

He let go a low wolf whistle. "God, you're beautiful."

She stopped and cupped her breasts. "My boobs are too small."

"No, ma'am, they're perfect. So's your gluteus maximus, your obliques, your adductor longus, your vulva, and your soft palate."

She gave him a completely baffled look. "What's with the anatomy mumbo jumbo?"

"You're a stud athlete, Coach Sticks. I was just trying to speak your lingo. Now show me that fine latissimus dorsi of yours?"

She turned her back to him and flexed her arms over her head.

"There it is! The hood of the cobra. As we say in Ignacio, magnifico!"

"That's Italian, you moron."

"So was Michelangelo, who immediately died after carving your statue."

She pursed her lips to keep from laughing and started again to the bathroom.

Sam acted like he was a sculptor, chiseling the last of his masterpiece with a final tap from his imaginary hammer. *"Dink. Magnifico!"* Then he clutched his heart and fell to the ground. "My life is over. Perfection."

She shook her head and closed the bathroom door.

*   *   *

As soon as they finished breakfast, they made love again. Afterward, they did an hour yoga practice and headed to the stables. Sydney's phone *pinged* as soon as they hit a good cell signal, then *pinged* again and again. She checked her phone and let out a long breath. Five messages from Blake, four from her parents, and one from Mary Beth. Obviously, Blake, trying to find her, had called everyone. Old guilt creeped back in. *For out of the heart come evil intentions, murder, adultery, fornication, theft, false witness, slander. These are what defile a person, but to eat with unwashed hands does not defile. Matthew 15:19–20.* What would the Church say about what she had done? Father John? Her parents? She glanced up at Sam, then back at her phone.

"Sorry about making things more complicated for you," Sam said. "But we both knew this would happen when you didn't go home."

She scrolled down and read the texts from Blake:

Hey, babe, where are you? I'm sorry about today. Allison is Eddie's girl. I was just being nice.

Bullshit, thought Sydney. She remembered the name from an earlier text. She scrolled down. *Hey, hon, it's 10:00. I said I was sorry. Where the hell are you?*

Next was … *Midnight, girl. If you don't reply in five minutes, I'm calling your folks.*

Then … *Your parents are PISSED. And so am I. Tell me where you are.*

And finally … *If I'm late for work, it's your fucking fault. I hardly slept last night. Get your ass home right now.*

She didn't even read the texts from her parents, knowing they would be full of worry and concern for her and for Blake. She scrolled to Mary Beth's.

Sydney. I'm sure you're okay, but Blake called and he was out of his mind. Accused me of turning you against him and thinks I'm hiding you somewhere. Just text me that you're safe.

She group-texted all three. *I'm fine. I just needed time by myself.*

Her phone immediately *pinged* several responses, but this time she didn't even look.

Sam put his arm around her shoulder and gave it a squeeze. "You okay?"

"Yeah," she muttered. She wanted to change the subject, wanted to forget about her troubles and stay in this wonderfully peaceful place that she had found with Sam.

He must have read her mind as he took off in a half jog toward the barn, smiling back at her. "Last one inside has to clean Leo's stall!"

She snorted back a laugh, knowing that no horse in that barn dumped more manure in a twenty-four-hour period than old Leo did.

"Hey! What'd I say last week? No head starts!" She bolted after him, happy that he was letting her gain on him, yet wondering a bit how this greater chase would eventually end. She was running after Sam Cloud-Carson. American League Rookie of the Year candidate Sam Cloud-Carson. One of Kansas City's most eligible bachelors, Sam Cloud-Carson. After what had happened last night, this would be a painful race to lose.

*   *   *

Sam kept it close but made sure he won, letting Sydney get within inches of catching him, before bursting through the barn door in victory. Infuriated, she pushed him headlong into a haystack, jumped on top of him, straddled his waist, and pinned his arms down with her knees.

"You big cheater!" she snarled, sliding her hands down to his armpits, and began tickling him. "I'm not cleaning Leo's power poop. That's your job, buster."

"All right, all right!" He opened his hands in surrender. "I give up!"

She stopped but planted her right hand firmly on his chest. "Admit it. You cheated."

"Actually," he said, lowering his voice as he ran a hand inside her blouse and up to her breasts. "I knew I'd win either way."

She felt her body respond to his touch and pressed down into him. "How so?"

"Because"—he waited for her eyes to come back to his—"win or lose, I figured I'd have a beautiful woman on top of me."

She punched him in the chest. "You're the worst. You're just a big tease."

"*Ahem,*" said a loud voice near the door.

Sam practically threw Sydney off him in sudden panic. They both stood up quickly and brushed the hay off their clothes.

"It's a good thing we don't do trail rides on Mondays," said Bette Tomlinson. "I'd hate for the kids to see their mentors rollin' around in the hay like two squirrels in springtime."

Sydney went beet red and glanced at Sam, then back at Bette. "Sorry, ma'am."

"You'll really be sorry after I tell ya what happened this morning." Bette knitted her brows and looked directly at Sydney. "Your husband came lookin' for ya about seven. Thankfully, I lock the gate every night, and he don't have the combination. But Blake laid on his darn car horn for about five minutes until I came out."

Sydney's shoulders slumped forward.

"I know your husband's a son of a bitch, Syd, so I covered for ya. Told him you weren't here. But that said, you gotta clean up your house before ya move on to another one."

"It's my fault," Sam cut in, but Bette raised her hand to quiet him.

"No, it's both your faults. I shoulda said something two weeks ago when I saw ya lookin' at each other like two high school kids on prom night."

She grabbed a pitchfork off the wall, walked over, and handed it to Sam. "I heard ya cheated to win, so you get first crack at Leo's shit."

*   *   *

As they worked the stables that morning, Bette was aware of them both: the sweet, naive, disheartened young lady brushing quarter horses in the corral, and the sensitive star ballplayer cleaning the stalls, looking so worried and regretful … yet not for himself.

After talking with her son, she knew a bit about Sam's backstory. A skilled Ute tracker, recruited by an American private military company to work his craft in the rugged mountains of Afghanistan. Bart hadn't offered any specifics of what Sam had seen or done, but he did say that the young man had arrived at Bagram Air Base depressed and that he may even have had a death wish.

Surely, she thought, *they've both been through enough*. Badgering them about this affair was only going to add to their guilt. From what she had assessed, they had a lot in common. Both loved sports, the outdoors, and working with kids, and they were kind, empathetic souls who looked for the good in everyone. And that quality made both of them vulnerable.

Bette picked up two saddle pads and walked out to the corral.

"Hey, Syd! Would you prep Leo and Jenny for a ride?"

"Yes, ma'am," she answered tentatively, making no eye contact.

Bette let out a long breath, then sat down on the mounting block.

"My husband was a fine man," she said. "Great dad, husband, lover, put me up on a pedestal as high as the moon … Three weeks before retirement, he dropped dead of a heart attack. Spoiled all our cool plans." She shook her head sadly. "Meantime, my sister married a bum like Blake. Drunk, couldn't keep a job, gaslighted her for thirty years. Then she died of cancer, and he got both her retirement and life insurance. I tell ya, life ain't fair."

Sydney stood frozen, her hand on Leo's withers, her eyes remote.

"I'd like to apologize for what I said earlier," Bette continued. "I also don't think it's a coincidence that you met Sam when you did."

"But I'm still an adulteress. And God punishes those who violate His laws—"

"Hogwash." Bette jumped to her feet. "God didn't make those laws. Man did. You made a mistake. You married the wrong guy. A guy who treats you like crap. Then somebody nice comes along, someone who has a lot in common with you, including the blues—"

"The blues?"

"Depression. Heartache. Grief. Sam's already been through his dark night of the soul, and fortunately, like the mighty alchemist, it transformed him into good. Maybe it's your turn."

Sydney swallowed hard. "You know about his losses?"

"I know enough." She picked up one of the horse pads and flipped it onto Leo's back. "I also know that he cares about you. He's in there cleaning stalls, lookin' like one of those Jane Goodall chimpanzees after their mate just croaked."

Bette placed the other saddle pad on Jenny's back and motioned for Sydney to follow her. "Help me with the saddles, honey."

They didn't say much after that, just saddled the two horses and untied the reins from the fence.

"Who are you riding with today?" Sydney asked as Bette handed her the reins to Jenny.

"I'm not going anywhere." She cupped a hand to her mouth and called to the barn. "Yo, Sammy! Get your butt out here!"

Not but five seconds later, Sam came hurrying out of the barn, still with that sad-chimp look on his face as Bette handed him Leo's reins.

"Why don't you and Syd check out that southwest trail," she said gruffly. "It'll take ya to the river, then head downriver about a mile, to a nice little spot overlooking a field of sunflowers."

He smiled shyly. "We know the place, ma'am. Thank you."

*   *   *

The next four days were quite possibly the happiest of Sydney's life. They rode horses every day, practiced yoga, and played catch in front of his cottage. Sam taught her where to place her fingers for a two-seam fastball, and when she got the hang of it, he stepped back another ten feet and told her to let it rip. She did, and unfortunately, missed her target badly, the baseball sailing high and away, clanging off the gutter of Sam's roof, which so startled Barney that their only fan quickly retreated inside the safety of the house.

Sam collapsed on the ground in hilarity, and she jumped on top of him, slapping him with her glove as he covered his laughter. Then he picked her up, carried her inside, and they made love again.

Could she just hit pause and stay here forever? Was it true what Sam had said one night, that *she was exactly where she needed to be right now*? There were moments she felt overwhelmed by what lay ahead: of returning to the tension of her marriage, of her parents' disappointment, and of her own self-doubt. In those times, it was as if Sam knew what she was thinking. He would wrap his arms around her and say, *Nothing is too big or difficult for you to handle if you seek the help of Spirit.*

"What do you think about when you're on the mound?" she asked him one morning as they lay in bed.

"Everything and nothing," he answered.

She gave him a look as if he needed to explain.

"I think about the situation," he said matter-of-factly. "Inning, score, outs, baserunners, hitter's strengths and weaknesses. Is he hot or cold? How have I pitched him in the past and how will I pitch him now?"

"And *nothing*?"

"When I decide what to throw, I clear my mind and concentrate on only one thing–executing my pitch." He paused in thought. "The mind is a powerful muscle. There's a fine line between conviction and doubt. Last week, we rallied from four runs down in the seventh inning to tie Houston. Even though the score was tied, you could feel the confidence in our dugout and the doubt in the Astros. Right then, I knew we'd win."

"What do you do when doubt visits you?"

"Breathe. Get back to the moment. Focus on doing my job."

"You do that very well."

He shrugged as if it were no big thing, but there was an intensity in his gaze that seemed to take him to that other world.

"I remember watching you on TV strike a guy out in a critical situation," she said. "It seemed like you knew what the hitter was looking for."

"I did."

"You did?"

"I'm a tracker, Syd. There are plenty of times I've lost a track–no print, no sight or sound telling me where to go. It's in those moments that I have to trust something beyond my five senses to tell me where the animal went. It's the same trust I have on the mound."

"Are you ever wrong?"

"Not much."

She turned in bed to face him. "Wow, you are an arrogant son of a gun."

He nodded. "When it comes to pitching and tracking, yes, I am."

She began to meditate with Sam, sometimes laying back in his arms as he read to her from Jenny's journal. She would listen with her eyes closed and her mind open, letting Jenny's wisdom wash over her and dissolve into her very soul.

Her favorite on Thursday:

May you Walk with the Wind and allow the spirit of love to flow through you. May it give you courage to choose love over fear, peace over attack, and the belief that there is no separation—that we are all connected—we are all one.

It was as if Jenny's words opened up an awareness of God that she had not known before. Jenny's God wasn't one of judgment, damnation, or wrath, but one of mercy, unity, nature, and healing. Her God was infinitely creative and had the power to rearrange time and space according to one's willingness to forgive and to love.

But as Thursday wore on, old doubts and fears began to creep back in. They would go their separate ways in a couple of hours. Sam, leaving for his road trip to Cleveland, and she, going home to resolve her issues with Blake. What would she say to her husband and parents, and where would she go? It was time to find out.

CHAPTER THIRTY-NINE

Stilwell, Kansas

July 2013

Sydney sat in the center of her parents' living room, forcing herself to look her mom and dad in the eyes. The room was a testament to her parents' strict Catholic foundation. From the needlepoint artwork her mother had crafted of St. Peter and St. Thomas Aquinas to the Virgin Mary statue on the mantel, to the crucifix of a dying Jesus above the fireplace, to the family Bible on the coffee table, open to this day's theme.

Wives, submit yourselves unto your own husbands, as it is fit in the Lord. Husbands, love your wives, and be not bitter against them. Colossians 3:18–19

She knew it was meant for her. *Be calm,* she told herself, inhaling deeply. *You can handle this. You're a coach, a leader, a child of God, and ... this couple's daughter.*

"I'm leaving Blake," she blurted out.

Both parents groaned in disappointment.

"Oh, Sydney." Her mother was first to speak. "Don't make a rash decision."

"And remember the vows you took," her father added, "before God and Church."

Sydney held up her hands to quiet them. "I know—for better or worse—but this isn't a rash decision. It's been building for over a year."

Vivian sighed. "What did Father John say when you went to him for counsel?"

"He was very understanding, but he only knows my side of the story. Blake refused to go with me and was furious that I shared our troubles with him."

"Have you talked to Blake yet?"

"I called him before I came here. He apologized profusely and begged me to come home, but it's too late. I don't want to be with him anymore."

"But he still loves you," Vivian said. "He's been by everyday, worried sick about where you were and why you left. I'm sure he'd be willing to get counseling from Father John now to save your marriage."

Sydney crossed her arms in defiance. "Did Blake tell you *everything* that happened last Sunday?"

Vivian shrugged, looking uncomfortable. "He said that you had an argument before church and that he went to a friend's house to cool off."

"Of course he did. That's Blake's MO. Always painting himself as the innocent victim and everyone else the villain." She paused to make sure they heard her next words. "Did Blake tell you that I found him at Eddie's making out with another woman? Did he tell you that they were doing cocaine?"

Both her parents' mouths fell open in stunned silence.

"I didn't think he told you that part." It took some effort, but she uncrossed her arms. "I'm not trying to bash him, but I think all three of us are guilty of ignoring his screwups and mistreatment of me, in hopes that he'd change."

"He—he can change," Vivian said.

"Only if he wants to, Mom. But I think it's time we all face the truth that Blake has had an addiction problem for years, and he doesn't want to get help." She shook her head sadly and let go a weary sigh. "I'm just—I'm just emotionally drained right now and could really use your support and a place to stay. Is that okay?"

Vivian moved quickly to her daughter's side and put her arms around her. "I'm so sorry," she said, as if finally understanding. "Of course you can stay here."

Her father nodded solemnly. "I'll talk with Blake. I'll tell him that it's best he not see you for a while."

CHAPTER FORTY

Kansas City, Missouri

July 2013

"If this is true we're going to have to suspend him," David Wilson said to Skip Charles and Andy Phillips. "Right now our lawyers are in the process of gathering all the information."

Phillips shook his head. "I don't believe it. I sat next to him on the flight home, and he was already game-planning his next start."

"Have you talked with him yet?" Charles asked.

"I left him a message to call me," Wilson said, "but I didn't tell him what it was about."

"He doesn't always get back with you right away," Phillips said. "He lives out in the country. Cell service isn't the best. He usually has to go to a corner of his porch when we talk."

Wilson turned in his chair to face his pitching coach. "Where does he live?"

"Stilwell, Kansas, about thirty miles southwest of the park."

"This doesn't make any sense. Why would he get off the plane at eight in the evening from the downtown airport and drive thirty minutes east on I-70 to go to a strip club when his house is in the opposite direction?"

Charles shook his head. "The club manager said he arrived drunk?"

Wilson nodded. "Drunk or stoned, waving hundred-dollar bills in the girls' faces. Then he paid one of the strippers for a private dance before he roughed her up and left."

"It's not him," said Phillips firmly. "I sat next to Sam for half of the flight, and he only drank water. He's been a model student. Ears open, mouth shut, totally focused. The veterans practically have to drag him out for a beer after a game."

"He's a morning guy too," added Charles. "I'm in the hotel gym by seven thirty, and Sam's already there, in the corner doing his meditation and yoga."

Wilson stared down at his coffee. It was already his third cup, and it was only nine thirty in the morning. He had received the call from the owner of Blue Temptations Strip Club at three in the morning. How the guy got his personal phone number he had no idea but that certainly would be part of this investigation.

"There's never a good time for these things to happen," he said, "but our team's coming together. Last place to second in two months, only six games back of Detroit."

"All with Sam leading our pitching staff," Charles agreed. "He's been the guy stopping our losing streaks, and even though he doesn't talk much, he's become a real leader. The guys respect him. Dude is fearless."

Wilson shook his head sadly. "We all have a dark side, Skip. Sam didn't exactly get a good reference from his previous employer."

*　　*　　*

Sydney bolted out the front door when she saw Mary Beth's car pull up in front of her parents' house. She leaped the three steps off the porch and acted as if she was a dribbling a soccer ball down the brick path.

Mary Beth reached across the passenger's seat and opened the door for her. "Who put an extra shot of espresso in your coffee this morning?"

"I've been up since six, MB. Stretched, meditated, ran five miles, made breakfast for my folks, and couldn't wait to see you!" She hopped in the car and closed the door. "How was your vacation? Did you hike Taos Mountain? Did the kids have fun?"

Mary Beth laughed and patted her friend's knee. "Wow, I didn't expect to find you in such good spirits after moving out."

She exhaled slowly. "I feel like I can breathe again."

They had talked only once in the last week, on the drive home from Mary Beth's family vacation in New Mexico. Sydney had filled her in about Blake, the girl, the cocaine, and her moving out. She left out the part about where she had stayed.

"How's Blake handling all this?" Mary Beth asked as she drove to the stables.

"Not very well—he's been by every day, apologizing every ten seconds, saying he's a changed man and will see a therapist. He went to church with us yesterday and charmed the socks off my parents like he always does."

"Do they believe him?"

"Yes."

"Do you?"

"No."

"Good." Mary Beth's voice was sharp with irritation as she banged her fist on the steering wheel. "Be strong, girlfriend. Don't let him con you anymore." She glanced over at Sydney and then back to the road. "I feel like my old spunky friend is back."

Sydney beamed at that, for she felt the same. Her confidence and sense of humor were returning. More importantly, she liked herself again.

"So, Syd, where did you stay before you went to your parents?"

The question caught her by surprise, and she turned away from Mary Beth, hiding her smile. She should tell her best friend, shouldn't she? She had never kept anything from MB as long as they'd known each other. That went all the way back to first grade, when she'd punched Joey Janesko after he made fun of MB's freckles. They'd been besties ever since.

"Sydney?" Mary Beth asked again, her voice low with interest. She pulled her car over to the side of the road just before they reached the Tomlinson drive. "Where did you stay last week?"

Sydney turned to face her, pursing her lips to keep from breaking out into a huge, silly grin.

"Oh my God, you didn't." Mary Beth gasped. "You were with Sam?"

She nodded shyly.

"Did you . . . do it?"

Sydney's face couldn't contain that silly grin she'd been trying to hide. Her face lit like a candle, like some teenage girl the night after her high school prom, waiting impatiently for morning so she could tell her best friend she'd done it. Done it with the coolest boy in school. Sweet Sam. Thinking about him now sent shivers up her spine.

Unfortunately, MB didn't share her friend's joy.

"Oh, Syd, that's, um, wow. That's—oh my."

Sydney sat up straight in her seat. "Aren't you happy for me?"

"Sure … I don't know what to say. I'm happy you're happy, but I'm concerned."

"Why?"

"I don't want to see you hurt. I mean, this isn't some rebound guy we're talking about. He's Sam Cloud-Superstar. Girls hold up signs at the ballpark asking him out for a date. Heck, what do you think it's like on the road?"

Sydney's shoulders slumped. "You don't think I've already thought of those things? That I'm not good enough? Not worthy of him. But maybe I am. I certainly don't want to live the rest of my life thinking this kind of love isn't possible."

"Love? You were with him for one week, Syd. One week. Is it love or infatuation?"

"I don't know. I just know I enjoy every moment I'm with him."

Mary Beth shook her head, put the car in gear, and turned into the Tomlinson drive.

*   *   *

Sam was in the corral, brushing the horses, when they drove up the lane. He waved when he saw who it was and followed a yapping Barney to greet the help.

"Welcome home, MB! Looks like you brought back a nice tan from New Mexico."

Mary Beth forced a smile and glanced over at Sydney, who was practically glowing at the sight of Sam. *Teenage crush at twenty-six,* she thought. *I don't want her getting crushed by this hunk.* Sam was indeed impressive to the eye, in those faded blue jeans that fit snugly around his rear and those biceps that were testing the elasticity of his royal-blue T-shirt. It was easy to understand why Sydney would be drawn to him.

Sam met them at the gate and gave MB a warm hug, practically lifting her off the ground.

"Glad you could come today," he said. "How are Phil and the girls?"

"Fine. Thanks for asking."

Sam shifted from one foot to the other, as if not knowing how he should greet Sydney, and then finally he just stuck his hand out and gave her a fist bump. "Yo, Sticks, how's it goin'?"

"Good. Very good." She looked over at the quarter horses as if beginning a protracted, scholarly study of the corral. "Is there anything you want us to do?"

"You guys are the worst actors ever!" Mary Beth exclaimed, and then turned to Sam. "Sydney told me she slept with you."

Sam looked at Sydney, who gave an embarrassed shrug and mouthed the words, *She asked me.*

Mary Beth clapped her hands. "All right, Sam, what needs to be done this morning?"

"Um, let the horses graze in the pasture, and stalls three and four need new hay."

She pointed at Sydney. "You do that while Sam and I go for a walk."

"What?" Sydney yelped, but Sam quickly raised both hands to calm her. "It's okay. I'll bring Barney for protection."

*　　*　　*

Mary Beth waited until they were out of earshot, and then grabbed Sam by the arm. "This isn't something to joke about, Sam. Sydney's extremely vulnerable right now. What in God's name were you thinking?"

"I was thinking about how much she deserves to be loved."

Startled, she released his arm and stopped in the middle of the path.

Sam walked on, and Mary Beth hurried after him.

"Wait up! Of course she deserves to be loved—when the time's right."

"Maybe my timing was perfect." He slowed to let her catch up. "Maybe last week gave her the courage to leave an abusive relationship."

Mary Beth's entire body softened. She hadn't thought of that and said nothing more until they reached the banks of the Blue.

"I'm afraid for her, Sam."

"But not for me?"

"No, nothing seems to bother you. You reek of confidence."

"Is that because you only see me as an athlete?"

"Maybe ... yeah. I guess that's mostly true."

"First impressions don't always tell the whole story," he said. "I was fortunate to have been raised in a strong and loving family. Then I lost my father in the war, my sister to kidney disease, and my mom in a car accident. Believe me, I wasn't very confident then."

"I'm sorry. I wasn't aware of all you'd been through."

"Have you camped the Rocky Mountains in winter time, MB?"

She shook her head.

"We have these wild winds that roar through the Rockies every winter. My grandfather used to tell me that those winds made our Ute people. They didn't defeat us; they didn't break us. Those winds made our people stronger so we'd be able to survive the storms that would come into our lives. What Sydney's going through right now is only going to make her stronger."

But Mary Beth was still afraid. She had seen firsthand Sydney gaslighted, belittled, abused, and intimidated by her husband.

"You don't think you're adding to her storm?"

"I hope I'm the eye of her storm." He leaned forward, picked up an acorn off the ground, and handed it to her. "Bur oak acorn."

She gave a confused look.

"The bur oak's called *Old Dependable* because it can tolerate just about any dirt," he said. "But an acorn is only potential. It has to fight through lousy soil, rough weather, drought, high winds, and other young trees to become the mighty bur oak. It's as if it needs to be broken down to break through."

"Do you think Sydney's broken through?"

"I don't know. I'd just like to be a friend she can count on."

"Oh, Sam, you took it waaay past the friend stage last week."

He shrugged. "Maybe like the acorn, a true friendship was planted. And, if Sydney wants to, I'm willing to ride out a little rough weather or a few high winds to see if it blooms."

She smiled up at him. "You're pretty smooth, you know that?"

He winked. "Old Dependable."

* * *

Sydney was sitting on the top of the corral fence when they returned, an inquisitive look on her face as she drummed her fingers on the wooden rail.

"Great timing," she teased. "Everything's done. All eight horses are grazing peacefully and stalls three and four are so clean I got a job offer from *Better Homes and Gardens*."

Sam chuckled, and Mary Beth walked over to give her friend a hug.

"He's pretty amazing," she whispered. "My only concern is how are your parents and Blake going to react when you tell them about him?"

"I don't know," she whispered back. "I just want to enjoy right now."

They separated, and Mary Beth held Sydney at arm's length, looking directly into her eyes. "Whatever happens, I'm here for you."

"Thank you."

Sam was standing off to the side, his arms crossed, his head cocked to the side, curious about their conversation.

"What did you say to her, MB?" he asked.

"I told her that you have a thing for acorns."

"Rrriiight." Sam rolled his eyes. "I see where this is going. Two old friends ganging up on the newbie. I got no chance."

"You're right about that," Sydney said, and then sauntered over and slipped her hand into the palm that Sam offered. He pulled her in for a hug, and for a moment, she didn't know how to respond. She glanced over at Mary Beth, as if to get her approval, and when MB winked, Sydney closed her eyes and relaxed into Sam's embrace. He smelled good: of hay and leather and musk and a hint of that cocoa-butter soap he showered with. *Calm down, Sydney.*

The *ping* of a phone jolted her back to the now, and she reached into her back pocket.

"I almost forgot." She handed Sam the phone. "You left this in the tack room. Apparently, you're Mr. Popular this morning."

"Who called?"

"I don't know. I'm not a snoop."

He checked and his face went blank.

"What?" Sydney asked.

"Two messages from my GM and one from my pitching coach."

"So?"

"Trade deadline's next week. Players don't get calls from the GM unless—"

"They're not going to trade you!" Sydney's voice was so sharp that Barney bolted behind Sam. "The Royals have been on a roll ever since they called you up."

It was the first time she'd seen uncertainty in his face.

"Oh no." He let go a defeated exhale. "Grandpa Douglas, Jose and Teresa, Whip, Hunoon, and Carlita are all flying in on Friday. I don't want to disappoint them."

"Would you stop with the Debby Downer. You're not going anywhere. The Royals are going to win the division, and you're a big reason why."

He gave a detached nod and clicked on to listen to the message. Ten seconds later, he clicked off. "Mr. Wilson wants me to stop by his office as soon as possible. That's not good."

Sydney put her hands on her hips and glared at him. "What happened to the confident, gutsy fighter we see on the mound every five days? Where's that sunflower searching for the light?"

Sam snorted back a laugh and looked at Mary Beth. "Dang, she's good. I can see why her Tigers have been to the postseason three straight years."

"Yeah." Mary Beth winked. "Sydney will go for the jugular if she thinks she's right."

"I'm fired up, Coach Sticks. Who do you want me to take out in the second half?"

"This isn't funny," Sydney said firmly. "Mr. Wilson's calling you about something else. What could it be?"

"Maybe it's about being pulled over by the police again?"

Both women's heads jerked up in surprise, and they said in unison, "What?"

"Last Thursday. On my way to the airport to catch our flight to Cleveland. Police pulled me over. Same story as before. Somebody called in, said a drunk guy with my license number was weaving all over the highway. I took the breathalyzer test and passed, but it's weird. I told the officer that this was the second time it's happened to me."

"Why didn't you tell me?" Sydney asked.

"It's no big deal."

"It is too. You'd better tell your GM about it."

"Naw, he's a busy guy. I can handle it."

Sydney narrowed her eyes. "Let me get this straight. It's okay for me to reach out to you for help when I'm going through a challenge, but when trouble comes your way, only *you* can handle it."

"That's not true. I just don't want to bother him with trivial stuff."

"Why do you think Wilson became a general manager, Sam? It's because he enjoys working with young people. From what I've read about him, he's not only an executive trying to win a championship, but a man interested in developing something our country sorely needs—future leaders—people like you."

Sam's eyes crinkled in amusement. "Are you recruiting me to run for city council or something?"

Sydney stormed over and hammered her index finger against his sternum. "Don't patronize me, buster. Here's the deal. Someone's trying to hurt you. You're going to tell your GM today exactly what's been going on. Got it?"

He raised both hands in surrender. "I promise I'll tell him." Sam bit the side of his mouth to keep from laughing. "Anything else, Coach Sticks?"

"Yes." She poked him even harder in the chest. "Tell him that if he even thinks about trading you, he'll lose every fan in Johnson County."

*   *   *

Sam knocked on David Wilson's open door. It was a simple office. Nothing fancy. Walnut desk with mounds of scouting and prospect reports strewn about. There were plenty of pictures covering the walls. Most were of Wilson's wife and three kids, but there was one of the Royals GM, his back to the camera, looking out at a packed Kauffman Stadium, as if dreaming about what it would be like when his team made postseason again.

Wilson looked up, his face serious. "Come in, Sam."

Wilson then called his executive assistant and asked her to send in some guy named Stewart. Thirty seconds later, a man in a dark gray suit entered and closed the door behind him.

"This is Stew Ecklein, our team attorney," Wilson said.

Sam shook the man's hand but had a foreboding sense that he was in big trouble.

"Did I do something wrong, sir?"

"Have a seat."

He swallowed once and sat down.

"We took a chance on you," Wilson said, "and you promised me that you'd do nothing to hurt this organization."

"Is this about being pulled over by the police?"

Ecklein leaned forward in interest. "Go on."

"One month ago, I was pulled over by the police on Eastwood Trafficway on my way to visit friends at the Plaza. The officer said he received a call from his dispatcher that a car with my plates was weaving all over the road and the driver looked drunk. Fortunately, he'd been listening to our game and could tell I hadn't been drinking. He let me go."

"What else?"

"It happened again last Thursday on my way to the airport. I was pulled over on I-35. Same story. Drunk driver weaving in and out of traffic. I took the breathalyzer test and passed. He apologized and let me go." Sam gave a confused shake of his head. "When it happened the first time, I thought somebody made a mistake. But twice?"

Ecklein was silent for a long moment as he studied Sam. "All right, now tell us about last night?"

Sam straightened up in his seat. "Last night?"

"Where did you go after we returned from Cleveland?"

"I went home."

"You didn't stop anywhere along the way?"

"No, sir. What's this about?"

His general manager stood up from behind his desk and came around to sit in the chair directly across from Sam. "I received a call from the owner of Blue Temptations Strip Club, at three in the morning, accusing you of roughing up one of their girls."

Sam was shocked. "What? I've never been to a strip club in my life."

"Can you prove that you didn't go to Blue Temptations last night? Did you stop on the drive home? Grocery store? Meet a friend? Anyone who could vouch for you?"

Sam rubbed a hand over his face. He couldn't tell them he was with Sydney. She had stopped by for a few hours before returning to her parents' house after midnight.

"Maybe Bo Chapman," he said. "He was behind me when we left the airport and headed south on I-35. We both live on the Kansas side."

"Did you stop anywhere?"

"No. Straight home. I have to get up early to work my landlady's stables."

This time it was Wilson and his lawyer who straightened up in their chairs.

"You have another job?" his GM asked.

"It's not really a job, sir. I rent a cottage on farm property owned by a woman named Bette Tomlinson. Part of my contract is to feed and water her horses and clean her stables every morning when we're home. It's no big deal. It only takes me an hour or two. And then, twice a week, we host the Urban Wildlife Academy for trail rides." He gave an innocent smile. "It's pretty cool seeing kids' faces light up when they ride a horse for the first time."

Ecklein looked at Wilson, then back at Sam. "Can Mrs. Tomlinson verify you worked this morning?"

"Sure. But shouldn't I talk with the owner of this Blue Temptations place so he can see for himself that it wasn't me there last night?"

"No, no, no, not until after we finish our investigation," Ecklein said. "But from what you've told us, somebody's got it out for you. Do you have any enemies in town?"

Sam's jaws tightened, and his soft brown eyes suddenly darkened. "Not in Kansas City."

Wilson seemed to catch the change in Sam's demeanor and waited for his eyes to come back to his. "What about a guy like Drake Dixon?"

The side of Sam's mouth twitched. Though he tried to remain impassive, there was an increased intensity in his gaze. He took a deep calming breath and wondered how to answer. They had probably surmised that he didn't like his former employer. Finally, he simply said, "I'm not a fan of his."

"Do you think he could be behind this?"

"I don't know."

Wilson nodded. "I got the feeling when I talked to him in March that there was some falling out between you two."

Sam didn't respond.

"He said you were a very talented employee, but that you had personal problems, fought with your coworkers, and that he tried to get you help—"

"And you believed him?"

"We don't know what to believe when we have only his side of the story."

Sam remained quiet. There was almost nothing he wouldn't give to reveal his history with Dixon. The man was a con artist who would cheat and steal from his own mother in exchange for money and power. Unfortunately, there was an innocent village in the Nuristan Mountains that was counting on Sam's silence for their protection.

"Can you at least tell us why you went to work for him?"

"No."

Wilson exhaled in exasperation. "C'mon, Sam. How are we going to defend you now, or in the future, unless you give us something?"

"I gave Dixon my word that I wouldn't talk about my time in Afghanistan." He paused and gave both men a long, level look. "And in my culture, a man's word is his bond. We don't break our treaties."

CHAPTER FORTY-ONE

Kabul, Afghanistan

July 2013

"China upped their offer another million, and Hazrat still turned them down," said Ullah Kardaar as they drove through downtown Kabul. "I don't think he's interested in money, sir."

"Bullshit!" Dixon hissed. "Everybody's got a price. It's your job to find out what that price is."

Dixon and his lawyer had flown all night on his company's private jet to meet with Afghanistan's Minister of Commerce and Industry, Nadeem Khattak. But when they arrived, they were greeted by Kardaar, definitely some low-level flunky.

Dixon glanced at his reflection in the glass. He looked exhausted. At least his limo was sufficiently defended. Two DiamondBar Security vehicles in front and two more behind, all filled with well-armed men. The streets had been partially cleared for Dixon's motorcade to travel from the airport to Minister Nadeem's office.

"Afghanistan isn't like the United States," Kardaar tried to explain. "We aren't adequately connected. Our government only controls sixty percent of our four hundred and one districts. Abdul Hazrat's mountain is part of a region that is very remote. Politically, it is beyond our jurisdiction, and legally, Mr. Hazrat holds all mining licenses to his mountain. Should we move too aggressively, the Afghanistan Natural Resources Oversight Network could be a problem."

Dixon shook his head in frustration. "What did the minister tell Hazrat?"

"He communicated the new offer from the Chinese corporation and was immediately rejected. I have Hazrat's statement." Kardaar reached into the breast pocket of his jacket and pulled out a letter. *"My people are the soil, the forest, the streams of this mountain. We will never let our land go. For that would be like selling our mother and father—"*

"They're nothing but a bunch of goddamn savages!" Dixon slammed his fist against the tinted bulletproof glass window of their armored limousine. As he stared out at the broken-down city, a helter-skelter display of new and old buildings, some pristine, some bombed out, most still under construction, he wondered if Kabul would ever return to its historic roots.

The city was said to be 3,500 years old. It was perfectly located at the crossroads of Asia, high in a valley of the Hindu Kush pass along the ancient Silk Trail, a mecca that had once connected East to the West. At one time, it was known for its gardens, bazaars, and palaces, but after three decades of war, it seemed as if Kabul was in a constant state of being rebuilt.

Afghanistan itself was one of the most unscrupulous countries in the world, and their extractive sector, which included oil and mining, was also corrupt. But corruption also meant opportunity, and Dixon had made a fortune gambling on other countries' mistakes. He was betting on it being his winning ticket again.

"When will Nadeem return?" Dixon asked as they pulled up in front of the minister's headquarters on Darul Aman Road.

"I do not know. He had a meeting with the president this morning, but that usually lasts only an hour or so."

Dixon opened the door and motioned for Kardaar to leave. "You tell him that I flew over seven thousand miles to meet with him. Phone me as soon as Nadeem arrives, or I'll call your president and tell him how poorly I've been treated in his damn country."

"But sir, I—" was all Dixon heard as he slammed the door in the young man's face.

He turned to his lawyer. "Something's not right. Our only solution may be to kill Hazrat."

"Not so fast." Barry King threw up his hands. "If Carson has damaging information, this could backfire."

"He has nothing, Barry. I've checked with our spies inside the Afghan government about the possibility of Carson having any audio or video of our negotiations with Hazrat, and they all said it was impossible."

"You checked with Almeida Zubair. The shill who was fired by the Afghan Interior Department after it was discovered he accepted a bribe from a Chinese mining company. Zubair can't be trusted."

Dixon waved him off with a flick of his hand. "Our only face-to-face offer with Hazrat was in 2008. A year before Carson arrived in Afghanistan."

"How do you know Hazrat didn't record that conversation?"

"Because the Afghan police we paid off made sure he wasn't wearing a wire, and we held the meeting in a completely secure location." Dixon gave a confident look. "Carson lied to scare me. At the time it worked. But now I have the leverage, and I will break him."

"I don't know, Drake. Only a strong man makes it to the Major League after all he's been through."

"He's strong in sports and tracking, but he has an Achilles' heel."

"Explain?"

"Carson lost it after his sister died. He was kicked off his college team, almost dropped out of school. My psychological counselors at DiamondBar said he was suicidal when he trained at our Virginia facility. Colonel Tomlinson thought he had a death wish too, and then of course, he had the nervous breakdown after rescuing the Afghan girl."

"That was actually pretty heroic."

"But it's his weakness, Barry. He'd risk his life to save a puppy wandering into traffic before defending himself. That's why I'm dropping bits of misinformation to dirty his reputation; a DUI here or an accusation from a stripper there. Rumors of him consorting with the Taliban. Eventually, I'll find someone besides Hazrat he's trying to protect, and when I threaten them, he'll go off the deep end again."

"It had better work," King said.

"It will." Dixon smiled. "I'll create doubt, and eventually, he'll make a mistake or have another breakdown. If I'm lucky, maybe this time he'll succeed in killing himself."

CHAPTER FORTY-TWO

Kansas City, Missouri

July 2013

"Why are you calling me again?" Sydney chuckled into the phone, "Did you hear another rumor about being traded?"

"One week till the deadline," Sam said as he turned off I-29 onto the Kansas City Airport exit. "I hear Houston's lovely this time of year."

"Would you stop it? Wilson told you Monday they weren't going to trade you." There was a pause before she added, "He's not stupid. He knows he can't win the Central without you."

Sam laughed. He was on his way to the airport to pick up Grandpa Douglas, Jose, Teresa, and his friends from Nicaragua. They had connected in Houston and would be on the same flight to KC. Sam had rented a van for them and booked two suites at the Hotel Intercontinental on the Plaza. His job today: pick them up, check them into the hotel, and head to the ballpark to prep for his 7:10 start against the Central-leading Tigers.

The Royals were making a big deal about their *Paint the K Blue* weekend series, encouraging fans to wear blue to the games and then handing out plastic blue thundersticks that they could bang together to show their support.

"I'm actually calling about something else," he said. "Are you still at the stables?"

"Just finishing up."

"I was wondering if you might drop by my place and pick up the SpongeBob socks I bought for Carlita. I left them on the kitchen table."

"SpongeBob socks?"

"It's a long story. Ask Carlita tonight. Hey, what time are you going to join them?"

"About six."

"Thanks, Syd. You have no idea how much this means to me. I really want you to meet them. And then maybe we can all go out after the game."

"Sure," she paused, and he could tell she was trying not to laugh. "Should I make a reservation at Blue Temptations?"

"Hey, that was a low blow."

"Sorry! I couldn't help myself."

"Yeah, right. Well, I just arrived at the parking lot. Time to pick up the strippers."

"Hey, Sam?" Her voice took on a serious tone.

"Yeah?"

"You really need to get to the bottom of this. Someone is trying to hurt you."

"Thanks, Syd. I can handle it. Gotta go."

*　　*　　*

The closer Sam got to baggage claim, the more excited he became. He hadn't seen his friends in six months and Grandpa Douglas in four years. Even though they talked two, sometimes three, times a week, he had plenty to tell them. And this was Carlita's first time away from Nicaragua, her first airplane ride, and tonight would be her first Major League game. He wanted to see her face when she stepped off that plane.

"Excuse me, Mr. Cloud-Carson?" asked a TSA agent by a security exit. "Could I get a picture with you?"

"Sure." Sam nodded and glanced over at the passengers who were beginning to trickle down the hallway. It was the fourth fan or airport employee who had stopped him for an autograph or photo while he was hurrying through the terminal.

He stood next to the agent and smiled for a selfie. The man clicked the photo and beamed. "Thanks! My son won't believe I saw you. You're his favorite."

"Tell him hi—" Sam froze when he saw the top of Carlita's head in the middle of a herd of travelers coming down the hall. He swept the three red roses he was holding behind his back and crouched down behind the TSA agent. "Do you mind if I use you for cover to surprise a little girl?"

"Be my pleasure." The agent straightened up tall, as if trying to turn himself into a human shield.

Sam peeked out from behind the big man, but Carlita found him and her face lit like a lantern.

"Coach EssCee!" she squealed and ran past fellow travelers to leap into his arms. He spun her around, then put her down and held her at arm's length.

"Look at you, girl! I think you've made it all the way to five feet."

She raised up on her tiptoes. "I'm almost as tall as Hunoon."

"Almost, but not quite," said a voice next to them.

Sam looked up to find the woman Carlita spoke of and her husband, Whiplash McCracken. Grandpa Douglas was behind them, and further back were Jose and Teresa.

Sam stood up and opened his arms. "Family hug!" he cried out, and all six of his dearest friends engulfed him.

"Hey, Mr. Cloud-Carson?" the TSA agent interrupted. "Do you want a picture?"

"I'd love one, thanks!" He handed the man his phone, knelt down in the middle of his entourage, and just as the TSA agent snapped the picture, Sam kissed Carlita's cheek.

* * *

As the afternoon sun drew the heat index over ninety-five, Sydney welcomed the shade of the oak and maple trees that lined the dirt driveway on her walk to Sam's cottage. Barney greeted her from the wicker couch on the screened-in porch, his tail wagging in joy, excited to see somebody who might give him some love.

"Hey, Barn," she said as she wiped the sweat from her brow and opened the front door. Barney hopped off and followed her inside. Sam never locked the place, saying he didn't have anything worth stealing and that if anyone made it past Bette Tomlinson's security gate and the near half-mile trek to his place, well then, they'd earned what they came to pirate. She knelt down and scratched Barney's ears and rubbed his belly, then picked up the SpongeBob socks for Carlita and looked about the place.

It was all Sam. Simple. No clutter. Economical. Dishtowel neatly folded on the sink, one coffee mug next to the coffee maker, a framed picture of his family on Pargin Mountain above the stove. She looked closer. His mom and dad were a handsome couple, and Jenny, despite her small, withered frame, had a look of absolute peace. It even appeared as if there was a soft glow about her head and shoulders. It was probably why Sam had chosen this photo.

Sydney moved to his bedroom, Barney on her heels. The bed was still unmade, but at least Sam had pulled the covers up so Barney wouldn't lay on the sheets. She pulled his pillow up to her nose and inhaled deeply.

Ah, heaven. It smelled of cocoa-butter soap and Sam. They hadn't been together since Sunday night. Well, she had seen him every day, even kissed him in the privacy of the stables several times, but they hadn't been *together* since Sunday.

She caught her breath for a beat, surprised by the kick of sexual intensity, and looked down at his nightstand. He had written something on a small notebook. It had her name on it.

Sydney. Dream. Biological father.

Why hadn't he told her about his dream? Then, below that, he had written:

Hazrat. Dixon. Construction. Parun to Kamdesh. Why? China?

Pakistan?

She knew the name Dixon, but nothing else.

"What's this all about, Sam?"

At his name, her phone *pinged* a text received. It was a picture of Sam and his friends at the airport.

*   *   *

"This is beautiful," Teresa said as Sam turned left onto Nichols Road, driving past elegant shops and busy restaurants that lined each side of the street.

"I'm probably not the guy to ask," Sam answered, "but word is the Country Club Plaza is the best place in KC to dine, shop, and people watch."

He turned right and crossed over Brush Creek and up Wornall Road to the Intercontinental.

"*¡Guau!*" Carlita's eyes went wide. "*Esto es como un castillo. ¿Nos quedamos aquí?*" *Whoa! This is like a castle. We're staying here?*

He winked back at the little girl. "*Los tengo a todos arreglados en dos suites con vista a la Plaza. Nada más que lo mejor para el lanzador estelar de los pequeños Duques de Diriamba.*" *I have you all fixed up in two suites overlooking the Plaza. Nothing but the best for the All-Star pitcher of the Diriamba Little Dukes.*

Sam valeted the van and luggage and followed the still wide-eyed Carlita into the lobby. She was touching everything: running her fingers over the top of the fine furniture, smelling every flower, sitting in every soft, comfortable chair.

Jose and Whiplash pulled Sam over to the corner of the lobby. "Hey, meat, this is way too fancy," Jose whispered. "This has to be costing you a fortune."

Whip nodded. "We'd be fine at the Do Drop Inn."

"Would you guys knock it off?" Sam frowned. "The Royals pay me very well, and you know me, I don't spend it."

"But—" Jose started, but Sam cut him off as he pointed to Carlita, who was now laying on a velvet couch, eyes closed. "Look at her. Having the time of her life. Her joy, and you guys being here, is my gift to me."

He then walked over to the porter who was waiting with their luggage, handed the man a twenty, and called out to Carlita. "Hey, *piña*, what time is it?"

Her eyes flew open, and she sat up straight on the couch. "It's focus time!"

He cupped his hands to his eyes as if he were a horse with blinders. "Big game tonight. First-place Tigers in town. *Paint the K Blue.*"

As he headed for the door, he said over his shoulder, "I left royal-blue jerseys for each of you in your suites. Tickets are at Gate C, dinner in the Diamond Club at five forty-five, and Coach EssCee's first pitch at seven ten."

*　　*　　*

Sydney was nervous. She was going to meet Grandpa Douglas and all of Sam's friends, and several probably knew she was married. Separated, but still married. Would they bring it up? How would she answer? And how much did they know?

As she walked down the Diamond Club aisle to row nine, seat eleven, she saw them. They were easy to find, all wearing their royal-blue uniform tops that Sam had bought them, each with their names on their backs. Two Lopezes, two McCrackens, one Rapino, and one G-Pa Douglas. Perfect. She inhaled a deep, calming breath, put on her best smile, and—

"You must be Coach Sticks!" Jose called out.

His greeting made her turn red. Obviously, Sam had told them even more than she imagined. "Get over here and meet the crew!"

Jose introduced her to each member of the party with a dramatic flair. She shook everyone's hand, sat down between Teresa and Grandpa Douglas, and noticed that Carlita was staring at her with particular curiosity.

"What happened to your mouth?" the little girl asked, and Hunoon smacked her knee.

"Carlita, where are your manners?"

Sydney laughed, actually relieved a bit. "It's called a cleft lip. I was born with it and had surgery to repair it when I was a baby. I still have this scar, but it doesn't bother me."

"Does it hurt?"

"Not at all." Sydney pointed to her teeth. "I had to have a lot of work done to get these straight, so several years in braces and a few more surgeries, but I'm all good now."

There were several more questions from Carlita about whistling, lipstick, and kissing, but for some reason the silly dialogue seemed to relax Sydney even more.

When there was a pause in the conversation, Grandpa Douglas leaned close. "I know why my Samuel would want you as a friend. You are very pretty."

Her heart jumped and she smiled shyly. This was going way better than she'd thought it would.

"Thank you," she whispered back, and then looked down at her purse, where the SpongeBob socks were peeking out. "Oh, I almost forgot." She pulled out the socks and handed them to Carlita. "This is from Sam. He said you would tell me what they're about."

Carlita had them all laughing when she mimicked Coach EssCee walking off the pitcher's mound singing, *"SpongeBob, Squarepannnts, Ahaa Hahaha."*

Dinner was served. They all ordered barbecue; Carlita chose the Rookie Sandwich, a KC classic of smoked, chopped brisket, smothered in barbecue sauce, on a hamburger bun with pickles. She was in heaven.

They chattered about baseball and Nicaragua, Jose's and Teresa's parents battling about who got to babysit the couple's now two-year-old baby boy, and about Grandpa Douglas volunteering at the Southern Ute Cultural Center. Then Whiplash and Hunoon suddenly stood up from their seats.

"Well, butter my butt and call me a biscuit!" Whip cried out. "If it ain't Colonel Bart!"

Sydney turned in her seat as Whip angled his way past knees and elbows to greet the man who was coming down their row with—oh my,

Bette Tomlinson. This man obviously must be her son. The Special Forces colonel who worked with Sam in Afghanistan.

"What a wonderful soo-prise!" Whiplash shook the man's hand excitedly. "I haven't seen you since me 'n' Hunoon had our hotel shut down."

"Mom told me you were flying in," the colonel said, "so she, Sam, and I decided it was a good time to ambush you."

By this time, Hunoon had joined them. Another round of introductions were made, and then the three of them excused themselves to find a more private spot to visit some three rows away.

Bette sat down next to Grandpa Douglas and shook her head. "My son has been part of Special Forces for so long he's paranoid that even a silly conversation about baseball is going to be spied on." As Sydney eyed the trio huddled close, she wasn't so sure they were discussing baseball. A tap on the knee brought her back to the present. It was Carlita, pointing up at the huge scoreboard beyond center field.

"Hey, Ms. Sydney, it's almost six thirty. What do you think EssCee's doing right now?"

As if preplanned, the two of them crossed their legs on their seat, placed their upturned palms on their knees, and began to hum, *"Ommmmm."*

*　　*　　*

The closer they got to first pitch, the more focused Carlita became. Hands clasped against her chest as she watched Sam walk out to the bullpen with his pitching coach, her eyes never moving from her hero as he stretched and long tossed, then warmed up in the bullpen. While every head was turned toward the American flag during the anthem, Carlita's eyes stayed with Sam standing in the pen next to his catcher, his hand on his heart, his head up, calming his breath.

When the song finished, Carlita reached into her backpack and pulled out a small brown scorebook. She dug down again as if searching for something else, and when she couldn't find it, a look of near panic gripped her face.

Sydney reached into her purse, pulled out two pens, and handed one to Carlita. "Is this what you're looking for?"

Carlita exhaled in absolute relief. "*Gracias.* Coach EssCee's never lost a game when I've kept score."

Sydney smiled and opened up her own game program. "Me too."

*   *   *

No Academy-Award-winning screenwriter could have written a more perfect script for that Friday night. Thirty-eight thousand fans, all dressed in blue, stomping and snapping their thundersticks together every pitch, were rewarded with a blowout. Sam worked a 1-2-3 top of the first, and the KC offense exploded for six runs in the bottom of the inning, knocking out the Tigers' starter with a Mason Falls grand slam. Sam was pulled after six, with his team up by eight runs. When the final out was recorded in a 13–2 Royals triumph, the Cloud-Carson crew danced up the aisle with their arms around each other, joining fellow fans belting out their favorite Kansas City songs.

*   *   *

Teresa grabbed Sydney's hand when they entered the Lopez suite at the Intercontinental. Everyone had agreed to meet up there after the game for beer, lemonade, chips, and salsa. Even though the curtains were open to a beautiful view overlooking Brush Creek and the Plaza, Teresa and Jose pulled over three chairs to a far corner of the room.

"Sit down with us," Teresa said. "You and Carlita were so busy scoring the game that we barely had time to talk with you."

Uh oh, here it comes, thought Sydney as she sat opposite the couple. *Twenty-one questions by Sam's closest friends.*

"How's your marriage?" Teresa asked.

The bluntness of the question had Sydney jerk back in her chair. "Excuse me?"

"Sam told us you've had a rough go of it and recently separated. We just wanted to find out where you are mentally and emotionally?"

Jose leaned forward in his chair. "Sammy's been through hell and back, yet he still has a heart so tender he tries to save anyone who's in trouble."

"You're"—Sydney tried to gather her thoughts—"worried about Sam?"

"We saw firsthand the depth of his grief when he lost his dad, sister, and mom over a two-year stretch."

"Sam told me of his depression—and thoughts of suicide."

"He probably wouldn't appreciate us asking you these questions," Jose said, "but we love him."

"He told us about the strip-club allegation," Teresa added, "and that the Royals' general manager asked if he could prove that he wasn't there."

"He had proof." Sydney looked down at her hands. "He was with me."

"Sam is a rare man," Jose said. "A man who has *always* put others before himself. Unfortunately, his tender heart has left him susceptible to certain kinds of people."

Teresa glanced at her husband, then back at Sydney. "Sam once saved a woman's life—protected her honor—and it almost ruined him. But he gave his word that he would never speak about that day, even though he could have freed himself."

Sydney didn't know what to say, a bit confused by the conversation. "You don't think I'm taking advantage of him, do you?"

"No." Jose made sure her vision stayed with his. "But Sam cares for you, and that makes him vulnerable. We don't want to see him hurt again."

At that moment, there was a knock on the door, and Carlita bolted off the couch to answer it, knowing her hero had arrived. She yanked the door open.

"The Royals are awesome!" she shrieked. "You're going to win the World Series!"

"It's only one game." Sam grinned as he gave her a hug. "Gotta do it again tomorrow."

"You beat the Central champs! You're going to be MVP!"

"Slow down, *piña*. Still over two months to go. A lot can happen."

Carlita kicked her right leg in the air and pointed to her foot. "I love my SpongeBob socks!"

Both of them sang out, "*SpongeBob, Squarepannnnts, Ahaa Hahaha.*"

Sydney watched the cute back-and-forth banter between this twelve-year-old girl and the strong, athletic, seemingly carefree baseball star through a new lens. Despite the confidence, poise, and fearlessness, Sam had displayed on the pitcher's mound earlier that evening, she wondered if he indeed was the fragile one in their relationship.

As Teresa raised up to greet Sam, Sydney put a hand on her arm.

"Whatever happened to the woman that Sam saved?"

"She's doing just fine," Teresa said in a voice so soft Sydney could barely hear her. "That woman was me."

*   *   *

Even though they had napped earlier in the day, the weary travelers were ready to close down the party by midnight. Carlita was curled up on the couch, her head on Hunoon's lap, already asleep. Whiplash was nodding off as well.

"I'll carry Carlita to your suite." Sam swept up the little girl into his arms and started for the door. "Try and be at the stables by ten. We'll go for a trail ride and then have a picnic before I have to head to the park."

"Bart and I will help you prep the horses," said Bette as she opened the door.

They said their good nights, Sam carried Carlita to the McCrackens' suite, and then Sam and Sydney headed to the hotel parking structure.

"You have great friends." Sydney looped her arm through his. "Kind, funny, supportive, they definitely have your back."

He grinned down at her. "Did Jose and Teresa put you in a full-court press?"

"A little."

"I figured. They can be a bit overprotective."

"That's funny. That's what they said about you."

He shrugged. "Just want to be a good teammate."

"You're an excellent teammate, Sam."

"Thanks."

Sydney didn't want to reveal any of the conversation she'd had with Jose and Teresa. That was personal. They were simply two friends concerned about a loved one. She understood their apprehension about Sam having an affair with a married woman.

Affair? God, that sounded awful. Affairs were sins her Bible study group talked about, but certainly would never include someone as prudish as Sydney Morgan—er—Harrison in. There was, though, another subject she wanted to discuss.

"I need to tell you something, Sam."

"Sure," he said, a bit distracted as he raised up on his tiptoes and searched the parking lot. "Did you park on level two or three? I'm right next to your car, so they should be easy to find."

She pulled him around to face her. "This is important. While I was in your house today getting Carlita's socks, I kind of read the notes on your nightstand."

His jaws flexed slightly. "What did you read?"

"Something about Dixon and Hazrat and construction and—"

He raised a hand to quiet her. "Those are just random thoughts. I'm trying to figure some stuff out."

"Do you think Dixon's the man behind the strip-club accusations?"

"I don't want to talk about it," he said, too quickly.

There it was, thought Sydney, *just as Jose and Teresa had said. Sam's trying to protect someone instead of defending himself. But who?*

He forced a smile. "Did you read anything else?"

She gave an embarrassed nod. *"Sydney. Dream. Biological father."*

"Oh yeah," he said, and his face changed as if he was relieved to move on from the previous topic. "I forgot to tell you. I had a dream about you meeting your birth dad. Seemed like a good guy. Lakota chief. Kind eyes.

He was teaching you the steps to your people's Sun Dance."

Her shoulders gave a little. "Why are you so interested in me meeting my birth father?"

"I'm not," Sam said sincerely. "I had a dream. And in my culture, dreams are important. We believe they're an extension of us, an opportunity to travel to other realms and communicate with ancestors and spirit guides that can help us heal."

"Maybe I'll meet him someday. But only when the time is right. I'm still working through my own stuff."

"There's never a perfect time, Syd. We're all working on something everyday. That's why we're here. Perhaps it's like that Lakota proverb I read in Jenny's journal: *To go on a vision quest is to go into the presence of the great mystery.*"

She mulled this over. "Do you think meeting my birth father is part of my vision quest?"

"I don't know. That's up to you."

He stood on his tiptoes again and scanned the garage. "Found 'em. Side by side, like two old friends dreaming about their ancestors."

His joke broke her melancholy, and she leaned against him as they walked to their cars.

"Sam?" she murmured softly.

"Mmhmm?"

"I'd love to stay with you tonight."

"But it's late. We have to be up early—and your mom and dad will worry."

"I'm twenty-six."

"You could be sixty-six, and your parents would still worry if you're late."

Her hand swept up and pulled his face down to hers, and she kissed him hard. *God, he wasn't even gone and she already missed him.* Both of them felt the sexual urge of one week apart, and Sydney sank against Sam and opened her mouth wider.

Lost in the heat of the moment, unaware of the black sedan on the other side of the parking lot with the window cracked a few inches, they didn't see a man with a camera taking their picture.

CHAPTER FORTY-THREE

Stilwell, Kansas

July 2013

It was almost one in the morning when Sydney parked her car in front of her parents' house. There was little breeze, and the blackness of the sky was softened by cloud cover. The waning moon in the eastern sky stretched long shadows of the maple and oak trees in the front yard into an eerie path toward the house. As Sydney hurried up the brick lane to the front door, she suddenly froze. Someone was sitting in her father's rocking chair.

"Hey, babe," Blake said and then stood up and slowly walked her way.

"You scared me." She put her hand on her chest to calm her breathing.

"You're out pretty late."

"I was with friends."

"Where?"

"Royals game."

"Yeah, I saw."

She paled.

"Saw you on TV. Camera was panning the crowd, and I thought I saw you in the Diamond Club. I had to rewind a couple of times to make sure—but it was you."

She remained quiet as he took a step closer and brushed a strand of hair away from her face. "You look beautiful. Even wearing makeup. Anyone special you want to tell me about?"

"No."

It was then that she realized, with a sinking feeling, that they were alone. Alone with her husband and she was scared. She could smell the whiskey on his breath and took a step back.

His hand slid down her left arm and grabbed her elbow. "C'mon, baby, it's time to come home."

Sydney felt her heart begin to pound as she struggled to steady herself. "I'm not going with you, Blake."

"I've changed, Sydney. I went with your dad to Bible study and even stopped by an AA meeting."

"Then why can I smell whiskey on your breath?"

"Because I'm lost without you. I cried when I saw you on TV enjoying the game without me. I just needed a little help to get over my broken heart."

She looked down at her hands, absent her wedding ring, and covered her right over her left.

"Who were those people you were sitting with?"

"Friends."

"Looked like Injuns to me. You tryin' to find your Lakota daddy?"

"Shut up," she said, her words coming out with more force than she expected. "That's none of your business."

His grip tightened on her elbow. "Don't you ever tell me what my business is. You're my wife. It's my job to protect you."

"You're hurting me, Blake."

He released her arm.

Her eyes darted sideways, to the front door. It was time to get inside. "We can talk about this later," she said firmly. "I'm tired."

He backed up to let her pass, but she felt his eyes following her every step.

"You'd better not be dressing up for someone else," he said in a low voice, "because that would be real painful."

*　　*　　*

She checked the rearview mirror every five seconds on her drive to the Tomlinson farm the next few days. As she punched in the code to open the gate on Monday afternoon, she was thankful that Bette believed in solid security, rarely leaving the one entrance to her property open. Only a few people knew the combination, and Bette could unlock the gate from her car or house on the days the Urban Wildlife Academy was scheduled. Sydney drove through the entrance and glanced up at the mirror to make sure the gate closed.

*   *   *

The Cloud-Carson party was setting up for a picnic in the shade of the barn. Sam, Jose, and Whiplash were by the Weber, grilling up everything from steaks to broccoli and corn on the cob. It smelled awesome. Grandpa Douglas, Hunoon, and Teresa were over by the corral, watching Carlita ride a quarter horse named Jenny. After her first trail ride on Saturday, the little girl had fallen in love with horses and had begged to go riding ever since.

Monday was a rare day off for the Royals, in the middle of the longest home-stand of the year. After taking two of three hard-fought battles from the Tigers, KC had moved within four games of first place, so the team welcomed a day to recover.

Instead, Sam had taken his crew on a tour of his adopted city. To the Nelson Art Gallery, to the Jazz and Negro League Museums, for lunch in the River Market, and then on a stroll around the Lewis and Clark Historic Park at Kaw Point, the site where the famed expedition camped in June of 1804 on their way to the Pacific Northwest.

"Ain't you wore out yet?" Whip asked Sam as he lifted up the grill's lid to check on the steaks. "You play hardball every day, and then on yer one day off, you hire on as a tour guide?"

Sam shrugged. "It was my first time seeing some of those sights too."

"He was the same way growing up," Jose said. "There wasn't enough time in the day for old Sammy. First to practice, last to leave, always trying to be better than everybody."

Sam gave him a sideways glance. "That wasn't the reason."

"I know, but you still couldn't understand why everybody wasn't as good as you. You were the fastest, strongest, most focused, competitive dude we ever played with."

"It wasn't easy."

"You made it look easy."

"I 'member the first time I caught EssCee in Afghanny," Whiplash cut in. "Long hair, baggy pants, tore-up tunic, filthy Chitrali cap, looked like he just fell off a turnip truck."

That got Jose and Sam to laughing.

"But then, shoot-fire, he threw that ball. I coulda taped a teacup to my kneecap, and Sammy woulda hit the center ten outta ten from a hundred feet."

Sam covered his face to hide his grin, but Jose kept the tease train rolling. "Yeah, Hunoon told me that his cutter broke so many bats that Señor Estevez had to take out a loan from Banco Lafise Nicaragua to buy new ones."

"And his curve hissed like a jungle pit viper—"

All three men stopped when they heard Sydney's car come up the drive.

"If it ain't Sammy's cutie pie," Whip said. "That girl's pretty as a speckled pup."

"And dense as one too," added Jose, "if she's got a crush on Sasquatch."

Sam crossed his arms over his chest. "What is this? Pick on Sam Day?"

"Not a bad idea," said Whip. He then leaned close to Jose and whispered, "Ten dollars says Sasquatch is too embarrassed to give her a hug."

"You're on."

Sydney walked over with a cherry pie in one hand and a cautious look on her face. "You two look like you're up to no good."

She handed the pie to Whip, who pulled her in and gave her a warm hug and kiss on the cheek. Jose then tapped Whip on the shoulder as if he were cutting in on a cotillion dance. He, too, gave Sydney an affectionate embrace, kissed her on the cheek, and led her over to Sam.

"Have you met the esteemed Coach Sticks?"

Sam narrowed his eyes. "What's going on, fellas?"

"Would you just give her a proper greeting?"

Sam stood awkwardly for a spell, his gaze moving from Jose to Whip, to the grill, and then settling on Sydney, as if unsure what it was he was supposed to do or say. Finally, he shrugged and stuck out his fist. "Hey, Sticks."

As soon as Sydney's knuckles touched his, Whip clapped his hands in delight and spun to Jose. "Ten dollars, brotha!"

Jose gave Sam a disappointed shake of his head and reached for his wallet.

"I thought you had evolved, dude. Guess I was wrong."

"What did you guys bet on?"

"Don't tell him," said Whip. "Let him guess."

Jose raised both brows to Sydney. "Or let his girlfriend guess."

Sam's face flushed, but not Sydney's as the wheels in her mind slowly turned in search of the answer. And when it arrived, she snorted back a laugh. "You guys are mean."

Sam gave a confused look.

"Shoot-fire, boy." Whip gave Sam a hearty pat on the back. "You got skeels that'll fool any hitter and can track wind over water, but Lordy, you'd search all day fer sunglasses that was a-sittin' on toppa yer head."

Sam still looked puzzled.

"They made a bet on how you'd greet me." Sydney grinned. "Jose bet that you'd hug me, and Whip bet that you wouldn't."

Sam's month fell open.

"We both gave her a hug and kiss when she arrived," Jose said, "but all three days she's been here, the most affection we've seen you give her was a high five or fist bump."

Whip winked. "And we know you been lockin' lips as soon as we outta sight."

Sam flamed red. "Geez, I thought the clubhouse was bad. You guys are the worst friends ever. Total turds. Sadistic scumbags. Heartless . . ."

"Hooligans?" finished Jose.

"Syd's birthday's next month," said Whip. "Waddaya think he gits her? I'm goin' with a spatula."

"Not romantic enough," suggested Jose. "How about a new shovel to clean the stables?"

Sam looked over at Sydney, who was covering her mouth to hide her own laughter.

"You're just as bad as they are," he muttered. He turned away from the trio and lifted the lid off the grill, not caring at all when the smoke billowed up to hide his embarrassment. "I'm only trying to be courteous and respectful."

That remark was greeted by another round of laughs, and then Sydney walked over to a still stewing Sam, leaned her head against his back, and silently mouthed to Jose and Whip, *"Isn't he cute?"*

*   *   *

As the sun dipped low in the west, the heat waves shimmered off the brome grasses that stretched all the way to the edge of the Tomlinson property. It was time to eat: steaks and catfish, baked beans and cole slaw, grilled peppers, broccoli, onions, and corn on the cob. Whiplash said grace, dinner was served, and Sam again became the target of everyone's barbs.

Jose told the story of Sam's first girlfriend, the former Miss Colorado, who sent heart-shaped brownies to the Mesa State clubhouse. Teresa shared a funny tale of Jenny ripping into Major League scouts for not drafting her brother, and Carlita had everyone in stitches telling of Coach EssCee's obsession with Nicaragua's jaguarundi.

"Coach was crazy," she said. "He'd stare at the track forever, then get out his knife and dig through the poop, and tell us what the cat ate and how old the poop was."

"That's pretty much how he was raised," said Jose. "From coyote to bear to bobcat scat, nobody digs crap like ole Sammy."

They all laughed until Carlita asked, "Does Coach have a Native American name?"

Sam's smile slipped. He glanced at Grandpa Douglas and gave a brief shake of his head.

"No, Samuel," Douglas said. "We're with the kind of people who would understand."

Sam took a deep breath, steeling himself to what came next.

"It was his sister's funeral ceremony," Douglas said. "Beautiful February day on our mountain. But we could see a storm coming swiftly over the San Juans. The temperature dropped, snow began to fall, winds roared, and a blizzard followed."

"Near the end of the ceremony," Jose said, "a mother cried out that her five-year-old daughter was gone. She had wandered off. We searched the grounds and the house, everywhere, but found nothing until Sam discovered her track near the woods. We called the police and rescue team, but by then, the blizzard was so fierce that no one could get up the hill."

Douglas nodded. "Sam went alone into the storm to find that little girl. He was gone for many hours, but I knew my grandson would not return until he found her."

Sydney straightened up on the bench, staring at Sam. His face was void of any emotion, and his eyes seemed remote with memory.

"The storm worsened, windchill minus-five, whiteout so bad you couldn't see five feet. We thought all was lost." Jose smiled at Douglas. "But not Grandpa D. Just past ten o'clock, he stood up, walked to the kitchen, opened the back door, pointed into the darkness, and said, 'I feel him.'" Jose looked again to Douglas. "What did you feel, Grandpa?"

A proud smile lit the old man's face, and he pointed to Sam. "I felt my grandson. The one who walks with the wind."

A chill went up Sydney's spine, part from the story, part from watching Sam, whose gaze seemed lost in some otherworldly place. She wanted to hear more but was afraid, if she said anything, the story would end. This was a side of Sam that she didn't know. His culture. His family. His people. His past.

"Walks with the wind," Carlita whispered, then raised up, walked over, and sat down next to Sam. "You're Walks with the Wind."

Sam smiled, the haze of his reflection gone.

"Is your mountain as beautiful as ours in Nicaragua?"

He nodded.

"When was the last time you were there?"

"Four years ago."

"That's a long time," Carlita said sincerely. "Why haven't you gone back?"

He paused for a long moment, unsure how to respond.

Finally, it was Jose who spoke. "Sam had a dream, Carlita. And in the dream, his sister told him he couldn't return to his mountain until he brought someone he loved."

"That's silly," Carlita said. "It's just a dream."

Sam put his arm around the little girl. "No, *piña*. In my culture, dreams are very important. Many times, they offer signs that we can apply to our life. I will respect my sister's wish."

Sydney flinched, as if Sam's words were meant for her. She recalled Sam's dream about her meeting her biological father. At the time, she didn't want to talk about it. Why was she resisting? Was she afraid of a sign? Afraid of what she might find? She raised her vision and saw that Sam was looking directly at her.

*   *   *

Barney curled up on top of Sam's feet during dinner, hoping his master might toss him a piece of whatever it was on that grill that smelled so good. Sam knew he shouldn't, but he stealthily reached down and gave Barney a generous chunk of steak. With his daily quest realized, the little dog trotted off behind the barn and happily dug in.

For those at the table, the playful teasing had moved on from Sam to Jose, to Whiplash, to Hunoon, until finally Grandpa Douglas clapped his hands and nodded to Carlita.

"Have you ever had homemade cherry pie with vanilla ice cream, young lady?"

She shook her head.

"Well, it's time you tasted the greatest dessert in the USA."

Carlita rubbed her belly in anticipation.

"Do you mind if we wait a bit?" Bart Tomlinson asked. The Special Forces colonel had been a quiet listener for much of the evening, but now it seemed as if he had something important on his mind. "I have an early flight tomorrow, and I'd like to visit with Sam before I turn in."

"You need a little privacy?" Jose asked.

The colonel nodded.

*   *   *

Sam led him to a quiet spot overlooking the river. He chose it not only because it had a couple of fallen elms they could sit on, but also because he had a clear view of any prying eyes.

"Before you left Afghanistan," Tomlinson said, "you asked me to update you on any renewed construction near Parun."

Sam's back stiffened. "What's going on?"

"When was the last time you talked with Mr. Hazrat?"

"Two weeks ago. He calls me on his sat-phone every three months. I just want to make sure his village is safe and that the government's kept their promise not to build on his land."

"What did he say?"

"Nothing but more offers from Chinese and US corporations. He's turned them all down."

"Then I have bad news." Tomlinson frowned. "Despite the investigation into private military companies by our government and the Afghanistan Natural Resources Oversight Network, there's been movement in the Nuristan Province. Three days ago, I received an email from the Special Forces officer who replaced me at Bagram letting me know that a Provincial Reconstruction Team had begun repairs on your old road."

Both of Sam's brows rose in interest. "Who's handling security?"

"It's not DiamondBar," Tomlinson said skeptically, "but that doesn't mean they're not involved. They could swap details with another company but still control rights to that region."

Sam pressed his right hand to his forehead and said nothing.

"The PRT crew chief told Major Garland that they're only cutting *across* Hazrat's land to connect Parun to Kamdesh."

"Parun to Kamdesh? That's in the middle of nowhere. Both districts combined serve less than thirty thousand people."

"Afghanistan's first oil production began last year, Sam. That means more roads will be needed for greater access to ports on the Arabian Sea."

"The Hindu Kush isn't oil country."

"Then whoever's behind this wants Hazrat's mountain for something else."

Sam's jaws flexed in fury. He wanted to tell the Special Forces officer everything he knew about DiamondBar: about his being blackmailed, about Dixon bribing politicians, circumventing Afghan and international mining laws, all in an effort to steal land from a poor mountain village. But Sam had no proof that Dixon was behind this new project. And until he did, he needed to keep his backstory quiet or Hazrat's village would be in danger.

"I know you can't tell me what happened between you and Dixon," said Tomlinson, "but with Chinese and Pakistani corporations maneuvering for control, American companies are obviously concerned … and that includes your old boss."

Sam shook his head sadly. "There are so many people who suffer unjustly—oppressed by systems over which they have no control."

"We may need some inside help then."

"You're not thinking about Hunoon?"

Tomlinson nodded. "She spent forty years in Afghanistan. Her brother's a policeman in Mitarlam, and his wife's sister is married to the mayor of Parun. If anyone can get to the bottom of this, it's Hunoon McCracken."

Sam rubbed his chin thoughtfully. "I don't want to bring them any trouble, but if they can find out who's financing the road through Hazrat's land, it sure would help."

The colonel glanced sidelong at Sam, as if trying to figure him out. "Maybe it's time you gave Dixon a call. Tell him to stop with the lies, or your deal is off."

Sam nodded absentmindedly but didn't answer.

"Just choose your words carefully because he'll twist anything you say to favor himself." The colonel paused and fixed his gaze at Sam. "Play him like you do when you're facing a bases-loaded, nobody-out situation. Don't go for the strikeout. Just minimize the damage."

*　　*　　*

Sydney tossed the last of the trash bags into the garbage bin and walked back to the picnic table. Sam had just finished cleaning the grill and was tightening the cover in case a summer storm blew in. *No threat of that,* thought Sydney. It was a humid but clear July evening, still only eight thirty as the sun slipped beyond the horizon.

The Cloud-Carson crew was already gone, back to the hotel after a long day of touring and eating. She'd felt uncommonly comfortable with everyone, particularly Teresa; they'd even shared contact information and promised to call each other in the coming weeks.

Then, of course, there was the meeting. Sam had barely said anything upon returning from a private counsel called by Colonel Tomlinson. There was one thing the two men had in common. Afghanistan. What had a Special Forces colonel and a simple private military employee seen in that war-torn country?

Sam rolled the grill next to the barn and turned around, still silent.

"Penny for your thoughts?" Sydney asked innocently.

He sighed heavily. "Nothing that would interest you."

"You mean like Drake Dixon?"

Her question was so unexpected, he took a step back.

"I asked Jose and Teresa if they'd heard of him."

His jaws tensed. "What did they say?"

"Not much," she paused, but held Sam's gaze. "Only that he's pure evil."

"Stay out of it, Sydney," he said in a low voice and then turned away.

Very tentatively, she walked over, slipped her arms around his waist, and rested her head against his back. "You were there for me, Sam. I want to be there for you."

He curled his arm around and kissed the top of her head. "I'm sorry. It's not something I can talk about right now." He then released her and forced a weary smile. "How about a lemonade?"

She looked up into eyes that were kind but tired. "I'd love to, Sam, but you've had a long day. You need to get some rest."

"No way." He took her hand and led her away from the barn. "I need me some Sydney time."

*　　*　　*

Neither of them said much on the walk to his cottage. She knew Sam's mind was still working overtime through a myriad of thoughts he wouldn't, or couldn't, share with her. But there might be another way to get his mind off what troubled him.

"I'll get our drinks," he said as he opened the screen door and followed her inside.

Sydney sat down on the patio sofa and picked up a catalog that was sitting on the coffee table. "Sundance?" she called out to Sam. "What are you doing with a Sundance catalog?"

"It's not mine," Sam yelled back. "I was picking up Bette's mail the other day."

"Bette shops at Sundance?" She flipped through a few pages of the catalog that featured stylish women's apparel, artisan jewelry, and expensive footwear. "I thought she bought her clothes from Field and Stream?"

He laughed and handed her a lemonade. "They have a Sundance store in Leawood."

Sydney cocked her head up at him. "How would you know?"

"I drove by it the other day."

She rolled her eyes and went back to studying the fashions. "Wow, these floral embroidered jeans are beautiful. Two hundred dollars–yikes … And these Sidewinder boots, four hundred and twenty-eight dollars. Ouch … This sterling-silver-and-stone necklace is stunning–four hundred fifty dollars! Outta my league."

Sam didn't speak for a long time. He watched Sydney, as if memorizing the pages that most interested her.

Finally, he pointed to a floral velvet top with antique brass metal buttons. "That would look good on you."

She closed the magazine and cocked a teasing eyebrow up at him. "Do you know what would look good on me?"

He shook his head and reached for the catalog.

She knocked his hand away. "*You*–Mr. Cloud-Carson–would look good on *me*."

He grinned suddenly and held out his hand. "Sounds pretty expensive, Sticks. I hope you're not outta my league."

CHAPTER FORTY-FOUR

Oakland, California

August 2013

Three days later, the Cloud-Carson party was over. Jose, Teresa, and Grandpa Douglas headed home for Colorado; Whiplash, Hunoon, and Carlita to Nicaragua; and Sam on a charter to California to play the Athletics and Angels. Even though he didn't think he'd be traded, Sam breathed a sigh of relief when the July 31 trade deadline passed. Exactly one minute past the three p.m. deadline, he received an *I told you so* text from Sydney.

He smiled.

What a cool friend, he thought. *I really enjoy her company, but where's this going? … Is Sydney emotionally ready for another relationship? … Will Blake suddenly realize what an incredible woman he's married to and change? … Am I making her decision more difficult? Am I inhibiting Sydney from the lessons she's supposed to learn? Should I back off? … I don't want to, but …*

The team landed in Oakland on Thursday night and checked into the historic St. Francis Hotel in San Francisco. Sam joined a few teammates for a beer at a nearby pub. The next afternoon, he took the early bus to the ballpark for his two-days-after-a-start workout: yoga, medicine ball, jog the stadium steps, sixty-yard sprints, and then a throwing session with his pitching coach.

"I'm still not used to this," he said to fellow rookie pitcher Bo Chapman as they stepped off the bus at the Oakland Coliseum. "Five-star hotels, free food, per diem, great facilities—we're spoiled."

"It beats the bush leagues," said Chapman, who had spent four years in the minors after being the Royals' first-round pick out of the University of Arizona in 2009. "But you don't know much about that, do ya, Sammy, since you only spent a month in the minors."

"Yeah, us five-thousand-dollar Nicaraguan bonus babies got it made in the shade." Sam elbowed his friend in the side. "What was your bonus?

"Oneponsen," Chapman mumbled into his hand.

"What was that, Bo? I can't hear you."

"One-point-seven—dickhead."

Sam glanced at Bo. "One-point-seven thousand? Or million?"

"Million, asshole who leads me in wins, ERA, and strikeouts."

Sam laughed and put an arm around Chapman as they walked down the steps to the clubhouse. "Me 'n' you baby, combined a bonus of one-point-seven-zero-zero-zero-zero-five, which means you get to buy lunch tomorrow."

"I walked into that one." Chapman scowled, then opened the clubhouse door. "But I'll take you to Chinatown and buy you some dumplings after dumping on me."

"That's a good plan," said Sam, who stepped inside and froze. Emblazoned on every television monitor in the visitors' clubhouse was a picture of Sam in a passionate embrace with a woman. He remembered the moment. One week ago. Hotel Intercontinental parking structure. Walking Sydney to her car. Someone had taken their picture.

"Turn it off," he said in a low voice as he scanned the room for who was responsible. The last thing Sydney needed was for someone to shame her by plastering her affair to the media. He could deal with it. But not Sydney. He headed for the computer in the corner of the clubhouse.

Relief pitcher Derek Cobb blocked his path. "Who's the babe, Sammy?"

He shoved him out of the way and powered off the computer. "Where'd you get that picture?"

Cobb recovered and straightened up. "Jesus, ya thin-skinned rookie, I was just having a little fun."

Sam's eyes glassed over as he glared at Cobb. "I asked you a question. Where did you get that picture?"

"It was texted to me today with the question, *Who's the babe with Sam Cloud-Carson?*"

Sam flinched. Drake Dixon. How far would his former boss go to crush him and hurt anyone along the way? Collateral damage. It was part of the DiamondBar code. Sometimes a village needed to be sacrificed to take out their leader. Colonel Tomlinson had warned him that Dixon was the kind of egomaniac who wouldn't rest until his vengeance was satisfied.

He had to steady himself. Calm down. Breathe.

But just as Sam inhaled a deep breath, Cobb said, "Was she the stripper you roughed up?"

The fury that had been building since he stepped into the clubhouse exploded. Sam grabbed Cobb by the throat, shoved him up against a locker, and drew back his fist to strike him. He was tackled from behind.

"What the hell's going on?" Charles demanded as he rushed out of his office.

Cobb stumbled from his locker, rubbing his throat. "Rookie went crazy on me."

"Just a little misunderstanding." said Chapman, still holding back an enraged Sam. "We got it under control."

Charles ignored Bo and pointed to the two combatants. "Cloud-Carson and Cobb. In my office. Right now!"

*   *   *

Once inside, Sam tried to steady himself; it was all he could do to remain standing. Finally, he leaned against the wall and looked over at his teammate. "Sorry, Derek."

Cobb continued to rub his neck. "It was just a picture of you kissing a girl. What's the big fucking deal?"

"Quiet," ordered Charles, who then nodded at Cobb. "What happened?"

"I got a text today. Unidentified number. Picture of Sam making out with some girl. You can't see her face because she has her back to the camera, but you can see his ugly mug." He hesitated, as if to make sure Sam didn't go rogue again. "Anyway, the person also texted, *Who's the babe with Sam Cloud-Carson?*"

Charles raised both brows to Sam. "That's why you choked him?"

He shook his head.

"Sam went after me," Cobb said, "when I asked him if the girl in the picture was the stripper he roughed up."

Charles narrowed his eyes. "How do you know about that?"

"It's a small clubhouse. People talk. I heard about it last week."

"Well, it's bullshit, Derek." Charles leaned forward in his chair. "Our lawyers investigated those allegations and found them to be complete lies. The owner of the strip club even admitted to receiving cash for an accusation against Sam."

"Did he say where the money came from?" Sam asked.

Charles shook his head.

"I think I should explain to the team what's going on, Skip."

"Let me talk to our GM first. This photo might have come from the same person who paid off the strip-club owner." Charles paused, making sure both players understood his next words. "But this can't happen again. We're a team. We fight for each other. Teamwork is why the Tigers are looking over their shoulder. They know we're coming for them. But the only way we're going to win this is together. Got it?"

Both players nodded, shook hands, and Sam opened the door. Waiting on the other side was the pitching coach, Andy Phillips.

"We have a situation," he said to the Royals' manager. "One of the writers was in the clubhouse and saw everything."

Charles exhaled and stood up. "Looks like I have to put out another fire."

*   *   *

Sam sat by the window of his hotel room, phone in hand, as he stared blankly out at the activity that buzzed around Union Square. Horns honked, shoppers hurried past beggars, and tourists took pictures. The St. Francis doorman whistled for a cab, and pigeons and seagulls circled over outdoor restaurants hoping for a crumb to drop.

Sam saw none of it. Instead, his mind was consumed by what had happened the day before. He'd let his emotions get the best of him. The result was a distracted clubhouse, and the lost focus led to a lost game. Oakland 7, KC 4. The Royals weren't good enough to win on talent alone. Much like Charles said, *The only way we win is together.*

The smears would not stop unless he called Dixon and demanded they stop. The police pullovers, the strip club, and now the picture of his affair with Sydney. It was only going to get worse.

He thought he had done a good job of moving on from his time with DiamondBar, but obviously Dixon had penetrated so deeply into his subconscious that he still had some hold on him. It was time to call him out.

*   *   *

Dixon clicked off the television and sat down in his leather chair. It was the second time he had watched his interview with CNN from two nights earlier. After a failed meeting with the Afghan government over mineral rights, he had called the network to offer his take on the war.

"Somebody has to put pressure on the Pentagon," he grumbled to his lawyer. "Thankfully, CNN let me rant about all the problems we're having in that fucked-up country."

"America needed to hear from a top official after last week's bombing in the Wardak Province," King said.

"Eight more deaths, Barry. Americans don't like to hear about their boys getting killed."

"They need to know how private military companies like yours can solve the problem."

"That's what I told CNN. It's time to bring our troops home, privatize the war, and pay proven veterans who served in Afghanistan, know the lay of the land, and get shit done. Hell, I'll bet PMCs could end this mess in two, three years, max"–Dixon winked–"and take control of the country's abundant natural resources in the process."

"Your comments did fire up the Afghan president. Karzai said your plan violates their national sovereignty–he called it a form of neo-colonialism."

"What's new? Every extremist in the world has been telling their followers for years that America's the imperial devil. That we're only interested in enriching ourselves while we take down Muslim countries."

"We do have a history of starting fights in their neighborhoods."

"Survival of the fittest," said Dixon, who then straightened up in his chair and looked directly at his lawyer, "Have you made any progress in finding out who Carson gave his intel to on what we were doing in the Nuristan Province?"

"Nothing yet. Our mole inside the Afghan government says no one at the Department of Commerce and Industry, nor the Natural Resources Oversight Network has heard of Carson."

"Then it has to be Hazrat and somebody else. Maybe a member of his Ute tribe or that Special Forces colonel."

King scrunched his forehead in concern. "Let's hope it's not Tomlinson. He's one highly respected man."

"But he's also a guy who's aware of Sam's troubled history," said Dixon. "He knows about the problems Sam had with coworkers, how he defied orders, and about his nervous breakdown–"

A buzz from the intercom ended the conversation. It was Dixon's executive secretary, Marsha Byers. "I'm sorry to interrupt, Mr. Dixon, but, um, it's Sam Cloud-Carson. He's demanding to speak with you."

"Put him through." Dixon leaned back in his chair and gave a sly smile to King. "Speak of the devil. Our boy must be starting to crack." Dixon pressed a button on his communications console. "I'll record the call in case he blows up or says something stupid we can use later." He then clicked on the speaker phone so his lawyer could listen in.

"Well, aren't I a lucky guy," Dixon said in a condescending tone. "Getting a phone call from a Big League star."

There was a long pause as Dixon waited for a reply. Then finally, from the speaker, came the deep, haunting voice of his enemy.

"I thought you and I had an agreement."

Drake took a deep breath and braced himself on the desk. "What agreement, Sam?"

"That I don't talk about your crimes in Afghanistan and you leave me alone."

"I committed no crimes, and I've left you alone."

"What about the random police stops? The reporter who asked me about Frank Weber? The strip club? And yesterday, the picture of me with the girl?"

"I don't know what you're talking about."

"Don't lie to me," Sam deadpanned. "Even your lawyer knows you can't be trusted. Hi, Barry, I'm sure you're listening to this call."

King winced but said nothing.

"I truly have no idea what you're talking about," Dixon said.

There was another long pause before Sam said, "Why don't we call CNN right now and tell them what you're really planning in Afghanistan?"

Dixon balled his fists in anger. "I take it you heard my interview."

"I did. Great propaganda. Would have made Benito Mussolini proud."

"Fuck you, Carson. I talked about private military contractors winning the war—not just my DiamondBar team. Our military has been over there thirteen years and accomplished nothing. It's time we bring our boys home and let PMCs get the job done."

"Cut the patriotic bullshit, Dixon. You wouldn't be in Afghanistan unless our government was lining your pockets. We both know you're still after their natural resources."

This time there was a long pause on Dixon's end of the phone.

"Guess that got under your skin, huh?" said Sam. "Any roads in the Nuristan Province you're doing security for?"

"Everything we've done is totally legit. We're working with the Ministry of Mines, we've followed the guidelines of the Extractive Industries Transparency Initiative, and–"

Sam cut him off. "Have you stayed away from Hazrat's mountain?"

"Of course!" He was furious with himself for letting this boy get to him. Again. He remembered the first time he had met Sam, at the doctor's office in Colorado, the day Carson's sister was diagnosed with a serious kidney disease that would eventually claim her life. He recalled Sam's unreadable face, even at seventeen years of age, his dark eyes studying him, as if a wolf locked onto his prey.

Dixon needed to remind himself that Carson was nothing. He came from nothing, and when this fiasco was all over, he would return him to nothing. Dixon inhaled another deep breath and said, "I've instructed my operations director to keep our people out of the Nuristan Province."

"What about other PMCs?"

"I don't have any control over them, but I've kept my word."

He heard a laugh on the other end of the line. "Your word is worthless, Dixon. Leverage is the only thing you understand. And I have the leverage because of what I know. Now, lay off with the police stops, the strip club, and having your goons take pictures of my girlfriend."

Then, just as Dixon was about to respond, the line went dead.

Dixon shook his head in genuine disbelief. *Who the hell did that son of a bitch think he was talking to?* After a moment to calm his anger, he said, "I think he's starting to crack."

King sat across from him, rubbing his chin.

"Twitter was abuzz today," Dixon continued, "ripping Carson for fighting with a teammate, and then the team played like shit. It's only a matter of time before he flips out again."

"I don't know." King shook his head. "He was pretty clever on the phone. Said nothing we can use to blackmail him."

Dixon silenced his lawyer with a flip of his hand. "I won't drop the hammer on Carson until after the Afghan government meets with representatives from the US, China, and Pakistan next month. I want to hear about their plans for new transportation routes for oil, minerals, and lumber. When that conference ends, we'll have a better understanding of which direction we want to go. Until then, we need to let a certain husband in Kansas City know that Carson's been having an affair with his wife."

CHAPTER FORTY-FIVE

Kansas City, Missouri

August 2013

As the Royals filed off the plane after a win-three, lose-four West Coast trip, Sam sidled over to where his manager was waiting for his luggage. Everyone was beat. They'd played an afternoon game in Anaheim and lost in twelve innings, 5–4. It was now two o'clock in the morning, and half the team had already hit the road, while the other half drowsily waited for their bags to be pulled from the plane.

"Hey, Skip," Sam said softly, "thanks again for letting me speak to the team about what's been going on."

"You handled it well, kid. Hopefully it will put to rest any gossip that was drifting through the clubhouse."

"I hope so, sir. The last thing I wanted to do was slow our momentum."

"This is my forty-third year in pro ball," Charles said. "I've never been on a team that went unbeaten. A hundred sixty-two is a grind. Highs. Lows. Distractions. Injuries. Attitude … My advice? Embrace the grind."

"Yes, sir. I also wanted to tell you that I called Drake Dixon. I told him to knock it off."

Charles turned to face Sam. "What did he say?"

"He denied it."

"But you still think he's behind it?"

Sam nodded. "I wish I could tell you why, sir, but I can't. I hope my silence doesn't hurt the team."

Charles put an arm around Sam's shoulder. "We're stronger than you think, Sam. Just focus on your job. Like I said earlier, highs, lows, good times, and bad—embrace the grind."

*   *   *

Sam checked his phone before heading home. One text from Sydney.

Bummer long game on getaway day. I would have dropped by had you gotten in at a decent hour. You're pitching tonight, so you need your rest. MB, Phil, and I will meet you after game at Gram and Dun. XOXO PS TV guys showed you blowing bubbles in dugout. You were terrible. We'll have to work on that.

He smiled. He wanted to see her too, talk to her in person about what had happened in the Oakland clubhouse. They had talked on the phone the day after the incident. Mary Beth was the first to see it on Twitter and had immediately called Sydney and read her the tweet.

Picture of Cloud-Carson with mystery girl leads to fight in Oakland.

He had apologized profusely. Apologized for not being aware that someone had followed him from the ballpark, had seen where he had parked, had waited over an hour for him to return, and had taken their picture. He had to protect Sydney, maybe cut back on how much time he spent with her. But not right now. Saturday was her birthday.

*   *   *

Sydney had just applied the last of the mascara to her eyelashes when she heard a knock at the door. Mary Beth and Phil must be early to pick her up. She hurried to open the front door and froze.

"Hey, baby." Blake was holding a bouquet of red roses. "I know tomorrow's your birthday, but I wanted to make sure the love of my life got an early gift."

Sydney stood in the doorway, unsure of what to do. MB and Phil would be there any minute to pick her up and go to the game. Then they'd connect with Sam afterward at Gram and Dun. She had her misgivings about meeting him in public, particularly after the media buzz about Sam with the unknown woman. But both agreed to keep this encounter cordial, simply four friends having a beer after the game.

"May I come in?" Blake asked.

"Yes, of course." She hesitated before taking the flowers, wishing he hadn't brought them. "I don't have much time. I'm going out with MB and Phil."

"Where?"

"Royals game."

"You've been going to a lot of those lately."

"How do you know?"

"I have my sources."

She paled.

"You look beautiful," he said sweetly. "Do you have a date?"

Her shoulders slumped forward. She didn't want to do this now. She just wanted him to leave. "Let me get a vase for these." She headed to the kitchen.

Blake sat down in front of the coffee table and saw a text pop up on Sydney's phone.

He knew her code, so he quickly typed the numbers and read the message.

Look forward to seeing you after the game at Gram and Dun. Go Blue!

He checked the phone number. Unfamiliar. The sound of Sydney returning made him pause. He placed her phone back on the table and stood up.

"I should let you go," he said, then leaned forward and kissed her on the cheek.

She flinched enough to make him notice.

"C'mon, babe, This is just a little speed bump in our marriage. We'll get through this. You and I were always meant to be together."

"It's over, Blake. I filed for divorce this morning."

His demeanor changed from the charming, boyish Blake Harrison to one she was too familiar with. Resentment. Judgment. Control. He stared at her, his lips beginning to turn white at the edges. "It's not over until I sign the papers, and that ain't happening. Why don't you just forgive me, so we can move on?"

"I've already forgiven you," she said in a tone with more force than she'd anticipated, "and I *am* moving on."

He continued to hold her gaze until a car honked from the Morgan driveway. It was Phil and MB. Blake stormed out of the house. He ignored their old friends and got in his car. When he finally drove off, Sydney felt herself exhale.

*   *   *

Sydney looked down at her scorebook. Another 6-3 groundout. Fourth of the game. Royals led 3–0 in the third. She loved watching Sam pitch. The man on the mound was completely different than the one she knew. Gone was the silly, teasing, flirting, loving Sam with his cute innocence and the touches and looks that made her heart speed up, and in his place, a foreigner. Sam Cloud-Carson. Face blank, body loose, supreme self-confidence, laser focus every single pitch.

She thought back to her husband earlier that evening, how his personality had changed as well, to a darkness that scared her. Sam's change was one that exuded a lightness and belief in oneself.

She watched him closely as the game progressed, admiring the way he made the game look easy. There seemed to be no self-analysis, no fear, no chaos, no questioning his decisions; there was simply a trust and conviction that every pitch he threw was the perfect one to help his team win. He was on a mission, and the closer he got to the end of the game, the more fixated he appeared to be. His control was more exact, his movement sharper, his changeup had more miss-hits.

According to Sydney's math, Sam needed only nineteen pitches to get the final nine outs of a 7–1 Royals victory. His line of nine innings, five hits allowed, one run, zero walks, five strikeouts in an eighty-two-pitch complete game, in two hours and four minutes was darn near perfection. Game over and it was only nine fifteen.

They didn't have to stay that long at Gram and Dun. MB and Phil would understand. Heck, she hadn't been with Sam in over a week. They could leave early and go celebrate her birthday at Sam's place. The thought made her heart thump like crazy.

*   *   *

The Plaza was packed. Many were fans who had come straight from the ballgame, still dressed in blue: caps, hats, T-shirts, pennants, and pom poms. Royal blue, navy blue, powder blue, everything some shade of blue. Sydney thought it wonderful how the team had energized the entire city, and now she wondered if Sam would even be able to make it through the crowd to their table.

They were lucky to find a place to sit on the patio overlooking Ward Parkway and Brush Creek. Great place to people watch. As she glanced back through the crowd, hoping to see Sam come through the door, she heard a familiar voice call out from the street.

"Hey, guys!"

Her head jerked around, and her eyes widened in shock.

"Blake? What are you doing here?"

He placed a hand on the short stone wall and hurdled over in one quick move. "I was out bar-hopping and saw you guys. I'll join you?"

Sydney glanced at Mary Beth and Phil, who held their own looks of distress as Blake sat down in the unoccupied chair. Sam's chair.

For an instant, she thought she might faint. She blinked once, twice, searching for something to say, when Blake yelled out, "Holy shit! Look who just came through the door. The King of Kauffman, Sam Cloud-Carson!"

Sydney closed her eyes tightly, hoping it wasn't true. But she knew it was as she heard other fans in the bar call out his name and then break out in that recognizable chant she'd heard only an hour earlier.

Let's go, Royals! Clap–clap–clap, clap, clap. Let's go, Royals! Clap–clap–clap, clap, clap.

She tried to breathe, tried to think, wanted to flee, but no … she had to face it, and finally, she opened her eyes and looked back at the bar.

Sam was talking with fans, shaking hands, signing autographs, but he was also glancing around. For the briefest of moments, their eyes met, and he immediately saw her dilemma.

"Hot damn!" Blake laughed. "Every hottie in this place is checking him out. I'll bet he gets his share of pussy."

His outburst was so startling that her words came out before she could stop them. "Shut up, Blake. You don't know him."

Blake shrugged, as if he knew what she'd say. "But I listen to sports talk radio, and all they've been talking about is who Carson was making out with in the hotel parking lot."

As she struggled for words, Blake rose up from his chair. "I'm gonna buy that boy a drink."

Sydney reached for her husband, but he was already gone, pushing past patrons, interrupting the couple Sam was talking to, and then introducing himself. She saw Sam nod and mouth the words, *I'll be right over.*

Dear God, she thought, *could this get any worse?* She tried to calm her breathing as she watched Sam start over, pausing along the way to shake a hand or say thank you to a fan congratulating him on his win.

When he arrived, Blake stepped behind Sydney and put his hands on her shoulders.

"This is my wife, Sydney, and our friends, Phil and Mary Beth."

Sam held out his hand. "Nice to meet you, Sydney."

She hesitated before grasping it, but didn't dare look him in the eyes. "Hello," was all she could manage.

"She's pretty shy," Blake said as Sam moved on to greet Phil and Mary Beth, who both looked dreadfully uncomfortable.

"Nothing wrong with shy," Sam said. "My father used to tell me that it was better to have less thunder in the mouth and more lightning in the hand."

"Well, you had lightning in your hand tonight." Blake grabbed a vacant chair from a nearby table and handed it to Sam. "Complete-game win. Not too shabby. Now, what can I get you to drink?"

Both Sam and Sydney answered at the same time. "Lemonade."

She turned red. "I'm sorry. I thought you were asking me."

Blake didn't seem to notice as he called out to a waiter. "Two lemonades, one Jack Daniels on the rocks"—he glanced at Phil who raised his now empty beer bottle—"and two Bud Lights."

Sam sat down next to Sydney and placed his hands on his knees, his left pinky gently touching the outside of her right thigh.

She swallowed hard and looked up at Blake, who had taken a seat across from them. He seemed to be studying her closely.

The conversation was stilted, almost uncomfortable at first, as Blake dominated both the questions and answers, telling stories of his high school football days, the knee injury that cost him a D-1 scholarship, and the life that had passed him by. Through it all, Sam's left pinky did not lose contact with Sydney, who now had dropped her right hand to her knee and looped her right pinky around Sam's left.

"Ya know my wife's part Injun," Blake blurted out. He took another long gulp of bourbon. "Sorry, I meant Native American."

"Blake, please," Sydney scolded him, but Sam tapped her leg to stay quiet.

"She's real sensitive about it," he continued. "Got Lakota blood in her—half-breed."

"That's enough, Blake."

But he was gone. Gone to some dark place that needed satisfaction. "She's half-everything—half-breed, half-woman, half-wife." He fired down the last of his bourbon and shot a menacing glare at Sam. "That's right—half-woman. She can't have kids. The only thing I wanted—but her girl parts are all fucked up."

Sydney's right hand shot to her mouth, and she felt the blood drain from her face.

Blake stood up, pulled a photograph out of his shirt pocket, and slapped it down in front of Sam. "I found this in my mailbox this morning with a note saying you've been fucking my wife."

Sam stared down at the photo. It was a picture he hadn't seen before. A photo of him with his arm around Sydney as they walked to her car in the Intercontinental parking structure. He couldn't take his eyes off the image of Sydney's face as she looked up at him. It was absolute joy. The smile she gave only to him.

"Now here's how this is going down," Blake said, his confidence on high as he leaned forward and wagged a taunting finger at Sam. "You, boy, are going to stay away from my wife. You don't want to soil her reputation, do you?"

Sam didn't answer.

Blake turned his attention to Sydney. "And you—wife—are coming home with me. If you don't do what I say, I'll crush your dreams. Your coaching career will be over, you'll be fired by your alma mater, and I'll make sure your parents and our church know all about the adulterous slut you've become."

It took every ounce of Sam's being not to leap across the table and rip the smirk off Blake's face. Instead, he sat for a long moment to calm himself, then he slowly stood up.

"I know how you treat Sydney," he said, his voice low but firm. "If you continue to hurt her—physically or emotionally—I'll not only call the police, but you'll deal with me. And believe me, you don't want that." Sam headed for the exit, never looking back.

*   *   *

"Talk about your arrogant prick," Blake scoffed as he watched Sam leave. "Dude can have any babe in town, and he tries to steal what's mine."

Sydney slowly rose up out of her chair, her eyes darkening as her gaze locked on to her estranged husband. "I. Am. Not. Yours." She said through clenched teeth. "And I dare you to go to the press. Let's tell them how *you* failed our marriage—failed as a husband, failed as a man. Go ahead and tell them why you couldn't hold on to your wife."

Blake took a step back from Sydney's fury. It was difficult to hear her words over the music and chatter of other patrons, but the intensity of her gaze rattled him.

"I'm done with you!" she seethed. "Done with your lies. Done with your control. Done with your abuse!"

Mary Beth moved quickly to her friend's side and matched Sydney's glare. "I took pictures of the bruise on Sydney's arm. Do you want to show those to the press, too?"

Blake looked to Phil for support but saw only disgust. He glanced around the patio. Most of the crowd was oblivious to their conversation, but a few heads turned in interest.

"Why don't we just calm down," he said softly. "We can settle this at home."

"Home?" Sydney snapped, an incredulous look on her face. "I'm not going anywhere with you!"

Paranoia flickered over his face, and he glanced once more about the place, sure that everyone was watching him, judging him, rejecting him. Humiliation rose in his belly like bile searching for release. He snatched his keys off the table and headed for the door, muttering over his shoulder, "We're not done. I'll deal with you later."

*   *   *

Sydney woke up with a headache. Unfortunately, alcohol had nothing to do with it. The strongest drink she had had the previous evening was lemonade. Now, she wished she had chased it with something stronger so she could have at least fallen asleep. But sleep had been impossible. Not after what happened last night.

She should have seen this coming. She should have known that whoever had taken pictures of her with Sam in the hotel parking lot would uncover her identity. And why hadn't she told Sam of her miscarriages and infertility earlier? Then he could have ended their relationship before it went too far.

She had been selfish. Her marriage was miserable and along came this knight in shining armor to save her ... and she had let him. What was wrong with her? She had deceived so many people the last three months. Her husband, her mom and dad, and now Sam.

She went to the bathroom and looked in the mirror. What a mess. Her eyes were red and swollen from crying, her hair looked like it lost a fight with a vacuum cleaner, and her cleft line seemed more pronounced. Old doubts began to creep back in. Why did she ever think that someone as remarkable as Sam would be interested in someone as unremarkable as her? School teacher Sydney Morgan. History Club Sydney Morgan. Sierra Club Sydney Morgan. Soccer coach Sydney Morgan. Cleft lip Sydney Morgan. Incapable of having a baby Sydney Morgan.

She did the best she could to fix up her disheveled appearance, slipped on her running gear, and went outside. Time to run. To escape. Run away from her troubles and fears. Just run.

She raced down Lamar, turned left on 159th, tears burning her eyes, then right on Nall, her heart slamming against her chest as she crested the hill and turned right on 167th. She stopped in front of the Tomlinson property, her hands on her knees, panting heavily. Her feet must have had a mind of their own. She wasn't running away; she was running *to* something. Dread pounded through her as she tapped in the code. The security gate lifted, and she headed down the gravel path to Sam.

He was in the tack room, fixing a leather strap that had come loose from one of the children's saddles. For a moment, with the morning sun flashing through the window behind him, he looked ethereal, silhouetted against the glare. She couldn't see his face but knew he was aware of her presence, as if he knew she'd come. He laid down his tools and walked over, but stopped a respectable distance away.

"Are you all right?" he asked.

She struggled to look at him. His face was grim, and there were dark circles under his eyes that said that he, too, had not slept well.

"I'm okay," she said, then swallowed hard, knowing the pain it would take to deliver her next words. "I'm sorry for all of the trouble I've brought you, Sam. I think it would be best if—if we took a break."

He shook his head sadly and gave her a look of utter disappointment. "Geez, Sydney, why would you go back to that jerk?"

"What? You think I'm getting back with Blake?"

"Of course. He's your husband. You've put up with his shit for years."

"Are you serious? After what he did last night?"

"He intimidated you, Sydney. I heard it all. I was so worried that I drove by your house twice after midnight to make sure you were okay."

"You did what?"

"I drove by your house. If I'd heard screaming, I was going to take care of business."

She crossed her arms over her chest and cocked her head to the side. "What do you mean by take care of business?"

"Well, I would have first knocked on the door. And if he didn't answer, I would have broken in and kicked his ass."

Startled, she shook her head as if she hadn't heard him right. "Are you—are you really that stupid, Sam?"

He took a step back, her insult stinging. "Well, somebody needs to protect you."

"But did you think about the consequences? How the press would've crucified you for breaking and entering, and then beating up your lover's husband?"

"Lover?" he asked incredulously, "Is that what I am to you?"

"Of course not. But had you broken in and I was there, I would've punched you in the nose to keep you from doing something so stupid."

"It's not stupid to protect a friend."

"I don't need you to protect me."

"Well, you've done a shitty job protecting yourself."

She slapped him across the face.

"Nice uppercut," he muttered. "Have you ever hit Blake like that?"

She went to slap him again, but he was too quick. He grabbed her wrist and held her gaze. "It's nice to see you finally sticking up for yourself."

"I stuck up for myself last night." She jerked her arm free. "I told him it was over, and MB and Phil dropped me off at my parents."

He blinked twice, unsure he'd heard right. "So you didn't go home with him?"

"Of course not. I'm not the weakling you think I am."

"I never said that you're weak."

"You drove to my house, ready to kick the door in, when I wasn't even there."

At this, his face went blank, as if deep in thought, trying to work through something.

"This is so *you*. Worried about me, when people are attacking you."

"I can handle it."

"Of course you can. You're Sam Cloud-Carson. You can handle everything by yourself. *Mr. In-Control-All-the-Time.* On and off the mound. Don't need any help."

He opened his mouth, speechless, then closed it. He shook his head sadly and headed to the tack room.

She followed, muttering. "God, what's wrong with me? I've gone from one control freak to another."

Sam spun back around, his eyes dark with fury. "I've never tried to control you! Not once. I know what that's like. I've been manipulated before, and it almost killed me."

Her entire body softened, and she looked up at him. She had struck a raw nerve. She knew who Sam was talking about. The man whose name he had written down on his bedside notepad. *Dixon. Construction. Parun to Kamdesh.* Drake Dixon was likely behind the strip-club accusations and the photographs. What other abuse had Sam endured and why was Dixon still tormenting him?

"I think you're right," Sam finally said in a defeated tone. "It's probably best if we not see each other anymore."

His words hit like a rattlesnake's bite. She didn't want that. Not now. Not ever. She just thought they should take a break. Get through their problems. She with Blake. He with the personal attacks. She tried to fight down the waves of nausea that came with the thought of never seeing Sam again.

"Being with me could ruin your life," he said. "Neither one of us wants that."

"But … I thought you cared about me?"

"I do care, Syd. I care so much I won't let you destroy your career and your relationship with your family and community because of me."

"Blake won't go to the press," she said. "I promise you. I know him. The truth would come out, and he'd look bad. Image is everything to Blake."

He shook his head. "It's for the best, Sydney."

A shock ran through her. She knew he cared for her. There had to be more. Was it something else that he had discovered last night?

"Sam, does your decision have anything to do with my not being able to have children?"

At this, his face tightened, and he slowly raised his vision to lock onto hers. "I can't believe you would think I'm that heartless, Sydney. I care for you. Deeply."

"I'm sorry," she said, with something like despair in her voice. "I–I didn't mean it that way."

He turned away, his shoulders slumping. "The kids will be here in an hour. I'd better go prep the horses."

He started to leave, then stopped. He went to the tack room and returned with a large shopping bag and handed it to her.

"Happy birthday," he muttered, then walked out the door.

She peeked inside and dissolved into tears. Inside were the floral velvet top, embroidered jeans, Sidewinder boots, and sterling silver jewelry she had seen in the Sundance catalog the week before.

*   *   *

It took her an hour to walk the three miles from the Tomlinson Ranch back to her parents' house. The last thing she wanted to do was ask Sam for a ride home. Or call her parents, or Mary Beth, or anyone for that matter. She wanted to be alone, to cool down from the breakup she'd just put herself through. Instead, her determination on what she would do next seemed to intensify. By the time she walked through the front door of her parents' house, she was as centered as if she was preparing her Blue Valley Tigers for a playoff game.

"Mom!" she called out. She put the gifts from Sam on the staircase.

"Where have you been?" came the reply from the kitchen. "We've been waiting all morning for you to return from your run so we could make your birthday blueberry pancakes."

Both parents hurried to the living room. "Happy birth—" Her mom stopped dead in her tracks. "Sydney? Oh my gosh, you look terrible. What's wrong?"

"I think she looks great," her dad said happily. He walked over and kissed her sweaty forehead. "Prettiest girl in Johnson County."

Typical Mom and Dad, she thought. *Mom found her flaws. Dad saw none. He'd say she looked cute even if she'd just been run over by a bus.*

Sydney inhaled a determined resolve. "I want you both to know that I love you, and there's nothing that will ever get in the way of how grateful I am to have you as parents. But there's something I want to know … and need to know."

Her parents stood quietly, bewildered looks on their faces as they glanced at each other, and then back at their daughter.

"Please tell me the name of my biological father."

Her mother blinked, entirely taken aback.

"Please, Mom." She then turned to her dad. "You'll always be my dad. Always. But it's time I met my biological father."

Vivian Morgan's mouth hung open for what seemed like an eternity. Sydney could almost hear her mother's heart pounding as she leaned against the chair to steady herself.

"Do you remember when I searched for baby pictures that showed my cleft lip?" Sydney asked her mom. "You didn't take any. It was as if you didn't want to remember that part of my life. My cleft is part of my history, Mom. So is this man. I want to meet him."

Vivian looked distraught as she glanced again at her husband. When he nodded, she sighed and said, "Louis … Louis Bear Shield."

Sydney nodded. "Thank you. I love you both very much."

CHAPTER FORTY-SIX

August 2013

Mission, South Dakota

Two days later, Sydney was on the road to Mission, South Dakota. She was surprised at the relative ease with which she was able to track down Louis Bear Shield. One phone call to the Rosebud Sioux Tribe switchboard operator was all it took. The woman told her that there was a Louis Bear Shield who was one of their Tribal Council representatives and that he could be reached at Sinte Gleska University in Mission, where he was a professor of Lakota Studies. Good. He had a job. That was a start. But this was still the unknown. *Don't take anything personally, Sydney. Don't make any assumptions. Don't feel guilty about what you might find.*

Was this the same Louis Bear Shield? she wondered when she had made the phone call. The university operator had told her the professor was in class and sent her straight to his voicemail.

"Hello, Mr. Bear Shield," she had said, and then almost forgot what else she had to say. "My name is Sydney Morgan Harrison. My mother is Vivian Morgan, and if that name rings a bell, I would love to talk with you."

She had left her number, but she wanted to kick herself for leaving such a lame message. This man could be her biological father. She crossed herself out of habit and settled back on her bed to calm her nerves. What would she say when he called back? If he called back.

He did. Not but fifteen minutes later.

A chill went up her spine when she saw the 605 area code. She inhaled a deep breath and picked up. "Hello?"

A deep voice said, "I have been expecting your call, Sydney."

Another chill went up her spine.

"I've had dreams of meeting you recently," he had said. "I was hoping you had similar dreams. Obviously, you did."

"Not me, sir, but a friend of mine had dreams of my meeting you. I thought it was time."

They talked only five minutes more. Sydney told him that she could drive up to Mission the coming week, but she had to be back for the start of her school session the following Monday. He said their school sessions coincided perfectly and that he would meet her at the Lakota Studies building at four on Monday. It would be easy to find, he had said. It was the building that looked like a big tipi.

*   *   *

Sydney felt her heartbeat quicken as she parked her car and walked to the lobby of the Lakota Studies building. She wiped her sweaty palms on her jeans and opened the front door. With the start of fall semester still a week away, there were only a few people inside, scanning the artwork or reading books. Her gaze traveled right to left and stopped suddenly on a man watching her from an office doorway. He was dressed casually in sandals, jeans, and a crisp white button-down shirt tucked in.

"Sydney?" he said with a pleasant smile.

The next five minutes seemed like she was outside her body, watching a film. Louis Bear Shield was nice. He had kind eyes and spoke in a clear, concise manner that was typical of most college professors as they made small talk about her drive, what she saw along the way, and about what his wife planned for dinner that night. It wasn't until they had sat down in his office that she asked, "What happened?"

He understood what she was asking. "Life happened. Your mother came up for the summer on a church mission. I was home after my junior year at South Dakota State. We worked together on a Native American aid program and fell in love."

"So you did love her?"

"Very much. But it was 1986. The red man was still looked on as a lower class. When the white missionaries saw us together, I saw fear in their eyes. I felt their judgment. Vivian ignored them until she became pregnant when she visited me over Thanksgiving break. Then the church leaders rushed in, removed her from the program, and silenced me."

"Did you try to stay in touch with her?"

"I called many times, but her parents wouldn't let me see her." His face was strained, his eyes remote with memory. "They wouldn't even let me talk to the woman who was carrying our child … all because I was Indian."

Sydney opened her mouth to respond, but there was really nothing to say.

"I later received a note from Vivian that she had given birth to a baby girl, met another man, and married."

"He's a good father."

"I'm sure he is. He raised you."

Sydney swallowed hard and looked down. Louis reached across his desk and touched her hand, as if asking that she raise her vision.

"I always knew we'd meet," he said softly, "but it had to come from you … when your heart said that it was time to find me."

She nodded. "It was time."

He smiled and squeezed her hand. "I think man's greatest challenge is to overcome the belief that we are separate from each other and separate from the Great Spirit. In our faith, we believe that God gave humans one sacred gift—the gift of choice. Free will. We can either walk forward or stay stuck in the past. To be born again is to start over."

*　　*　　*

She stayed with the Bear Shield family the rest of the week. Louis' wife, Shelley, and their two sons, Will, sixteen, and Connor, fourteen, knew of his other child. They welcomed Sydney with an openness that surprised her.

"You have Dad's smile," Will said at dinner that first night. "Both of you start your grin on the left side."

She laughed, and Will's arm jerked up, pointing first at Sydney, then at his father. "Right there! You're doing it now!"

Connor leaned forward. "And they both cock their head to the side whenever someone says something stupid."

"That is your perception," answered Louis with a teasing smirk, "but as any psychologist would tell you, when a person tilts their head, it's a way of respectfully questioning how that individual came to such a harebrained conclusion."

Sydney covered her mouth to hide her laugh, then gave an exaggerated tilt of her head. "I wonder if this conversation is designed to delay one from doing the dishes?"

"Astute observation," said Louis as he slid his empty plate across the table to his youngest son.

"No fair." Connor picked up the plate and headed to the kitchen. "Total setup."

Will picked up his mother's plate and followed his brother. "You walked into that one, Connor."

The playful conversation made Sydney happy. There was no bitterness about her coming to see the Bear Shield family. No judgment, no resentment, no jealousy. Just genuine acceptance—of a new friend they could tease.

The next morning, Louis gave Sydney a tour of the university and Lakota lands. He showed her both the good and bad, the hope and hopelessness, the persecution and the blessings. They visited abandoned buildings the government had used to assimilate the Lakota into white culture.

"It was a sad time," Louis said as he kicked shards of broken glass that littered the floor. "A time when Indian children were taken from their homes, forced to attend white schools, and were severely disciplined if they spoke their native language."

Sydney didn't know what to say as she glanced over at the chalkboard, riddled with pockmarks and graffiti, likely from past students or their descendants who had returned to release their anger at the federal government's assimilation program. What had these students endured? How were they forced to change?

"It wasn't easy growing up Indian," Louis said. "Always running, always hunted and hiding. Kicked off our land or herded onto some godforsaken territory far enough away to keep the white man less afraid."

He paused for a long moment, his face emotionless. But the hurt was evident. "I taught myself never to become comfortable with what I knew was wrong. Sometimes it's easier to just go along, accept mediocrity, ignoring the pain and injustice of a fearful world. But there are times we must stand up and say no. No to the crushing of our spirit. No to the oppression of our culture. No to the abuse of Mother Earth. The time has come for us to choose what is right for our future."

He took her as far west as the Black Hills, formerly part of the reservation, but because of broken treaties, the Sicangu Lakota lands had shrunk farther east and south.

She delighted in the ease of their conversation, for they had much in common, both being educators and lovers of history and the outdoors. She told him of her childhood, her passion for sports, of her failed marriage and meeting another man. Through it all, Louis listened intently, rarely speaking, as if knowing she needed to be heard.

"I'm very happy that I finally called you," she said as Louis walked her to her car on the morning of her departure. "I have to admit that I was worried that you might not accept me, and now I question why it took me so long."

Louis put his arm around her. "Your timing was perfect."

"Thank you." She paused, searching for the right words for her next question. "I hope you'll come visit me in KC."

He gave her shoulder a squeeze. "We both have semester breaks in December. Why don't you talk with your mother first to see if she would be comfortable with me visiting?"

Sydney nodded, and Louis pulled her in for a warm hug. When they separated, he looked her in the eyes and said, "The Elders say the Native American women will lead the healing among the tribes. That we especially need to pray for our women, and ask the Creator to bless them and give them strength. For, inside them, are the powers of the moon and Earth. When everyone else gives up, it is the women who will sing the songs of strength. You are the backbone of our people."

When she left on Friday morning, she practically flew home, her heart full, feeling that her family had doubled. She knew that every reunion didn't go this way, but she was grateful that this one had. Louis Bear Shield's final words left her overjoyed with happiness and gave her confidence.

"You have a good heart, Sydney … trust it."

CHAPTER FORTY-SEVEN

Stilwell, Kansas

August 2013

Sam pulled off a chunk of grilled catfish and tossed it into Barney's bowl. The little mutt immediately went to work on his treat. The two had gone fishing on the Blue that morning and caught three channel cats at least two pounds each. Sam gave two to Bette Tomlinson and filleted and grilled the biggest one for lunch with Barney.

This was Sam's favorite kind of August afternoon, not too hot, plenty of elms and oaks providing a canopy of shade as he listened to the cicadas, frogs, and birds in the distance. The only thing that would have made it better would have been to share it with someone special. But he had not seen or heard from Sydney since their unpleasant exchange one week ago. She had left him a thank-you card for the birthday gifts, making sure to tape it to his door after he had already left for the ballpark.

He touched the icon on his cell phone to check for messages. There was one from community relations on what time to meet at the children's hospital tomorrow, and one from teammate Kevin Cimoli asking about Sam's interest in meeting his girlfriend's friend.

"No," he said out loud.

Barney rose up from his treat and cocked his head at Sam.

"Really? Now you're giving me the Sydney look?"

Barney ambled over and placed his chin on Sam's knee, as if understanding his master's plight.

"She wanted a break from me, remember?"

Dark brown eyes stared up at Sam.

"I think it was the right thing to do." He scratched behind the little dog's ears. "She has her family and career to think about."

Barney stuck out his tongue.

"It's not all my fault." Sam leaned back in his chair, palms up as if asking for forgiveness. "I miss her too."

The dog sat back on his haunches, but his gaze never left Sam.

"Do you think I should call her?"

The little guy barked, just the sign he was hoping for. Sam reached for the phone.

"I'll bet she doesn't answer, but at least I can leave a nice message."

Barney barked once more.

* * *

"Hi Sam! How's it goin'?" The voice on the other end of the line took Sam by surprise, and for a moment, he stared at the phone, wondering if he had called the wrong number. He hadn't expected Sydney to pick up, and even more surprising was her unabashed enthusiasm.

"Good—I'm good. How are you?"

"Fantastic!" came her delighted reply. "Guess where I am?"

"I don't know. Soccer practice?"

"Soccer doesn't start until Monday. I'm on Highway Twelve, just south of Yankton, South Dakota."

"Okay," he mumbled, still confused. "What are you doing up there?"

"I did what you encouraged me to do. I went to meet my biological father."

Sam straightened up in his chair. "You did?"

"It was aaaah—mazing! His name is Louis Bear Shield. He's a professor at Sinte Gleska University. He has a really nice wife and two funny sons. They're my half-brothers, y'know ..."

Listening to Sydney talk was like drinking from a fire hose, going from nothing to full blast.

"I feel like I have two families now!" she continued to gush. "It's like having a totally new insight into who I am. New unity, new awareness, new adventure!"

Sam didn't know how to respond. He had expected a different Sydney. One more reserved, somber, perhaps still hurting from their breakup. But this Sydney was overflowing with joy, and that hurt a little. Had she already moved on?

There was an awkward pause in the conversation, then she said, "I'm sorry, Sam. You called me. What's up?"

He shook his head to collect his thoughts. "I just wanted to thank you for the nice card. I didn't think you'd pick up. I was going to leave a message. I'm really sorry about the way I behaved last week."

"Both of us said some things we probably regret," said Sydney.

Sam could tell from her tone that she was serious.

"But I know your heart, Sam. You're such a good guy, and Louis said something that jolted the way I think. He may have been talking about Lakota culture in general, but I felt like it was for me. He said that we should never become comfortable with what we know is wrong. That sometimes it's easier to accept mediocrity, ignoring the injustice and pain of a fearful world. That there are times we must stand up and say no."

Sam opened his mouth to reply, but he couldn't think of anything to say.

"What did Jenny tell you this morning?" Sydney asked thoughtfully.

"What?"

"Your sister's journal. What did she write?"

"Um ... uh," he stuttered, racking his brain to remember. "Something about choosing joy instead of pain."

"There you go. That's perfect. Your sister was ravaged by her kidney disease but still had the guts to say, *No! You're not the boss of me. You don't get to choose my attitude.* Jenny's a rock star, Sam. You're lucky to have her as your guide."

"Yes, yes, I am." Sydney's words about his sister made him feel good, and he wanted to know more about what she'd discovered in South

Dakota. "Hey, Syd, I'm truly sorry about last week. Can we meet up to talk? Maybe have a cup of coffee or something?"

This time the silence was on her end, for an uncomfortably long moment, and then she said, "Okay, but can we wait a couple of weeks? I'm still working through some personal stuff, and school starts Monday. That means teachers' meetings, soccer tryouts, conditioning, and practice. Not a lot of time right now, and you have to lead the Royals to a championship—by the way, how did you pitch this week?"

The question jarred him back to the present. He was hoping she'd agree to meet him for coffee, but instead she wanted to know about the Royals. "I was awful. Five runs in five innings. We've lost four of our last six."

"I'm sorry you're going through a rough stretch, but you'll get through it—because if there's one thing I know about you, Sam Cloud-Carson, it's that you're not mediocre. You're constantly searching for your higher self. It's what drives you both in baseball and life. That's a gift. If you're strong enough to survive what Drake Dixon's been throwing at you, then you're strong enough to survive a little losing streak. Hang in there ... the team needs you."

*   *   *

Sam was in a lousy mood when he drove home from the airport in early September. The team was still in a slump, having lost ten of fifteen to fall six games back of Detroit with twenty-five to play. Sam contributed to the slump, losing both of his decisions with an ERA over eight. The Kansas City papers and talk shows were tearing into the Royals for another late-season collapse.

He was well aware of the fact that both the team's and his struggles coincided with his breakup with Sydney, but no way was he going to let that be an excuse. He sucked because he sucked. She had nothing to do with it. *Focus, dude, focus.*

He tried to concentrate on his breathing as he drove home ... *Why hadn't she called? Or even texted? She said they could meet up in a couple of weeks ... Was that a couple of weeks since they had broken up or a couple of weeks since he had called her?*

Hmm, only one way to find out, because this concentrating on breathing stuff wasn't working. He checked the clock. 9:07. *It's early. She's still up … hopefully alone. I need a game plan.*

He pulled off to the side of the road, put his car in park, and texted *I suck.*

Thirty seconds later came a reply: *You do with that attitude.*

All right, we have a connection. He quickly texted back: *Coffee?*

Her response: *My first class is at 8:30. How about 7 a.m. your place?*

He typed back. *Perfect. I'll get one of those bran muffins that you like.*

Thanks. See you at 7.

He put his phone down and smiled triumphantly. Time to come up with a game plan.

*   *   *

Sydney felt like she was in a good place. She'd finished organizing her classroom space for the best cooperative-learning potential, soccer tryouts were going well, and she'd only gotten three phone calls and one box of "I'm sorry" chocolates from Blake. After ten years together, he still didn't know that she wasn't crazy about sweets. Typical.

One month ago, her world seemed upside down after her break with both Blake and Sam. Finally, she listened to some inner voice that said *go!* And go she did, to meet Louis Bear Shield. It wasn't anything her biological father said or did; it was simply the awareness to get out of the way and let Spirit guide her. When she made that choice and didn't worry about how it would affect someone else's happiness, she found peace.

Now, as she drove down the lane to Sam's cottage, she tried to calm the pounding in her chest, as she anticipated seeing the man she truly cared for. She was in a good place. Not great, but good.

He was sitting on the first step of the porch with Barney by his side. She glanced at her phone. It was 6:58. *I'll bet he had everything set up fifteen minutes ago. Clean kitchen, table set, coffee hot, and bran muffin in the microwave, ready to be heated.*

"Hey," he said when he stood up. Faded blue jeans, black T-shirt, flip-flops. *God, he looked good. Keep it together, Sydney, show some discipline.*

As he approached the car, she found herself staring at him, admiring the athletic grace of his stride, the warmth in his eyes, and that awkward indecision he always had in how he should greet her. She loved it all.

He opened the car door and offered a hand. When she took it, she felt the warmth and strength in it.

"Hey, yourself," she said as he helped her from the car and stood quietly, waiting.

He shuffled his feet, then lightly touched her shoulder. "C'mon in, coffee's ready."

"Thanks, anything I can do?"

"Nope. Just have a seat on the porch, and I'll warm your bran muffin."

There was something so endearing about Sam's predictability. A person you could count on. His grounded sense of right and wrong, never wavering, relentlessly dependable.

He returned with her muffin in one hand and two coffee mugs in the other. "Advantage of having big hands." He winked. "I don't have to make a second trip to the kitchen, and I get better spin on my curveball."

"It always gets back to baseball with you." She laughed and helped him with one of the mugs. "It's your zen garden."

"Baseball's a great example of how one can redeem their mistakes. As long as you have a good game plan."

She gave him a sidelong glance. "Game plan?"

"Yep." He paused to take a sip but held her gaze. "Us."

She leaned back on the sofa and crossed her arms over her chest. "You put together a game plan for *us*?"

He gave a self-assured nod. "Both of us get organized for a baseball or soccer game by putting together a plan to beat the opponent. I think this little break thing is silly. We're good friends. I enjoy your company and you enjoy mine. Why are we letting outside forces keep us apart?"

"Am I the opponent, Sam?"

"It's a metaphor, Sydney, don't be so literal."

"Sorry I got in the way of your game plan."

"C'mon, you're a coach. If anyone should understand this conversation, it's you."

"Of course. On behalf of coaches everywhere, I humbly apologize."

"Thank you." He leaned forward, confident she was finally getting his message. "Now, when I game plan for, let's say the Minnesota Twins, I look at data on their strengths and weaknesses, how I'm going to pitch to them, maybe set up their big slugger, Carlos Cruz, with something soft away, so then I can come inside hard with a fastball on his hands."

"Am I Carlos Cruz?"

He exhaled loudly. "Metaphor, Sydney, metaphor."

"Okay, so what you're saying is what happened on the Plaza, what my soon-to-be-ex-husband discovered, and our breakup is just a little foul ball in our friendship?"

"Exactly," he beamed. "We're still in the game, ahead in the count, but we have to realize that the results still may not go our way. It's time to think ahead, execute the next pitch. The better we execute, the higher percentage we have of a positive result."

She cocked her head to the side, eager to ask the obvious question. "What if you miss with a pitch?"

His head jerked up, as if he was shocked by the question. "I don't miss."

"That's why you're so good?"

He shrugged. "I'm not bad. Two point seven ERA. Ten-to-one strikeout-to-walk ratio is considered elite."

She pursed her lips tightly to suppress a laugh and rolled her hand for him to continue.

"Think of all the things I do when I'm on the mound. Breath work, balance, delivery, focus. It's just like life. We're always preparing for the next pitch, so that when there's a difficult time, tension, fatigue, mistakes made by ourselves or others, whatever, we can always get back to breathing and balance. Letting go of the past and focusing on right now."

"What if right now is the wrong time to play?"

He gave her a look as if she had two heads. "There's never a wrong time in life, Syd. We're always playing that game."

"But a relationship isn't a game, Sam. And, right now, as much as I'd like to play, I'm on the injured list. I'm going through a divorce and need time to rehab and recover before I can return to the field."

Sam rubbed his chin as if he was deep in thought, then slowly, a devilish smile creased his face. "Eventually, a guy gets healthy enough to go out on a rehab assignment. Are you close to a bullpen session or two?"

She picked up a crumb from her bran muffin and threw it at him. "You're impossible, Sam! You need to focus on right now too. And right now, according to your own admission, you're not pitching very well, and consequently, the team's losing. What's your game plan for that, Coach EssCee?"

Flustered, Sam sat back. This was not working out as he had planned.

"I think my game plan this month will be about getting my act together," Sydney said. "Finalizing my divorce, finding a place to live, organizing my class schedule, and coaching soccer." She placed her hand on top of his. "And your game plan should be about doing whatever you can to help your team win the American League Central. This final month of the season needs *your* complete attention."

He jerked his hand away from hers. "You don't think I know that? But it sure would be nice to spend my free time with someone I like ... who I think likes me."

When he pouted in that cute way where his brows drew down in disagreement, Sydney realized how much she'd missed him. Yet, as much as she wanted the same thing, she had to stand her ground ... for the well-being of both of them.

"I miss you too, Sam, but it's for the best. I've been on an emotional roller-coaster the last few years, and I need some time to find my own breathing and balance. You need this time to focus on your job as a Kansas City Royal. You're six games back with twenty-five to go. If you're really serious about winning a championship, then you might want to start by putting together a game plan on how you're going to beat the Minnesota Twins tomorrow night."

He stared at her for a moment, then grabbed at his chest as if he'd been shot. "Geez, you really know how to kill a guy's game plan."

She shrugged. "Sorry."

He didn't reply, but it was clear her nixing his game plan bothered him. In the silence, she could almost hear the wheels turning inside his brain as he thought of what to say next. Finally, he shook his head and mumbled, "Maybe my new plan should include somebody else."

Sydney thought her heart had stopped for a second, not sure she'd heard right. Then, as the realization of his statement settled in, she swallowed hard and placed her coffee cup back on the table. "Okay, I understand—if that's what you want."

Then, with all the strength she could muster, she stood up and headed for the door. "I'd better go. I have class in twenty minutes."

*   *   *

Sam was pissed. Why the hell did he say that he wanted to game plan with somebody else? No, he didn't. He wanted to spend time with Sydney. He said that to hurt her. Dammit, that wasn't him. His words were both insensitive and cruel. And then, he didn't even walk Sydney to her car when she left. He just sat alone, stewing about his own wounded ego while she drove off. What a jerk.

What was it about Sydney that messed with his head? The last few times they'd been together, she'd thrown him off his game. He was out of control, like some rattled rookie pitcher with the bases loaded, just raring back and throwing the ball as hard as he could to get out of a jam. Jenny had called those guys BDHs—Brain-Dead Heavers. Was he being a BDH? The very notion infuriated him.

I don't need her, he thought when he washed and dried the breakfast dishes that morning. "I don't need anyone." Then he stubbed his toe on a chair while leaving the house, tore his T-shirt on an exposed nail at the stables, and it took him two hours to corral the horses after he'd absentmindedly left the gate open and they'd run off. Not even Barney joined him for lunch or dinner on his one day off … alone again.

As he lay in bed that night, struggling to find a comfortable position to fall asleep, he thought back to something his mom had always said. *Words have the power to heal or harm. If you speak with your mouth, others will only hear with their ears. But if you speak from your heart, others will hear with their hearts. That's why it's important to stay silent when you're angry. Wait until the anger passes, then from your heart will the right words flow.*

"Thanks, Mom," he muttered as he readjusted his pillow for quite likely the twentieth time. "Now I really feel guilty."

But his mom was right. As much as he wanted to see Sydney, now was not the right time. She had her stuff to sort through, and he had his. He rolled over, flipped the light on, and reached for Jenny's journal. Opening to a random page, he read:

To join with others is a holy connection. Get quiet. Let Spirit guide you.

Okay, he thought. He crossed his legs and placed his open palms on his knees. *Let's see where Jenny's words take me.*

*   *   *

A crowd of thirty-one thousand buzzed Kauffman Stadium that Friday night. It was Kevin Cimoli bobblehead night. Game one of a three-game series with Minnesota. Even though the Twins were out of the race, and their lineup was peppered with September minor league call-ups, Sam prepared as if it was game seven of the World Series.

He had meditated on Jenny's message when he woke up that morning, then while doing yoga, eating breakfast, cleaning the stalls, on his drive to the ballpark, studying the scouting report, and as he warmed up in the bullpen. He could feel his mind, body, and spirit locking in.

To join with others is a holy connection. Get quiet. Let Spirit guide you.

The Royals scored four runs in the first inning and three in the second, and the rout was on. The Twins were never in the game. Sam was pulled after six innings with the home team up by eight. When bobblehead boy, Kevin Cimoli, scooped a grounder and touched first base for the final out of a 9–1 Royals win, both players and fans let out wolf howls that could be heard a mile away.

*　*　*

The Royals went on a roll after that, winning fifteen of their next twenty, to tie Detroit for first with three games to go. Tigers and Royals at Kauffman for the Central Championship. Their mojo was back, they had a self-assured swagger every time they took the field, and the guys were feeding off each other. If Blackwell struck out, Falls picked him up. If Falls grounded out, Hawkins picked him up. If Hawkins popped up, Contreras picked him up. Keep the line moving.

While Cimoli and Ramirez had become the leaders on and off the field, Sam had become the unwavering force of the pitching staff. He didn't say much, but the team seemed to have an extra edge, a heightened confidence, on the days that he pitched. And he rewarded them by winning each of his next four starts, pushing his record to 16–5 with one start remaining. He was also spending more time with his teammates, joining them for a card game on the plane or a beer after the game … and finally saying yes when Cimoli invited him to meet a friend.

*　*　*

Sydney sat on her bed, staring at her phone. Should she text Sam? Just send him a *Congrats on the Royals' success* greeting. Their last conversation three weeks ago had not ended well, with Sam inferring that perhaps it was time he dated someone else. She had left his house fighting back tears.

But now, she had just gotten off the phone with her biological father, and there was something Louis Bear Shield had said that nudged her to text Sam. She had called Louis to let him know that her mother had reluctantly agreed to host the Bear Shield family when they came to visit over Christmas break.

"Mom went to the Bible for her decision," Sydney told Louis. *"I think she must have come across 'Judge not and ye shall not be judged, forgive and ye shall be forgiven.'"*

"Oh, be gentle with her," said Louis in an understanding tone. *"Your mother didn't intentionally steer you in the wrong direction. She only taught you what she learned."*

"She kept you from me."

"Let it go, Sydney. Your mother did the best she could with what she knew at the time."

She sighed. "I suppose."

"I know it's not easy to let things happen without our direction. We were taught to believe that the smarter, or more organized, we were, the greater was our chance for success. Simply stepping aside and letting experiences unfold seems irresponsible. Yet sometimes it's best to get out of our own way and believe that we're already good enough and ultimately prepared. We have to trust our inner guide to show us the right path. Why not trust your inner guide right now?"

Her fingers hovered over the cell phone, and then she typed …

*   *   *

Sam leaned back on his patio sofa and stared up at the moon that seemed to be resting atop the trees, leaves flickering in the breeze like tiny shards of gold. Autumn had arrived. Those leaves would soon turn brown, break from their source, and flutter to the ground, knowing that they would be nourishment for the next generation. As Black Elk had said, *Everything the Power of the World does is done in a circle.*

Even happiness, he thought. Things were going well for him: he'd won his last four games, the Royals had tied the Tigers for first in the Central, the news from Afghanistan was civil, and there were no personal attacks by Drake Dixon in over a month. All good. Yet, he felt a bit of melancholy as he sat alone on this beautiful September evening … alone again … wondering . . .

His phone *pinged*, snapping him out of his quiet reflection. It was probably Cimoli about what time Kevin and the girls would be coming to the stables tomorrow. He checked the message, and his melancholy vanished. Sydney!

Congrats on the way you guys are playing. Tied for first place! Not to nitpick, but you would have thrown a shutout in your last start if you hadn't hung that slider to Ruiz. Grinning face emoji.

He laughed and said to himself, "I swear Sydney's channeling Jenny. Same kind of stupid humor."

He texted back. *Hey, Coach Sticks! How's soccer going?*

Good. We scrimmage BV North Saturday. Can you ref?

He laughed again. *Sorry. We play the Tigers that night.*

Aw, c'mon, Sam. It's just one game. They won't miss you.

"Geez, what's gotten into her? Sassy and sarcastic—I like it."

Sorry about my stupid game plan idea, he texted back. *Are we still friends?*

Don't be silly, Sam. How could anyone hold a grudge against you?

He shook his fist. Dang, this night couldn't get any better. Sydney wasn't mad at him anymore. Before he could answer, she texted.

How about lunch?

Sure. When?

Is tomorrow okay? Our school district has a Board of Education meeting, so I have the day off. I can meet you at the stables.

He gulped. He couldn't meet her tomorrow. Cimoli had set him up with his girlfriend's friend. He'd already turned down Kevin's first three attempts at introducing him to Tiffany. The three of them were coming over tomorrow morning, on the team's first off day in two weeks, to go riding. He wasn't sure how to respond to Sydney's text, but he wasn't going to lie. He'd handle this the same way that he pitched. *Stay calm, trust your stuff, and let 'er rip.*

He texted back. *Sorry. I have plans with Cimoli and a couple of his friends. Rain check?*

For what seemed like a painfully long moment, there was no reply. Then: *Okay. Maybe another time.*

Sam stared at her text, wanting to explain. Instead, he texted back, *I'd like that. Good night.* Then he stood up, powered his phone off, and went to bed.

*   *   *

"My family had horses growing up." Tiffany Conrad beamed. She sported tight white jeans and a low-cut orange tank top as she stood in the corral, sipping an iced dirty chai latte. "My daddy bought me an Arabian for my birthday."

"Mmhmm," mumbled Sam as he hooked the left stirrup over the horn and tightened the cinch strap on Jenny. He was questioning himself on why he'd agreed to this trail ride with Kevin's friend. Yeah, Tiffany was gorgeous. A twenty-four-year-old long-legged blonde with a tanning-bed bronze glow who looked as if she'd just come from Venice Beach rather than the suburbs of Kansas City. They were a half hour late because Tiffany just couldn't start her day without stopping by her favorite coffee shop.

"What kind of horses will we be riding today, Sam?"

"Quarters," he said succinctly.

"As in four for a dollar?" Tiffany giggled and took another sip.

He gritted his teeth. "Quarter Horses are great for new riders."

"I'm not a new rider." Tiffany batted her eyelashes at Sam. "I rode in the American Royal Parade when I was twelve."

"I was thinking about KC." He nodded to his teammate. "Can't let our All-Star first baseman fall off Ladybug."

Both girls laughed. Sam pulled one more time on the cinch and then glanced down the drive when he heard a car headed their way.

Sydney! What the heck is she doing here?

In the shock of the moment, all he could think of was protecting Sydney from being hurt.

She stepped out of her car wearing her usual: faded overall jean shorts, a wrinkled yellow T-shirt, and a Blue Valley Tigers ball cap pulled low. He thought she looked adorable.

"Hey, Syd!" He ran over to greet her. "Why aren't you at school?"

"I told you I had the day off," she said, her tone sharp. "Board of Education meeting. Bette called me. Said you needed help."

"Help? I only asked her for permission to ride her horses."

"She didn't tell me you had guests—just said you needed help before you went out to lunch."

"But we're eating here." He looked past Sydney to the main house. Bette was watching them from her garden. When she saw that Sam spotted her, she turned away and acted as if she were checking a tomato plant.

What a busybody, thought Sam. *Bette wants me back with Sydney.*

"Well?" Sydney put her hands on her hips,

"There's really not much to do, but I guess you can … clean and fill the water buckets?"

She shot him a scathing glance.

"What?" he asked, still flustered.

"Would you at least introduce me to Barbie and her friends?"

"Her name's not Barbie."

She shook her head. "It was a joke, Sam."

"Huh?" He gave a befuddled look as they walked over. This was a complete reversal from the last time he saw Sydney. One month ago, *she* was horrified when he had met her husband. Now, *he* was the one worried about how Sydney might feel seeing him with another woman. She was both angry and jealous … and that bothered him.

"Hey, guys," he called out, his voice a bit higher than normal, "Say hello to my coworker, um, friend, Sydney Morgan—I mean Harrison. Or is it Morgan?"

She rolled her eyes and held out her hand to Tiffany. "My friends call me Sticks."

Sam gulped, then the phone in his back pocket rang. He checked the number.

Kabul, Afghanistan? Not now!

"Sorry, guys, I—I have to take this. Sydney, could you help get everyone ready to ride?" He ran to a part of the corral that had better cell service.

"Hello?" he said softly, then he heard the familiar voice of Abdul Hazrat.

When Sam switched to Hazrat's Dari-Nuristani dialect, all four heads turned his way in surprise.

"Sam speaks like seven languages," Sydney said, trying to give him privacy but also trying to figure out what language he was speaking. "It sounds Persian, and Sam did spend time in Afghanistan."

He glared at her to shut up, and when she caught his drift, she led the riding party over to their horses. There was nothing Sam would rather do than tell Abdul to call back at a more convenient time, but that was impossible. Hazrat's family could be in danger, and the only American he trusted was Sam, the guy who had rescued his kids from a Taliban warlord some three years earlier.

"I've received two more offers," Hazrat said. "One from a Chinese corporation and the other from an American firm."

"What are their demands?" Sam asked.

"That we relocate to Kandahar, so they can begin construction on our mountain. They said we would be allowed to return when the project is completed."

"They'll never let you go back to your land."

"I know. That's why I'm calling you from Kabul. I'm meeting with our country's Minister of Commerce and Minister of Mines. Without their help, all may be lost."

"Don't commit to anything yet, Abdul. Let me first visit with a man I have complete faith in. Colonel Bart Tomlinson, who was in charge of Special Forces at Bagram. He's the one who told me that a Provincial Reconstruction Team had resumed construction on your land."

"The PRT manager said it has nothing to do with our mountain. That they're only building a road from Parun to Kamdesh."

"They're lying."

"I know. Does this colonel know who's behind it?"

"No. But I'd like to connect the two of you. May I give him your contact information?"

For a long moment, there was only silence. Then Hazrat said, "Yes."

"Thank you, Abdul. Please believe me. The colonel is a man you can trust."

When they finished their conversation, Sam leaned back against the fence and stared at his phone, a thousand thoughts flashing through his brain. Drake Dixon was somehow still involved, but what about the Chinese corporations, or other American mining companies, that might be planning similar operations in the Nuristan Province? How could he stop them? He thought about Hazrat's children, Malala and Mateen, and how their lives would change if they were pushed off their land and forced to live in some big city like Kabul or Kandahar. Lives ruined because of money and power. Someone had to stop this madness.

"Sam—Sam?" Sydney snapped her fingers in front of his face, and his head jerked up.

"Oh, sorry, just thinking."

"Afghanistan?"

He nodded.

"Do you want to talk about it?"

"No."

"You can't do this alone, Sam."

He stood up. "I'm fine. All good. I don't want you involved."

She looked away and shook her head sadly. He could tell she was annoyed by his refusal to elaborate. Or was she irritated about something else?

Finally, Sydney gave an impassive nod to his party, who were waiting on their horses inside the corral. "I think your date's ready for a trail ride."

"It's not a date, Sydney."

"None of my business," she muttered and headed for the barn. "Time to do my job—clean and fill the water buckets."

He followed her. "I can do that."

She spun back around. "No. You have guests. Take them on a ride."

Venice Beach tan Tiffany exhaled in exasperation, from astride her horse. "Excuse me, young lady. Can you chitchat with Sam some other time? I'm sure there's something for you to do inside the barn."

Sam winced as if he'd been stung by a bee. He glared up at Tiffany, holding her gaze for an excruciatingly long moment.

"What?" Tiffany finally said, forcing an innocent smile. "She has work to do, and you have a trail ride to lead."

By now, Sydney had already gone to the corral, returned with Sam's horse, and handed him the reins.

"Don't make things worse," Sydney whispered. "Just go."

With no further comment, Sam put his left foot into the stirrup, swept up into the saddle, and led his horse toward the line of dark oak trees that edged the farm to the east. *Be calm,* he instructed himself. *Be present, breathe, let it go.*

But, darn it, this morning was like a ballgame he'd lost complete control of. He was with a girl he had no interest in, who could cost him a girl he *was* interested in; trouble was brewing in Afghanistan; Dixon was likely behind it; and, oh yeah, there was this little pennant race with the Tigers this weekend. Tied for first with three games to go.

Focus, dude, focus. One pitch at a time, one inning at a time, one game at a time. Right now ... trail ride.

CHAPTER FORTY-EIGHT

DiamondBar Headquarters, Southern Virginia

September 2013

Dixon leaned back in his chair and yawned. He and his lawyer were twenty minutes into a video put together by some Afghan environmental group. It was a presentation of all the mining regulations that Afghanistan required from both domestic and outside interests. The new laws demanded greater detail for each type of license, tendering process, royalty fees, and environmental and social protection issues.

Yeah, yeah, whatever, Dixon thought. He knew all about the laws that prohibited Afghan politicians and senior government officials from acquiring any mining contracts, yet he knew of five cases alone where such persons, or their close relatives, were involved. One was a member of Parliament he had already paid off.

But what he didn't know and couldn't understand was why Abdul Hazrat had not taken the bait. An Afghan Provincial Reconstruction Team was back on his land and had even begun construction on the bridge that had been destroyed three years earlier. Dixon wanted Hazrat to attack the PRT crew, giving the Afghan Army or NATO forces justification to retaliate against violent insurgents.

As the video came to a climactic conclusion, complete with melodramatic music and images of the pristine, raw beauty of the Hindu Kush, Dixon flipped on the lights in the DiamondBar conference room and turned to his lawyer.

"Our mole inside the Afghan government believes that Carson has been communicating with Hazrat," he said. "If that's true, we have to make sure no one believes a word he says if he attacks me in the press."

"It's a critical time," replied King. "There are a lot of players bidding for your mountain now. It's not only foreign corporations, but members of the Afghan parliament, security forces, local government officials, and the Taliban, all positioning themselves to claim the spoils of a dysfunctional nation."

Dixon's mouth curled into a wicked smile. "Bob Dalley will release his story about Carson on Saturday morning. I'll bet within hours of it breaking every sports talk show in America will be demanding that son of a bitch be suspended."

*   *   *

The Royals beat Detroit on Friday night as Mario Fuentes and three relievers controlled the Tigers' potent offense in a 6–2 win. Kansas City now led the Central by one game, with two to go, and if they lost on Saturday, their rookie ace would be available to start Sunday's clincher.

On the drive home, Sam found himself glancing at his phone that lay silently in a cup holder. He'd already checked twice to see if Sydney had called or texted, but nothing. He wanted to talk to her. Explain yesterday. He noted the time. 11:03. Geez, how could he be cold-blooded on the mound yet feel like some nervous teenage boy calling a girl? He was tougher than that. He grabbed his phone, scrolled down to the contact that read *Sticks*, and pressed call.

She answered on the second ring. "Hi, Sam. Nice win. You guys are playing great."

"Yeah." He paused to calm his breathing and muster up some moisture in his dry mouth. "The stadium was pretty loud. All we need is one more win."

There was a long silence on the line before Sydney said, "So, what's up?"

He grimaced. He forgot that he was the one who had called her. "Oh yeah, I wanted to apologize about yesterday. Cimoli wanted me to meet—"

"Was Barbie high-maintenance?"

It took him a moment to figure out her question. "Why do you keep calling her Barbie?"

"Because she looks like a Barbie doll I once got for Christmas ... every girl had one."

"Not my sister. Jenny wasn't a doll person."

"What did she like?"

"Books. She loved books ... read everything."

"I need details, Sam. What books did you get her?"

"Pretty much every year I bought her a subscription to *Baseball America*, and then books like *Black Elk Speaks* or books by other spiritual masters."

"Of course, baseball and spirit, a Cloud-Carson twofer!"

He laughed. He was feeling much better now. "What about you, Syd? Only Barbies?"

"No, I wasn't much of a doll person either. I loved sports, so I always got a new soccer ball, cleats, and shin guards."

"Ooo, sexy."

"I thought so."

He paused for a long moment. He wanted to ask to see her but wasn't sure she was ready to see him. Just as he was about to speak she said, "Hey, you'll be happy to know that my mom approved of my biological father's family visiting over Christmas break."

"That's awesome, Sydney. I'm glad you reached out to him."

"You'd like Louis." She paused, and he sensed pride in her voice. "He's a well-respected man in their community. He's not just a professor, but a leader who truly believes that traditional Lakota values have much to offer our world—from the beauties of nature to the power of forgiveness."

"Wow, sounds like your conversations are pretty inspiring."

"To go on a vision quest," she said in a melodramatic tone, "is to go into the presence of the great mystery."

"Cool—did Louis say that?"

"No, that was you, Sam, six weeks ago in the Intercontinental parking lot, when you encouraged me to find him."

He smiled. Talking with Sydney was so easy. There was no pretense, no attempts to impress, no holding onto old grievances, like yesterday's embarrassment. They were truly good friends. And, for a brief moment, he thought of them having a hundred conversations like this in the future.

"I hope you can meet Louis someday," she said.

His smile widened. "I'd like that Sydney. I really would."

*　　*　　*

Sam lay in bed, his mind flooded with thoughts of Sydney. He'd barely spent five minutes on the phone with her, but he couldn't stop grinning. Sydney was funny. Smart. Thoughtful. He loved the way she teased him about Barbie—er, Tiffany. To watch her transformation from June's desperation to October's contentment was a testament to the power of choice.

He could relate. He'd been there himself. Pulled so low after his mother's death that he'd almost taken his life. He admired Sydney for conquering her demons. She was no longer the beaten down, frightened, emotional wreck he'd met four months earlier. In her place had emerged, as Mary Beth had said, the *real Sydney*, the spunky girl MB had grown up with ... and the one Sam missed.

CHAPTER FORTY-NINE

Stilwell, Kansas

September 2013

Buzzz … buzzz … buzzz …

Sam jerked up in bed, hearing the phone ringing from the kitchen. He checked the clock on his nightstand. Six a.m. Who would be calling at this hour? He had finally drifted off to sleep about two and was dead to the world when the phone started buzzing.

He checked the caller ID. Walt Swanigan, the Royals' vice president of communications. The guy who dealt with the media on a daily basis.

Sam rubbed his eyes and walked to the corner of his house that had the best cell service.

"Mornin', Walt,"

"Hello, Sam. Have you read the *Sporting World* this morning?"

"No, I was sleeping."

There was a long pause from Swanigan. "Bob Dalley of the *Sporting World* wrote a pretty damaging story about you. It came online a half hour ago. I've been getting calls from local and national media wanting a comment from you."

Sam stood bolt upright, his heart pounding. "What'd he write?"

"About your time in Afghanistan. He's got quotes from DiamondBar associates, Charlie Whitson and Frank Weber. Allegations of drug use, fighting with coworkers—and consorting with the Taliban."

"What!" Sam exclaimed in absolute astonishment. He knew who was behind it. Drake Dixon. He should have known that bastard would pull something like this before the Royals' biggest game of the year.

Damn it, why couldn't he just go after me? Why would he go after the team? My teammates had nothing to do with this.

"Sam? Sam? Are you there?" Walt asked.

"Yes–yes, sir–I'm here."

"David's on a call with the commissioner. They're trying to decide what to do."

"I don't understand. These are just accusations."

"This is some pretty bad shit, Sam. The commissioner has to do what he feels is in the best interest of the game."

"You mean I may not be allowed to pitch tomorrow?"

Another long pause from Walt. "I think you should talk to David first. But we'll likely need you to come in and give a statement to the press."

"A statement? You know I can't talk about my time in Afghanistan."

"I know, Sam. I've been defending your silence ever since you arrived. But I'll be honest with you–it sure would help if you could say something to prove Dalley's story is wrong."

Sam took a deep, ragged breath, fighting the urge to explode.

"Stay close to your phone," said Swanigan. "David will call you as soon as he finishes with the commissioner." Then he clicked off, leaving Sam staring at his phone in disbelief.

The anger he'd been holding inside boiled to an uncontrollable level. His mind was back on Pargin Mountain, blackmailed by Dixon to force him to track for his private military company; it was back in Afghanistan, uncovering Dixon's plan to steal Hazrat's mountain; it was at the DiamondBar station outside Bagram, where Dixon had promised to leave Sam and Hazrat alone. Fucking liar. He was losing control, beyond fury, his eyes blood-red with hate.

"Goddamn you, Dixon!" He fired his phone across the room. It ripped through the screen door and flew out onto the drive. He kicked over the kitchen table, shattering dishes and glasses, then slammed his left fist through the side wall, cutting his hand from middle knuckle to wrist. He collapsed on the floor, dropped his head into his hands, and squeezed his temples as if trying to force the rage out of his mind.

"Sam?"

He raised up slowly and looked full into the face of understanding.

Sydney stood in the entryway, his phone in her hand. She walked to the sink, soaked a towel in water, and returned to clean his bloody hand.

"I guess you read the story?" he said, his voice heavy with anguish.

She nodded.

"Drake Dixon has beaten me. I may still have time to save an Afghan family—but my career is over. Dixon doesn't need facts to get what he wants. He only needs people to submit to his deception. He conned our government, he conned Afghanistan, and he conned me."

Sydney didn't respond. She continued to clean his wound, pressing the towel tightly just below the knuckle to stop the bleeding.

"Afghanistan is a country of broken promises," he said in a bland tone, as if he were talking to himself. "A hundred years ago, it was the Russians and Brits who ignored Afghan laws to steal what they wanted, and now it's unscrupulous corporate bosses, like Dixon, who bribe government officials or shape contracts to favor themselves. All you have to do is accuse someone of being Taliban, or in my case, consorting with the Taliban, and your life is over. The baseball commissioner can do what he thinks is in the best interest of the game. He has the power to suspend me for life."

Sam glanced over at her, unable to read her expression, and shrugged.

"What the hell was I thinking? Believing I could take down a man as powerful as Dixon? With all his money, all his lawyers, all his political cronies manipulating international laws I know nothing about. What a fool I am."

"You're only a fool if you give up," she said.

His eyes darkened, demanding she explain.

"I've never met a fiercer competitor than you, Sam. You took a perennial loser in the Diriamba Dukes to the Nicaraguan Championship.

You pitched so well in our minor leagues that the Royals called you up after only one month. You led a team that hasn't been to the postseason in three decades to within one game of a division title"—she paused and looked him directly in the eyes—"and you're going to quit now?"

"I can't beat him."

"He beat you—*this time*." Her voice was low but firm. "He bribed some unethical journalist to write lies about you. But if you let him take your attitude—your spirit—*you* are letting him beat you a second time."

He swallowed, recovering himself slightly.

"You were the one who convinced me to meet my biological father, Sam. It was at the Rosebud Reservation where I learned about the persecution of the Lakota ... *Kill the Indian and Save the Man* was the white man's justification." She shook her head sadly. "Drake Dixon is trying to break you ... trying to ruin your reputation so that no one will trust your word."

The color began to come back to Sam's face, and he sat up straight.

"Your strength, Sam, is your ability to focus in times of crisis. In situations where other pitchers struggle—you thrive. It's as if some otherworldly force takes over, commanding every sense within you to throw a baseball with even greater precision and movement." She inhaled a deep breath and went to a place she wasn't sure she should go. "Unfortunately, your weakness is your belief that you alone can save others, the belief that you could have done something to save your father, your sister, your mother, and now a family in Afghanistan ... and your baseball team."

She stood up, went over to his nightstand, and returned with Jenny's journal.

"It was you who told me the world works perfectly without us directing it—that acorns become oaks, sunflowers turn to the light, hearts beat, lungs breathe, and the sun comes up without our help. When you're on that mound, you let the same force that moves the universe direct you. To trust in that power takes faith, and your willingness to surrender to it allows you to do amazing things—whether it's to get out of a bases-loaded jam, or to get out of the mess you're in today." She smiled at him. "Have faith in that power again. Turn your anger into something positive." She flipped open Jenny's journal to a random page and read:

"Life can break you, my brother. You have always felt most comfortable with being alone. The mountains and the pitching mound have been your churches. But solitude can also break you with its yearning to stand with others. Trust them, Sam. It is the reason you are here."

His phone buzzed. It was his general manager.

She put her hand on his chest. "You'll know what to say—listen with your heart."

*   *   *

Sam paced the screened-in porch, looking like a caged animal in a zoo walking back and forth in front of the bars, as if searching for some way to escape. He had finished his conversation with his GM and had come away relieved that the Royals and Major League Baseball had yet to make a decision about suspending him before his final start of the season. The league wanted answers. They requested that he give his side of the story at a noon press conference.

Sydney swept the last of the broken glass into the dustpan and emptied it into the trash can. She walked in front of Sam to get him to stop pacing. "What do you usually do when your mind's not right?"

"Go for a walk," he grumbled.

"Then go."

"I can't."

"Why not?"

"Well, you're here."

Typical Sam, she thought. *Even in his darkest moment, he was thinking of others.* She needed to be firm to get him out of the house.

"I don't need you hovering over me like a mother hen." She pointed out the door. "Go. Get out of here. Leave me alone."

A thankful smile spread across his face as he opened the screen door and looked back at her. "You're pretty cute when you're mad, y'know that, Sticks?"

"Shut up." She frowned and then yelled after him. "Clear your mind. Kansas City needs you mentally, physically, and emotionally ready for tomorrow."

As soon as he was out of sight, she called Teresa Songbird-Lopez. Since they'd met back in July, the two had become good friends and called each other practically every week.

When Sydney told her about the Dalley story and Sam's reaction, Teresa broke down in tears. She told Sydney everything: about the two thugs, Billy Cutthredge and Rob Marcus, booking Sam for hunting expeditions, about Marcus stalking Teresa, about the accident, about being kidnapped, and finally, how Sam had hunted them down on Pargin Mountain and saved her from being raped.

Sydney had to fight to keep it together when she listened to that part; it was as if she were hearing about a completely different person than the tender, sweet man she'd come to know. Sam had killed two men? How could that be possible? Yet perhaps they were all capable of such violence if pushed to the limits in which Sam had been driven.

"Why didn't he just tell the police?" Sydney asked abruptly. It was hardly tactful, but she had to know.

"You have to understand elite trackers," Teresa said. "When Sam locks onto his prey, all of his senses become completely absorbed in one singular purpose. It's the same hyperfocus that makes him a great pitcher. Unfortunately, that strength is also his weakness. The belief that if left alone, he can get through any crisis … so when he discovered my track at the crash site, he fixated on nothing else except finding me."

"And then he killed Cutthredge and Marcus to save you."

"While Dixon and his team videotaped everything."

Sydney inhaled a startled gasp.

"While Sam was tracking me, Dixon was tracking Sam. He told Sam he'd take care of the bodies, cover everything up if Sam signed on with DiamondBar … and that if he refused he'd make sure Sam went to prison for manslaughter or second-degree murder."

I can't believe what Sam went through in one day, Sydney thought. *Tragedy. Murder. Deception. Blackmail. Lost dream. No wonder he had been suicidal.* She pinched the bridge of her nose with her free hand to force out her own growing fears for Sam. This was no time to lose it. She had to stay focused. Be the coach. Fix the problem.

"Why did Sam spend only two years in Afghanistan?" she asked.

"He said that he finished his contract and that Dixon agreed to release him if he promised to never talk about his time with DiamondBar."

"Then why is Dixon spreading these lies about Sam if they came to some *mutual agreement?*"

"I—I don't know."

"There has to be more, Teresa. This doesn't add up. When Sam blew up earlier, he mentioned something I've long suspected."

"What's that?"

"He said that his baseball career was over, but that he *may still have time to save an Afghan family.* Have you ever heard the name Abdul Hazrat?"

"No. Why?"

"I saw his name on a notepad in Sam's house, and then two days ago, I overheard him talking to Mr. Hazrat on the phone."

"Sam always changes the subject when Jose and I have asked him about Afghanistan," Teresa said. "Maybe Whiplash would know, or Hunoon, or—"

"Colonel Tomlinson." Sydney finished Teresa's sentence, then glanced up at the picture over the fireplace. It was the only piece of artwork that Sam displayed in the entire house: a photo of Sam on Pargin Mountain with his mom, dad, and sister. Three of the four were gone. Was Sam now risking his career to protect someone else's family?

"I have to go, Teresa," she said firmly. "I have to make another call."

CHAPTER FIFTY

Kansas City, Missouri

September 2013

Royals General Manager David Wilson looked out the window of his fifth-floor office at Kauffman Stadium. First pitch was still four hours away, but the parking lots were already beginning to fill with tailgaters hoping to be part of Kansas City's first division-championship celebration in thirty years. Plastic cups were being filled with beer, parents were playing catch with their children, and smoke billowed from grills barbecuing chicken and brisket and ribs.

It was everything Wilson had dreamed of as he had patiently built a team of talent, character, and integrity the last seven years. They had drafted skilled athletes, developed them through the system, then signed or traded for players who would fit perfectly into the Royals' climb: 74 wins in 2010, 78 in 2011, 82 in 2012, and 91 so far this year. All they had to do was win one of the next two games, and the Central would be theirs.

Wilson had always believed 2013 would be their year. A core group of winners had come up through the minors together. Cimoli, Ramirez, and Hawkins had become All-Stars, and they had the best defense in the American League and a solid bullpen. The only question when the season began was did the Royals have enough starting pitching? And then, as if the baseball gods had smiled down on them, an unexpected gift fell out of the sky.

Sam Cloud-Carson was the type of workhorse who took teams deep into the postseason. He was smart, fearless, and competitive. He raised his teammates' confidence, and if need be, he could win one game by himself. It would be a huge loss if Major League Baseball suspended him before tomorrow's game.

Wilson checked his watch. Eleven fifteen. Cloud-Carson's press conference was forty-five minutes away. Sam better have some answers to Bob Dalley's scathing story.

"Excuse me, David?"

Wilson looked up to find his executive assistant, Emily Sanders, at his open door.

"There's a Colonel Bart Tomlinson on line two wanting to speak with you. He says he worked with Sam in Afghanistan."

"I'll take it," Wilson said quickly, then motioned for Emily to give him some privacy. As soon as the door closed, he picked up the phone. "This is David Wilson."

"Thanks for taking my call, Mr. Wilson. I'm Colonel Bart Tomlinson of the US Army. Is this a secure line?"

"Yes."

"I was in charge of our Special Forces Unit at Bagram Air Base in Afghanistan. It was my honor and privilege to have Mr. Cloud-Carson help my team on several assignments. I'm calling to tell you that Bob Dalley's article that came out this morning is complete bullshit."

Wilson heaved a sigh of relief. "Thank God! Can you join our press conference today and tell the media what you just told me?"

"No."

Wilson straightened up in his chair. "No? Why not? The kid's getting hammered on every talk show in the country—idiots with no facts calling him a traitor, demanding we suspend him."

"Mr. Wilson, at this particular time, that's all the information I can give you, but you might want to call Baseball Commissioner Stevens. A member of my staff is meeting with Mr. Stevens as we speak, and he's agreed not to suspend Sam until Major League Baseball does a complete investigation into Bob Dalley's story. It's time to get to the bottom of where Mr. Dalley got his information, who were his sources, and why his story broke one day before your biggest game of the year."

Wilson gritted his teeth in frustration. "Why won't Sam just break his silence and defend himself?"

"Because he gave his word to Drake Dixon that he would never talk about his time in Afghanistan. And with Sam Cloud-Carson, his word is everything."

The Royals GM pounded his fist on his desk. "Damn—what am I going to tell the media at today's press conference? Our organization's going to be blasted for doing nothing."

"Tell them the commissioner's office and the Royals are beginning an investigation into Bob Dalley's story. Believe me, Sam's tough enough to take the media and talk-show hits. I witnessed firsthand that son of a gun survive some crazy shit in Afghanistan. But do you know what he may not be able to survive?"

"What's that, Colonel?"

"Not being able to help his team win. You gave him a chance to play in the Majors when no one else would. Not allowing Sam to pitch tomorrow could break him."

*　　*　　*

The rest of Saturday did not go well. Even though owner Jonathan Ewing and GM Wilson flanked Sam at the press conference, his answers were short and clipped. He offered up the same evasive clichés he'd given the media all season long:

I gave my word not to talk about my time in Afghanistan … yes, Frank Weber was a coworker … no, I didn't cut off his ear … Charlie Whitson was the operations chief at our Bagram site … I followed his orders to the best of my ability … I've never been involved in drug trafficking or consorted with the Taliban … I have no idea if the owner of DiamondBar is behind these allegations … I will honor Mr. Dixon's request that I stay silent on this matter … I'd like to thank Commisioner Stevens, Mr Ewing, and Mr. Wilson for letting me start tomorrow's final game …

The press conference lasted all of fifteen minutes, leaving the media grumbling with frustration and Sam and the Royals receiving harsh criticism from sports talk shows and social-media sites across the country.

The Royals lost that night, 6–2. Detroit and Kansas City now had identical 91–70 records with one game to go.

CHAPTER FIFTY-ONE

Stilwell, Kansas

September 2013

Sam was gone. Lost in his breath. Falling deeper and deeper into the present moment. Pure consciousness. Perfectly relaxed. Completely at peace. He was home on Pargin Mountain, first snowfall, deer and bear tracks everywhere. Three faint lights in the distance slowly drew near, shimmering with power. He recognized them. His mother, his father, and his sister, dressed in their finest Ute colors and feathered plumes, dancing to the songs of the bear. He knew he was being blessed, for the spirit of the bear was good, and to respect the bear spirit would ease his anxiety and give him strength. Jenny took his hand and led him inside the ceremonial corral.

"*Oh Great Spirit,*" she sang out, "*let my brother know that he is never alone as You bless him with Your everlasting love. What need has he for anger or fear when You created him in holiness as perfect as Your Own? Straighten his mind so that he may claim the gift of freedom that You offer him this day.*" Jenny then removed the plumed robe he was wearing and hung it on a cedar tree.

He understood. For as the Utes say, *leaving the plume on the tree is to leave your troubles behind and start your life anew.*

His eyes opened to the Blue River. It appeared as if there were little edges of light around the plants and flowers that grew on its muddy banks. These light episodes were something he'd become familiar with since his time in Afghanistan, and they'd always happened after a deep meditation. Perhaps it was a sign that he was seeing in a new way.

*　　*　　*

Kauffman Stadium was rocking on the late September Sunday afternoon. Fans waved blue towels over their heads, and speakers blared music to pump up the crowd as Sam slowly walked in from the bullpen after his pregame warm-up.

"How'd he look?" Charles asked when pitching coach Andy Phillips stepped into the dugout.

"Last twenty throws, Tony never moved his glove," Phillips said.

"You don't think the negative press will get to him?"

"He doesn't read the papers, doesn't have a TV, and says he visualizes the opponent's lineup to shamanic flute music on his drive to the ballpark."

"Shamanny what?"

"Don't worry, Skip, he's ready. He's got that dead-eye blank stare of his that tells me he's locked in."

Charles scanned the sellout crowd at Kauffman. "I hope you're right because the fans and the press will really tear into us for starting him if he gets bombed."

*　　*　　*

Sam wrote the initials of each member of his family on the back of the mound, then he raised up and curled the bill of his cap tight. He wanted complete tunnel vision on his catcher's glove to eliminate any outside distraction as he played an elevated game of catch with Ramirez. He'd always been able to hit his target. It didn't matter if it was a rock, a stick, a snowball, or a baseball, he had the innate ability to throw any object exactly where he wanted.

The Tigers' leadoff batter, Cesar Rubio, was a light-hitting lefty, inside-out swing, who rarely swung at the first pitch. He did this time, rolling Sam's sinker down the third-base line, just by a diving Rex Blackwell for a leadoff double.

The crowd groaned, and the voice of legendary Royals broadcaster Matt Denny echoed throughout the stadium concourse. "Certainly not the way you want to start a game that's for the division title … speedy Rubio on second base with nobody out and a guy hitting over four hundred the last week coming up."

Sam pressed the bill of his cap tighter and stared in to get the sign from Ramirez. His brown hawk's eyes darkened as he shook no for the first sign and then nodded for the second. Rarely did Sam throw his curve first time through the order, but in this case, he would.

He checked the runner at second, and then spun a slow sixty-five-mile-per-hour bender that surprised Greg Stanley, buckling his knees for strike one. The right-handed hitter called time and stepped out of the box, glancing out at the pitcher who gave no tell.

Sam followed with a four-seam fastball, up and in, that Stanley fouled off for strike two, and then he threw a hard, down and away, slider that finished a good eight-inches off the plate for a swing-and-miss strike three. Rubio held at second. Sam got Detroit's number-three hitter to fly out to left and then struck out MVP-candidate Eduardo Suarez on three pitches to end the inning. The crowd roared.

*   *   *

Ramirez sat down next to his first baseman in the dugout and leaned in so only he could hear.

"You seeing what I'm seeing?"

"Dude's in another world," Cimoli said. "Nine pitches, nine strikes. It's like he's got the ball on a string."

"That breaker he threw Stanley slid like it was on black ice."

"I've never seen Greg swing at a pitch that far off the plate."

Both Ramirez and Cimoli looked down at the end of the dugout, where their rookie right-hander sat alone, staring at a small notebook, oblivious to his teammates' chatter, the buzz of the crowd, and the stadium music blaring some classic rock and roll.

"Just give him a good target," muttered Cimoli, "cuz he's in a zone."

"Shut up, here he comes."

Sam walked past his first baseman and stopped directly in front of his catcher, his eyes deathly intense. "No more breaking balls until third time through the order. Two-seam, four-seam, changeup. I might cut it to Suarez if I fall behind in the count, but that's it."

Ramirez nodded. "You got it."

Then Sam walked back to the end of the dugout and studied his notebook again.

"Damn," Cimoli said. "Have you ever met a rookie like him?"

"No. Glad he's on our side, because I'd crap my pants if I had to face that slide piece he threw Stanley."

Cimoli clapped to the beat of the rock music blasting from the stadium speakers and sang out, *"He makes the Tigers cryyy–yie … He makes the Tigers cryyy–yie . . ."*

*   *   *

The game was scoreless through six. After giving up the Rubio single to start the game, Sam retired the next eighteen batters on only sixty-one pitches. Unfortunately, Detroit ace Chip Townsend matched him pitch for pitch, scattering three singles.

With one out in the top of the seventh, the Tigers' three and four hitters chopped seeing-eye hits past diving infielders to put runners on first and third. Pitching coach Phillips asked for time. He jogged out to the mound and waved for the entire infield to join him.

"How you feeling, kid?"

"Great," answered Sam bluntly. "Here's what we'll do. Santiago's a dead-pull hitter. Four-seam low outside corner, strike one. Changeup in, he'll yank it foul for strike two. Then I'll take a little off a down-and-in sinker, he'll pull it to Rex for a five-four-three, and we're outta the inning."

Startled, Phillips didn't reply for a second. He saw the no-nonsense look in his pitcher's eyes and patted him on the back. "Hell of a plan.

Make sure to keep that off-speed in." Then he headed back to the dugout.

Sam looked at his third baseman. "Play straight up on the first two pitches, then move two steps to your right on the third." He turned to his second baseman. "Santiago runs well, Terry. Be quick with your turn."

His infielders all nodded and headed back to their respective positions.

*　　*　　*

"What'd he say?" Manager Charles asked his pitching coach when he returned to the dugout.

"Fastball strike one, off-speed pulled foul, strike two, sinker grounded to Rex for the double play."

Charles narrowed his eyes. "No shit?"

Phillips chuckled lightly. "No shit."

Sam's first-pitch fastball barely touched the outside corner for strike one. Second-pitch changeup, Santiago turned on savagely, blasting a long drive down the left-field line, well over four hundred feet … but well foul. Strike two. Sam glanced over at Blackwell, who took two steps to his right and readied himself.

"C'mon, EssCee!" yelled Rex, pounding his fist into his glove.

Sam placed his right foot off center of the rubber to get a better angle on the hitter and nodded yes to Ramirez's sign. *Deep inhale, slow exhale, check the runner at first, and let her rip.* The baseball spun off his long fingers with an extra revolution, knifing down and in, to the right-handed hitter. Santiago pulled the ball directly to Blackwell, who flipped to second for one out. Ayers' turn was perfect, Cimoli stretching for the ball like a ballerina doing the splits.

The umpire jerked his right arm up. "Out!"

The crowd went wild.

Cimoli hopped up and pointed his glove at Sam. "That was awesome!"

Both Charles'and Phillips' mouths fell open in stunned disbelief. The Royals' manager slowly turned to his pitching coach. "Did I just see what I think I saw?"

Phillips nodded dumbly.

Charles gave a wolf howl and then high-fived his players returning to the dugout.

"Let's get Sammy some runs, boys! Right here! Right now!"

Hawkins lined a single to left to start the bottom of the seventh. Cimoli moved him to second on a soft grounder to first. The crowd picked up, the scoreboard demanded more noise, and every Royal leaned over the dugout fence, sensing something big was about to happen.

Manny Morales stepped into the batter's box, windmilled his bat, and inhaled a deep breath. He told his skipper that he was going to swing at the first pitch. He blasted a long fly to center, barely missing a home run as the ball hit off the top of the wall, easily scoring Hawkins. One, nothing. Royals.

Both sides went three up, three down in the eighth, leaving Charles with a tough decision. He could stay with his in-the-groove rookie, or bring in closer Kevin Andrews, who had saved thirty-two games this year. Charles made up his mind when he looked down at the end of the dugout and found his starting pitcher staring back at him, eyes dark with intensity. Sam mouthed the words, "Leave—me—in. Leave—me—in."

Cloud-Carson would pitch the ninth.

Sam felt eerily calm when he warmed up for the top of the ninth. He thought of his family watching him play. They would be proud. He had surrendered his old ways of isolation, finally understanding that it was not enough for a man to depend simply upon himself. He was part of a team. He trusted his ability, but he also trusted the men behind him. The men who had played flawless defense all day.

He thought of Sydney, whose words yesterday had inspired him:

When you're on that mound, you let the same force that moves the universe direct you. To trust in that power takes faith, and your willingness to relax into it allows you to do amazing things.

Three more outs.

His second pitch of the ninth was chopped up the middle. Sam jumped high but missed it. Hernandez bolted in from short, barehanded the ball, and flipped to Cimoli for the first out.

He thought of Jenny:

Life can break you, my brother. You have always felt most comfortable with being alone.

Rubio was next, lining a one-hop smash to right. Cimoli made a diving grab, rolled over, and flipped the ball to Sam covering first, barely catching the speedy Tiger. Two outs.

The mountains and the pitching mound have been your churches. But solitude can also break you with its yearning to stand with others.

The count went to two balls and two strikes on Stanley, the Tigers' hottest hitter in September. Sam's one-hundredth pitch of the game was his signature sinker, but unlike the others, it didn't bite down, catching too much of the plate. Stanley's bat caught it flush, driving the ball to the right-center gap. Center fielder Hawkins took off in a dead sprint, twice taking his eyes off the ball to check for the wall …

Trust them, Sam. It is the reason you are here.

Hawkins leaped. The ball hit his glove just as he smashed into the wall and collapsed in a heap on the warning track. The crowd hushed, waiting … and then, finally, Hawkins took the ball out of his glove and held it up for the umpire to see. Game over. For the first time in almost thirty years, the Kansas City Royals were going to the postseason.

CHAPTER FIFTY-TWO

DiamondBar Headquarters, Southern Virginia

September 2013

Dixon clicked off his TV and hurled the remote at the screen, batteries and plastic pieces exploding across the room.

"Bastard pitches the best game of his life after getting destroyed by the press! Why didn't the fucking league suspend him? Damn traitor!"

Dixon was alone in his office on a Sunday afternoon. Alone … again. His marriage was over, the woman he'd been seeing had gone back to her husband, and his lawyer and most trusted confidant was home with his own family. This was unfamiliar territory.

Dixon was used to getting his way. So much so, that when people didn't submit to him, he made their lives so miserable that they finally gave up and gave him even more than he'd originally demanded. Yet, every once in a while, he'd run into a rebel like Carson, but it didn't take long to crush them and get his way. He thought Sam was beginning to crack after the Oakland clubhouse fight, but the kid had somehow recovered and pitched even better down the stretch.

Dixon backhanded a glass of scotch off his desk, ice, alcohol and glass joining the batteries and plastic on the floor. "Son of a bitch better stay quiet, or I'll do whatever it takes to see his murdering ass in prison."

*　　*　　*

That was the best game I've ever seen. You were incredible.

Sam read Sydney's text at one in the morning. It was the first time he'd looked at his phone since hours before the game. There had been prep, game, win, on-field celebration, clubhouse celebration, press conference, and finally team party at the Power and Light District. By the time Sam climbed into his Prius at twelve fifteen, he was better off than most of his teammates. Exhausted, but sober.

He read Sydney's text again and smiled. He wanted to text her back, wanted to call her, but it was one in the morning. She'd be up early to go for her run, and then she had class. It wouldn't be right to wake her, but … he thought of her sleeping, the way she lay on her side, mouth slightly open, smooth, even breaths, long, black hair caressing her face, neck, breasts—

"Aw heck, I'm texting her."

Sorry to wake you. I just saw your text. Thanks for the kind words.

Thirty seconds later: *Hey, party animal! Congrats on the huge win!*

He replied: *You know me. One beer and I'm gone.*

She texted back: *You're really good. It's so much fun watching you compete.*

That made him feel good. *Your words Saturday got my head right.*

The little texting bubble in the corner of the screen told him that she was writing something. Finally:

I didn't want to tell you this until after you pitched. I called Teresa. She told me what happened.

Sam's eyes flew open, and he immediately called her.

"I'm sorry, Sam," she said when she picked up. "I was worried—"

"What did Teresa tell you?"

"She told me that you saved her from being raped. That you killed the men who kidnapped her. That Drake Dixon videotaped it—and blackmailed you."

For a long time, he didn't speak. He didn't know how to explain the worst day of his life. How do he put into words how he felt the day both his mother and his dream died?

"Sam," she said cautiously, "you can't do this alone."

"Stay out of it, Sydney."

"But Colonel Tomlinson needs to know *everything* that happened. Not just what you're willing to tell him."

"You didn't talk to him too, did you?"

"Yes."

"Did he mention a letter I gave him the day I left Afghanistan?"

"Yes. He read it while I was on the phone with him. He said that he needed to call Whiplash."

"Damn it, Sydney! You have no idea what you've done! I gave my word I wouldn't talk about my time working for Dixon."

"And you've kept your word. I'm the one who told him."

"You don't understand. I don't have much proof of what Dixon was doing in the Nuristan Province. I only have a few copies of mining contracts he violated, but the rest were veiled threats I made to force him to stop construction on a mountain and to release me from DiamondBar."

"Call the colonel and Whip. They'll help you."

"It's not about me, dammit! It's about an innocent Afghan family who Dixon threatened to kill if I broke my word."

"Then trust your friends. You can't save the family alone. It's like your ninth inning tonight. Who helped you win? Hernandez, Cimoli, and Hawkins all made great plays to bail you out."

"This isn't a damn game, Sydney. It's life or death."

"That's exactly why Tomlinson and Whip need to know *everything*. Trust them."

Sam gripped his phone so tightly he thought he might crush it. "I—I have to go," he said, his voice desperate with emotion. "I can't talk with you right now. Just—just stay the hell out of it!" Then he clicked off and stared at his phone, his face tense with fury.

*　　*　　*

For the second time in three nights, he couldn't sleep, his mind wild with this new information. Was Sydney right? Was this about some arrogant belief that only he could protect Hazrat's land? That his knowledge of Dixon's illegal activities in Afghanistan and subsequent leverage over the DiamondBar owner could keep foreign investors away? His hope had been that Dixon's political clout inside the Afghan government would hinder any prospecting of Hazrat's mountain.

It had worked for a while. Hazrat had had two years of peace … But now the riches in the Nuristan Province were drawing interest from multiple international mining companies and Sam wondered if Dixon was one of the hunters. A new Provincial Reconstruction Team had begun work on the old road through Hazrat's territory, and the scandalous story about Sam's past had broken. Adding to the trouble was that Tomlinson and McCracken now knew that he had killed Cutthredge and Marcus. It didn't matter that he had done it to save someone. At the very least, he had committed manslaughter and then had consorted with Dixon to cover it up. The revelation of that conspiracy would not only end his baseball career but would send him to prison.

He called Tomlinson. The colonel picked up on the fourth ring.

"Hell of a game, Sam. Congrats on winning the Central."

He ignored the compliment. "I understand Sydney called you."

"Yes, she did. You have a good friend in that young lady."

Sam didn't know what to say. His emotions were all over the place when it came to Sydney. Yeah, she had tried to help him, but at what cost?

"Colonel," he said firmly, "I made a simple request two years ago that you not open that letter unless I was killed or disabled."

"What do you think Dixon's doing to you right now, Sam? Attacking you with these shameful stories in the press, drop by drop, like water on rock, slowly trying to break you."

"I can handle it."

"Of course you can," Tomlinson scoffed. "Just like Afghanistan—you can do *everything* by yourself. Discover Taliban hideouts in the mountains by yourself. Disobey orders and turn off your sat-phone so you can do recon by yourself. Go into a cave to take pictures of enemy weapons caches by yourself–"

"I got the pictures," Sam said defensively, "and–and you destroyed the weapons."

"Admit it, Sam–you had a death wish. You refused to take anyone with you because you didn't want to be responsible for *them* getting killed. You didn't care about *your* life. At the time, you were hoping that someone else might end your misery."

Until Sam heard the words, he had forgotten how much he had suppressed his depression when he arrived in Afghanistan. He had boldly told his DiamondBar boss and coworkers that he worked alone, that he couldn't track if he had to worry about the safety of others. Even when Frank Weber lashed out at him, saying he wouldn't last one day alone in the field, Sam had cryptically replied, *That, sir, would be a relief.*

"You did the same thing when you saved that little girl from being raped in the village near Kamdesh," Tomlinson continued. "Yeah, it turned out fine, but one mistake and that entire village could have been wiped out."

"But they weren't."

"Sydney's right, Sam. You're trying to save the world by yourself. You've come a long way since we first met, but you have to help me do my job. An FBI national security unit is now on the case. The information you had in that letter revealed more than you know."

Sam hadn't been expecting that and was genuinely curious. "How? The only intel in that file that you didn't know about was me killing Billy and Rob."

"That was the first piece of the puzzle. It led us to the next piece."

"What did you find?"

"Still working on it, but quick question. What was the name of the DiamondBar coworker who was captured along with Frank Weber when the Taliban blew the bridge?"

"Scott Thornton."

"Do you know what happened to him?"

"I have no idea. Why do you ask?"

"Just doing my job. Now, why don't you get back to doing yours."

"What's my job, sir?"

"To pitch your ass off for the Royals ... that's it. Regardless of the attacks that may come from Dixon, stay cool and do whatever you can to help your team win."

CHAPTER FIFTY-THREE

Oakland, California

October 2013

When the Royals flew to Oakland for the first game of the American League Division series, Kevin Cimoli motioned for Sam to join him in the last row of the plane.

"We believe you," the Royals' unofficial captain said.

"Thanks."

"I don't know if you knew this, Sammy, but we were pissed when they called you up from the minors back in May. We were playing lousy, and our starting pitching was a mess. We wanted the front office to trade for a veteran starter, and instead they called up some bootleg turd from Nicaragua who had spent all of four weeks in Double-A ball."

"Those are pretty good reasons to be pissed," Sam said.

"But the way you pitched that first game, then the second and third, the way you competed, kept your mouth shut and listened, the way you defended Manny in Detroit, the way you step up in big games—you're a warrior, man. We're damn lucky to have you."

Sam didn't respond.

"You also got a great endorsement from my man, Roberto Francisco."

Sam smiled, thinking about the Royals scout who had signed him. "He's a great guy."

"The best." Kevin's voice was filled with respect. "Robby signed me too. He called me when you were promoted. Told me about the first time he saw you pitch in high school—said we would have drafted you in the first round back in 2009 if not for a family tragedy."

Sam nodded.

"He told me what you've lost."

Again nothing from Sam.

"How do you do it?"

Sam blinked, startled by the question. "Do what?"

"Stay calm when people talk shit about you?"

"You should have seen me Saturday morning when Walt called about the story. I wasn't so calm then. I broke about everything in my house." He pointed to the Band-Aid on his left hand. "This is from punching a hole in the wall."

"Really? Dang, I would have paid good money to see that. Outside of the time you jumped Cobb in Oakland, you're always so zen."

"I'm not very zen when someone goes after our team. We worked our butts off to get back in the race and then some jerk wrote lies before our biggest game. I was beyond angry."

"But when you came into the clubhouse that day, you acted as if nothing had happened."

"A friend helped me get my head right," Sam said. "She came over that morning when I was going ballistic and calmed me down … told me not to let the story beat me. She said that I had to somehow channel my anger in a positive way that would help our team win."

"Whoa—when do I get to meet your motivational guru?"

Sam laughed. "Yeah, she's pretty cool."

Kevin studied him. "It's that girl who was at the stables last week when we went for the trail ride, isn't it?"

"How'd you know?"

"I might be a dumb jock, Sammy, but I'm not blind. I saw the way the two of you looked at each other—and the way it made Tiffany jealous."

Sam looked about the plane to make sure no one was listening. "Unfortunately, she's going through a divorce."

"What? Don't you have enough shit on your plate right now?"

"I've only seen her a couple of times since August. She thinks she needs to work through her stuff—and that I need to focus on pitching."

"Smart woman." Cimoli winked. "She must see what we see. A good man … and a winner."

*　　*　　*

He texted Sydney when they landed. *I'm sorry for yelling at you. I was wrong.*

He didn't get a reply for a couple of hours. It was only three words. *Yes, you were.*

He texted back. *Are we still friends?*

Yes. But you hurt me. Don't do it again.

He grimaced, recalling their last conversation. He had taken his anger out on his best friend, the person who had driven over to his house at six thirty in the morning to make sure he was all right after a damaging story had been written about him. *Geez, what a jerk I am.* He waited a few minutes before texting: *Can I leave you tickets when we return home?*

Thanks very much. Maybe game four.

Wow, he thought, *that's rather blunt. I wasn't that big of a jerk, was I?* He texted: *Can I call you?*

She replied: *No. Concentrate on your job. You don't need any more distractions.*

*　　*　　*

A distraction showed up the morning of game one of the division series. Another Bob Dalley story about the July rumor of Sam roughing up a stripper in a nightclub off Interstate 70. There were no facts. No proof. No quotes from the nameless stripper. No confirmation from the owner of Blue Temptations Strip Club that Sam had even been there. It didn't matter if it was true or not. The allegation had been made and now was being shared and retweeted on every social-media site on the internet.

Another story broke the same morning that didn't get as much attention. It was a simple letter to the editor of a Tacoma, Washington, newspaper. The writer, a Lieutenant Dan Snyder of Army Special Forces, now stationed at Fort Lewis, recalled a DiamondBar scout named Carson having saved his rescue team in the Nuristan Province in August of 2011. The story told of Carson radioing for help when the DiamondBar crew providing security for a Provincial Reconstruction Team was overwhelmed by Taliban forces.

Carson was the only one from his unit to avoid capture and had warned Snyder's Black Hawk helicopter rescue team to hold back just before the Taliban destroyed a bridge the PRT had been constructing. Lieutenant Snyder then wrote that Carson went alone into the mountains to track down his captured teammates and said that he would radio back for help when he found them. The story ended there. No finish. No ending. Like a fish lure in the water, leaving the reader wanting more.

*   *   *

The media room at the Oakland Coliseum was packed when Sam walked in to meet the press. He sat with his manager, Skip Charles, and players Cimoli and Hawkins, all hoping to answer baseball questions. There was an awkward moment of quiet, as if the media was expecting a statement.

Finally, the rep from MLB said, "Any questions?"

A writer in the front row raised his hand. "Sam, could you address the Bob Dalley story about you roughing up a stripper at Blue Temptations?"

Sam pulled the microphone close. "It didn't happen. I've never been to a strip club in my life."

"Then why these accusations?"

"I don't know. You're the journalist. Have you questioned my accusers, or do you just want a quote from me that you can retweet?"

A reporter in the back called out, "What about the Lieutenant Dan Snyder story about you saving his Black Hawk team in the Nuristan Mountains?"

"I can't talk about my time in Afghanistan."

"But it's a positive story."

"It doesn't matter. I gave my word. If I betray my word, I'm not much of a man."

"Do you know this Lieutenant Snyder?"

Cimoli reached over and grabbed the mic. "Hey guys, any baseball questions? We kind of have a pretty big game today."

The rest of the media session was about baseball, and the four Royals at the table answered each question respectfully, yet with a chip-on-their-shoulder, terse edge. As soon as the four returned to the privacy of their clubhouse, Cimoli let loose a volley.

"Screw Bob Dalley!" he screamed and then waved for the rest of the team to join him in front of Sam's locker. "That lying piece of shit never played behind this man!"

"Yeah!" his teammates roared.

"Look into these eyes!" Cimoli pointed at Sam, who began to flush red with embarrassment. "They're the eyes of a warrior!"

Sam bit the side of his mouth to keep from smiling, which only fueled the Royals' unofficial captain more. "They're the eyes of a winner! A champion! Our champion!"

The team crowded around Sam: players, coaches, trainers, even GM Wilson, slapping him on the back as they shouted words of encouragement…

We got yer back … you're our brother … we play for each other … win this moment … this inning … win tonight . . .

The Royals won that night, bailing out Mario Fuentes' rough start with four home runs in a 9–7 victory. They won again Saturday night as Sam threw a complete-game five-hitter in a 5–1 win, and the Royals returned home to finish off the sweep with an 11–4 trouncing of the A's on Monday night.

*   *   *

As the team flew to New York to begin the American League Championship Series against the Yankees, another story broke in a Boise, Idaho, newspaper. A retired Army unmanned-aerial-vehicle pilot validated Lieutenant Snyder's account, saying he piloted the week the PRT bridge was destroyed. He confirmed that there was a second explosion three days later. The first was set by the Taliban, but the second was detonated by a member of the DiamondBar team to alert US forces that insurgents had returned to the area. Black Hawk choppers were sent to investigate. A battle ensued, and the enemy was driven back toward the Pakistan border. The drone pilot didn't know the name of the DiamondBar man who ignited the second blast, nor did he know what happened to him. Once again, there was no ending to the story.

With all the media speculation and attention now directed at the reticent rookie from southwest Colorado, the rest of the team went about their business. The Royals seemed to take on Sam's personality, playing with a quiet, determined, professional focus: throwing strikes, playing great defense, stealing bases, moving runners. If a Royal made it to second base with nobody out, they got him to third; if a runner made it to third with less than two outs, they found a way to score him. And Sam was spending more time with his teammates: on the plane, the bus, working out, at meals. He sat with a different player or coach, asking them about their life, their family, where they grew up, and how they fell in love with the game.

Sam started the opener on Friday night, frustrating the vaunted Yankees offense with his dipping and diving sinker, cutter, curve, and changeup. Seventeen of the twenty-seven outs recorded were groundouts, including four rally-killing double plays. The Royals won 7–2.

The next morning, the *New York Times* reprinted a story from the *Afghanistan Times Daily.* There were quotes from a woman named Hunoon Sanjari, praising Sam Cloud-Carson's volunteer work at a local mission called the Friends of Everyone Hotel. Ms. Sanjari said that Mr.

Cloud-Carson helped coach their children's programs and used sports as a way to *"help heal the wounds of war."* She said that the children adored Sam.

The Royals won both games over the heavily favored Yankees in New York and took two out of three in Kansas City to win the American League pennant.

Now it was on to the nation's capital for the World Series. Time to face the winningest team in 2013, the 108-win Washington Nationals.

CHAPTER FIFTY-FOUR

Washington, DC

October 2013

"We have to find out who's leaking these damn stories," grumbled Dixon as he tossed a copy of the *New York Times* into the trash can of his luxury suite at Nationals Park. It was thirty minutes before game two of the World Series. The Nats had taken game one, 6–4, and Drake and his lawyer had come early to make sure their suite was spotless for his important guests.

"Who the hell is Hunoon Sanjari?" Dixon said. "And why would some Afghan woman give a shit about baseball in America?"

"It is called the *World* Series," King said. He slid the glass door shut that faced the field to give them greater privacy. "And it does involve tonight's starting pitcher, who at one time served in Afghanistan."

"He's still an American. The *Great Satan* to Islam."

"Damn, Drake, you sound like some Taliban warlord."

"It's an age-old recipe to control the masses. Create a common enemy and give them someone to hate—a person, religion, culture, or country they can blame for their miserable lot in life. If you can make people believe they're victims, and that only you can save them, it's much easier to control them."

King shook his head. "Yet when it comes to Carson, you've made *yourself* the victim. I sometimes wonder if your infatuation to crush him will come back to bite you."

"He has to go down. Son of a bitch cost me millions. He embarrassed my company. DiamondBar's dropped from seventh among the most profitable private military companies to thirty-fifth because of what he did."

"We're doing fine, Drake. As long as America is involved in two wars, we'll make money. PMCs have become the fifth branch of the military. They represent the private sector, and you know the corporations—they want a return on their investment."

"They'll get it. My connections in Afghanistan are paying off. The Minister of Mines agreed to work with our shell company in the Cayman Islands, giving us complete control of Hazrat's mountain, and our old friend, Almeida Zubair, found a warlord willing to accept our bounty to kill Hazrat." Dixon rubbed the tip of his index finger and thumb together. "It's amazing what one can buy from a country in chaos."

"Don't push it, Drake. We don't want Integrity Watch Afghanistan or the US Defense Contract Audit Agency looking into what we're doing."

Dixon snorted. "There were over a hundred investigations last year into fraud, illegal kickbacks, bid-rigging, and overbilling. How many prosecutions, Barry?"

"None ... Still no reason to draw prying eyes by going after a star baseball player that all of a sudden is getting good press."

Dixon's jaws flexed in anger as he stared out of his luxury suite to the field, where the Royals' starting pitcher was long-tossing in the outfield with his catcher.

"You take care of our shell company, Barry. I'll take care of Hazrat and Carson. Just let me enjoy tonight as our team kicks his Royal ass."

*　　*　　*

Overland Park, Kansas

Sydney placed the bowl of salsa next to the tortilla chips and sat down on her parents' couch. It was almost game time, and she was already a nervous wreck. Mary Beth and Phil were there, not only to watch the game, but to give her moral support for what she was about to tell her parents and brother. As soon as Tom found out his sister had scored tickets for games three, four, and five of the World Series, he'd caught the next flight to KC.

"Law school can wait." Tom handed Sydney a napkin. "You're my hero, sis. I mean, how the heck did you find six seats for the Series?"

Sydney glanced at Mary Beth and then back at her brother. "That's what I wanted to talk with you guys about—"

"Can I get you a beer, Tommy?" their dad interrupted and started to get up before Sydney reached across the table and pulled him back down.

"Dad, I need to tell you something—"

"Here's my boy!" Her mom unmuted the TV as the broadcast came back from a commercial break to show the game's starting pitchers. "Sam Cloud-Carson. He's awesome—and what a nice young man too. Did you read the stories about Sam visiting children at hospitals, coaching kids in Nicaragua, and warning that helicopter pilot in Afghanistan?"

"What about him cutting off that guy's ear?" Tom teased. Even as a child, he had taken delight in needling his mom. "Or the trouble he got into at the strip joint?"

"Hogwash!" Vivian's voice was sharp with indignation. "Our owner and general manager are men of integrity. They'd never let Sam play if any of that were true."

"I dunno, Mom. In my business, where there's smoke, there's usually fire. I'll bet you wouldn't want Cloud-Carson dating your daughter."

Sydney's shoulders slumped forward. This was going to be a lot harder than she'd thought. She snatched a tortilla chip, scooped up a large chunk of salsa, and stuffed it into her mouth.

"Hey Syd?" Her dad looked down at his phone. "I just got a text from Blake. He wants to join us tonight. Is that okay?"

She practically choked on the chip and raised her hand to let them know she needed to finish chewing.

"I'll get you a drink, honey. You need something to wash that down."

She turned to Mary Beth and gave her an absolutely defeated look.

"Stay strong, girl," MB whispered. "You're doing just fine."

Her dad returned with a beer, and she took a long drink.

"*No* on Blake coming over," she said firmly. "You do remember that our divorce will be finalized tomorrow?"

Mr. Morgan shook his head sadly. "It breaks my heart that you'll be all alone. Are you sure this is the right decision?"

"Please, Dad, it's over."

"I'm glad she's leaving him," her brother said. "Blake's a jerk. I never liked the way he treated Syd in high school, and I thought he got meaner after they were married. Always making fun of her, criticizing every little thing she—"

"Can we please just watch the ballgame?" Vivian interrupted.

It was just like her mom, thought Sydney. Avoid any confrontation, whether it was about tomorrow's divorce or discussing her daughter's biological father, Vivian Morgan wanted no part of any tension. Just close your eyes and cover your ears and pray that bad stuff would go away.

The Royals went three up, three down in the top of the first, and the television broadcast broke for commercials. *Time for a quick family discussion,* Sydney thought as she muted the TV. "Have any of you noticed a change in me since I left Blake?"

"Yeah," Tom said. "You seem happier."

"I am."

Vivian cocked one brow at her daughter but said nothing.

"I'm happy with me. I like *me* again … I didn't before."

"Why?" Her mom finally seemed interested.

Sydney traced her cleft line from her upper lip to her nose. "I felt less than, felt different than you and Dad and Tom because of my cleft and because of my blood … and Blake reminded of those imperfections every day."

Her father's face tightened and he turned in his chair to face his daughter. "But you know we love you."

She nodded. "But I didn't love me. I didn't feel worthy of your love, didn't feel worthy of Blake's love. I tried to do everything to get him to love me more, and even when he treated me like crap, I thought it was my fault, something I said or did."

"What happened that made you like yourself again?" her mother asked.

By now the broadcast was back from commercial break, and there was a full-screen shot of Sam on the mound. Sydney pointed to the TV.

"*He* happened."

Vivian narrowed her eyes, as if not understanding.

Sydney let out a long breath. "Sam's the one who got us tickets for the Series. He's a good friend."

Her parents' mouths fell open and so did her brother's.

Sydney glanced up at the TV to watch Sam throw strike one.

"He rents a cottage on Bette Tomlinson's property. We met working the stables and prepping the horses for the Urban Wildlife Academy."

Vivian glanced at Mary Beth, who nodded that what her daughter said was true.

Sam's next pitch was popped up to short. One out.

"We had great talks," Sydney continued. "Those conversations gave me confidence to examine my life: my past, my faith, my marriage. I realized it was okay to question every value I'd held before—and to move forward rather than stay stuck in the past."

Her mother cleared her throat. "Is *he* the reason you're leaving Blake?"

"No—Blake's the reason I'm leaving Blake. Being married to him is a constant battle. Every day is exhausting. I decided I didn't want to live that way anymore."

A Sam changeup was grounded to deep short. Hernandez made a nice backhanded stop and threw the runner out.

"I've only seen Sam a couple of times in the last two months," Sydney said. "That was my decision because both of us had stuff we were working through."

Her mother gulped. "Do you … have feelings for him?"

She nodded.

Both of her parents sighed heavily.

"I don't know where it's going, but I do know one thing—Sam renewed my faith in myself. He's more than a baseball player. He's a really good guy." She paused to watch Sam get the final out of the first and then high-five a teammate as he left the field. His smile made her smile. "I used to carry around a lot of shame about who I thought I was: half-white, half-Lakota, cleft lip, not pretty enough, history nerd, soccer geek, failed wife who can't even have a baby. It was always something. There were times I even felt as if I was in competition with God. What was He thinking when He made me?"

Her mother looked like she might cry. "I'm sorry. I never knew you felt that way."

"There's nothing to be sorry about, Mom. It got me to where I am today. Only when I let go of those old doubts did I discover the power that was already in me. I still struggle some days, but most of the time, I don't think about my self-perceived flaws anymore because I like who I am now. I'm a good person. Blake may not see that in me, but Sam does. And I'm grateful that he likes me just the way I am."

*　　*　　*

Washington, DC

Dixon poured himself another glass of Glenlivet and looked out at the scoreboard. Sixth inning. Royals 5, Nationals 0. A Cloud-Carson two-seamer that looked like it would hit the Nat's left-handed slugger, suddenly darted back, barely grazing the inside corner of the zone. The umpire's right arm jerked up for a called strike three, the hitter slammed his bat down, and the home crowd howled their displeasure.

"Shit! Your former employee is making us look like minor leaguers," Senator Richardson grumbled. "It's like he's playing darts out there, hitting the bullseye every damn time."

Dixon's face was a mask, his mouth set in a harsh line. "Can we talk about something else?"

"What happened between you two?" Richardson asked. "Five years ago, you couldn't wait to sign him. When you did, you raved about his work in Afghanistan, then bam—he was gone, and you've hated him ever since."

"He screwed up our plans to claim Hazrat's mountain."

"How exactly?"

Dixon hesitated and loosened the knot of his silk tie. He couldn't tell the important senator every detail of his failed attempt to control the mountain, of the bounties he had paid to eliminate Hazrat, and the deaths of Cutthredge and Marcus.

"Carson uncovered why we were building the PRT road," Dixon said, "and blackmailed me for not having a mining license in that region and for violating the Afghan Mining Regulations Act."

Richardson snorted back a laugh. "That's nothing, Drake. I could take care of that with the stroke of a pen, and no watchdog committee would ever see it." He slapped Dixon on the back. "This is Washington, DC, boy. Hell, I take a hit every damn day. I just climb back up Capitol Hill and renegotiate. Everybody's got their price. When the Supremes passed Citizens United three years ago, it gave corporations like yours unlimited power. All you have to do is get those mining contracts from Afghanistan's Minister of Commerce and Industry, and we're in fat city. You get the mountain, and the company I was CEO of before I became senator gets the contract to provide all the construction equipment for our little project."

"Nadeem Khattak hasn't returned any of my recent calls, Ed. We have a verbal agreement, but nothing official. I don't know why he's being so slow. I'm paying him big bucks not only for those contracts, but to grease his friend at the Natural Resources Oversight Network to look the other way."

"Just don't do anything stupid." Richardson paused to make sure he had Dixon's full attention. "That's why those stories about Carson you've been dropping through Bob Dalley have done nothing."

Dixon winced. "How'd you know *I* was behind it?"

"It's right out of your playbook, Drake. Accusations of strippers, drugs, prostitutes, fights with coworkers. Unfortunately, you picked on a man who's become a star. All your attacks have done is draw out people who want to defend Carson—American soldiers, a Muslim charity worker, children at a mission. What the hell were you thinking?"

"What do you suggest?"

"Get off the damn sidelines. Go after him. Tell the press with that silky-smooth voice of yours that everything you did was only to help Carson. That you were worried about him after he lost his entire family—that you gave him a chance when no one else would."

The crowd groaned as a National turned on a Cloud-Carson breaking ball and lined out to third. Two outs.

"Create even greater mistrust in him," Richardson continued. "Take something that was said by one of those American soldiers and stretch the truth to favor you. As an example, what happened when Carson went alone to rescue his coworkers?"

"He was supposed to radio back for support when he found them but claimed his sat-phone was broken so he captured the bad guys himself."

"Did he get credit for the rescue?"

"No, he didn't want it."

Richardson gave an amused grunt. "There's the mistrust you've been looking for, Drake."

Dixon's face changed from one of frustration to the look of an oil tycoon who'd just hit a gusher. "You're a genius, Ed. The press reported that Frank Weber and Scott Thornton were responsible for capturing a Pakistani Taliban leader. There was no mention of Carson because he deserted his team."

"Where'd he go?"

"He discovered Hazrat's kids at the hideout. They'd been kidnapped by the Pakistani warlord a week before." Drake paused for a long moment. He couldn't tell Richardson that Carson didn't bring the children to DiamondBar headquarters because he knew Dixon would use them as leverage against Hazrat. Instead, he said, "Carson disobeyed orders and returned the children to their father."

Both of Richardson's bushy gray eyebrows rose in surprise. "How'd he know where Hazrat's village was? Had he been there before?"

"He's a skilled tracker, Ed. He probably knew every inch of that territory."

"Don't waste your time with facts," Richardson scoffed. "Just manipulate information so people believe you over him. Had Carson been consorting with a warlord without your knowledge? What was he doing in an enemy camp?"

Dixon's smile widened. "Carson went AWOL for more than a week. Then he randomly showed up at Camp Blessing in Nangalam looking like a terrorist. Security made him lay on the ground while they searched him. They wanted to be sure he wasn't playing for the wrong team."

The senator put a hand on his heart in mock concern. "Alas, now you can act as if you're the understanding parent trying to help a wayward child." Richardson paused to make sure Dixon understood the importance of his next words. "Because, if Carson truly does have damaging information on what we were doing in Afghanistan, well, that could get us into some hot water. That's why it's important that you make him sound like some disgruntled, corrupt former employee."

Dixon swallowed hard, and then glanced again at the field, where another Nationals hitter fired his bat down after swinging and missing at a Cloud-Carson changeup. The sixth inning was over. The enemy still led 5–0. Dixon cursed under his breath. *Time to drop the hammer on you, boy.*

*   *   *

Overland Park, Kansas

Sydney shook her fist when Sam struck out the Nationals batter and smiled at her dad.

"Ten strikeouts in six innings. He's on a roll."

Her father gave her a stiff smile but said nothing. Both of her parents seemed to have settled into an almost numb silence after hearing their daughter's startling revelation that she had a relationship with the Royals' star pitcher. She had told them almost everything: the cute story of how they had met, the prank he pulled on her at the Royals game, how they worked together at the stables, and their conversations about sports, life, and faith. But they had stayed away from anything even closely resembling romance. She could tell that her parents' didn't want to know.

"Does anyone need anything?" Sydney picked up the empty basket of chips and headed to the kitchen.

"Brewski, please." Her brother winked and then stood up when there was a knock at the door. "Dang, who could this be? I figured everyone in town would be camped in front of the TV."

*　　*　　*

He opened the door and—

"Tommy boy!" Blake cried out happily. "How you doin', bro?"

Tom stood in the doorway, unsure of what to do. There was no doubt his brother-in-law had been drinking, but—until tomorrow—he was still his sister's husband.

"Sorry to drop by so late, Tommy, but I was in the neighborhood and knew you'd be watching the game. Pretty cool, huh? Up five runs?" He slid past Tom to the living room and opened his arms wide. "Mom and Dad! Waddup!"

Both Jeffrey and Vivian stood up when their son-in-law entered the living room, but Phil and MB remained seated, only offering cool glares.

"Where's my bride?" Blake asked.

Sydney was in the entryway to the kitchen, a beer in one hand and a stunned look on her face.

"Now there's a good wife." He winked. "Ready with a cold drink as soon as I walk through the door."

"It's not for you." She walked by him and handed the bottle to her brother.

Blake put on his sweetest smile. "Can you at least fulfill your duties one more day and get me a beer?"

"You know where the refrigerator is." She pulled a dining-room chair over next to her brother and sat down.

"I'm not signing any papers tomorrow," he said with a smug look. "Our marriage ain't over till I say it's over."

Tom raised his hand. "I may only be in my first year of law school, but I believe you needed to file a response within thirty days. If you don't sign tomorrow, the judge will stick you with a pricey legal fee for the delay."

The smug look suddenly vanished, and Blake glanced at his in-laws, as if hoping for support. When he found none, he stormed to the kitchen, returned with a beer, and sat down in a huff.

All eyes were glued to the TV, watching Sam deliver a first-pitch strike to the Washington cleanup hitter.

Blake took a long drink and nodded up at the screen. "How much do you guys know about him?"

"I've heard that he's a very nice young man," Vivian said sweetly.

Blake was irritated and made no trouble to hide it. "Did you know that he's a big time womanizer? And that one of the babes he's been chasing is your daughter?"

His words were like a blow to Sydney's gut, and for a second, she only stared at him. She was about to respond when her mom stood up and pointed to the door.

"That's it, Blake. Time for you to leave."

He ignored her, his arrogant smirk returning, as if he now had the upper hand.

Vivian took a step closer. "I said it's time for you to leave."

"Not until you hear the truth." He glanced over at Sydney, then back at her mother. "The truth about Sydney whoring behind my back with Sam Cloud–"

Before he could finish, Vivian slapped him sharply across the face.

"Don't you ever talk that way about my daughter! You've bullied Sydney for the last time! Now get out!"

Her outburst was so surprising that the rest of the party jerked up from their seats. The only sound that broke the silence came from the TV:

The Royals' rookie star from southwest Colorado can't pitch much better as KC tries to even the series with the Nationals at one win each.

Then, very slowly, Sydney's dad and brother walked over and put a hand on each of Blake's shoulders.

"Let's go, Blakey boy," said Tom, who, along with their dad, pulled Sydney's soon-to-be ex-husband out of his chair and escorted him to the door.

"We'll see you at the courthouse at nine a.m. sharp." Jeffrey gave him a fatherly pat on the back. "Tommy and I will be with Sydney to make sure everything goes smoothly."

CHAPTER FIFTY-FIVE

Kansas City, Missouri

October 2013

The Royals' success brought joy to Kansas City, and the fans wanted to share that joy. The town had always loved baseball. Before the Royals, there were the A's; before the A's, there were the Monarchs; and before the Monarchs, there were the Blues. With heroes like Satchel Paige, Jackie Robinson, Buck O'Neil, George Brett and Willie Wilson, KC was baseball, barbecue, and the American Royal.

During the 2013 postseason, 80 percent of televisions in the metro area were watching baseball. Everyone was talking Royals. Every TV in Westport, the Power and Light District, and the Crossroads were tuned to the games. Hippie cashiers at Whole Foods were talking about Rex Blackwell diving into the stands for a foul ball, and priests in Catholic churches were praying a novena for every game the team played. The town was happy and proud; proud of a team that played the game right. The *esprit de corps* seemed to be contagious. People said please and thank you more, opened doors, and honked horns when they saw a blue Royals flag flapping in the wind outside a car window.

There were more smiles, kindness, and gentleness, and more giving to charity. It didn't matter if someone wasn't in the mood to be gracious to the person who cut them off in traffic. They did it anyway. After Sam's complete-game shutout in game two, the Royals and Nationals split the next two, and the price to be inside Kauffman Stadium for game five went up considerably.

"How you doing on tickets, kid?" Jack Celine, the director of team travel and clubhouse operations, asked.

Sam reached into his locker and showed him his phone. "Thirty-eight calls or texts, most congrats from friends and old teammates. I'm trying to get tickets for some college buddies."

"How many?"

"Naw, you have enough on your plate already."

"That's my job, Sam. Take care of the clubhouse, travel, and tickets. Your job is to pitch. What do you need?"

"Well, I have my usual six for Sydney Morgan—"

"I thought her last name was Harrison?"

"It was. She, um, got a divorce."

Jack was wise enough not to press further. "So six for Morgan and who else?"

"Three for Jose Lopez if it's possible. He was my college catcher and drove all night with a couple of our Mesa teammates to see tonight's game."

"Three?" Jack raised a brow in surprise. "That's it? With the way you've been dealin', I thought you might ask for twenty."

Sam laughed. "I wouldn't do that to you. Thanks."

"No problem. That's what the Royals are all about. I got your back."

"Hey, Sam!" Andy Phillips called out from across the clubhouse. "I need you in Skip's office."

He could tell by the tone of his pitching coach's voice that it was important, so he hurried to his manager's office. Inside were Charles, Wilson, and Walt Swanigan. Phillips closed the door behind them.

Sam gulped. "Don't tell me another Bob Dalley story broke?"

"No," Wilson said, "this is team related."

Charles leaned forward in his chair. "What are your thoughts about going tonight on three days' rest?"

"What's wrong with Mario?"

"Shoulder's barking. He can barely lift his arm."

"Then I can go," Sam said matter-of-factly.

"We could start Eduardo, but he hasn't pitched in ten days."

"No, I'm good."

"You sure, Sam? You threw a hundred sixteen pitches last time out, and you've never pitched on three days' rest before."

"I did in Nicaragua. Threw a hundred ten in a complete game on a Sunday, came back on a Thursday and threw a hundred thirty-seven in a five–one win." He winked at his pitching coach. "Ump squeezed me."

Phillips snorted back a laugh. "Damn, you're an arrogant cuss. This is game five of the World Series, y'know?"

Sam nodded toward the clubhouse. "Every guy out there is hurting in some way. Sore arms, legs, backs, whatever … but they keep on grinding. Who I'm fighting with has always meant as much to me as what I'm fighting for. I can do it."

No one said anything as they all seemed to take in Sam's words. Then his pitching coach clapped his hands. "Well, if you're going tonight, we better start prepping. Six hours till first pitch."

Sam looked at his communications director. "Could we wait a couple of hours before announcing that I'm starting tonight?"

"Sure—may I ask why?"

"My gut tells me that my old employer was planning to drop another bomb before I was supposed to start tomorrow."

Wilson held his hand up. "Hang on, Sam. What are you talking about?"

He shrugged. "Just a feeling—that's the way Dixon works. Attack enemies when they're most vulnerable. Allegations, conspiracy theories, no facts." He took a deep breath and stood up. "I think if we wait a few hours to announce the change, he won't have time to release anything before the game."

Walt nodded. "Is five o'clock okay?"

"That'll work." He opened the door to leave, then nodded at his pitching coach. "I'll be in your office in ten minutes to game plan."

Sam went back to his locker to get his scouting book and phone. There were another five messages. Four from 970 area codes, friends from Colorado, and one from 913. Sydney.

My divorce is final. Great support from family. Thank you, God.

He typed back: *I'm glad it's over.*

Twenty seconds later: *Thanks again for the tickets tonight. My family is excited. Any chance to see you after game before you fly to DC?*

Probably not. Mum's the word about this, but I'm starting tonight, so I'll likely have a press conference after game and scramble to make bus.

What? They're starting you on three days' rest? Are they crazy?

He grinned and typed back: *C'mon, you're a coach. Take one for the team.*

Her reply: *You're right. Sorry. You'll do great. We'll be cheering every pitch!* Thumbs-up emoji.

He shook his head. *Really? No heart emoji?*

Ten seconds later, he received five heart emoji.

I feel better now. Any words of inspiration?

Nothing from Sydney for a couple of minutes.

Sam had a meeting to get to so he texted: *Yo, Sticks, I've gotta game plan with my coach and catcher in two minutes . . .*

Thirty seconds later: *If you knew who walked beside you on the path that you have chosen, fear would be impossible.*

His smile widened. *That's from* A Course in Miracles.

She replied: *I know. I remember reading it in Jenny's journal but had to google to make sure I got it right.*

He typed back: *It's perfect. Thank you.*

As he got up to leave, his phone *pinged* one more time. *Early count outs, Sam. Keep those sinkers low.*

He laughed, tossed his phone in his locker, and headed to the coach's room.

*   *   *

Senator Richardson's Georgetown house was ten minutes from Dixon's office. He and King had been invited to watch game five of the Series with some of the top power brokers in Washington. There would be at least four senators with close ties to the mining industry or companies that sold heavy construction equipment overseas, and with super PACs all the rage in DC, dark money was pouring in.

It was getting close to nut-cutting time too. Afghanistan's Minister of Mines and Petroleum had met recently with representatives of the US, China, India, and Pakistan about extracting Afghanistan's coal, oil, timber, and minerals. A decision would be made soon on who would build the transportation routes to move those resources. Both Dixon and Senator Richardson were maneuvering to have their old company, Dixon Industries, be the one selected by the Afghan government.

As the limo driving Dixon and his lawyer turned left, King scanned his Twitter feed and groaned. "Check out this tweet from Major League Baseball, Drake."

Dixon read it and slumped back in his seat. "Carson's pitching tonight? Shit. Tomorrow's press conference won't have near the impact."

"Then call it off. I never thought it was a good idea to go public and trash him."

"No. This is fucking personal."

"That's your ego talking, Drake. Leave him alone and focus on nailing Hazrat."

Dixon's face flushed with anger, and he glanced at his reflection in the limo's window. He looked older than his forty-eight years. This entire Afghan situation had worn on him. His last trip to Kabul had been fruitless, and his attacks on Carson, through Bob Dalley's stories, didn't have the desired effect. Now images of Carson's icy glare from the last time he saw him in Afghanistan were haunting his sleep. He had to take him down.

To succeed in Drake's world, one had to be totally ruthless. There would always be some other corporation or power trying to stop him from claiming his prize. Right now, Carson was that power. He knew too much … and that scared Dixon. He believed that unless men feared you, you became a target.

"One p.m. tomorrow in the lobby of our DC office," he muttered. "Carson won't have enough time to prepare a rebuttal when baseball has their pregame meet the media."

*   *   *

It was a cool, but pleasant late October evening at Kauffman Stadium. Field-level seats twenty rows behind the Royals' dugout provided a perfect view to watch the game. Sydney had every necessary item, both rational and superstitious, with her: Royals cap, Royals scarf, blue sweatshirt, binoculars, scorebook, three pens, water bottle, tub of lightly salted popcorn—she didn't want buttery hands to smudge her scorebook—and the rabbit-foot bracelet her brother had given her on some past birthday.

Top of the fourth. Game tied at one. Sam knifed a two-seam fastball down and in on the Washington right-handed batter. Ground ball to short. Three outs. Sydney wrote down 6-3 in her scorebook and counted the number of groundouts. Ten of twelve. Wow. His sinker was certainly dipping and diving.

She felt a tap on the shoulder and turned to find Sam's boyhood friend standing in the aisle.

"Jose!" She jumped up and gave him a warm hug. "What a wonderful surprise."

"Thanks. Sammy came through with tickets for me and two college buddies. He said you'd be behind the home dugout. I found you with my binoculars and thought I'd come down to say hi."

"Well then, say hi to my family." They all stood up as Sydney continued. "Mom, Vivian; Dad, Jeff; brother, Tom; and friends Phil and Mary Beth . . . this is Sam's best friend and catcher in high school and college, Jose Lopez."

They each shook his hand, but Tom held his grip a little longer. "How long do you think we'll stay with Sam? His velocity's down from his last start."

"He's fine." Jose chuckled, then pointed to his head. "Sammy's strength is up here. He showed the Nats sliders and ninety-two to ninety-four heat last week. Smart hitters adjust. So tonight, eighty-eight to ninety, late-life sinkers, cutters, curves, changeups, and an occasional four-seam up and in to keep 'em off balance."

Jose showed them the palms of his hands. The base of his left thumb was fatter than his right. "That's from ten years trying to catch Sam's sinker. His ball moved so late that I'd have to ice my left thumb after every start. Believe me, it's tougher to hit late-life eighty-eight than straight ninety-seven."

An usher came down the aisle and asked them to sit down because the bottom of the fourth was about to begin. Jose squatted next to Sydney and whispered, "Do you have a second? There's something I need to tell you."

*   *   *

They walked along the concourse, eyes glued to the field but conversation elsewhere.

"Your phone call to Teresa got the ball rolling," Jose said. "Colonel Tomlinson called me later that day to do some research for him."

Sydney slowly nodded. "Teresa told me how Sam …"

"Saved her life," Jose finished her sentence in a low voice that hinted at suppressed rage. "Billy Cutthredge and Rob Marcus were flat evil. But until the colonel told me they worked for DiamondBar and that Dixon had sent them to watch Sam, I didn't know the extent of it."

"What did you find out?"

"Teresa remembered them coming into Mercy Medical looking for a drug dealer named Tommy Sherman. I'm with the Southern Ute Tribal Police, so it wasn't hard to track him down."

"Is he still dealing?"

"No. He stopped about the same time Cutthredge and Marcus went missing. He now works part-time for a roofing company in Durango. As soon as I said the names Cutthredge and Marcus, he got scared … told me everything. How they beat him after he swindled Cutthredge in a deal. He said that Marcus was with a woman named Valerie Quintana the day she died from a drug overdose. I checked with the Durango police. Valerie died the same day Sam's mom was killed in a car accident. When I shared the story with Teresa, she said that Susan had befriended Valerie—tried to get her help."

"Do you think Valerie reached out to Susan that day?"

"I know she did. At the time, the police thought it was an accident. Someone simply driving too fast on a dirt road. They didn't see the tracks of Cutthredge's truck that Sam found. They didn't listen to any messages on Susan's phone. But Grandpa Douglas never canceled her service plan and has been using her phone ever since the accident. He never listened to her old messages either. I did. Valerie called Susan to say she needed help to get away from a man named Rob Marcus. I haven't told Sam what I discovered."

Sydney's chest felt tight, and she put her hand on Jose's arm to catch her breath. She looked up at the television monitor. Sam was back on the mound, his dark eyes fixed on his target. What else had he been through, had he seen, had he experienced that he hadn't shared? Yet, through it all, somehow, some way, for three hours on the days he took the mound, with millions watching, he was able to push it all aside and focus on one thing. Doing his job. Executing the next pitch. Helping his team win. He was there again. On three days' rest. Whatever it took.

When the root is deep, there is no reason to fear the wind. God, she loved him.

"There's one more thing," Jose said, jolting Sydney back to the present. "I told Tomlinson what I uncovered about Cutthredge and Marcus, and he found out who was helping to move the heroin from Afghanistan to the port in Southern Pakistan."

"Let me guess—the DiamondBar coworker in the Bob Dalley story, Frank Weber."

Jose nodded.

*　　*　　*

"You got another inning in you?" Phillips asked Sam when he came off the mound after the top of the fifth.

Sam held his gaze, mildly irritated. "You've asked me that the last three innings, Andy. I'm fine."

"Jordan got a hold of that sinker you left up."

"It was three inches off the plate. Give him credit. He's a darn good hitter who made an adjustment and stayed with the pitch. I won't make that mistake again."

Phillips suppressed a smile. He loved getting under Sam's skin. It seemed to tighten the screw to his rookie right-hander's hyperfocus. By now, Ramirez had taken off his catching gear and joined the conversation.

"All right." Phillips clapped. "How do you want to work the sixth?"

Sam glanced up at the flags in right field. The wind had shifted. It was now blowing in hard from left and out to right. The temperature had also dropped ten degrees from the start of the game.

"Four-seamers, up and in, changeups low and away to Alfaro. Sliders to Markowitz. He couldn't hit my slider if I told him it was coming. Everything in to Castillo. I dare him to hit it out to left." He nodded to the flags. "Not tonight, dude."

The sound of bat squarely meeting baseball and fans screaming made them pause. They stepped up to the rail and watched Rex Blackwell's towering shot arc high into the night sky. The wind caught it, carrying it fifteen rows beyond the right-field bullpen for a 2–1 Royals lead. As Blackwell rounded the bases, Sam looked back at his pitching coach and catcher and shook his head. "Fastball thigh-high to a left-handed pull hitter. That's like reaching into a snake pit, hoping it won't bite. Big mistake."

*　　*　　*

"When was the last time you saw Sam?" Jose asked as they continued their stroll around Kauffman.

"The final weekend of the regular season. The day he had the meltdown after the Dalley story broke."

"That was a month ago, Syd. I thought you guys were good friends?"

"We are. We text—occasionally—but I needed to finish my divorce. And I didn't think Sam needed another distraction."

Jose gave her a sidelong glance. "You're not a distraction."

"I don't know. He was pretty mad at me for calling Teresa and Colonel Tomlinson."

"Yeah, he was." Jose laughed. "Called me later that day madder than a barefoot centipede on a hot rock."

Her shoulders slumped forward.

"Don't worry about it, Syd. He used to do the same thing with me. Blow up at me when he was angry with himself." He gave her a playful nudge. "He'll get over it. He likes you."

She turned away. She didn't want Jose to see the disappointment on her face. He circled around and stopped directly in front of her.

"What's going on, Syd?"

She shrugged. "He *likes* me."

"Isn't that what you want?"

"I don't know. Yes, I do. No, I don't. Oh God"—she curled her fingernails into her palms and forced herself to look at Jose. "Please don't tell him this, but I'm head-over-heels, fastball-to-the-heart, completely, totally crazy in love with him."

He laughed out loud. "What's wrong with that?"

"Because—because sometimes the person you fall for isn't ready to catch you."

"You don't think he cares for you?"

"Yes, he cares, but I know that Sam eventually will want a family and … I can't have children."

Jose blinked, entirely taken aback.

"I didn't think you knew." Sydney hung her head. "Most guys prefer a new car over a used one that doesn't work."

"Don't say that," he said, recovering himself slightly. "Both of you have been through a lot. You've been through a lousy marriage, and he's lost just about everyone he's ever loved."

The crowd roared, so they turned to see what had happened. The Royals had scored two more runs on a Cimoli home run to take a 4–1 lead. While Kauffman was a sea of delirious joy, Sydney stared off into space. Her declaration of loving Sam was like a scab being ripped off an old wound. All her old doubts, fears, and pain were now exposed to the world. She thought that if she could control her heart, she might be able to stop loving him, but she knew her feelings were like the baseball Cimoli had just struck—long gone.

CHAPTER FIFTY-SIX

Washington, DC

October 2013

Dixon dabbed the high-priced concealer to the dark circles under his eyes and checked his image in the mirror. He still looked tired. It had taken him five hours to fall asleep because he was so angry about his Nationals losing to the Royals and Cloud-Carson 5–2. The kid was depressingly good; 5–0 in postseason with a 0.91 ERA. 7–1 strikeout-to-walk ratio. Thinking about those numbers wanted to make him punch the mirror.

Dixon couldn't stand anything he couldn't control, and he couldn't control Carson. He dabbed another layer of concealer under his eyes and then picked up the face powder. It was time to look good for the cameras.

The lobby of Dixon's Washington, DC, DiamondBar office was packed for his one o'clock press conference. His marketing people had done a great job of letting the media know that the subject would be about his former employee, now the leading candidate for World Series MVP. And, with the Fall Classic shifting to Washington, Dixon knew attendance would be high.

"Thank you very much for being here today," he said as he pulled the microphone on the podium closer. "I know many of you have been reaching out to me in recent weeks for a comment about Sam Carson's time working for me as a tracker for my DiamondBar Security team in Afghanistan." He paused and surveyed the room, as if letting every reporter present know how important they were to him.

"First of all, let me say how proud I am of the way Sam has pitched this postseason. Absolutely sensational. He's come a long way from the boy who signed on with DiamondBar after his mother died in a car accident in 2008." Dixon clasped his hands in prayer at his chest. "Very sad … I've known his family for years. Sam's father, Daniel, served for me from 2005 until 2007, when tragically, the helicopter he was in was shot down over the Langham Province. Daniel was a great man. I attended his funeral and insisted that a plaque honoring his memory be displayed in our Heroes Room at our DiamondBar headquarters in Southern Virginia.

"I was also at Sam's sister's funeral when she passed from a kidney disease in 2008. I took care of all expenses for her Celebration of Life at the Durango Holiday Inn and made a generous donation to both the Kidney Foundation and the Ute Cultural Center."

He looked down for a long moment, giving the impression that he might dissolve into tears if he continued.

"After his mother passed, I knew that Sam was very depressed. I wanted to help him any way I could. I offered him a job with DiamondBar at double the starting salary of any of my previous employees. Unfortunately, I did not realize the depths of Sam's depression. My medical staff was worried that he had suicidal tendencies during training. We tried to get him help, but unfortunately, he refused."

Another long pause from Dixon as he looked down at the podium and then back up. "That's why I'm so proud of the young man I watched on the mound last night. He's come a long way."

"Mr. Dixon! Mr. Dixon!" Several reporters raised their hands to ask a question. Dixon pointed to the pretty blonde from ESPN.

"Is the story about Carson cutting off a coworker's ear in a fight true?"

Dixon sighed. "I don't know. But, much like baseball, not everyone gets along inside a clubhouse. Next question?"

"What about the Army officers who said Carson saved their troops?"

"Sam is a talented tracker, particularly when he follows orders. But those assignments you're referring to are classified, so why don't we move on."

"Was he involved with drugs and prostitutes?"

"Only rumors, but, when you hear something once, twice, three times, you have to do an internal investigation. Our findings are private."

"What about consorting with the Taliban?"

"Once again, rumors. There were times he went absent without leave, and some troubling stories floated around. There was also his nervous breakdown. Near the end of his contract, we just felt that it was in the best interests of both Sam and DiamondBar that we go our separate ways."

Dixon scanned the room, giving each and every reporter his most sympathetic and understanding look. "There's no ill will on my end. I love Sam like a son and pray that he's finally over the demons that haunted him in Afghanistan. Thank you very much. Now, if you'll excuse me, I have to get back to the important matters of protecting our great country. God bless America."

He left, ignoring the barrage of questions that followed him out the door as he hurried down the hall, to the elevator waiting to take him up to his private suite.

*   *   *

Two hours later, the Cloud-Carson press conference at Nationals Park went much differently.

"I didn't watch it … I can't comment about something I didn't see … Yes, he did attend my father's and sister's funerals, but he wasn't invited … I have never consorted with the Taliban, nor have I ever been involved with drugs or prostitutes … Any questions about yesterday's win? I mean, we are getting ready to play game six of the World Series."

Sam left the media bash, called Colonel Tomlinson, and somehow found a quiet spot for a meditation. Clearing his mind wasn't easy.

*   *   *

Game six was a classic. Fifteen innings, thirty-seven hits, twenty-five runs, eighteen pitchers used. The only two Royals pitchers who did not take the mound that night were Sam and game-seven starter, Bo Chapman. Washington won 13–12, tying the series at three wins each.

CHAPTER FIFTY-SEVEN

Washington, DC

October 2013

"Welcome to Nationals Park in Washington, DC, for game seven of the one hundred and ninth World Series," announced the play-by-play broadcaster.

Sydney raised her lemonade over her head. "Here's to our Royals winning it all!"

She touched her glass to her mom's and dad's and sat down on the sofa. It was just the three of them tonight. Her brother was back in Chicago, studying for the bar, and Phil and Mary Beth couldn't find a babysitter. Sydney didn't want to watch the game with a big group of people anyway, where someone would shout their managerial advice, while others might argue about a nacho recipe or the best beers in KC. Not tonight. She wanted to be able to focus on every single pitch of this decisive game.

"Have you talked to him?" her dad asked.

"No." She opened her scorebook and made sure she had the lineups correct. "I texted him *good luck*. He texted back *thanks*.

"Will we ever get to meet him?" her mom asked.

"You guys!" She looked crossly at her parents and pointed to the TV. "Game time. C'mon, we need to lock in."

Jeffrey pursed his lips to keep from laughing. He loved this about his daughter. Competitive, disciplined, supreme concentration for every event she played in or coached. Sports had always been their connection.

He would honor her wish tonight. Be quiet, watch the game, and only open his mouth if the Royals did something good.

Just before the first pitch of the game, Sydney's phone rang.

"*Arrrgghh,*" she growled. "Who the heck would call right now? Geez Louise!" She looked at her phone, and her eyes went wide. It was Colonel Tomlinson. "I—I have to take this." She tossed the scorebook to her absolutely stunned father and ran up the stairs to her room.

"This is Sydney Morgan," she answered breathlessly. "How may I be of service, Colonel Tomlinson?"

She heard him chuckle. "I'm not calling to ask you to captain the Eighty-Second Airborne in storming Normandy Beach, Sydney. I just wanted to update you on some things."

"Yes, sir. I'm listening."

"Well, I'm sorry to bother you during the game. I have it on too. One out, nobody on, Terry Ayers up."

"Thank you, sir."

"Please call me Bart. Did you see the press conferences with Dixon and Sam?"

"No, sir. I was teaching. I did see the highlights on the news though."

"Dixon's scared. He's trying to lure the media back after they've gone soft on his enemy. I thought Sam handled his conference perfectly because he didn't attack Dixon or defend himself. He just stayed with the facts. Believe me, if Sam were involved with drugs or prostitutes in Afghanistan, my Special Forces team would have known about it. And I was the one who witnessed firsthand his breakdown. Not one of his DiamondBar cronies even came to visit him while he was recovering at the Bagram hospital."

The colonel paused, but Sydney knew he wasn't finished. "I'm calling to let you know that we're at a critical point in our investigation, and I want you to be prepared if Dixon goes after you."

"Me? Why would he go after me?"

"Because he's scared. And like any narcissist when accused of wrongdoing, they'll burn down everything around them in their battle to survive."

She gulped. "Do you think that he'll reveal the pictures of me with Sam that I told you about?"

"I wouldn't put it past him. I'll do my best to keep that from happening, but you might want to prepare a statement for the press just in case Dixon lashes out."

"Okay, sir … thank you for warning me."

"This all should be over soon, Sydney. Please don't share our conversation with anyone. I just felt it important to keep you in the loop—hey, Ayers just doubled. The Royals have a rally. Now, go enjoy the game."

"Thank you, sir—I mean Colonel Bart."

After hanging up, Sydney sat on the edge of her bed, staring at the phone, Colonel Tomlinson's revelation still ringing in her ears.

*   *   *

Dixon picked up a celery stick, swept it through the ranch dip, and took a bite. After what he considered a successful press conference, he was feeling pretty good. It didn't matter that Carson's response wasn't what he had hoped for. Dixon was able to control the media, and that's what was important. He made sure that everyone stayed on topic, focused on Sam's dark side, with no questions about what DiamondBar was doing in Afghanistan.

"Get your butt out here, Drake!" Senator Richardson called out from the front row of Dixon's luxury suite at Nationals Park. "Bases loaded, one out, and our boy Kingman's about to bust this game wide open."

Dixon filled his plate with munchies and joined his allies. Richardson and King were flying solo tonight, their families at some posh party in Georgetown. The senator's chief of staff, Mark Sommers, had brought his entire family, including three obnoxious brats who were eating everything in sight. Also stopping by every half-inning was a different mining lobbyist or politician ingratiating him or herself with Drake in hopes of receiving a sizable campaign donation.

The Royals led 3–2 in the fifth, with starter Chapman wiggling out of jam after jam through his first four innings. He would need a miracle to get out of this mess.

"Big hit, right here!" Richardson yelled. "Big hit!"

The Nats' first baseman lined a one-hop smash between short and third. Hernandez backhanded the ball, leaped in the air, and fired a strike to Ayers for the force, but they had no chance to double up the runner at first. Tie game.

"Damn!" Dixon slapped the railing so sharply that Sommers' six-year-old daughter in the row behind them buried her head in her dad's chest.

Alfaro flied out to end the inning. Richardson shook his head in disgust and then headed inside to use the bathroom.

Dixon glanced over his shoulder and then leaned close to his lawyer. "When are we nailing Hazrat?"

"Tonight," King whispered. "Zubair found a warlord from the Kunar Province who agreed to our price. His men detonated a bomb on the PRT road through Hazrat's land this morning. The Minister of Mines, Nadeem Khattak, blamed the strike on Hazrat, and our military has approved of a drone hit on his village at midnight."

"How many casualties?"

"Just Hazrat's family. Medium Hellfire missile with a precise drop on his home."

"Any chance it will be tied back to me?"

"None. DiamondBar wasn't providing the security for the PRT crew, and nobody in America cares about Afghans getting killed anyway. Hell, there have been over eight thousand drone strikes since January of 2004, killing over five hundred civilians, many of them women and children. Only a handful of those stories got a passing mention in American media. Some US general will call it a 'tragic mistake,' and it will be old news within a week."

"Good." Dixon smiled wickedly. "It will be so much easier for our construction team to do their job with Hazrat out of the way."

*   *   *

"Bo's done," said Andy Phillips to his manager. "A hundred and three pitches in five innings."

"I was hoping to save Sam until the eighth." Charles looked down at his lineup card. "Andrews and Kahal each threw over sixty pitches last night, Mario's arm is a no-go, and Ramsey and Guerrero are slumping."

"Asking Sam to go four might be pushing it, Skip."

"I know." Charles looked up at the scoreboard. 3–3. Game seven of the World Series.

"Want me to get him ready for the sixth?" Phillips asked.

The Royals' manager nodded.

*   *   *

"Is Charles out of his mind?" Sydney jerked up from the sofa when the game came back from commercial break with a shot of Sam on the mound to start the bottom of the sixth. "He threw ninety-five pitches on Monday! Ninety-five! He's only had two days' rest. They're going to kill him."

"I thought you said you didn't like it when fans criticized the manager," Jeffrey said.

Sydney gave her father a look that could have frozen steam. She sat down in a huff and turned up the TV volume.

"I don't know how much more the Royals can ask from this twenty-six-year-old rookie, who only eight months ago was pitching in the jungles of Nicaragua."

"Exactly!" she snapped. "His arm's gonna fall off."

"He does have four months' rest after tonight," Jeffrey teased her. "That should be enough time to recover for spring training.

"Dad!" She turned to her mom. "How have you lived with this—this knucklehead for twenty-six years?"

"Twenty-seven." Vivian grinned. "Twenty-seven stupidly glorious years."

Sam only needed thirteen pitches to shutout Washington in the sixth.

*　　*　　*

Sam's head was down, and he was absorbed in his scouting book. His pitching coach and catcher knew it was best to stay quiet when he studied his book. It wasn't as if Sam wouldn't take advice, but their rookie phenom had a definite plan on how he wanted to get hitters out. And he was rarely wrong.

Finally, he raised his head and said, "Markowitz loves the heat. He's only seen my sinker, slider, and change. I want to start him off with a slow get-me-over curve for strike one. That'll put him on the defensive. Then I'll bust him in with cutters. Castillo opened up his stance two inches on Bo—probably because he throws harder than me. I still think we should go sliders away and sinkers down and in."

"What about Jenkins?"

"Good low-ball hitter for a right-hander, but slider bat speed. My four-seam's got good arm-side run tonight. I'll get him to pop up or strike out."

The seventh and eighth went exactly as planned, and the game was still tied at three going to the ninth.

*　　*　　*

Sydney sat with her head in her hands, half listening to the commercial singing about how tough their trucks were.

She raised up and glanced at her dad, who was smiling back at her.

"I've never been this nervous before any game I've played in or coached." She shook her head. "This is absolute torture."

He rubbed his hands together. "Three, three. Bottom of the ninth. Here we go."

She checked her scorebook. "Nine up, nine down, three strikeouts, forty-two pitches. Erasmo Rodriguez coming up. Sprays the ball around. Tough matchup."

Her mother turned a page in the *Art of Eating* magazine she was reading. "Does Sam like Italian food? You should invite him over for my lasagna and your homemade Caesar salad."

Sydney rolled her eyes. "Not now, Mom. Not now."

*   *   *

The tension rose inside Nationals Park. Scoreboard music cranked high, fans screamed at the top of their lungs, and the inebriated ones swore at the man on the mound. Sam was oblivious to it all. The same quiet focus he had while tracking in the woods also empowered him on the mound. Instead of his awareness opening to allow all of the wild's elements to help him track, his center of attention narrowed to where all of his concentration was consumed into one solitary objective. The middle of his catcher's glove. His breathing slowed, his heart rate dropped, and every cell in his body came together as he readied to throw his first pitch of the ninth.

Erasmo Rodriquez. Right-handed, speedy, spray hitter. Liked the ball up. First pitch, fastball, low outside corner, strike one. Second pitch, curve, low, but unable to check swing, strike two. Third pitch, fastball, up and in, taken for a ball, now a 1-2 count.

He bit on the curve that wasn't close to the zone, Sam thought. *Let's go back there.*

Fourth pitch was in the exact same spot as the second, but Rodriquez dove over the plate and somehow got the sweet part of the bat on the ball, hitting it sharply past a diving Cimoli at first and down the right-field line.

*   *   *

"Noooo!" shrieked all three Morgans as they watched the Nationals runner cut first sharply and hustle to second for a leadoff double.

Sydney pressed her palms to her forehead and looked at her father. "They have to walk Kingman to set up the double play."

"And face cleanup hitter, Alfaro? I don't know. He's had a good series."

"Not against Sam."

*   *   *

The Royals intentionally walked Kingman, and Alfaro swung at the first pitch he saw, grounding a slow roller past the mound. Second baseman Ayers' only play was first. The runners advanced. The winning run was now ninety feet away with one out.

Charles called time and jogged out to the mound. "What do you think about walking Markowitz to set up the double play?"

"Castillo will be tough to double with his speed," Sam said, "and he's a good bunter. He might squeeze."

"You want Markowitz?"

Sam nodded. "I won't throw him a strike. If I walk him, no big deal, but if I get him to chase, I'll walk Castillo and pitch to Jenkins. I've struck him out four times already."

Charles patted him on the back. "Go get 'em, kid."

Sam struck out Markowitz on four pitches and walked Castillo. Bases loaded, two outs. 3–3, bottom of the ninth, game seven of the World Series. Rookie Sam Cloud-Carson against ten-year veteran Freddie Jenkins.

First pitch, slider, check swing, strike one. Next, sinker low for a ball. Third pitch, slider, fouled off for a 1-2 count. The crowd was on their feet, pleading for a hit. Every home in Kansas City was praying for an out in anyway possible.

Sam inhaled a deep, calming breath, bent low at the waist, and stared in to get the sign from his catcher. Ramirez dropped his pinky finger next to the inside of his right thigh. Sinker, outside corner. Sam nodded, straightened up, and glanced at the runner at third. He placed his right foot off center of the rubber to get a better angle on the hitter and came set. A deep inhale and exhale was followed by a textbook delivery.

Every part worked perfectly: the legs, the balance, the hips, the trunk, the separation of hand from glove to form a perfect *L* that hid the ball from the hitter. His front foot landed in a straight line toward his target as his upper body exploded toward home plate. The baseball spun off his long fingers with an extra revolution, his wrist snapped down, and the ball zipped out of his hand, spinning down and away from the right-handed hitter.

Jenkins tried to check his swing, but he'd already gone too far, the bat catching the underside of the ball and popping it only twenty feet down the first-base line. Sam broke for it and dove, snow-coning the ball at the very end of his glove, but as he slammed to the ground, the ball rolled free. He snatched it with his right hand and back-hand flipped it to Ramirez for the force just as Rodriquez's foot touched home.

The umpire swept his hands out. "Safe!"

Ramirez jerked around in rage and let loose a stream of obscenities at the ump as the Nationals poured from their dugout and dog-piled Rodriquez. Every Royal, save one, charged the ump, who raised his arms to let them know they would review the play.

Sam lay on his back, staring up at the night sky, both joy and fury swirling around him.

He knew the runner was safe. He'd seen Rodriquez's right toe touch the plate before the ball hit the back of Ramirez's glove.

*   *   *

All three Morgans stood in front of the TV in disbelief. The discussion between the umpires on the field and the video umps in New York seemed to take forever. Finally, the crew chief took off his headset, spread his arms wide for the safe sign, and Nationals Park went crazy.

*   *   *

"Yes! Yes! Yes!" Dixon roared from his luxury suite and high-fived everyone near him: Barry King, Senator Richardson, a freshman congressman from Texas, a mining lobbyist from Wyoming. Even Mark Sommers's kid, who he had scared earlier, gave him high fives.

"What a perfect fucking day!" he screamed. "Winning the Series and beating that piece of shit, Carson!"

Sommers' wife glared at Dixon as she helped her children on with their coats. She motioned for her husband to join them, and together they left the suite.

Twenty minutes later, Dixon, King, and Richardson were in their stretch limo, heading home. Drake leaned back in his seat, a Cheshire grin on his face. Everything was falling into place: Carson had been conquered, an Afghan mountain rich in natural resources would soon be his, and Hazrat would be dead. And he'd done it all without Senator Richardson discovering that he'd put a bounty on Hazrat's head. The only thing that he was waiting on now was a call from Nadeem Khattak saying that their mission had been accomplished.

"We're going to make billions off this deal." Richardson beamed. "Our old company will provide the equipment to carve that mountain, and we'll take fifty percent of everything the extraction team gets—all with money provided by American taxpayers."

Dixon pulled out his phone and checked for messages. Nothing.

"It's about nine thirty in the morning in Kabul. What do you say I give Nadeem a call?"

Richardson nodded.

As Dixon began to type in Khattak's number, he heard sirens in the distance, fast approaching. Their limo lurched to a stop, and Dixon looked outside. They were surrounded by dark vehicles flashing blue-and-red lights. Ten seconds later, there was a knock on the window.

Dixon opened the door. "What's this about?"

A man in a dark trench coat ignored him and stepped inside. He was followed by a man Dixon recognized, but he couldn't remember from when or where.

"Hello, Drake," the second man said. "I'm Colonel Bart Tomlinson. We met at Bagram Air Base a few years ago."

"Yes, uh, of course." Dixon stuttered. "I—I authorized the use of my security detail to help your Special Forces—"

"Shut up," Tomlinson cut him off and then nodded at the man next to him. "This is Jason Odom, executive assistant director of the FBI's national security branch. Your private military company in Afghanistan has been under investigation the last year."

"We've done nothing wrong," said Richardson. "Our investment is all above board."

"That's not what your chief of staff said." The FBI agent paused as if to read the senator, who shifted in his seat uncomfortably. "Mark Sommers has been part of our investigation since January. He downloaded information from your laptop about illegal kickbacks, bid-rigging, and violating the War Profiteering Prevention Act." Odom opened the door and motioned for the senator to leave. "There are a couple agents outside who have a few more questions for you."

When Richardson left, Odom closed the door and turned to Dixon and King. "Have you gentlemen heard of Scott Thornton, Nadeem Khattak, Almeida Zubair, and Abdul Hazrat?"

Dixon gulped but remained quiet.

"It took us a while, but we found Mr. Thornton working for your company in Sierra Leone. He admitted that it was Mr. Cloud-Carson who was responsible for capturing a Taliban warlord, not himself and Frank Weber. He said that you changed the facts to get good press for DiamondBar and to make it look as if Sam went AWOL."

Dixon said nothing.

"Afghan's Minister of Commerce and Industry, Mr. Khattak, told us you offered him bribes for mining licenses, and the former Interior Department hack you kept in your employ, Mr. Zubair, said that you paid a warlord from the Kunar Province to detonate a bomb on the PRT road through Mr. Hazrat's land. By the way, our military was never going to order a drone strike on Hazrat's village. That was just part of the sting."

"You have no proof I'm behind any of this!" Dixon hissed.

"Actually, we do." Tomlinson gave a wry smile. "Courtesy of Ethan Conway ... You know Ethan, Drake. The man you had videotape Mr. Cloud-Carson when he killed two of your employees on Pargin Mountain back in 2008. The same employees you discovered were smuggling heroin in from Afghanistan, the same men who kidnapped a young lady Mr. Cloud-Carson saved from being raped. Then you blackmailed Sam into working for your company by threatening to have *him* thrown in prison for murder."

Dixon's shoulders slumped forward.

"With help from a detective from the Ute Tribal Police, we were able to tie a few loose ends together and give Mr. Conway a call. Unfortunately for you, he had a copy of the tape, which is now in our possession." Tomlinson clapped his hands. "Now, here's how we're going to handle this. There's no reason to get Mr. Cloud-Carson involved in a crime from five years ago. That would only hurt his reputation. But both you and Mr. King will be tried for your crimes in Afghanistan. You'll be forced to sell DiamondBar and probably have to do some jail time."

Tomlinson paused and looked directly at Dixon. "I know your type, Drake. I've dealt with egomaniacs like you my entire professional life. You're no different than a terrorist: suspicious at best, vicious at worst, in your thirst for power, and when backed into a corner, you'll burn down everything and everyone around you in your madness to survive. If you even think about revealing what happened that day on Pargin Mountain, or try to smear the reputation of any of Mr. Cloud-Carson's friends, I'll make sure you spend the rest of your life in prison."

Tomlinson opened the door, where two more FBI agents were waiting. As Dixon and King were being handcuffed, the Special Forces colonel waited again for Dixon's eyes to come back to his.

"There's one more thing you should know, Drake. The President of Afghanistan, the Minister of Mines and Petroleum, and the Afghan Environmental Protection Agency will make an announcement tomorrow. The Nuristan National Forest will be extended another one hundred square kilometers in order to protect Abdul Hazrat's village and mountain. Apparently, the Afghan government, as parochial, chaotic, and corrupt as it is, would still prefer to rule itself rather than sell their land to some foreign two-faced con artist like you."

CHAPTER FIFTY-EIGHT

Kansas City, Missouri

November 1, 2013

As the Royals' charter began its slow descent to Kansas City International Airport, Sam looked out the window at the dark flatland, glistening patches of water, and the soft glow on the horizon of his adopted city. It was almost four in the morning, and he figured by the time he got his bag and drove home it would be well after five.

He was exhausted. Both physically and emotionally. He'd watched video of his final, fateful pitch at least fifteen times. It was a good throw: a sinker, three inches off the plate and down … but somehow Jenkins had made contact and hit a soft pop between home and first.

Perhaps his biggest mistake was trying to make a play on the ball. Had he let it go, the spin likely would have taken the ball into foul territory. But competitor that he was, he was sure he could catch it. Almost. That fatal word. Almost.

His teammates had been terrific, consoling him in the clubhouse and on the plane. It had been quiet for much of the flight, but as they got closer to KC, veterans Cimoli, Ramirez, Blackwell, and Hawkins had started firing guys up, talking about next year, being together again, and making another run at the championship.

Cimoli pointed at Sam and let loose a wolf howl. *"Ah-wooooo!"*

The rest of the plane joined in. *"Ah-wooooo!"*

What a team, he thought. *What a great, great team.*

As the plane touched down, a symphony of *pings* erupted from cell phones throughout the cabin. Phones flashed messages and texts of congratulations about how far the team had come, from ten games back and last place in May to almost winning the World Series. Almost.

Sam scrolled down his phone. Texts and voicemails from Jose and Teresa; high school and college coaches and teammates; Whiplash, Hunoon, and Carlita, leading the Little League Dukes in the Kansas City song, twenty-five tiny voices shrieking, *"They got some crazy lil' women there and I'm gonna get me one."*

It made him smile. He scrolled down further. One from Sydney.

Tough loss. I know you wanted more, but you made all of Kansas City proud. You guys competed every second on that field, and that's all anyone can ask. I'm proud of you too. Very proud. You're a good man.

*   *   *

Sam squinted through the fog as he turned off the highway and headed home. The morning was chilly, still a couple of hours before sunrise, and he couldn't wait to lay his weary body down in bed. As he turned onto the Tomlinson property, a slight smile began to crease his face. He was happy. Content. At peace.

But why? He'd just lost the biggest game any baseball player could lose, game seven of the World Series. And he was smiling.

His life was still a mess of unanswered questions: Would Dixon drop another bomb? Was Hazrat's family safe? Would Major League Baseball continue its investigation into his background? And where was he with Sydney? He had no idea. Yet, in this instant, he was fine with it all. He was completely, totally, at peace.

Barney greeted him when he drove down the lane to his cottage, his tail wagging joyfully as Sam parked the car, lifted his bag out of the back, and followed the little dog inside. He slipped out of his clothes, washed his face, brushed his teeth, and sat down on the edge of his bed. Jenny's journal was on the nightstand, open to whatever he'd last read. He glanced down, and his smile beamed even brighter.

Are you ready for the Bear Dance, Sam?

He chuckled lightly and read on. *We celebrate the Bear Dance every year, not to celebrate the bear, but to celebrate rebirth … the rebirth of our soul, the awakening of our spirit to all that is good in the world.*

It was true, Sam thought. *I am on the right path. I have found the Great Spirit within me. I am an expression of His love. I was never without it. I may have forgotten it for a while, but it was always there, waiting patiently for me to remember.*

He had finally surrendered, let go of his fears, brought his darkness to the light, and burned through the pain of his past. That past, as painful as it had been, had created the man he was today. He was good. He had forgiven himself, and he had forgiven those who had hurt him. It was time to move on.

"Thank you, Jenny," he whispered, then turned off his phone, collapsed in bed, and fell asleep within seconds.

*　　*　　*

The noon sun peeking through the curtains hours later woke him. Barney was next to him and rolled over, demanding his belly be scratched. Sam obliged, then got up, put the coffee on, let Barney out, and powered on his phone. Within thirty seconds, it started beeping: messages and texts from his GM and manager, pitching coach, several players and friends, and the Royals' VP of Communications. There was one from Colonel Tomlinson, and others from TV and radio stations.

He figured he'd better listen to the message from Swanigan first.

"Hello, Sam, call me ASAP. There was a big press conference this morning in Washington, DC. We need to talk."

Uh oh, Sam thought. *This doesn't sound good. I hope it isn't another Bob Dalley story.*

He called Swanigan, who picked up on the first ring.

"Jiminy Christmas, Sam! Where the heck have you been? We've been trying to reach you the last two hours!"

"Sorry, Walt, I was tired—turned my phone off. What's going on?"

"There was a press conference this morning in DC. The Secretary of Defense, Bill Clifford; the assistant director of the FBI, Jason Odom; and a Special Forces colonel, Bart Tomlinson; talked about a year-long investigation into private military companies. They arrested your old boss and his lawyer after last night's game."

Sam jerked up in his chair. "What?"

"Yeah. Apparently, Dixon was involved in some pretty nefarious stuff in Afghanistan. The colonel made you out to be some kind of superhero. Did you really warn two Taliban soldiers guarding a weapons cache that a missile was minutes away from blowing them up?"

"That's, uh, classified, Walt."

"Unclassified now. Tomlinson said that you also saved an Afghan girl from being raped by a Taliban leader. Then he told a wild story of how you single-handedly captured an enemy compound, rescued your DiamondBar teammates and two Afghan children being held for ransom, then risked your life returning the kids to a village leader in the Hindu Kush."

Sam snorted in amusement. "Colonel has a big imagination."

"Well, Super Sammy, the media wants your side of the story. How soon can you be here?"

"You mean, like, today?"

"Of course. Everybody's on hold. Our owner, the GM, the entire organization, and the media are all waiting to hear from you."

Sam hesitated as he glanced at his fridge. "Okay. Can I eat first?"

Swanigan laughed out loud. "Sure, just get your butt to my office by two, so I can show you the DC presser you missed. You'll meet the media at three."

*　　*　　*

The Crown Club was packed when Sam walked in, flanked by the Royals' owner, Jonathan Ewing, and the general manager, David Wilson. Sam flushed red when the crowd rose up from their chairs and gave him a standing ovation. His teammates in the back, led by Kevin Cimoli, let loose wolf howls, and Sam bit down hard on the side of his mouth to keep from laughing. He raised both hands to calm the crowd, then he sat down and pulled the microphone close.

"I've seen the video about twenty times and still think I should have caught the ball."

The room broke up in laughter, giving Sam time to calm his nerves.

"I'd first like to thank Mr. Swanigan, Mr. Ewing, and Mr. Wilson for supporting me this year," he said, then nodded to the man next to his owner and GM. "A special thanks to Roberto Francisco, the scout who followed me from high school to college and then to Nicaragua. Thank you for believing in me and giving me a chance to play for a great organization. I love my teammates, and I love Kansas City." He looked down at the microphone and then back up. "Now, to get to the point of why we're here ... I'm very sorry, but I can't talk about my time in Afghanistan."

There were a few murmurs from members of the media until Sam raised his hand.

"As many of you know, I am Ute. In my culture, your word is everything. I gave Drake Dixon my word that I would not discuss my time working for him. I will continue to honor his request."

The room went silent as Sam inhaled a deep breath. "My people have gone through many challenges. Our land, our people, and our religion were taken from us. We were put on reservations, our children were forced to attend white schools, and we were disciplined if we spoke our language, sang our songs, or practiced our faith. Yet, through it all, we did not break our word."

The media seemed unsure how to respond.

"Any questions?" Sam asked.

Finally, a reporter in the back raised his hand. "Can you at least tell us if you were part of this investigation into private military companies?"

"I communicated with Colonel Bart Tomlinson, but I was unaware of their findings and had no idea they would be making any arrests in Washington, DC, last night."

"But you were part of this one-year investigation?"

"I guess a little bit. I think much like our Royals getting to the World Series, I was just one of many people involved. There were others in Afghanistan, Nicaragua, and here in America, all working together, not only for justice, but to do what was right for both the citizens and the environment of the Nuristan Province."

"Were you trying to protect the Afghan warlord, Abdul Hazrat?"

"Mr. Hazrat is not a warlord. He's simply the leader of a mountain village that wants to live peacefully on land that has been theirs for hundreds of years. Land that ten years ago was discovered to have valuable natural resources ... and ever since has been pursued by foreign investors."

A reporter from the *Kansas City Star* asked, "How did you become friends with Mr. Hazrat?"

Sam arched one brow. "You are very clever, Mr. Gibson. I can't tell you how we met, but I can tell you that Abdul is a good man—a good man and a good father. His daughter, Malala, is now ten, and his son, Mateen, is seven. They are two of the most courageous children I've ever met."

"Aren't they the kids you rescued from the Taliban?"

Sam suppressed a smile but didn't answer.

There was more laughter until another reporter called out, "What are your thoughts about Mr. Hazrat's land being made part of the Nuristan National Forest?"

"That was the best news I received today," he said proudly. "To have the Afghan government and their Environmental Protection Agency work together and extend the park to protect the Hazrat land forever, well, that made my time in Afghanistan worthwhile."

He looked down at his hands. The room quieted as if they sensed the young man had more to say. Then Sam raised his vision, his dark eyes gazing sightlessly about the crowd. "I want to thank all of you for being patient with me this year. There were many questions you had that I could not answer because of a promise I made ... and other questions that I refused to answer because it was too painful to talk about, like the loss of my parents and my sister. They were my everything." He reached into his jacket pocket and pulled out a slip of paper. "My sister, Jenny, was considered a medicine woman in our tribe. She wrote a journal of daily inspirations to help me move on after she died. I would like to share with you her words I read this morning: *The Great Spirit is my only goal. And the only way to reach God is through forgiveness. There is no other way.*"

Sam's gaze fixed on the scout who had signed him, then returned to the crowd. "I believe my experience with Mr. Dixon has been my greatest lesson in forgiveness. Now it's time to move on." He then winked at his teammates in the back of the room. "What do you guys say we win the whole thing next year?"

His fellow Royals let loose another round of wolf howls, and when order was restored, the press conference moved on to questions about his family, his tribe, Colonel Tomlinson, Whiplash, the Friends of Everyone Hotel, the Estevez Casino and Orphanage, and the Little League Dukes. There were even a few inquiries about baseball and losing game seven of the World Series. But by then, he no longer looked at *the catch he didn't make* as so devastating. It was part of what got him to this moment. The Drake Dixon headache was over, and the Hazrat family was safe. Peace.

It was almost six o'clock by the time the final one-on-one interviews were over, and as he walked to the players' parking lot with several teammates, a cold November wind swept in from the north. He pulled his coat tighter, but the wind blew harder, and he grabbed Bo Chapman's shoulder for balance.

"Hang on, Sammy," Bo laughed. "Where's that wind blowing you?"

"Maybe like those stories today," added Cimoli. "A blast from the past."

Jenny, Sam thought. Yes, his sister was in the wind. Her spirit had been with him every step of his long journey. Nudging him. Prodding him. Encouraging him. Protecting him. An invisible tap on the shoulder to warn him of danger one day, or a blast of cold wind redirecting his steps on this night.

"I'm starving," Cimoli said. "Who's up for a burger and beer at Power and Light?"

"I'm in," replied Chapman, Fuentes, and Ramirez.

"I'm out," muttered Sam.

All four of his teammates turned to face him, their eyes pleading for him to join them.

He shook his head. "Sorry, guys. I'm exhausted. It's been a long day … time to go home."

*　　*　　*

As Sam drove away from Kauffman Stadium, his mind was much like the weather, a whirlwind of random thoughts roaring by, not one he could grasp before it would fly off and another take its place. He opened the windows and turned the radio up, trying clear his head, until a gust from the north almost blew his Prius off the road.

"Two hands," he said to himself. "Ten and two. Don't kill yourself now. Eyes on the road."

A shower of brown and yellow leaves tore against the side of his car as he continued south on Route 69. His exit was still a mile away, but his car seemed to have a mind of its own as it turned down 151st Street and headed east. It was dinnertime. He wasn't sure if arriving unannounced would be rude, but he felt they would understand.

It was 6:40 when he found the house, walked up the sidewalk, and knocked on the front door. Twenty seconds later, a middle-aged man opened the door.

"Sam Cloud-Carson." The man smiled brightly and extended his hand. "It's nice to finally meet you. I'm Sydney's dad, Jeff."

"Sorry to drop by without calling first, sir." Sam wiped his sweaty palm on his pants and shook Jeff's hand. "My car just kind of drove itself over here. I was wondering if I could have a word with you and your wife and, uh, maybe Sydney."

"Come on in. Sydney's upstairs getting ready to go out with friends, but I'm sure she'd like to see you."

"Thank you, sir." Sam followed him into the living room.

"Vivian!" Jeff called out.

"I'm in the kitchen, finishing the dishes you forgot to wash."

"Dishes can wait. We have a guest."

"Phil and Mary Beth aren't guests, they're family."

"It's not Phil and MB, honey."

Sam ran a hand over his hair to smooth it. The wind had done a number on it from car to house, and he wanted to look presentable for Mrs. Morgan. Coming straight from the press conference, he was wearing a nice introductory outfit. Gray slacks, white shirt, navy jacket.

"Who would be out on a wild night like—" Vivian paused midsentence as she stopped in the kitchen entryway, staring at who was in their living room.

"Hello, Mrs. Morgan. I'm Sam—"

"I know who you are." She hurried over and shook his hand enthusiastically. "We watched your press conference. You are one amazing young man."

"I'm just happy we were able to help a family."

"You saved an entire mountain," Vivian said.

He gave a bashful shrug and didn't know what to say. He'd hardly done anything. Maybe connected a few people, but it was the Afghan government and their Environmental Protection Agency that had saved Hazrat's village and mountain by putting it under the protection of the Nuristan National Forest.

"I just did my job," he finally said, feeling an awkwardness he hadn't experienced since asking a girl out in college, a notion that seemed foolish at the moment, and he pushed his hands into his pockets so they wouldn't see them shaking.

Vivian held up a hand as if to change the subject. "I know you can't talk about what you did in Afghanistan, so why don't we talk baseball. We're very proud of you and the Royals."

"You'd be prouder if I'd made that catch—"

"Don't you say another word about that play," she scolded him. "You did your best. That's all anyone can ask."

"Thank you, ma'am." He licked his dry lips.

"May I get you something to drink, Sam?"

"A glass of water would be wonderful, thanks." He tugged at the collar of his shirt. *Geez, the Morgans must keep their thermostat at eighty-five. I'm burning up in here.*

Vivian returned with a glass of water, and Sam took a long drink.

"You have a lovely home." It was all he could think to say.

"Thank you." Vivian grinned, seeming to enjoy Sam's discomfort.

"You, uh, did a real fine job raising Sydney. She's a—a very good person."

"Yes, she is," Jeff said. "Sydney looks for the good in everyone."

"Yes, sir." Sam wiped the beginning of perspiration from his forehead. "I was wondering, um, y'know, with, uh, all that she's been through with, um, her marriage over"—he inhaled a deep breath—"I was wondering if, um, it would be okay to, uh, ask your daughter out for a date?"

"I'm twenty-seven, Sam," said a voice from the top of the stairs. "I think I can speak for myself."

He jerked around and looked up to find Sydney. She was wearing the outfit he had bought her for her birthday. The Sundance velvet top, the floral embroidered jeans, the Sidewinder boots, and the sterling-silver-and-stone necklace.

"Wow." He stared. "You look beautiful."

"Thanks. It's a gift from a friend."

"Your friend"—he couldn't take his eyes off her as she walked down the stairs—"has good taste."

She chuckled lightly. "Why, if I didn't know any better, Mr. Cloud-Carson, I'd think that you were nervous."

He took another sip of water. "How could you tell?"

She nodded to the glass of water he was failing to hold steady. "Because I've never seen your hand shake like that when you're on the mound."

"I'd feel a lot better if this glass was a baseball."

They all laughed, and then the room quieted.

"So"–he paused, unsure what to say next–"you're all dressed up. Do you have a date?"

"I was going to meet Phil and MB." She stifled a grin. "But I don't think they'd mind if I canceled. I'm kind of a third wheel anyway."

Vivian put one arm around Sydney and the other around Sam. "Let me walk the two of you to the door. I'll text MB." She winked up at Sam. "And you, sir, have permission to date our daughter."

*   *   *

Sam opened the passenger door, grabbed the food wrappers and baseball glove that were on the front seat, and threw them in the back. "Sorry–I didn't know you'd say yes."

"Really?" She gave him a sideways glance and sat down. "You didn't think I'd want to see you?"

"How was I supposed to know? Your last few texts weren't very encouraging."

"I was going through a divorce and you were trying to win a world championship. I thought we both needed to stay on task."

He put his hands on his hips. "Do you ever stop being a coach?"

"No. Now stop talking and get in the car."

He shook his head in amusement and did as he was told.

"Where do you want to go?" he asked as they drove off.

"I don't care. I just want to be with you."

"Good. Me too. How about wine and cheese with Barney?"

She laughed. "Looks like I'm the third wheel again."

*   *   *

The wind picked up as they drove down the street, weaving around maple and elm branches that littered the road. He turned into the Tomlinson drive, punched in the code to open the gate, and drove through. He suddenly stopped and pointed out the front window.

"Two white-tail," he whispered. "Buck and a doe."

She squinted out the window and saw nothing but the silhouette of bent brome grass and trees swaying in the wind.

"Most deer don't stray on windy nights," Sam said. "They will during the day, but not so much at night."

Sydney turned back to Sam and watched him, his dark hawk's eyes following two invisible creatures in the black abyss.

"When I'd hunt in this kind of weather back home," he went on, "I'd always track the lee side of a downwind thicket where mule deer would hunker for better feeding and—"

"I love you—" she blurted out, surprising herself at the boldness of her words.

He continued to stare out the window.

"I'm sorry," she said, suddenly afraid. "You didn't want me to say that, did you?"

His face warmed as he turned her way. "When I was driving over to your house tonight, I thought of all that had happened to me the last ten months: winning the Nicaraguan Championship, signing with a Major League team, being part of our run to the World Series, surviving allegations from my old boss, helping save an Afghan village … and meeting you. It seemed impossible a year ago."

He put the car in gear and continued down the lane. "Yet there was one trait that made the impossible, possible. Family. I may have lost my blood family, but I was blessed to find a new one, brothers and sisters from all over the world. If Jenny taught me anything, it's that we're not separate from anyone—that we're all on the same team, longing for some connection, the trust and love of others. Our people believe that the power of the world is done in a circle, from childhood to childhood, uniting us like the whirling of the wind."

He turned down through the archway of trees that lined the path to his cottage, the storm thrashing branches and leaves against the car.

"Even though I like being alone, I wanted to share today with someone—someone who would truly understand what I was feeling." He gave her a bashful glance. "That someone was you. *You* were the one who came over early in the morning to make sure I was okay after that awful story broke. *You* were the one who told me to go for a walk to calm down, and then stayed to clean up the house that I had trashed. *You* were the one who, despite my objections, called Teresa and Colonel Tomlinson. Your phone call triggered the arrest of Dixon and helped save an Afghan village."

Sydney's cheeks flushed with pride.

Sam patted her leg. "You did well, Coach Sticks."

They arrived to the beginning of a storm. Tiny, icy pellets merging with the wind, stinging their faces and hands as they ran inside. He swept the sleet off Sydney's hair and helped her off with her coat. She knew he wanted to say more as he stood quietly in the kitchen, head bowed as he opened a bottle of red wine and poured each of them a glass. She prepared a plate of crackers and cheese and followed Sam to his couch. He handed her a glass and raised his own to her.

"To our first date."

She laughed, then touched her glass to his and took a sip.

"I didn't think it possible to love again after losing my parents and sister," he said softly, "and for a long time, I didn't think I was worthy of love." He took another sip and placed his glass on the table. She did the same. His eyes slowly moved up to meet hers.

"I haven't been home to Colorado in five years, and your Thanksgiving break is three weeks from today. I was wondering if you'd like to go with me for a walk on Pargin Mountain?"

She inhaled a startled gasp, knowing exactly what his words meant. Jenny had told her brother that he couldn't return to his mountain until he was ready to share his heart.

Tears began to spill down her cheeks as she reached up and drew his face to hers. He opened his mouth to say something more, but she kissed him hard, her tears mixing with his as she closed her eyes and tried to let go. But there was one more thing she needed to say, needed to know, before this relationship went further.

"Sam." Her voice was suddenly strained. "You do remember—I can't have children."

He stared at her for a long moment, then a smile curved his wide, soft mouth. "What a coincidence. And me with friends who run an orphanage in Nicaragua." He touched his forehead to hers. "If you still like me after our first date, we can adopt."

This time, the dam of tears broke free as she fell against him in a giggling mess, kissing his eyelids, his cheeks, his mouth as she whispered, "I love you, I love you, I love you."

At last, she let go and leaned back on the couch. "Okay, Mr. *Walks with the Wind*, since we're now dating, do you have a name for me?"

"Hmm …" He rubbed his chin, as if deep in thought, then put his feet up on the coffee table and lay back in her arms. "How about *Catching the Wind*?"

THE END

The idea of writing *Walks with the Wind* and the sequel, *Catching the Wind*, first came to me some twenty years ago … but I didn't put pen to paper until 2017. I had always planned to have the story end with the Afghan government and their Environmental Protection Agency saving Abdul Hazrat's fictional mountain village by extending the Nuristan National Forest. Needless to say, I was both surprised and quite happy when, on World Environment Day, June 5, 2020, the Afghan government designated *all* of the Nuristan Province as a national park to protect the environment and local culture. #MiraclesHappenEveryday #ThereIsGoodnessEverywhere

More from Steve Physioc

Did you read the first book in this series,
Walks with the Wind?

Track Sam's trials and adventures before he made it to the mound.
Winner of the Writer's Digest Self-Published eBook Grand Prize.

Don't miss Steve's historical fiction saga about a pair of families
whose fates are intertwined in WWI and WWII Italy. Both winners of
2019 Reader's Favorite Fiction awards.

All available on Amazon.

Follow Steve online
BookBub | GoodReads | Facebook | Twitter | Instagram
stevephysioc.com

ACKNOWLEDGMENTS

It would be impossible to begin any acknowledgment without first thinking of my mom, Bette Physioc. She was the one who read me my first book and inspired my love of storytelling. Even though she's physically gone, her spirit is with me always.

Thanks to Beth Kallman Werner of Author Connections, my guide to understanding this crazy world of publishing and the book biz.

To Kerri Holtzman, my incredibly patient marketing guru, a friend I completely trust, who protects me from making rash decisions and answers my countless questions about publishing, book covers, social media, and advertising. I'm very fortunate to have Kerri leading me every step of the way.

To Nicole Ayers, my brilliant editor, who has been with me from the very beginning, pushing, prodding, encouraging me to make my dialogue stronger and storylines more dramatic. I don't know how much of my books are me and how much are Nicole, I am just honored to work with someone as wise and helpful as she.

To my beta readers: Colonel Scott Fehnel, who helped me with all things military; my "show don't tell" buddy Mark Mendizza; apostrophe queen Seja Bajich; spiritual advisor Sister Rosie Kolich; and Royals Hall of Fame pitcher Jeff Montgomery. As Monty always reminds me, "Radar guns don't get people out, quality pitches do."

To my friend and fellow author, Joel Goldman, a kindred spirit who makes me laugh and challenges my thinking in all things authorish.

To my sister, Cathe, the cover artist for all four of my books. Cathe always seems to capture the soul of each story in her art. I love having her along on this journey. What a gift.

Thanks to the Southern Ute community in Ignacio, Colorado. In particular, Hanley Frost, the former Sun Dance Chief and Southern Ute Cultural Education Coordinator. I wanted to make sure I was both accurate and respectful of the Ute culture with the way I wrote about Ute traditions, ceremonies, family connection, and the spiritual awakening of my protagonist, Sam Cloud-Carson. Hanley was very patient in answering my many questions, and his answers were both informative and inspiring. Here are a few of my favorite quotes from Hanley…

"I want our children to understand our history."

"Don't ever forget where you come from. Remember that you are Ute."

"Our spiritual beliefs and our songs are what kept us going."

"I want to let our people know that our traditions are a way to find yourself."

"When you find your inner spirit, you will find peace."

Finally, I am indebted to my best friend and wife, Stace, who has encouraged me every step of the way on this writing adventure. I'm blessed to have her by my side on our own vision quest. For many years I wanted to write stories based on the principles of a book Stace and I have been studying the last twenty-five years, A Course in Miracles. ACIM is a spiritual self-study that teaches that the way to love and inner peace is through forgiveness. I wanted characters emblematic of that philosophy, people who despite all odds would be vigilant to choose love over fear, forgiveness over attack and light over darkness. I hope those qualities came out in the writing of this series, for we are all on a journey without distance to a goal that has never changed. As is written on a sign that hangs in the Southern Ute Cultural Center, "If the songs are not sung and the stories not told, our Mother Earth will die." We are all One.

About The Author

Steve Physioc has been telling stories for the past forty years. He has been a play-by-play announcer for football, baseball, and basketball for both college and the pros. Physioc is currently the radio-tv broadcaster for the Kansas City Royals. He won an Emmy in 2013 for his excellent announcing. Steve and his wife, Stace, have two children, Ryan and Kevin, and three grandchildren. They make their home in Stilwell, Kansas.

www.ingramcontent.com/pod-product-compliance
Lightning Source LLC
Chambersburg PA
CBHW072037190726
48294CB00005B/1290